HOW WE MET

Katy Regan worked for various women's magazines for two years before joining Marie Claire in 2002 as Features Writer going on to become Commissioning Editor. In 2004, at the height of her career as the office swinging reporter singleton, she fell accidentally pregnant by her best mate (who just remained a friend). Seeing the creative possibilities in this unconventional situation, her editor commissioned her to write a column *And then there were three . . . sort of.*

Which proved so successful it ran for two years and inspired many a reader to write in to Katy with their own story. She has now taken her loyal following to her blog on the Marie Claire website www.marieclaire.co.uk. When she is not writing fiction she writes features for the likes of Stella Magazine, The Times and Marie Claire. She lives in Hertfordshire with her son.

Also by Katy Regan

One Thing Led To Another
The One Before The One

KATY REGAN

How We Met

HARPER

Harper
An imprint of HarperCollins*Publishers*
77–85 Fulham Palace Road,
Hammersmith, London W6 8JB

www.harpercollins.co.uk

A Paperback Original 2013
3

A catalogue record for this book
is available from the British Library

ISBN: 9780007237449

Set in Sabon LT Std by Palimpsest Book Production Limited,
Falkirk, Stirlingshire

Printed and bound in Great Britain by
Clays Ltd, St Ives plc

MIX
Paper from
responsible sources

FSC C007454

For my friends, with love.

ACKNOWLEDGEMENTS

It's finally here! The book about friendship I've been trying to write for years. I would definitely still be trying without the following people: my agent, the very talented Lizzy Kremer and everyone at David Higham Associates; Laura West, Harriet Moore; my brilliant editor Sarah Ritherdon.

Sarah, (and all the team at HarperCollins – Louise Swannell, marketing, sales and anyone else I've left out) I truly could not have asked for more passion and enthusiasm behind this book and I am so grateful. Also I want to thank the art team for doing such a beautiful job on the cover.

I am also grateful to my family and parents for their continued support (particularly all the looking after Fergus whilst I tapped away all year! I couldn't have done it without you, Mum and Dad.) My lovely Fergus, for inspiring some of the special mother–son moments in this book and Louis – without your time and support I could definitely not do this job.

I also want to thank: Jenny Matthews, Jean Fish, Roger Snow and Renata Simoes for specifics.

Lastly, all my brilliant friends – I'm so lucky to have the lot of you. Our shared times have inspired lots of this book (in fact, thanks for any anecdotes supplied, or just unearthed by me. . .). I really wrote this for us.

PROLOGUE

August 2006
Ibiza

Outside the bar, the silence rings in my head; like the delayed echo of a lone guitar string. The air is warm and gluey and smells of sea salt and those flowers again – they're everywhere you go. Cancan skirts of frothy pink blooms.

I kick off my shoes and, carrying them, take the stone steps down to the sand. It's still warm and sugar-soft after another baking day. Behind me, I can still hear the throb of the music. Ba-doom! Boom! Faint laughter from further down the beach. Lasers streak the sky.

I'm walking quickly towards the sea now. The moon is high and fat as a pumpkin. It's bleeding pearly light across the sky and across the water but there's not much time left for it now, today will soon be gone. And then there'll be tomorrow. Another brand-new day.

I don't bother to take off my clothes at first, I just

1

wade straight in. The water's cool and delicious around my thighs, my stomach, my chest, and now I am swimming out, out towards the light.

And it's beautiful. So beautiful. The cool water; the black, silky sky. At either side of me, the cliffs rise up and glitter in the moonlight, like giant-sized precious stones. The water dances with a million needles of white light. It makes me think of music, of notes alive on paper, and every molecule of me tingles with pleasure, so much that I have to stop and catch my breath.

Push, glide, I am swimming beneath the water with every stroke now – like a mermaid. Except I'm not a mermaid because my white dress has ballooned around me so that I must look like a giant jellyfish, shifting and morphing, a glowing orb in the middle of the sea; alone but not lonely. Not wanting now. I'm swimming further out now, I slide the straps of my dress down and slip out of it, as if I'm shedding a skin. And suddenly I am totally free, the water caressing every inch of me, my dress floating alongside me, in my hand. I can still hear the throb of the music back on shore and when I put my head beneath the water, the b-dum-dum of my heart. I turn onto my back; I am floating, weightless. I imagine the stars are tiny pinprick holes, windows into another universe, a world where people are dancing and smiling too and don't know, don't care, where one day starts and another begins. And then they start to go off – the small explosions, deep in my belly, little bubbles of light working their way to my throat and out across my mouth and I make a mental note that this, THIS is what it tastes like. For the first time ever, I know this is it.

Life has brought me so much more than I ever

imagined. So much more than I ever thought possible. Friends I could *marry*, whom I'd die for. What did I do to deserve that? I imagine them now, dancing like those in the world above me; one great universe of dancing people and me, in the middle, dancing in the sea. I think of him back at the bar, hands pumping the air now. That grin across his face, the beautiful almond-shaped eyes. Lost in music. It makes me smile.

I swirl and tumble, feel the seaweed feather my skin. The moon is sending iridescent rays of light through the water; it's like electricity darting through my legs.

I should feel tiny out here but I don't, I feel bigger than ever, every last cell of me filled right up. I imagine the deep green bed beneath me, and the domed sky above, and imagine I am suspended, held in the centre of it all. A tiny being, spinning in orbit.

The music has stopped now, so it's just the sound of the waves and me and everything feels perfect. Everything feels right.

Above me, stars are going out, one by one. Night is giving way to day. Any time now, a brand-new day and I can't wait. I CAN'T WAIT.

THINGS TO DO BEFORE
I AM THIRTY

1. Sleep with an exotic foreigner – (in an ideal world, Javier Bardem). Night of heady, all-consuming passion: getting lost, snogging amongst lemon groves and being drunk on something thick and hugely alcoholic that I can't pronounce.

   (*Do this without becoming completely neurotic about what it's supposed to 'mean'.)

2. Learn to do SOME sort of dance: jive, tango, birdie . . .

   Don't tell anyone am having classes then wow them at random event and watch as they go, 'Oh, my God, Liv, you didn't tell me!'

3. Learn a foreign language.

4. Learn how to make a Roman blind.

5. And the perfect Victoria sponge . . .

6. Read all works by William Wordsworth and be able to recite lines at will. (Not including 'I wandered lonely as a cloud'.)

7. Use up all seven Scrabble letters in one fell

swoop! BUFFOON, for example, which would be great.

8. Go to Venice, properly this time, and have a bellini at Harry's Bar.
9. French kiss in Central Park.
10. Climb Great Wall of China and learn a bit of Chinese (should be able to do this whilst climbing the Great Wall).
11. Vegas, baby!
12. Live in Paris, listen to Edith Piaf, smoke Camels, drink pastis and have a torrid affair. Then leave, crying eyes out in Paris Gare du Nord.
13. Learn how to pluck eyebrows so that they 'frame the face'.
14. Swim naked in the sea at dawn.
15. Get a six-pack (or at least a two-pack) Something better than the one-pack I currently sport.
16. Learn how to meditate. To live in the moment.
17. Have a massive party for my wonderful, wonderful friends. Just because . . .
18. Learn how to use chopsticks. Asking for cutlery is getting embarrassing at twenty-seven.
19. Go to airport, close eyes and pick a destination at random, then GO! Even if it's to Stuttgart or Birmingham.
20. Make homemade porn video. Can't believe I just said that.
No really, I can't.

ONE

6 *March 2008*
Williamson's Park, Lancaster

Mia put the brake on the buggy, walked around the front
and checked on Billy. Thank God for that, *finally* he was
asleep. His fat little cheeks red with cold, a puddle of
drool collected in his chin.

With any luck, she might have time for a cheeky half
outside the Sun on the way back home. It was her best
friend's birthday after all and, 'be rude not to, Woodhouse,
be rude not to . . .' She knew what her best friend would
have to say about that.

'Hi, Liv.'

Mia took off her rucksack, sat down on the bench
and took in the view for a second, once again congratu-
lating herself on finding this corker of a spot, Ashton
Memorial white and gleaming in the sun, like a provincial
version of the Taj Mahal. The whole of the city laid out
below; the River Lune a snaking, silver ribbon through

the middle of it all and, in the distance, the Lakeland hills. She often thought they looked like big hairy mammoths from some ancient land.

She took the pint glass and bottle of water out of the rucksack and the tulips from the Morrisons bag. She set the glass down on the floor, poured in the water and tried to arrange the yellow flowers. She tutted at herself for not thinking to bring scissors, since the stalks were too long and so they didn't sit in the glass at all, but splayed all over the place, most of them toppling out onto the grass.

She leant back on the bench and looked at them.

'Well that looks shit, doesn't it?' Then she laughed, mainly at the predictability of it all. Where was Olivia Jenkins when you needed flowers arranging?

Mia moved right to the other end of the bench so she was nowhere near the buggy and took the packet of Golden Virginia and the Rizlas out of her jacket pocket. She pulled her hoodie over her knees – bloody hell it was freezing, why hadn't she worn a coat?

She was often doing this of late, already being out somewhere before realizing she was wearing completely inappropriate clothes for the weather. Last week, she'd looked down in the Post Office to see she was wearing odd shoes.

She rolled a cigarette, glanced at the back of the buggy, felt a slight tug of guilt but pressed on. 'Must press on!' as Olivia would say. Frankly, what with Billy's fascist policy regarding sleep lately (i.e. allowing her to have none, ever), it was either the odd fag to keep her sane, or adoption. Put like that, she felt much better and lit it.

'So it's your birthday today, Olivia Jenkins. Happy bloody Birthday.'

She blew the smoke up into the clear March sky, which seemed to hum, it was so cold.

'Now, I know what you're going to say. You should be ashamed of yourself, Mia Woodhouse, smoking now you're supposed to be a responsible mother. But honestly, Liv, after the week I've had with David Blaine over there – the baby that resists sleep for so long, he should do a show so people could come and watch – you'd let me off. And actually I can now inform you with confidence . . .' she inhaled enthusiastically . . . 'this is what you would, at one time, have called a twenty-quid fag.'

She laughed, then began to cry when with no warning whatsoever – this was also happening more often of late – she had a sudden memory: Liv, lying on Fraser on the beach in Ibiza, topped by that ridiculous visor she'd insisted on wearing for the whole fortnight, so she looked like an OAP from Florida, coming out with just that: 'Twenty-quid fag, this.' A fag so good she'd pay twenty quid for it.

Everyone had laughed and laughed.

'D'you remember how you always used to say that, Liv?

'Anyway, I've got news on that front.' She pulled herself together. It could easily go one of two ways up here, especially when she was suffering from acute sleep deprivation and she wanted to keep it light and entertaining. It was Liv's birthday, after all. 'Fraser's given up! Would you believe it? I'd be happy for him if he wasn't so smug. Honestly, it's *killing* me. The other day, he called me at seven a.m. – just as Billy had gone back off to sleep; I

9

could have murdered him had he not been two hundred and fifty miles away – to say, "Guess where I am? Go on, guess, guess!"

'I was like, "Dunno, a police station? The zoo? Buckingham Palace?" And he was like, "No. Hampstead Heath."

'And so I said, "Oh, well done. So clearly you haven't been to bed yet after some brilliant night out and are just ringing to nauseate me. That's not very nice." But *he* said, "No. I'm at Hampstead Heath Running Track." Then he said it again, just in case I hadn't heard: "RUN-NING TRACK. I've just been for a RUN."

'He didn't sound very out of breath, which I pointed out, and then he hit me with it: "Ah, but then I wouldn't be, would I? Because I've given up smoking. Three weeks, and five days!"

'Which turned out to be the real reason he was calling me at that hour.'

'Like I said, just unbearable. Horribly, horribly smug. It was all I could do not to be sick in a bag.'

'So that's Fraser.'

She looked around just to check she was alone. She had to admit, she did feel moronic on occasions, sitting here, talking to herself. But it was the only real place she had to come – a place that was Liv's (unless she wanted to traipse all the way to the cemetery in Peterborough every month. She knew what Liv would have to say about that too.) She also knew, if this were the other way round, Olivia would have rallied the troops, weeks in advance, marched them all up that killer hill to Williamson's Park, bringing cake, candles – probably a personal choir, knowing her. She could picture them all

10

now: Liv at the front carrying everything, Melody struggling behind in heels and a slightly too-tight skirt-suit, complaining that the cake was too chavvy, why didn't we get one from Marks's? Norm at the back, breaking into a light jog, Anna . . . Well, Anna probably wouldn't be there yet, having only left some random bloke's bed in Tooting about an hour ago, and finally Fraser – lovely Fraser Morgan . . . what would he be doing? Probably pegging it to the nearest offy, having decided right at the last minute that this occasion called for booze.

Mia thought of Fraser now, alone in his flat in Kentish Town – the one he used to share with Liv – and felt a rush of love. Poor Frase – she must give him a call as soon as she was finished up here, because today would be extra tough for him. She imagined him waking up, the date hitting him and then the aching absence of Liv in the flat and the memories, flooding back, more acute and painful than ever. It was at times like this that she wished Fraser would move back to Lancaster, just so she could keep an eye on him.

'So what else is new . . .?' Mia pulled her sleeves down over her hands and blew on them to keep them warm. 'Oh, yes . . . Billy. My son. Almost forgot! He's almost eight months old now, I can't believe it, Liv. Where the hell has the time gone since July? I look back and I can't remember anything. Must have blanked it out. Anyway, the good news is, he hasn't got my bacon ears or prominent chin – yet . . . although it's hard to tell since currently his entire jaw line is covered in fat. The bad news is, he's got Eduardo's everything else. Literally, he is his double, which as you can imagine, I am seething about: same beautiful green eyes, same Brazilian monobrow, same permanent look of wounded entitlement. I just hope to God he doesn't inherit total disrespect for women, too.

'Oh, Olivia, why didn't I listen to you when you said never trust a man who wears sunglasses inside?

'So, Eduardo has turned out to be a useless cock – no surprises there – although I suppose, in some part of my tiny pea-brain I did, at one point, think he might change. Sadly not. Since I've had Billy, he's seen him eight times. *Eight* times in nearly eight months! Pathetic or what . . .?'

Mia could feel the familiar rage bubbling up inside her, the sort that made her want to punch a wall – no, actually, just Eduardo's stupid, face; the maddening sense of injustice she always got when she thought about Eduardo. What really got her goat was that Eduardo was meant to be a summer fling, not the (useless-at-that) father of her child. She'd been seeing him for getting on a year by the time she fell pregnant, but Mia had always just thought he was 'good enough for now', that they'd eventually fizzle out. If she were really honest, she was kind of banking on that.

They rowed constantly for a start, but although she was ashamed to admit it now, part of her had thought that was cool and romantic. If she couldn't have a tumultuous, impulsive relationship with a hot-headed Latino in her twenties, when could she? She imagined them in one of those black-and-white foreign films she dreamed of writing one day, where nothing much happened except for two, very beautiful people shouting at each other in a spartan room in Provence or Andalucia or, well . . . somewhere very hot, anyway. It didn't quite translate into a flat in Acton that smelled permanently of ragù, but then she'd got pregnant. If it had been up to her she would have had a termination, but Eduardo's Catholic upbringing had suddenly made an appearance. It made her feel guilty: *It's a life, Mia, as soon as those cells start to divide.* She'd fallen for it at the time, she thought he actually wanted this baby, that it might even bond them. Now she realised he was calling her bluff. Well that backfired pretty spectacularly.

'Anyway . . .' She told herself to rein it in. She'd promised herself this birthday visit to Liv's bench today was not just going to turn into a rant-athon about Eduardo but, look at her, she was at it already.

'. . . The thing is, whatever I think of him, he's still Billy's dad, isn't he? And I want Billy to have a relationship with his dad. It's just I'm not that sure his dad wants to have a relationship with him, which is the most heartbreaking thing of all, do you know what I mean?

'But hey, let's see, he's promised me he'll be here at five p.m. today to take Billy off for the night because everyone's arriving for YOUR do.

'Which brings me onto everyone. I guess you'll be wanting an update:

'One. Anna. You'll be glad to know everything is exactly as it was in Twelve Station Road days, Livs, except she's gone north of the river now and inflicts it on some other poor, unassuming flatmates in Islington. She still has dubious hygiene, walks round with toothpaste on her spots, picks plaque from her teeth when she thinks you're not looking and eats gherkins straight from the jar. And yet still scrubs up to look like Florence Welch – how is that?

'She still reads *The Economist* in bed, too – like we

were ever impressed – and I still maintain she hasn't got the faintest clue what it's on about, but we love Anna Spanner, she's good value. Oh, and she's still single, *obvs*.

'Who else? Melody and Norm . . . Well, it's all change in that camp, Melody having almost completed her total transformation from Indie mosher to hotshot lawyer (as you will know, Norm was far more impressed with the Indie mosher version). They're doing really well for themselves: Norm's 'Entertainment Correspondent' for the *Visitor* these days. I know! Get him. It pays peanuts, of course, and occasionally he has to go and cover groundbreaking front page stories about people turning a hundred, but the rest of the time he gets to go to free gigs, so he's not complaining. They've got a swanky, three-storey townhouse up on that posh estate by the university. Clearly, it's only a matter of time before all those rooms are filled up with mini-Normantons. Fraser reckons they'll have twins: a boy who looks like Melody and a girl who looks like Norm.

'It's bizarre though, Liv, it's like Melody came back from travelling and Ibiza, started her law course and said, "Right, I want to be a grown-up now." The fags went, the drugs went – although you'll be pleased to know she still drinks inordinate amounts of cider. Nowadays, if you go round to theirs, it's like a beauty spa waiting room.

'She's got that room-fragrance, joss-stick thing going on – you can smell lily of the valley from half a mile away and everything's beige, sorry *stone*. And I do not just mean the house. Gone are the Arctic Monkeys and Green Day and the Foo Fighters, now it's Norah Jones all the way. Even I – musical Philistine – know you would not be impressed.

'Oh, and she does these "Pampered Chef" parties now, sort of Tupperware parties but with kitchen implements where you're forced to pay fifty quid for a garlic press. Norm's still the same, thank God – he's usually in some mild stage of intoxication to block it all out – but the "change" has already begun on him too. She's started buying him clothes from places like Aquascutum and Gap (she calls it THE Gap) and so you've got Norm, 90s but cool with his lamb-chop sideburns in a chino and a moleskin jacket. Wrong, in so many ways.

'Other than that, motherhood's treating me well, even if it's like living with a fascist dictator, and sometimes I actually catch a whiff of my own BO because it's very hard to have a shower of a morning with a baby hanging off you, I can tell you. But he does make me laugh, Liv. And he is *really* cute, even if he looks like his dad. If I was to describe motherhood to you, I'd say imagine what it's like to want to throw someone out of the window one second, and eat them up with love the next. And as Mrs Durham said to me the other day (Mrs Durham is an old dear I look after on a Tuesday. She's pretty revolting. I found a pellet of cat poo in her knicker drawer the other day . . .) "You're never—"'

Then Mia stopped. She stopped because what Mrs Durham had said hit her. 'You're never really a grown-up until you've had a child yourself.'

But then, of course, some people didn't get the chance to grow up at all.

Billy was still asleep when Mia left the bench. It was 1 p.m. – he'd been asleep half an hour; if she played her cards right, she probably had another half-hour yet. She

15

held tight onto the buggy as she walked down the steep hill from Williamson's Park, the wind blowing so hard from behind, it made her break into a run. It was one of her greatest fears: accidentally letting go of the buggy and watching helplessly as Billy careered into the traffic. It made her breathless with panic just thinking about it.

She walked down through town. It was the start of the Easter holidays and all the students had gone home. Mia liked Lancaster best like this – vacated of eighteen-year-olds with far too much confidence for their own good. Then she could pretend this was her town again; their town, when the six of them had been brimming with confidence and it felt like they owned it all too.

Same day
Kentish Town, London

'Sssh, don't move.'

Still half asleep, Fraser Morgan had the vague notion that he was being held up at gun point in his own bed. Something was pressing firmly into his back. And he had an erection, which was a *bit* odd. He could even get an erection when his life was in danger?

'That nice hun? Mm?'

It was only when the voice spoke again, whispered into Fraser's ear, a warm flood of breathiness that *Jesus Christ* that *stank* of booze, that he woke up, with a start, the awful truth hitting him in the face. Or was that the back?

KAREN. Fraser's eyes shot open.

Karen from the Bull was in his bed. She was naked,

16

pressing her pelvis into him and playing with his cock, which went without saying was really quite pleasant.

Fraser lay there, motionless, blinking into the half-light, staring at the radio alarm clock on his bedside table: 10.53 a.m., 6 March 2008.

Sixth of March.

He closed his eyes again.

How? How could he have let this happen? Exactly at what point of last night did he ever think this was a good idea?

'I said, is that nice . . .?' She was purring, kissing the nape of his neck now. Breathing pure alcohol fumes into his skin. Fraser tried to speak but it came out a couple of octaves higher than intended, so that he sounded like a pre-pubescent boy on the brink of his voice breaking. He cleared his throat and tried again.

'Yeah, that's um, yeah, very nice.'

Fuck it. Fuck IT! Panic consumed him. How the hell was he going to get out of this? How had he even got *into* this?

'Good, good, very glad to hear it. Well don't go away, handsome, I'm just popping to the loo but I'll be right back to carry on the good work.'

Karen leant over, pecked him on the cheek and got out of bed.

Fraser turned his head, very slowly. Ow, that *killed*. Why did his neck hurt? Just in time to see what was – it had to be said – a rather sizeable arse disappear round his bedroom door.

Thank fuck for that. Fraser turned onto his back, pulled the duvet over his head and let out the breath he'd been holding since he woke up. GOD he felt tragic.

17

His heart was palpitating, his head throbbing as he tried to piece together the events of last night. It was all very vague, involving beer, wine, tequila and, at one point, her showing him her yogic headstands, which he'd then tried too, before breaking the coffee table, and very nearly his neck. Oh, that's why his neck hurt.

He vaguely remembered coming to his senses for one brief moment after that – must have been the rush of blood to the head – to say to her, 'Come on, you don't want to go to bed with some drunken stranger . . .' just as she was removing her blouse (he'd noted with some alarm that that was *definitely* what you'd call a blouse). But she'd just sat on his bed in the white bra that Fraser imagined he could fit his head into and said: 'Oh, I think I do.'

So at least he'd made some effort to avoid this. However, the fact remained that he'd slept with her. He'd slept with Karen from behind the bar of the Bull – was this really the end of the world? She wasn't a horror story; in fact she was a perfectly lovely girl. God knows, she'd scraped him off the floor of that pub enough times in the past eighteen months, chucked him in a cab well past closing time after another night of him drowning his sorrows and talking shit to whoever he could find in there – mainly her.

But she was also forty-two. Shitting hell, forty-two! That was practically middle-aged. Old enough to be his mother in some parts of her home town of Hull, Fraser felt sure. As old as . . . Fiona Bruce.

He winced as he remembered a conversation – the bit where she'd asked him how old he thought she was and

18

he'd said (thinking he was being flattering, this was before beer goggles took over and he'd even considered doing anything with a woman in her forties), 'Don't know, Forty-two? Forty-three?' And she'd blinked at him and said, 'Forty-two,' which was followed by a nasty silence before he moved swiftly onto . . . DOLPHINS! Oh, God, how could he forget the dolphins? Karen from the Bull had two-inch nails with dolphins painted on them. Was this a normal girl thing to do and he'd just never seen it before?

He winced again as bits of that particular conversation also came back to him: her telling him she'd adopted a dolphin from a sanctuary in Florida, that this dolphin was like the baby she'd never had, and he, in an effort to appear interested and engaged, telling her he once swam with dolphins in Zanzibar. Which was a lie. A pointless, outright lie. He'd never even been to Zanzibar. Why the fuck had he said that?

Oh, God, she was back now, padding towards the bed, naked except for a pair of lacy, black knickers that had largely disappeared up her behind and clutching her massive, Christ, GIGANTIC breasts. Fraser sat up, pulled the duvet right up to his chin and arranged himself in the most asexual, un-come-to-bed position he could muster. But she got in anyway, so he moved right up against the wall.

'So,' he said, brightly. 'Coffee?'

Brilliant. There was no better feeling, decided Mia, ten minutes later, than sitting down with a half of Carling and a baby still asleep – even if it was minus five and blowing a gale. This is how she got through the week, these days, by finding the odd little pocket of time to herself and guarding it with her life. At least there was that about being a single mother – you really got to appreciate your own time. What on earth had she done with it all before she had a baby? Work and drink she imagined. And lots of face-packs.

Sometimes, Mia dreamt of her old life, before she'd moved in with Eduardo in Acton – not one of her better ideas – and Liv had moved in with Fraser to start her new teaching job in Camden, when she, Liv and Anna had shared a flat in Clapham and she was working all hours God sent for Primal Films as an art department assistant.

She'd wake up when it was still dark, thinking she was back in her old bedroom on the Ikea futon and that she had ten minutes to chuck on some clothes before jumping in the car and driving through the silent city to Shepperton Studios for another thirteen-hour day. She'd loved those days. She loved the exhaustion she'd felt, an excited kind of exhaustion, totally different to the tiredness that comes with motherhood.

Barely conscious, she'd then imagine the noise she could hear was Liv and Anna making a racket downstairs in their gloomy Victorian kitchen with the huge table all six of them had spent so many hours drinking at. Then she'd come to, realize it was Billy crying and that it was just the two of them, alone in their boxy new-build flat in Lancaster with its woodchip and ubiquitous laminate.

Still, things had improved lately. Yes, definitely, things had improved. She still wondered occasionally if her son didn't rate her that much, or wasn't that impressed with the whole set-up, really, what with it being just the two of them in a poky flat and a dad who only turned up when he felt like it.

She still didn't really know how to talk to him and found herself stuck for words when it was just him and her. She marvelled at mothers who seemed to be able to coochie-coo so naturally in public, whereas she just felt like a dick a lot of the time. Then Billy would get that look of wounded entitlement on his face as if to say, 'Seriously, is this all you've got?' And she'd wonder if she was really cut out for this motherhood thing at all.

But at least the panic had gone. She didn't worry about him dying every night any more, which was something, and now Melody and Norm had moved back up North to Lancaster, they sometimes offered to help, which was really sweet, even if Melody drove her mad by suggesting single motherhood was somehow 'romantic', that Mia was like J. K. Rowling, writing an award-winning film script in a freezing cold flat she couldn't afford to heat, when in reality she wasn't writing anything at all, was reading OK! magazine and tucking into the wine in a flat she couldn't afford to heat and feeling thoroughly guilty that her brain was probably half dead by now.

Mia put her hood up, took a sip of her lager and took her mobile out of her pocket so she could text Fraser to see if he was still on track for tonight, and check he was surviving the day so far. When she looked at her phone, however, there was a text from Anna:

was at a party in Kidderminster last night so there's a SMALL chance I might be late but WILL BE THERE I promise. Start without me.
Spanner x

Mia rolled her eyes; she knew 'a SMALL chance' translated as 'am still in Kidderminster and will be two hours late', and composed her message to Fraser, wondering whether she had time for another rollie.

Then her mobile went. It was Eduardo. Her heart sank. Do not do this to me, she thought. Please, please, do not do this to me. Not tonight. To add insult to injury, him calling had also woken Billy.

She picked up.

'Hi, Eduardo.'

'It's me.'

'I gathered that.'

She told herself to keep the tone neutral, but it was hard – so very, very hard.

'What's going on?' he said.

Oh, fuck off, she wanted to say. Why did he always have to use that accusatory tone?

'Nothing's "going on".'

'Why is Billy crying then?'

Because I'm strangling him, what the hell?! He was a baby. Babies cried. He'd know that if he spent any time with one.

'Where are you?' said Eduardo, sharply, before she had time to answer.

'At the pub.'

He snorted.

'The pub?'

Yes. We're having a pint – three in fact – and we might follow that with a tequila chaser. She thought better of it. She wasn't in a position to piss Eduardo off. She needed him, that was the most galling thing of all.

22

Eduardo sighed, in that martyred way he did. She knew just from that sigh what was coming next.

'Anyway, look Mimi . . .'

Mimi? Stop calling me bloody Mimi.

'. . . work have just called and—'

'Er, NO.' Mia felt the rage rise like bile in her chest. 'Come on, Eduardo, you are not doing this to me.'

Billy was wailing now, rubbing his eyes. Mia pushed the buggy back and forth.

'You know how important tonight is, what day it is today, you've known for ages.'

Silence.

'Mia, this is not about choice, is it?'

She hated how he did that. Always put 'is it?' on the end of everything, so subtle and yet so successful in making her doubt herself. 'I need the money. I'm late on my rent, I'm fucking desperate here, I don't have the luxury—'

Luxury? HA! Don't fucking talk to me about luxury, thought Mia, you total lying, manipulative bastard, but she stood there, the wind howling, Billy crying now, and she knew it was pointless.

'Whatever, Eduardo,' she said. 'I can't be arsed any more. Go. You go to work.'

Then she hung up, tears of frustration already running down her face. And what she really wanted to do was to call her best friend, but of course she couldn't.

Where were those fags? He could have sworn he'd hidden a couple in here. Fraser was now in his freezing kitchen, rummaging futilely in the kitchen drawer in his dressing gown. The fridge. Maybe he'd put them on top of the

23

fridge? Right at the back so he wouldn't be tempted but they'd still be there, just in case of real emergencies like this one he was currently facing, a moment of true, genuine need.

He patted his hands on top but couldn't feel anything. Perhaps they'd fallen down the back? He steadied his feet and wrapped his arms around the fridge to move it, giving it an enormous hug, relishing the coolness against his hot, toxic skin, thinking maybe it would be nice just to stay here for a few minutes, just him and the fridge in their cool embrace. He pulled and pulled but he was too weak, too sleep-deprived, too fucking hungover to manage it. When he finally let go, the door flew open and a cucumber shot out, hitting him on the chest like a missile.

He gave up, leant against the kitchen worktop, breathless, his head pounding, thinking what to do next. Maybe he could go to the corner shop for cigarettes? Then just do a runner? Just not come back! Ah, that only really worked when you were in someone *else's* house though, didn't it?

Fuck it. Fuck it, you moron.

He was giving himself a talking-to now, firm but sort of kind. He knew who that reminded him of.

He held the heels of his hands to his face, stretching the skin outwards, watching his reflection in the greasy microwave door as if, if he did it for long enough, he might actually be able to escape his own skin. He thought of tonight, of approximately eight hours from now, of walking into the pub to face his mates. God, he wanted to hurl.

What was really bothering Fraser was how comfortable Karen seemed to be in his bed. How *happy*. No sign of post-bender jitters whatsoever.

24

If she'd just been some flirty barmaid who'd wanted a bit of sexy time then that would have been fine. Not fine, but *finer*; he would have felt less guilty. But she liked him, she'd liked him for ages, she'd told him last night. Which was just brilliant, just the absolute best.

He considered his options:

- Be nice, go for breakfast with her, ask for her number then never call her. Of course all this meant that he could never drink in the Bull again; or, if he did, he'd have to wear a disguise. He briefly went through how this might work in his head and decided it never would.
- Say he was going out (which he was, just not for another four hours but Karen didn't need to know that . . .) wait till she was safely out of view then go back to bed. The thought of bed, alone, right now, was amazing. Truly amazing.
- Tell her the truth: Say he's sorry, she's a lovely girl but he was drunk, he's still grieving his girl-friend and it should never, ever have happened. Can they be friends?
- Fuck that. He didn't want to be friends!

Anyway, right at this point, all three sounded hideous. Especially the last. He felt sure the last would guarantee tears and the last thing he could handle today – especially today – were tears from a barmaid he barely knew.

Norm. That's who he wanted right now: simple, unjudgemental, chilled-out Norm. Norm, who he'd known since he was nine.

25

He took his phone off the side, sank down onto the kitchen floor in his dressing gown and texted him:

So guess who woke up today in bed with Karen from the Bull? What a cock. Head in bits. Need some Norm wisdom.

A reply buzzed immediately:

You cock.

Fraser groaned and half laughed at the same time – he knew Norm didn't really mean it, that that level of genuine harshness was beyond him.

He texted back:

I know, it's not normal. Today. Any day but today! What's wrong with me?

He held the phone in his hand, waiting for a reply, and something caught his eye: the photo of Liv held against the fridge door with a magnet in the shape of a beer bottle. He reached forward and took it in his hand. This was his favourite photo of her. They were at a fancy dress party – Anna's twenty-third birthday. It was a 'come as a London Underground Station' party and Liv had gone as Maida Vale.

'I *simply* made myself a veil . . .!' she'd said, standing on his front doorstep, in a voice like a posh, wooden TV presenter from the 1970s . It made Fraser giggle even now.

He stared at the photograph. She was wearing her

homemade veil and a French maid outfit that revealed her comely thighs – she always had fantastic legs – and which plunged at the neck (her cleavage was pretty fantastic too). She was holding a cocktail with an umbrella in it and standing in a naughty-postcard-type pose, doing an exaggerated wink, her wide mouth half open, revealing her lovely teeth. Liv had the best teeth: big, naturally white teeth with a tiny gap in the middle. That was his favourite bit of her – that little sexy gap. Fraser smoothed out the frayed corners of the photo, kissed it and put it back.

A text from Norm:

Mate, chillax. Nothing's normal for any of us today. See you at 8 in the Merchants, you oaf. Cuddles and kisses Norm x

Fraser smirked and shook his head. Cuddles and kisses? Norm was such a plonker. Then he stood up, rather too quickly so that the blood rushed to his head and he had to put his head between his knees so he didn't pass out, climbed the stairs to his bedroom, and prepared to face the music with Karen.

TWO

That evening
Lancaster

Mia walked into the Merchants with Billy at gone eight. For some reason, she was thinking of the film *Look Who's Talking*, and winced as she imagined what her son must be thinking now: *The pub, twice in one day, Mother, and now for the evening? Classy!* And wished so much she could explain without sounding embittered and abandoned. This is what Mia most resented about this whole situation, the opportunities it held for mental behaviour: screaming in the middle of the street at Eduardo, slamming phones down, revenge plots and murderous thoughts. She spent far too much of her time, these days, feeling like a character from *Coronation Street*.

Of course it pissed her off whenever Eduardo let her down, but tonight felt especially cruel. Although she was not one to drag out self-pity too long, she couldn't help but feel a bit sorry for herself as she pushed Billy past the cosy, candlelit arches, looking for her friends.

This was one night, *one night* out of the whole year, for remembering her best friend whom she didn't even have any more, and he thought the customers of Bella Italia needed him more than she did? And she'd had a *baby* with this man?

She had considered cancelling – there was nobody else she could call to look after Billy, after all, since Melody was coming too – but she was too angry, too *sad,* too at risk of binge-drinking alone if she stayed in tonight and, anyway, she wanted to come, she *had* to come. Surely, Bruce, the landlord, would relax the rules on the baby front just this once?

But then perhaps not; not after last year's reunion, which had been utterly grim. Melody and Anna had drunk far too much, got far too maudlin and ended up literally rocking, clinging onto each other in a sentimental sobbing wreck, people openly gawping at them, and Mia had found herself actually cringing at her friends' display of grief.

Norm had been unusually quiet – said barely a word, in fact, and spent the entire night at the jukebox putting Green Day on a loop (he and Livs were bonded in their mutual love of Green Day), until he got shouted at to literally 'fucking change the record!' by some hard-nut local who Fraser – also steaming drunk – then decided to punch, resulting in two broken fingers and them all getting chucked out.

Through all of this, of course, Mia was four months pregnant with Billy, and sober. She'd tried to reason with them that perhaps that second round of sambucas was not the best idea, that Fraser had had enough to drink, that quite possibly, Liv wouldn't have wanted him to take a swing at a bloke twice his size on her behalf, but they wouldn't listen. Of course they wouldn't listen, they were steaming and Mia had gone home feeling utterly deflated, sure that two broken fingers and a police caution was definitely *not* how her best friend would want her birthday to be marked.

Also, perhaps due to being pregnant, she felt blocked. She couldn't let her grief run riot like the rest of them. Everything was too much – life event overload – and even though everyone else had piled back to Melody and Norm's, she'd gone home to Eduardo (who was still with her at this point, preferring to wait until she was thirty-six weeks pregnant to tell her, actually, this whole baby thing wasn't really going to work for him . . .) and lay in bed, staring into the dark.

But tonight was a whole year later, wasn't it? Their grief was less raw; it would be more of a celebration, a celebration of her life! A chance to reminisce about the good times – so many good times – and a chance to get together. Then she located Melody and Norm at the end of the final tunnel, clearly already in the throes of a row, and her heart sank.

Melody turned dramatically when she saw Mia, who thought, if she were turning into a character from *Coronation Street*, then her good friend Melody Burgess was fast becoming one from *Ally McBeal*. All power dressing and courtroom drama.

'Nobody's here yet,' she said, breathily, with what Mia couldn't help but feel was a slightly staged flick of her hair. 'Twenty past eight and not a peep out of anyone.'

31

'Well, I'm here,' said Mia, brightly.

'Right, yes, I suppose so and er . . . Billy,' said Melody, somewhat begrudgingly, clocking the buggy, as if Mia had a choice in this matter. Mia gritted her teeth.

Norm groaned. 'I've told her to take a chill-pill,' he said. 'I've told her this is about Olivia, REMEMBER?' He fired daggers at Melody, and Mia found herself thinking – not for the first time in the last year: what happened to my friends? Jolly old Norm and Melody? Inseparable. Bonded for years in their love of cider and singing appalling indie anthems on karaoke?

Melody folded her arms indignantly. 'Well, I'm disgusted, frankly. I mean, Anna's no surprise but *Fraser*? Liv was *his* girlfriend, remember?'

'I think we do,' said Mia, in a way that was supposed to be helpful and calm her down but didn't.

'So why the fuck isn't he here then? No phone call, no text, *nada*!'

'Um, do you mind putting your foot down, mate?' Fraser was sitting in the back of a black cab travelling from Preston to Lancaster, jiggling his legs up and down, which he always did when he was nervous. Honestly, what was wrong with these provincial types? No sense of urgency. Liv was doing this, he thought. She knew all about his overactive conscience and she was having a laugh. He imagined her looking down at him now, sweating and toxic and wracked with guilt, and thinking, you muppet, Fraser Morgan. All this guilt for a fumble with a barmaid? Deep down of course, so deep down he couldn't bring himself to admit it, Fraser Morgan knew this tardiness and stress was entirely of his own making. In fact, the last twenty-four hours were entirely of his own making.

He was supposed to have caught the four o'clock from Euston – which would have got him to Lancaster and the Merchants in plenty of time, but because he was far too nice and far too hungover to put up a fight, he'd somehow become embroiled in a Tarot reading from Karen, which overran (he wasn't sure how long the average Tarot reading was, but felt sure an hour and a half was overrunning), missed the four o clock, so had to catch the five o'clock, and only realized when he was on the train that it didn't go further than Preston.

He now felt wretched, having thrown up in the train toilets and fielded three texts from Karen – are you on the train yet? How's the hangover? He'd finally broken when she'd told him what she was having for tea and switched off his phone.

Still, at least in the end he'd told her the truth; he'd been nothing but a gent. At least there was that.

'Unfortunately,' (he was now somewhat regretting the 'unfortunately' line. You give these people an inch and they take a mile) 'I can't hang out all day because I'm going to a reunion with my university mates – we do it every year.'

All true, nothing but the truth. But even that had backfired when Karen had propped herself up on her elbow, shaken her head slowly and given him that look – the look of love – and said, 'Do you know what? That doesn't surprise me one little bit. I can tell that Fraser Morgan is the sort of person who, once he is your friend, is a friend for life, do you know what I mean?'

Oh, Jesus Christ.

* * *

'So this is Ollie. Ollie, these are my friends . . .'

Fraser practically skidded into the Merchants, locating his mates in the last arch, just as Anna was introducing some new . . . boyfriend/fuck-buddy/future husband – it was hard to know what to expect where Spanner was concerned.

'Ollie,' thought Fraser, standing in the doorway of the arch, they're always called Ollie and I *bet* he works in the media and lives in Ladbroke Grove.

It took him another few seconds to register the reality of the situation. Spanner had brought some idiot in red skinny jeans – no doubt last night's conquest, a bloke nobody knew from Adam – to Liv's birthday reunion? He felt a sudden, overwhelming blackness of mood that crashed down on him like a tonne of rock involving anger on Liv's behalf, fury at his friend's audacity, mixed with a horrible, *horrible* wave of self-loathing – an ugly sense of his own double standards as the reality of what he'd done last night hit him again.

What Anna had done seemed suddenly outrageous, and yet, was what he'd done actually any better? And these were his friends, his best and oldest friends. They'd just know.

Nobody said hello to Ollie, who had the most unfortunate hairstyle Fraser had ever seen: dyed a reddish-pink and pulled forward around his face, like a giant crab-claw had him in a headlock.

'Right, wicked . . . well, er, I'll just go to the bar then?' he said, eventually, to nobody in particular.

Anna stroked his arm repeatedly as if he was a cat. 'Can I have a vodka and lime, please? Proper lime juice, not lime cordial?' she added, lowering her lashes at him, and Ollie nodded, locking eyes for far longer than was natural. (Or necessary, or fucking appropriate, come to think of it, thought Fraser. Who did he think he was? Playing out his postcoital dance, here?) And went to the bar.

'So you got here then?'

Fraser was still boring a hole in Ollie's back when he realized, back inside the arch, that Melody was talking to him.

'A call would have been appreciated, Fraser, we've been worried sick.'

Ha! this was rich. What about Anna? Why was nobody angry with Anna, who was busy removing her various bags (Anna always seemed to be carrying an assortment of bags, since her life was one big impromptu sleepover) like nothing had happened? Anna had always been flaky and selfish and Fraser had always forgiven her, not least because Liv always had ('I understand her, Fraser,' she always said. 'She's a mass of insecurity inside.') Also, Anna compensated by being gutsy and fearless; she appealed to Fraser's passionate side. Anna came from a socially aspiring, lower-middle-class family who had as good as bankrupted themselves to send her to private school. She and Fraser would have awesome 'heated debates', i.e. blazing slanging matches, in the kitchen of 5 South Road, where she would accuse him of being an inverted snob and he would accuse her of being a shameless social climber with a massive chip on her shoulder.

They disagreed on many things: Fraser incensed her with his tendency to always play devil's advocate. But Fraser loved her passion, how she wasn't remotely interested in life's subtle emotions: it was all pain and death and love and torture with Anna. But these days, she seemed to be using Liv's death as an excuse to be even more flaky and selfish, and Fraser wasn't having it.

He felt rage rise within him.

'Um, *Anna*.' He rubbed at his head hard, as if this would somehow get rid of it. 'Can I have a word with you? Like, outside? In private, please?'

Anna froze. Everyone had gone quiet and was staring into their drinks.

'Why?' she said, defensively.

'*Why?* Fucking hell, Anna. If you don't know why, then there's something wrong with you.'

'Oh, look, we'll just leave,' Anna snapped, standing up and gathering her stuff. 'Jesus Christ. If I'd thought this was going to be such a big deal . . . if I'd thought—'

'Anna,' Melody broke the silence. 'How can you say that? Of course this is a big deal, this is Liv's birthday.'

Anna let out an incredulous little gasp.

'Oh, my God, you're at it too! What is this? Gang up on Anna night? You lot have such double standards. HE was forty-five minutes late.' Anna was standing up now, pointing at Fraser. 'Later than me, and Liv was his girlfriend!'

'She does have a point, Fraser,' said Melody, grimacing, but Fraser didn't want to know about logic or who had a point; he was just angry, really fucking angry, and he didn't know why but it was taking over him, becoming bigger than him, as if he was being engulfed by a fireball.

The words came out in a torrent before he could help himself. 'God, you're selfish.' Anna stood there open-mouthed as he laid into her. 'You're like a fucking

36

teenager. You want so much back, and yet YOU, you, just do what you want, when you want. Bring who you want – twats in red jeans . . . some bloke you probably shagged last night.' He was on a roll now and he didn't care. 'No respect for Liv, for me . . .'

Out of the corner of his eye, Fraser clocked Norm staring at him and looked away.

'Fra*ser come on* . . .' It was only when he heard her voice, alarmed but still soft, that Fraser clocked that Mia was with Billy – why was she with Billy? Oh, he knew why she was with Billy. Eduardo. Such a useless pile of shit. Why she'd ever got together with him was beyond him.

Then Mia got up – Billy was crying now – and went over to him, putting her arm around Fraser as if trying to soothe him.

Anna exploded. 'Oh, that's nice, that is. You just take sides, Mia, go on – you always look after him, don't you? Have you noticed that?

'Anna, I do not . . . I—' Mia tried to defend herself, but Anna cut her dead.

'It's not all about you, you know, Fraser. I know Liv was your girlfriend, but she was our friend too; we all miss her. She wouldn't have given a shit if I had wanted to bring a friend along, or someone I shagged last night for that matter . . .' She was shouting now and Billy was crying harder. 'I'm sure she would have liked Ollie actually.' Ollie had come back from the bar now, and Fraser could feel him looming behind him. 'She *liked* new people, unlike some people I know. Some very angry and tormented people.'

What the hell was that supposed to mean?

She carried on and all hell broke loose. Anna was shouting at Fraser, Melody joined in and Fraser was shouting back. Then Mia was arguing with the landlord, Bruce, who said she couldn't bring a baby in a pub after 7 p.m., to which she shouted, 'DO YOU THINK I WOULD UNLESS I HAD TO? Unless it was a very special occasion? Do you not *remember* last year?' Then ate her words when a look of realization crossed Bruce's face as last year's escapade came flooding back. In the middle of all of this, Fraser had a flash of lucidity, something he found very uncomfortable when he got like this, which was getting more, not less, often, because he knew, deep down, that they'd done it again, *he*'d done it again. He thought of Liv. *Jesus wept, you lot, get a grip*, and he felt a trickle of shame run down his spine.

It was Norm who finally snapped and got them all to shut up. Including Billy.

'Look, people . . .' He slammed his pint down, a good deal of which splashed all over his shirt. 'Shit,' he mumbled, wiping it away. 'Don't you think this is pretty lame?'

He shifted on his feet, looking slightly uncomfortable. Voice of authority and reason was not a natural role for Norm, but circumstances called for it.

'I mean, if Livs could see us, you know, if she was looking down on us now – on her twenty-ninth birthday, in case you've all forgotten; if she had her feet up watching *Countdown*, having one of her cheeky Tia Maria coffees and maybe a twenty-quid fag . . .' There was a murmur of laughter and recognition from the group. 'Do you think she'd be impressed? Do you reckon she'd be like. Awesome. Look at my mates, aren't they just the best?

'I don't think so somehow.'

Fraser looked at his friend and felt a bloom of pride in his chest. Norm must think I'm a dick, he thought. I AM a dick. Norm had been so good to him in that text, going out of his way to make Fraser feel better, and then he'd still let the side down: rocked up an hour late, hungover, taking his guilt out on everyone else. He really hated himself sometimes.

'Look . . .' said Norm eventually.

Everyone was shuffling and staring at the ground, as if they were being told off by the headmaster.

'I found this.'

He reached inside his pocket and pulled out a tatty piece of A4.

'It's a list that Liv wrote – Things To Do Before I Am Thirty. I thought it might be nice for us all to read it later, pass it around or whatever and raise a drink to her. But since everyone's being idiots now . . .'

There was a sheepish mumble of apology from the crowd. Fraser was staring at the piece of paper in his friend's hand.

Norm looked at him, realization crossing his face.

'Oh. Totally innocent, mate, found it in the pocket of my old parka that Liv must have borrowed some time.'

Fraser smiled and waved his hand away. He didn't care where he'd got it from. He had a list. A list with Liv's handwriting on.

'Can I have that?' he said, stepping forward. Norm handed him the piece of paper.

THREE

Lancaster

Mia piled banana-and-mango purée into Billy's mouth, most of which he then regurgitated back onto the spoon, too busy watching *Peppa Pig* to concentrate on swallowing. She looked over at her friend on the sofa – just a tuft of brown, slightly matted hair poking out of the top of her orange sleeping bag – and felt a warm rush of nostalgia. When was the last time she'd had anyone stay the night on her sofa? (Except Eduardo after a row.) Or talked to someone in a sleeping bag late into the night? God, must have been years ago. University probably. They were always talking late into the night in sleeping bags back then.

Who did she talk to now? NatWest Debt Management Centre (although technically, that was more shouting), Virgin Media, Ashley at the Benefits Office. In fact, Ashley at the Benefits Office probably knew more about her life than her friends did. Definitely more than her mother did. No, if she really thought about it, Mia didn't really

41

talk to anyone these days. Not *proper* talking, anyway, just for the sheer fun of it. These days, talking always had to have a purpose.

She had a sudden memory – these were coming more often, like now the heavy numbness of early motherhood was lifting, clarity was gradually returning and, with it, memories and feelings, some of which she'd kept down for a reason. V Festival in Leeds – 2000, or was it 2001? She wasn't sure, but she knew Coldplay were headlining and that Melody pooh-poohed them as dullsville. Now Melody couldn't get enough of Coldplay.

It was warm and getting light – 4.30 a.m. or thereabouts – and she, Liv and Fraser were the only ones awake, sitting in their sleeping bags outside their tent, talking in hushed voices and drinking flat lager, the sound of Norm's pneumatic snoring coming from the tent next door.

'Let's play a game,' said Liv, suddenly. 'I know a brilliant game.'

Mia and Fraser had groaned: Liv was always coming out with new, strange games and 'takes' on things. Once, she'd tried to combine strip poker with the children's game Frustration – moving little men around a board in their bras and pants. Liv and Fraser were big on taking their clothes off when drunk – it was one of the many traits that made them perfect for each other. Whereas, Mia? Good God, no. She'd rather chew off her own arm than reveal her body to her friends. And that was before she'd had a baby.

'It's called I Have Never,' Liv continued. 'And it's a bit like Truth. Basically, the person whose turn it is says something they've never done in their life. For example, I might say . . . anal sex.'

Fraser had laughed. It sounded extra-loud in the soft dawn. 'Do you have to be quite so crude, Olivia?'

'So if you've done whatever the person whose turn it is is saying – i.e. you have had anal sex,' she carried on, ignoring him, 'then you have to down your drink, and then it's your turn, and so it goes on.'

They went through the usual repertoire: saying I love you when you don't mean it (they'd all done that one); threesomes – nobody had had one of those, which seemed a bit of a poor show. Mia had felt disappointed that at twenty-one, nobody in the group had fulfilled this particular rite of passage, but had comforted herself in the knowledge that good old Anna would no doubt have had one, if not that very evening in her tent.

Then it was Mia's turn: 'I have never . . . snogged anyone famous,' which Fraser drank to because Floella Benjamin, a distant family friend – they all thought this was hysterical in itself – had once given him a peck on the cheek at a country fair when he was eight. They'd all agreed that didn't really count.

It was almost light now; a rosy mist hovered above the field, illuminating their faces. Norm's snoring from the tent was reaching crescendo levels. Then Liv said, 'I have never . . . snogged any other member of our group of friends except Fraser.'

'What, not even Anna?' Mia blurted out, almost on automatic. 'Everyone's snogged Spanner.' Which was true. She'd kissed her back in their first year at Lancaster, at the height of her very fleeting foray into lipstick-lesbianism, which she was quite proud of if truth be told.

'No, I have *not* snogged Anna!' said Liv, outraged, and yet Mia suspected, ever so slightly jealous. 'When the hell did you snog Anna?' Mia was in the midst of answering when it all came flooding back, it dawned on her. She glanced at Fraser, whose face was covered with the can of lager he was now drinking from.

Liv looked at Mia, then at Fraser.

'Oh, my God, *you've* snogged Anna?' she said, smiling, but it was a sliding smile – half intrigue, half . . . what was that look? Appalled? Mia didn't like to think about it too much.

Fraser had spluttered beer everywhere.

'What? No. I haven't snogged Anna. Or anyone else for that matter. Sorry, I was just drinking my beer, is that allowed? I just forgot the rules.'

Then they'd all sort of moved on, the question lost in booziness and early morning confusion, but Mia was thinking about it now as she shovelled banana-and-mango purée back into Billy's mouth. It was coming back to her. Lots of things were coming back to her now.

Fraser stirred, made some sort of grunting sound – an attempt at speech, and Billy, on cue, did the same, which made Mia laugh.

'Morning, Fraser Morgan.' She'd been up since 5.50 a.m. with a grizzly baby, but then grizzliness was more or less Billy's default mode. It was now 9 a.m. and she felt as though she'd lived a day already.

'What?' He stuck his head out of the sleeping bag and grimaced at her, squinting into the light that flooded through the Velux window, a look of pure confusion on his face.

'How you doing?' Mia dodged a bit of purée as Billy smacked his podgy little hands up and down on the

44

high-chair top. ''Coz you look shocking, to tell you the truth.'

'I didn't ask for the truth, but cheers, I feel like death,' croaked Fraser, easing himself up on his elbows. There was a brief pause before they both registered what he'd said and laughed awkwardly.

'Well, I can tell you, you've done very well indeed.' Mia turned her back to carry on feeding Billy. 'You've slept through a box-set of *In the Night Garden*, a phone row with Eduardo and a meltdown from Billy who lobbed a rusk at your head at one point and you still didn't wake up.'

Fraser laughed weakly, then coughed – he'd smoked last night and could feel it on his lungs – and pulled the sleeping bag up around his chin, staring blankly out at the bare trees, dark and arrested as if frozen in time. The stark whiteness of another winter's day.

And I do feel like death, he thought. I really fucking do. He remembered this from last year, the days after the anniversary of Liv's death and her birthday.

The actual anniversaries themselves weren't that bad; they certainly weren't that good, either, but he was drunk for much of them. Also, they were occasions and, like all occasions, there was a momentousness, some degree of specialness involved. People called and fussed around him, Mia especially. On the first anniversary, she'd called practically every hour to check he was out of bed and dressed. Actually, he was in the Bull by midday, halfway down his second pint, Karen listening patiently as he blathered on. His parents, Carol and Mike, had called too. That was one good thing to come out of Liv's death, he supposed: he'd become closer to his parents. Before

45

he lost Liv, their relationship was stuck in teenage mode, where he told them nothing except the absolute essentials and they didn't ask much except about when he was going to get a proper job like his brother (Shaun Morgan ran *Top Financial Solutions*. Why he'd never come up with a 'top solution' to his little brother's financial problems, Fraser would never know).

Fraser was a dutiful son – i.e. he did the bare minimum, visiting them in their spotless ex-council house in Bury every few months, where he'd sit and read the paper whilst Liv talked to Mike about his job in the world of tap fittings and to Carol about her gallstones, but they weren't close. They didn't really know each other. In fact, if Carol Morgan were honest, she'd lost her youngest son the day he went to university, when his friends and his girlfriend became his family.

But that was before grief dismantled Fraser, ripped him open then hurtled through him like a freight train, making him furious and self-destructive and self-pitying. That was the worst. After his mother had to pick him up from Manchester Royal Infirmary, where he was admitted with a broken ankle after being so drunk he had fallen down a fire escape at a club in Manchester, Fraser knew the game was up. There was no room for his teenage self, full of misplaced pride and embarrassment. He needed her again like he had when he was a blond, corkscrew-haired five-year-old, and he'd curled up in her arms that night and cried like one.

So, in a strange way, the actual anniversaries were doable. At least everyone was there. But this – the day after – was worse, because what now? Where now? Life still carried on, but the phone stopped ringing, and when the specialness had gone, what did he have left? Except himself. And he was a mess. He couldn't settle anywhere; his flat scared the shit out of him, a place he just rattled around in, wandering from one room to another, in some state of intoxication most of the time. He had told himself, countless times, he'd use this time alone to learn to cook, because Liv was a fabulous cook, but eventually got bored of buying lemon grass only to stop off at the Bull on the way back and leave it there. the Bull in Kentish Town must have the biggest stock of lemon grass in north London.

He couldn't watch TV any more, couldn't concentrate on films – something he and Liv had loved to do; daft comedies were their favourite, cuddling up on a Sunday to watch *Meet the Fockers*. Nowadays, he'd totally lost the ability to look at a screen for any length of time and, sometimes, although he never admitted this to anyone, he went to bed at 8 p.m. because he couldn't deal with any more day.

Then there was the job, or excuse for one, really, since life as a freelance sound engineer – holding a fluffy mike whilst some geezer did a piece to camera about local history, or a party political broadcast – didn't actually require much skill, and it was a far cry from being a sound engineer for bands, too, wasn't it? Let's face it. That dream, along with his dream to be an actual rock star himself had shifted, as he moved through his teens to his twenties, from a dead cert to still doable if he really pulled his finger out, to now, aged thirty, simply a comforting fantasy he liked to indulge in occasionally.

The worst thing was, it had been over a year now, he should really have pulled himself together. But life had become one big long promise to himself that tomorrow would be different. Tomorrow he'd get it together. Sometimes he wondered if his grief was becoming a habit rather than a need, but it didn't matter because now he was breathless with it – the emptiness – as if he'd woken up entombed in concrete.

'Fancy a tea? Bacon sandwich?' Fraser could hear Mia's voice and he could see her but couldn't really compute what she was saying; it was all muffled as if he were looking at her through a glass screen, and yet he was so glad she was here, suddenly overcome with gratitude in fact because it occurred to him – what the hell would he have done with himself today if she *wasn't*? For a second he wanted to reach over and grab onto her legs. He shook the feeling away.

Billy was sucking on a bottle of milk now, not very enthusiastically, and Mia took it off him for a second to shake it, so he started wailing, a cry that turned into a raspy scream. It reminded Fraser of something and he was aware of his heart pounding as though it might leap right out of his chest. Mia gave Billy the bottle back and he immediately stopped crying. Fraser could still see his little flushed cheeks sucking greedily and happily, and yet he could still hear something. He could still hear a terrible noise.

'Oh, God, Frase. Oh, shit . . .'

It wasn't until Mia had her arms tight around him, that he realized the noise was coming from him.

FOUR

Mia got Fraser up and out of the flat as soon as possible – which in reality, Fraser had noted with some amusement, took about an hour, half of that trying to get an incensed Billy into his snowsuit. 'Told you I lived with Mussolini,' Mia shouted over the racket, whilst Fraser looked on, gobsmacked. She was right. Bloody hell. How could such a small thing make so much noise? Did Mia really have to do this every day, just to get out of the door? In the months that followed Liv's death they'd spent a lot of time together – first when Mia was pregnant and then those difficult months after Billy was born, but he didn't have a clue about the day-to-day, the reality of which now shocked him.

Still, Billy looks like I feel, thought Fraser.

'Can I do that now, please?' he said. 'Roll onto my back and scream whilst someone puts me into a straightjacket?'

They went directly into town to the Sunbury Café. It was bitingly cold, the sky sharp and blue as stained glass. The Sunbury Café – housed in one of Lancaster's sandstone Georgian houses down a cobbled alley – was where they used to go as students. They'd have millionaire's shortbread and cappuccinos, sit out the back on the terrace on wrought-iron chairs, like they were ladies who lunched, not poverty-stricken students, discussing the big topics of the day (back when talking was just for the fun of it): whether Phillip Schofield dyed his hair, whether Prince Harry was the love-child of James Hewitt, but also marriage, kids, what order they'd do everything in.

Even though Mia liked to think of her style as 'thrown together arty' (although admittedly, of late, it was more single mum on benefits), she was a traditionalist at heart and had said yes to both, in the right order. Liv had said yes to marriage but definitely no to kids, 'Over my dead body!' How those phrases came back to them now.

Mia had loved those times, when everything was hypothetical, when it felt like life was a game and they could press 'reset' at any time. These days, of course, it all felt so real.

Mia walked back towards the terrace from the café, carrying a large black coffee for Fraser and a cappuccino for herself and eyed him in a motherly way. This was the thing: she had no problem feeling naturally maternal towards her friends; it was just her son she sometimes struggled with.

Fraser was all wrapped up in his parka like a duvet and was pushing Billy back and forth in his buggy – a bit too hard if Mia was the sort to be pernickety, which she wasn't – trying to get him off to sleep, and Mia thought what a cute dad he'd make and whether, if Liv had still been around, he might even have changed her mind and they might have made a baby together by now.

'So basically, I'm a mess,' he said suddenly. It took Mia by surprise. Fraser wasn't one for outbursts of self-awareness, it was all going on inside with him, all being secretly brooded about.

She put the coffee down in front of him.

'Um, yeah, I'd say so. But that's OK, that's workable with.'

He smiled, weakly.

'Can I come clean about something?' he said.

Mia sat down.

'You're in love with me. That's OK.'

Fraser sighed, wearily.

'Sorry.' Mia grimaced. She knew she did this; this was her coping mechanism – humour in dark times. In some ways, she often thought Fraser was more in touch with his raw emotions, that his were somehow closer to the surface than hers, Norm's, Melody's and Anna's put together.

'I've stooped low,' he said.

'Oh?'

'With the whole grief, mess, not coping thing, I've stooped low, Woodhouse, Really low.'

'Well, it can't be as low as I've stooped in the last twelve months,' said Mia, scooping the froth from her coffee onto the saucer (Fraser noted this, and once again wondered why she insisted on ordering cappuccino when she hated the frothy bit, the whole point of a cappuccino, surely?). I once left my son with a seventy-eight-year-old batty old woman who lets her cat poo in her knicker drawer.

He blinked and shook his head.

'What?'

'Mrs Durham. You know the old lady I look after on Tuesdays? Billy was teething – well, that's always been my excuse, but I just think he's one of life's screamers, to tell you the truth. He'd have about ninety-two teeth by now if he'd really teethed at the rate I had people believe . . .'

Fraser laughed, properly, for what felt like the first time in ages, and once again felt a rush of gratitude that his friend was here, that he wasn't alone.

'Anyway, he'd been at it, nonstop all weekend. It was round about the time of Liv's anniversary last year and I was desperate to have just twenty minutes on my own, so I took him round there in desperation, practically chucked him in her doorway like a rugby ball. She's stone deaf anyway, so an ideal child-minder.'

They both laughed.

'*Anyway,* as I was saying . . .' said Fraser. Mia could see he was eager to get back to his point. 'You know last night when I was in that taxi? I'd fucked up, I was hungover, nearly an hour late because the stupid train didn't stop at Preston and you know what? I blamed Liv. I *actually believed,*' he said, enunciating his words as if this was the most preposterous idea ever, 'that she was stirring things up from heaven, having a laugh at me. At one point, I said out loud in the taxi – the taxi driver had his screen up so he didn't hear: '"Right, enough now, Olivia, you're not funny any more."'

Mia smirked with recognition. On the day of the funeral, all sorts of nonsense had gone on, and she'd said the very same thing. For starters, in one of those 'you couldn't make it up' moments, the night before, Eduardo had been walking home from the pub, fallen through an open trap door in the street, into the beer cellar of a pub, and broken his leg, so didn't even make it to the funeral. Then the battery of Mia's car was found to be flat for no apparent reason and she'd had to get a lift with Fraser instead. Yeah, that was Liv, always the practical joker. But that was the day of the funeral, that was eighteen months ago. The most strange and dark day – like a scene in a film: she still couldn't believe it had actually happened.

She said, 'But that's kind of nice, isn't it? To feel she's still with us? The Olivia Jenkins effect?'

'Yeah, but I'm finding myself blaming her for loads of stuff,' Fraser said. 'How I feel, what I do – or *don't* do, which is more to the point. But it's not her fault, is it?' he continued. 'None of this: how I feel, how you feel, the total pig's ear I seem to be making of my life – it's not her fault she left us, is it? Or . . .'

He stopped.

'Or what?' said Mia.

'Nothing. You know.'

'Fraser, you have to give that up, seriously.'

'Yeah, yeah, I know.'

'I know it's hard – I think about it too – but it's really unhealthy. Plus,' she leant over to check on Billy who had fallen asleep, his head lolling to the side, 'it's bollocks and it's irrelevant.'

Fraser didn't say anything.

'Isn't it?' she said again, peering into Billy's buggy. 'It's irrelevant?'

'Yeah, guess so. Survivors' guilt and all that. And anyway, it changes nothing.'

'Exactly,' said Mia. 'So, no, it's not her fault, Fraser. The wallpaper in your lounge is her fault and the fact we saw in the new Millennium in a queue for a kebab, but nothing else.'

Fraser rolled his eyes.

'You've never forgiven her for that, have you?'

'Nope and I never shall,' she said, a twinkle in her eye to tell him she didn't mean it.

She watched him as he drank his coffee in the crisp, winter sun, feet up on the chair – he could look like someone enjoying après-ski if he didn't look so shocking. His hair had obviously not been washed for days so that the waves clung together in a greasy mess, gathering in an unsightly duck's arse at the nape of his neck. His skin had a deathly pallor today and definitely lacked the elasticity a man barely turned thirty should possess. But she couldn't deny, he was attractive too. Or appealing, maybe that's what it was. Whatever it was, Mia found herself inexorably drawn to his face. Maybe it was the symmetry thing she was always reading about in the vacuous magazines she liked to numb her brain further with after Billy had gone to bed. Maybe he looked like her dad – not that she knew what her dad looked like.

There was something real about him, something, what was it . . .? Northern, perhaps? He certainly didn't look like the Home Counties rugger-buggers she'd been to school with, or even the artsy lot with their foppish hair and 'ironic' jumpers. No, he was definitely more real than that. You'd never cast him in a Richard Curtis romcom, she thought, but maybe a Mike Leigh.

He had charm rather than being beautiful or ruggedly

handsome, or even particularly good-looking, now she came to think of it. Thick, darkish hair that had a nice, almost wartime wave to it when he actually washed it. Blue, almond-shaped eyes – his best feature – if it weren't for the fact they were half blind, but he never got round to getting his eyes tested, meaning he was permanently squinting. This often got misread as a scowl by people who didn't know him, which was something Mia thought was a great shame and easily remedied, but Fraser seemed to prefer to go through life with impaired vision.

He had a cute, sort of squishy nose, which was scattered with freckles and, she noted today, broken capillaries, hinting at the excessive drinking he'd been doing of late. A nice mouth. The teeth a bit discoloured after a long and intense affair with Silk Cut, but a nice mouth all the same, with expressive lips. This morning, sporting a shocker of a coldsore.

'What?' said Fraser suddenly.

'What?' She came to. 'Nothing. You've got a coleslaw, that's all.'

He smiled – that's what Liv always called them – and put his finger to it, self-consciously. 'I know. I started with it last night.'

'You make it sound like labour and don't touch it! You'll spread herpes all over your face.'

Fraser tutted.

'Anyway, I was just thinking,' she continued, 'about what you said, about Liv having a laugh at you. I mean, besides it being a bit morbid, why would she want to have a laugh at you? She loved you.'

Fraser took a deep breath; there was no point dragging

this out any longer, it was killing him. He covered his face. 'Oh, God, I slept with someone.'

Fraser didn't know what he expected Mia's reaction would be, but three small words that conveyed neither sense nor feeling, and a face like he'd just told her he had a fungal infection, wasn't really it.

'What? Oh. *Eeeew* . . .' She was actually recoiling, screwing her face up.

'What's that supposed to mean?' he said.

Mia didn't really know what *that* was supposed to mean. They were just the first noises that came out of her mouth.

'Nothing. It doesn't mean anything, it's just . . . God, OK.' Something strange was happening to her facial muscles and her voice but there seemed little she could do about it. She attempted to smile. 'So who was it?' she slapped her knees with her palms. 'Come on!'

'Karen,' said Fraser.

'Karen?'

'Yes, you know, Karen from the Bull.'

A cruel 'Ha!' escaped from Mia's mouth. That didn't seem like something she could help either. 'What? The really old one who looks like Ness from *Gavin and Stacey*?'

'She's not really old, she's forty-two.'

Mia felt her eyebrows rise involuntarily and put them back, sharpish.

'And she looks nothing like Ness from *Gavin and Stacey*.'

'She so does!' *Rein it in, rein it in.* 'A bit. I mean in that she's got dark hair and she's, you know . . . curvy . . .' REIN. IT. IN.

'You mean fat.'

'I did NOT say fat, you did. Also, she's . . .'

Fraser cocked his head.

'What? Easy. Bit of a slapper?'

'I did NOT say slapper, you did! No, I was going to say bubbly, actually.'

'Bubbly,' said Fraser, flatly.

'Yes, bubbly. You know, outgoing, chatty . . .?'

'Mmm,' said Fraser, unconvinced. 'Anyway, crucially, she's not Welsh, she's from Hull.'

There was a long and sudden pause.

'Well, I'm sure she's very nice,' Mia said, eventually.

'She is and she's got a very pretty face.'

'Well, we all know what *that* means.'

Fraser's mouth dropped open.

'Oh, Fraser. It was a joke!'

Neither of them said anything for a moment. Fraser was confused and yet he wasn't even sure what he was confused about; he just knew he'd expected a proper discussion or even a motherly telling off about one thing – i.e. the fact he'd slept with someone, *anyone*, the night before Liv's reunion – and he'd got something else entirely.

'I just think it's a bit disrespectful,' Mia blurted out when she'd tucked Billy in as much as she could and the silence was getting too much. 'Not just to Liv but to Karen. I mean it's not like you intend to see her again, is it?'

Fraser felt sick. What was it about girls that meant they could always do that? Psychologically strip you in a flash – it really pissed him off. This was exactly how he felt, exactly what was driving his guilt, but still, the way this whole conversation was going . . . it was making him defensive.

'I was drunk,' he said. 'I was pissed. I didn't know what I was doing, did I? And she's been really good to me. She's a nice person.'

Mia looked at him. 'But you don't fancy her.'

'I don't *not* fancy her.' Fraser was getting more agitated. 'Anyway, what's with the double standards?' This was another thing girls did that really got his goat. Double standards, left, right and centre. 'I mean look at you and Eduardo. He's such a tit, Mia, he lets you and Billy down constantly and yet you still let him sleep on your settee.' He jabbed a finger in her direction. 'And I bet it's not your settee every time, young lady.'

Mia fidgeted uncomfortably – how could he possibly have deduced that when all she ever did was slag Eduardo off? He was far more perceptive than she gave him credit for. Still, she was riled now. She hardly thought him sleeping with Karen and her letting Eduardo – the father of her child – stay over now and again were quite the same thing.

'Fraser, it is actually quite hard on my own, you know. Really bloody hard, actually.' She hated doing the poor single mother thing, but she was really hacked off now. 'If I had the luxury of being able to wipe Eduardo from my life, then I would, course I would, but, as it happens, I rely on every scrap of support and help I can get.'

'Oh, God, look, I'm sorry,' said Fraser, getting up. 'I'm going for a fag.'

'I thought you'd stopped,' Mia called after him.

'I started again.'

Fraser walked around the front of the café and leant against its façade, cupping his hands to light his cigarette.

Well, *that* went well. Clearly, he'd been deluded to think Mia would ease his guilt – she'd basically just made him feel worse! And the awful thing was, she was the most objective and reasonable of the group (except Norm perhaps. Norm was Switzerland. But that was more down to being stoned than any political decision to remain neutral.) If *she* thought what he'd done was bad, there was no hope for everyone else. And yet, it had to happen some time, didn't it? Presumably, he couldn't swear himself to celibacy all his life? Become a monk, one of those shaven-headed 'Tibetan' ones he often saw in Lancaster town centre, who weren't Tibetan at all; more ex-drug dealers from Skerton – Lancaster's answer to Moss Side – who wanted to turn their life around and still spent all day hanging outside Greggs, waiting for food handouts. Presumably, he had to get laid some time? Surely, Liv would have wanted that? Wouldn't she? He didn't know any more.

Fraser put his lighter back in his coat pocket and, as he did, felt the piece of folded-up paper – Liv's List, the Things To Do Before I Am Thirty – that Norm had given him the night before. He must have felt pretty special to find that, it must have been a big deal for Norm, and yet he'd just nabbed it from him. He felt a twinge of guilt at his crassness and, not for the first time recently, wondered if he was just not that nice any more.

He unfolded it, JULY 15TH, 2005 it said at the top – two and a half years ago, she would have been twenty-six – and read downwards, touching Liv's elegant, left-handed writing that sloped to the right. *Liv Jenkins woz 'ere.* He said it quietly. She was here and now she's not. It was the maddest concept ever.

He read on and, for a moment, standing outside the café, the cold numbing his fingers, it felt like she *was* there; he could hear her voice in the writing and yet he also felt disloyal, as though he was snooping. They always discussed everything. Liv couldn't go for a wee without informing him first. How come she'd never discussed making this List with him?

He read on: Sleep with an exotic foreigner (in an ideal world, Javier Bardem). He smiled, whilst vigorously fighting a niggling dent to his ego. *What's so special about this Javier Bardem character?* He sounded like a knob. *And what did he have that Fraser didn't? Besides an international film career and millions in the bank?*

Learn how to make a Roman blind. Fraser frowned, genuinely puzzled. She'd never shown any interest in home furnishings when she was around, hence the disastrous wallpaper choice with the embossed bunches of grapes all over it – a sort of wine-induced migraine in wall-covering form.

Climb Great Wall of China and learn a bit of Chinese (should be able to do this whilst climbing the Great Wall).

Fraser sniggered at that one. He could really hear Liv now. Her very specific breed of deadpan, random humour.

Vegas, baby! Swim naked in the sea at dawn . . . A picture of Liv and her phenomenal legs and her glorious boobs was just coming into view when Mia appeared with the buggy.

She looked up at him, shielding her face from the sun. 'You OK?'

Fraser nodded, sheepishly.

'Yeah, just about.'

'Give us a drag on that, will you?'

Fraser did as he was told and Mia inhaled, blew the smoke sideways, then stubbed it out.

'Oi, I hadn't finished that!'

'You gave up,' she said. 'I'm helping you.'

A group of five or six teenagers – almost certainly students – arrived at the café, chatting and laughing. They went inside and Mia and Fraser looked at each other, both knowing instinctively they were thinking the same thing.

'Anyway, what you up to?' said Mia, eventually.

'Oh, just reading this . . .' Fraser folded the piece of paper up self-consciously. 'It's that List that Liv wrote, the one Norm had last night?'

Mia knew exactly what it was. She'd already had an idea about what to do with it, too. Looking at Fraser's face now, she was even more convinced it was a good one.

She put the brake on the buggy and went to stand next to him, leaning against the wall, lifting her face to the sun.

Fraser sighed.

'It's just shit, basically, isn't it? All these things she'll never do. All this life she'll never live.'

'The world is certainly going to be a much darker place without Liv's perfect Victoria sponge and her home-made porn video, that's for sure,' said Mia, and Fraser couldn't help but laugh, although Mia inwardly chastised herself. She was doing it again.

Fraser said, 'I just think . . . I think we were robbed. Life's just not the same any more, is it?'

'No,' shrugged Mia. 'And yes, we were robbed, course we were, but without sounding harsh, nothing's going to bring her back, Frase, is it?' She looked across at him. 'So what are we going to do about it now?'

It was a suggestion rather than a statement, since she had one idea about what they might do.

For a moment, Fraser said nothing. There was the sound of plates clattering inside the café, orders being called from the kitchen. Life. Then he slowly unfolded the List again and read it through.

'It's not exactly, get married, get a pension, get a Tesco's Clubcard, is it?' he said.

'What do you mean?' said Mia.

'I mean these ideas are Blue Sky, ambitious.'

'It's like the annual schedule from Red Letter Days.'

'Well exactly,' said Fraser. 'And yet it's all I can do to get up in the morning.'

The idea nagged urgently in Mia's head. Would he just think it was silly and pointless? Or naff, even? Nothing would bring Liv back, that was true, but at least this would be a project and a distraction, something for them all to focus on. She could definitely do with some focus in her life.

'Can I say something?' she said.

'Go for your life.'

'Promise you won't take offence?'

'No, but I'll try.'

'Well, it's just you say that. You say you can't get out of bed in the morning, but it wasn't you who died, was it?'

Fraser frowned. 'No. If it had, I definitely wouldn't be getting out of bed, would I?'

'I don't think that's my point,' said Mia, thinking God, he could be facetious when he wanted to.

'So what is your point?'

'My point is, we are still alive, aren't we?'

'Yeees . . .'

'We still have our lives so, in a way, all we can do is get on with it. Liv would have wanted that. I know she won't be able to do all those things on the List but maybe . . .'

'What?'

'Well, maybe we can do them for her?'

She looked at him, unsure. Fraser pulled a face.

'If you think I'm making a Roman blind or learning how to meditate, you have got another thing coming.'

Mia rolled her eyes.

'Well, nobody's going to make you do anything you don't want to do, but don't you think it would be a laugh? A bit of structure at least. A project? We could get everyone else roped in too.'

Fraser considered this for a second. 'What, Norm and Melody making a homemade porn film at some dodgy B&B in Morecambe?'

'Yes, if you think that would work for you, put a smile on that face.' She got hold of his cheeks and tugged them.

Fraser stuck his tongue out.

'Promise me Spanner will not get the swimming naked in the sea one. She'd love it too much and we'd never get her out – which would defeat the object.'

'If you insist. You can be List secretary if you like.'

'Hey, we could all go to China together! We could all climb the Great Wall together – me and you, what do you reckon?'

'I reckon this is much more like it.' Mia smiled.

And so they went on. They ordered more coffee, they stayed at the café and they hatched their plan. Fraser baggsying, 'Vegas, baby!'

FIVE

Fraser stands outside Top Shop on Oxford Street, occasionally craning his neck to see if he can make out Karen coming towards him, out of the crowds. They've been seeing one another for five weeks now, although Fraser doesn't quite know how this happened. One minute, Karen was just a friendly, regular face behind the bar, someone who listened patiently as he got more drunk and morose; the next, she was his girlfriend, all seemingly without him having experienced any cognitive processes whatsoever.

As he stands there, April blossom scurrying around his feet, Fraser suspects it's happened simply because he couldn't come up with a good enough, fast enough reason why it shouldn't.

Karen called him the night after he got back from Lancaster, asking him if he fancied going for a curry as she had a two-for-one voucher at the Taj Mahal. Fraser said yes, mainly because he had no food in the house and somehow the voucher thing made it seem more innocuous, and that was that. They went for a slap-up Mexican the week after that, then 'a beer' one Monday night that somehow ended up in Karen's bed, her giving him a back massage to the strains of Enya and, before he knew it, he had himself a girlfriend – as well as, he feared, the onset of heart disease. Karen isn't really one to pick at lettuce leaves, put it like that, but then he's always liked that in a girl.

And it's nice to have someone to go out for curries with. He likes having another body in the house, someone who calls him at work, who comes round and cooks for him – *finally*, someone who knows what to do with lemon grass. It's comforting and grounding.

However, she started, about a fortnight in, to buy him random 'love gifts', as she calls them, which makes Fraser feel special and anxious in equal measure: a four-pack of Ambrosia Devon custard, for example, after he said this was his favourite childhood dessert (this is the sort of question Karen likes to ask, often after sex: What was your favourite food as a child? If you were an animal, what animal would you be?), and a photo frame in the shape of a guitar, which was disgusting, truly foul, but which he felt pressurized to fill with a picture of him and Norm. He just hoped to God he remembered to hide it if Norm ever came round.

Fraser knows Karen is a ridiculously kind, thoughtful and giving woman, and he lives in hope that one day, preferably this week, he might wake up to find he has fallen in love with her, even if he cannot shake the feeling when he is with her that all his dreams are going up in smoke.

Not that he really believes his dreams will come true any more, but they are still there, lurking at the back of his mind like forgotten treasure on a sea bed: the one about him writing that one incredible song that will get the Fans signed. They'd started one before Liv died – called 'Hope and Glory' – about youth – all their songs seemed to be about youth, and living forever, back then – and never finished it. But Norm doesn't even live in the same city any more, so band practice is out of the question. These dreams feel idiotic and delusional when he is with Karen, and he doesn't know if this is just because he's growing up or because she is wrong for him, but it suits him fine at the moment because feeling the way he does, so depleted and traumatized, his dreams feel too scary to contemplate, like gigantic, terrifying foreign lands that he has neither the strength nor motivation to conquer.

He looks down at his filthy running trainers and wonders if he's wearing the right footwear for a salsa class – what do people wear at a dance class anyway? God forbid it's bare feet. Fraser felt, in his bones, he would be against any physical activity that warranted bare feet.

He moves away from the doorway of Top Shop so he's standing in the middle of the pavement and he can see her now, grinning, her dark head bobbing down the road, weaving her way through the evening crowds with her arms above her head, carrying several shopping bags.

Karen is an enthusiastic shopper – and enthusiastic, thinks Fraser, is the word. He's always presumed all girls were born shoppers, like boys were born knowing how to put up shelves, but Karen seems to be the exception to this rule, bringing home something new to wear, or getting a delivery from eBay on an almost daily basis but then promptly sending it back.

Evenings at Karen's largely consist of Fraser sitting alone on her sofa, the TV drowned out by the sound of masking tape being pulled then torn with teeth, like she's performing some sort of medieval operation next door.

Fraser waves slowly at her and she gives him a big smile back since she can't wave due to the number of bags hanging off her arm. He walks towards her; she holds his face in her hands and kisses him when they meet.

'Hello, Fred . . .'

She has a sheen of sweat on her top lip from the effort of rushing but is also flushed and bright-eyed, which Fraser is encouraged to note makes her look pretty and fecund in a milkmaid kind of way.

'Fred . . .?' says Fraser, lost.

'Astaire, innit.' She laughs, looking up at him with that look again – he really wishes she wouldn't do that – and, despite his best efforts not to (it's a daily battle), Fraser cringes.

Karen has taken to putting 'innit' on the end of sentences but, like other little nuances of hers, she is slightly slow on the uptake – wasn't Ali G famous in about 2005? Immediately he has this thought, Fraser chastises himself for it. This is the other thing he is finding about Karen. She brings out the petty in him; small, inane things make his toes curl and he hates himself for it. Who are you anyway, he thinks, the Cool Police?

He says, 'Oh, right! Yeah. Got yer. Fred Astaire, mmm . . .' He raises an eyebrow, as if to say, I don't think so somehow. 'Well, I think I'm as ready as I'll ever be.'

But Fraser knows he'll never be ready for this. Ever. In his life. In fact, right now, standing in the street on a warm Tuesday evening in April, every molecule in his body is telling him he'd rather be doing anything – undergoing a life-threatening operation, for example – than going to a salsa class.

But 'Learn to do SOME sort of dance' is one of the four tasks he's been allocated from Liv's List to complete and he is determined to do this for her.

After he and Mia hatched their plan that awful day after Liv's birthday, they got everyone over to Mia's, where they tried, for a fruitless hour, to give free rein and let everyone choose four things each from the List.

But this resulted in nothing but shouting and Melody and Norm almost filing for divorce when it was decided, as the only couple, that they should do the homemade porn movie one and Melody burst out laughing: 'Chance would be a fine thing. We haven't had sex since October!' Norm was not amused.

They'd gone round in circles, until finally, Mia had the ingenious idea that they should write down all the tasks on bits of paper, put them in a hat and let fate decide.

So this was the outcome:

Fraser: Learn to dance; sleep with an exotic foreigner: do this without becoming completely neurotic about what it's supposed to 'mean' (Fraser felt – at a push – he could probably manage this); use up all seven Scrabble letters in one turn; make a Roman blind.

Norm: Learn how to make the perfect Victoria sponge; Vegas, baby!; get a six-pack; climb Great Wall of China.

Mia: Go to Venice, properly this time, and have a bellini at Harry's Bar; swim naked in the sea at dawn; learn a foreign language; learn how to pluck eyebrows.

Anna: Read all works by William Wordsworth, learn how to meditate, to 'live in the moment'; live in Paris for a while; learn how to use chopsticks.

Melody: French kiss in Central Park; make a home-made porn film; have a party for all my wonderful friends.

Number nineteen, they planned to do as the very last one, together as a group:

Go to airport, close eyes and pick a destination at random, then GO! Even if it's to Stuttgart or Birmingham.

Of course, Fraser hasn't told Karen about the List, which he does feel guilty about, since if there were no List – if there were no Liv, essentially – there'd be no way he would voluntarily sign up for a salsa class. Today, against his better judgement and only to liven up the most boring day at work this year (eight hours spent holding a microphone to someone's head as they made a party political broadcast about obesity outside McDonald's), he'd told the boys at work – John and Declan – and they'd ribbed him mercilessly, said they didn't know anyone less likely to be going to a 'gay' salsa class . . .

But Karen doesn't know this and what she doesn't know, he's reasoned, can't hurt her. Besides, she was ecstatic when he asked her.

'Really? You're not jesting me?' ('Jesting' is one of Karen's favourite '90s expressions, along with 'mint' and 'yes way'.) 'You actually want to go to dance lessons – with

70

me?' She looked dumbfounded, as though he'd just asked her to marry him, and squealed before hugging him so tight she almost suffocated him with her enormous, no, really *enormous*, amazing and wondrous breasts. It doesn't matter how many times she says 'innit', Fraser doubts he will ever get irritated by those.

So, he felt absolved of his guilt, but now, what with Karen's obsession with *Strictly Come Dancing* and calling him Fred Astaire, he is starting to worry she might think he can *actually* dance. After all, who suggests starting a hobby they don't already have some aptitude for?

Fraser clings to the hope that salsa might just be his big, untapped talent, but realistically, chances are slim. Small children have been known to laugh at him at wedding receptions.

'Been shopping again?' says Fraser, cheerfully.

They're walking side by side up Oxford Street now, towards the class, which is somewhere tucked behind Little Portland Street.

'Ohmigod, have I been shopping.'

'Really?'

'*Really.*'

'You've really been and done the shopping thing this time?'

She squeezes his arm. 'Just you wait and see.'

They are prone to little exchanges of inane conversation like this, where Fraser feels as if he's in that programme, *Whose Line Is It Anyway?*, but just can't think of any good lines.

He lights a cigarette for want of something better to do.

'So . . . do you wanna see then?' says Karen, after Fraser clearly hasn't taken the hint.

'Yeah, why not, go on then.'

She moves to the side of the street and opens up one of the plastic bags, which is pink and has the word FREED written on it. Fraser's hands go clammy, his throat goes suddenly dry. It's a shoebox and inside the box is a pair of leather dance shoes with a strap across and a square heel. The leather looks soft – he can smell it – and, even with his untrained eye, he can tell they cost a fortune.

Karen holds them up proudly, like a cat making an offering: 'I just thought, do you know what? Bugger it. If we're going to do this, we're going to do it properly. I'm telling you, this dance thing is like a whole new world of retail opportunity!'

Thank you, Lord, they're not for me.

'Do you like them? The lady in the shop said they were the same as professionals wear.'

Fraser isn't really au fait with dance shoes or what there is to like about them, so says the first thing that comes into his head: 'They've got a very nice heel.'

Her face lights up.

'Really? Do you think so?'

'God, yeah, totally, a really, really good heel. Really good heel.' Jesus. I hope you can see me, Olivia Jenkins, he thinks, and I hope you're happy.

Fraser has seen adverts on Sky TV for salsa classes – in fact, he's done a broadcast for one before; something about multicultural London – and they are always held in a dimly lit, buzzy bar, throbbing with Latino beats and unfeasibly attractive people: taut-bottomed men wearing cumberbunds and raven-haired beauties, that sort of thing. Not this one. This one is held in a mirrored

72

studio, four flights of stairs above a shop selling bridal wear, and is complete with sprung floor and ballet *barres* around the edges – so bright, it makes you squint when you come in from the outside. Fraser may as well be naked, he feels so exposed, and wishes he'd done a bit more research than googling Salsa Classes in London and booking the first that came up.

To make matters worse, they're early, so have to hang around whilst everyone arrives.

'Gosh, this is very proper, isn't it?' whispers Karen excitedly as she takes off her trainers and gets changed into her new, professional shoes. 'Takes me right back to dancing classes when I was little.'

Fraser feels a bit sick.

'You didn't tell me you'd done dance classes.'

'Didn't I? Oh, yeah. Distinction in Advanced Modern, me. Intermediate Ballet, gold medal three years running at the Hull Festival, I'll have you know. I was going to audition for ballet school at one point before these buggers grew . . .' She turns around and pushes her boobs together and Fraser has a flash of hope, once more, that maybe he is already a little bit in love with Karen after all.

It seems to take forever for everyone to arrive. Karen goes straight to the front where she starts chatting to a tall man in small, round glasses, whilst Fraser loiters at the back, feeling like a twelve-year-old at an adults' party. He dares to look at himself in the mirror and regrets it. He looks ridiculous, like a youth offender brought in for 'dance therapy'. He had no clue what to wear, so went for general fitness attire and is wearing shiny tracksuit bottoms, his running trainers and a FILA

T-shirt bought in about 1991 which is too big for him and smells of his bedroom floor.

Everyone else is wearing normal, *fashionable* clothing, or professional dancewear. In particular, there's a woman next to him who looks as if she's pirouetted straight in from the set of *Fame*.

He smooths down his hair in a vague attempt to make himself look more presentable and sees Karen smile warmly then wink at him through the mirror. She seems to be getting on famously with the tall man in glasses. This is something Fraser greatly admires in Karen: her ability to be sociable and chirpy at all times – it's why she makes such a good barmaid. Fraser has always found that hard, even more so these days. They are quite high up here and for some reason, as he looks out of the window, over the treetops thick with blossom, the evening spring sunshine glinting through the branches, he has a brief rush of something he remembers as happiness. Or hope. Is it hope? He closes his eyes, feels the warmth of the sun on his eyelids. He can do this. He can. He will do it for Liv.

'OK, if you're ready, shout, "SALSAAA!"'

Fraser nearly jumps out of his skin. Suddenly there is really loud music and a man at the front wearing a headset and wiggling his hips in a way that looks un-natural, not to mention painful.

'SALSA!' everyone shouts back, including Karen. How the hell does she know when to shout salsa?

'Are we HAPPY?' yells the man again – obviously the teacher or coach or instructor – what did they call them in the World of Dance? Fraser has no idea. The man's gyrating his hips and shouting into the no-hands microphone that comes around the front of his face and reminds Fraser of the head-brace Norm used to have to wear at night when they were kids because his front teeth stuck out.

There's a weak, affirmative dribble from the group.

'Not GOOD ENOUGH!!!' he tries again. 'I said are you HAPPYYYYYY!!!?'

'YES!' everyone shouts, much louder this time.

Fraser remembers something Mia always tells him: 'Fake it till you make it.'

Still, he can't quite bring himself to shout 'Yes' back.

The instructor's name is Calvin. He has a glorious Afro like a lion's mane, a disgustingly toned body, which he is showing off to full effect in a tight, white vest, and buttocks that – as Liv would say – 'you could crack a nut with'. Fraser could well hate his guts, were he not also in possession of the sunniest, most disarming smile he's ever seen.

Calvin's beauty, decides Fraser, is the sort that transcends a lifetime's sexual orientation and he wonders if he might actually fancy him, just a tiny bit.

'OK, hands up people if this is your first time today.'

His accent is hard to place – transatlantic mixed with something Latino: Brazilian perhaps, or Columbian. Whatever it is, it's very, very cool.

Fraser puts his hand up, along with Karen, and is relieved to see at least ten other people out of the class of twenty or so doing the same.

'Cosmic. Awesome. Right then, guys, well, we're not going to worry, yeah?' says Calvin, and Fraser can't help but nod and smile. This man is like the sermon-giver of salsa. 'We're not going to cry, or let aaaanything get us down. We are going to salsa ourselves happy, OK?' He flashes another amazing smile and lets out a laugh that sounds like pure sunshine. Again, Fraser feels the sides of his lips turn up – amazingly beyond his control.

'I said, OK?' He cups his ear, still shaking his hips, and this time Fraser manages at least to say the word 'OK'.

'Good. Awesome, my friends. THIS is what I like to hear.'

Five minutes in, any hopes Fraser had of possessing some untapped talent for salsa are dashed when it becomes clear he has no natural ability whatsoever. He is an appalling dancer – so appalling, it's even a surprise to him. He's musical; he can play the guitar and sing in tune, so how come this does not translate to his limbs, which are making erratic and alarming jerking movements, as if he's desperate for the toilet or suffering from a neurological disorder. He catches sight of himself in the mirror again, blinks in disgust and looks the other way, only to be greeted by his red-faced reflection once more, his mouth hanging open in concentration. This is like a grim exercise in public humiliation.

He looks over at Karen. She's a natural, of course she is, her hips and the rest of her body working in harmonious, fluid movements, which make her look sexy and stylish. He'd be proud of her if he wasn't so busy being bitter. Why didn't she tell him she was some Darcey Bussell wannabe as a kid? That gives her a totally unfair advantage. Not that this is a competition or anything.

He looks up, just at the moment that she does, and she gives him a tight-lipped smile that kills Fraser because he knows it's a sympathy smile, and there's nothing worse than a sympathy smile, except perhaps a sympathy snog.

He wouldn't mind, but they're only trying to master the 'basic salsa step' on their own as yet. If he can't do that, what hope does he have for proper dancing in a pair? Or of ever achieving his goal?

Fraser is not a gracious loser and has a tendency to become despondent quickly when he can't do something, especially in a public situation like this where his dignity is on the line. He remembers – just as the mood descends – that he also tends to become sullen; get a 'face on like a smacked arse', as Liv used to say, and he doesn't want Karen to see him like that. 'Smacked arse' is one thing in front of your long-term girlfriend, but quite another in front of your new squeeze. He tells himself to get a grip and imagines what Liv would say if she could see him now: 'Wipe that look off your face, Fraser John Morgan. It's *deeply* unattractive.'

It's not helping that the woman next to him in a leotard – a fucking leotard, for crying out loud – is muttering something and giving him funny looks. Fraser's sure she's trying to get his attention, but he's choosing to ignore her. If it's just so she can tell him he's cramping her style, she can bugger off. How rude. He perseveres, concentrating as much as possible on Calvin's feet and encouraging smile, but then she jabs him in the side with her bony little elbow.

'Ow!' He turns round, annoyed. 'What?'

She's pointing at the floor, jabbering on about something in a foreign language, but he can't tell which one because the music's too loud.

He frowns at her, shrugs his shoulders, and tries to

turn back the other way, but she starts pointing more angrily, throwing her hands in the air, and Fraser begins to think she must just be mad, until the next thing he knows, Calvin is beneath his feet with a dustpan and brush.

It's only then that he looks down and sees that all over the floor are little clumps of dirt – like molehills or animal dung. All sorts of terrible, unspeakable things come to mind, until Fraser realizes it's just mud, mud that his filthy trainers have been depositing for the last fifteen minutes; half of Hampstead Heath all over the pristine white floor.

By the time they have a break, halfway through the class, Fraser has fought the sullen mood all he can and is in the full grip of smacked arse.

After the humiliation of the muddy trainers scenario (Calvin said not to worry but Fraser still feels mortified), they did pair work, the girls moving round the circle so that they got a chance to dance with every bloke. Woman-in-a-leotard refused to look at him when it got to her turn because he stepped on her toe by mistake. She was lucky he didn't stamp on both feet, silly cow. There was some light relief when it came round to Karen, who was sweet and encouraging, but all in all, he feels like a loser.

'Buddy, don't worry, it is much, much harder than it looks.'

Now he is having to go through the further humiliation of perfect strangers sympathizing with him. And calling him 'buddy'.

Joshi – the tall man with the glasses that Karen seems to have struck up an immediate rapport with, has been coming for six months and is certainly proficient, but only in the way that anyone who'd done the same steps for six months would be. There wasn't much in the way of natural flair.

It may just be his foul mood, but Fraser also finds Joshi really annoying. He's wearing one of those cheese-cloth 'granddad' shirts with mother-of-pearl buttons and a plaited, raffia bracelet – both of which tell of time spent in Third World countries, probably with Raleigh International building schools or wells. Not getting off his face at full-moon parties, that's for sure. And also, what's with 'Joshi'? What's wrong with Josh? Or Joshua? Why the name like an Indian guru healer?

He also has the most enormous Adam's apple Fraser has ever seen, and which he can't take his eyes off when he speaks, as it goes up and down like a giant walnut in a lift.

They're sitting down now, sipping free Liebfraumilch in plastic cups and eating Twiglets like they're at a sixth-form party.

'Calvin's phenomenal, isn't he?' says Joshi, rather unnecessarily. 'He's an awesome teacher, I think, especially good with the weaker students. If you watch, he doesn't patronize, do you know what I mean?'

Karen agrees and looks at Fraser, as if urging him to say something, which he does, mainly to stop Joshi before he gives him any more patronizing words of encouragement.

'So, er . . . Josh, how come you decided to come to salsa classes then?'

'Well, it's interesting you should ask, buddy, actually.' Joshi swallows the Twiglet he's eating and Fraser stares as his Adam's apple goes up and down. 'Because I'm going to Bolivia next month – three months on a volunteer project doing irrigation systems – and I wanted to learn salsa beforehand. I think it's so important to embrace the culture. To have the authentic experience, do you know what I mean?'

'Wow,' says Karen, shaking her head in a wowed kind of a way. 'An irrigation system? In Bolivia? That is amazing. Amazing, isn't it, Fraser?'

Fraser downs his wine.

'Wouldn't it have been better to do a course in plumbing?'

It's an innocent enough question, he thinks. OK, maybe a little facetious, but it's funny, too, and he couldn't resist it.

Joshi stares at him blankly, biting into a Twiglet. Karen lets out a nervous giggle.

'I think what Fraser's getting at is that maybe you won't have time to go out salsa-ing if you've got so much other, more important stuff to be doing.'

That's not what I was getting at all, thinks Fraser, but anyway, he's lost interest now, so that when Joshi eventually says, 'I think the irrigation systems in Bolivia are somewhat different to those in the UK,' he's busy filling up his cup with more wine.

Joshi goes to the toilet leaving him and Karen alone, and Fraser detects a rather awkward silence. She looks up at him over her cup, swinging her hips in a strange, coy sort of way.

'Can I ask you something?' she says, and Fraser fights the little frisson of anxiety he gets whenever she looks at him like that from under her heavily mascara-ed eyes.

'Sure, go for it.'

'Have you got a problem with . . .?' She makes a strange jerking movement with her head.

'With what?'

'With a certain *someone*,' she hisses, nodding towards the door.

'What, Joshi? No. Why would I have a problem with him?'

'Well, no, you wouldn't.' She blushes, as if she's back-tracking now. 'I mean not that you have, obviously. It's just if you think there's anything going on, like you know, I fancy him or he's flirting with me . . .'

Fraser frowns at her. 'No, not at all . . .'

'What I guess I'm saying is that, if you're jealous, Fraser, you don't need to be, all right, hun?' She takes his hand and squeezes it. 'Because I don't fancy him. Like, what-so-ever.'

Fraser can't help but think she doth protest too much, but a little part of him still dies inside because he wishes he were jealous: that's the problem.

The second half of the class is a definite improvement on the first, with Fraser at least managing the basic salsa without injuring himself or a third party.

By the time it ends, he's almost enjoying himself, and he and Karen decide to go for a drink to celebrate. Drinking, Fraser is finding, is the key to his relationship at the moment. As long as there is booze, he can just about manage to put any doubts to the back of his mind. It's only at 3 p.m. on a rainy Sunday, the two of them stuck for conversation, that he really starts to panic.

They go to Las Iguanas on Dean Street, have three – Fraser has four – Coronas, so that by the time they emerge out into the cool evening and make towards Oxford Street for their bus, he's feeling much better, much more *carpe diem* and *que será* and other foreign phrases he often vows, when he's drunk, to live his life by.

He takes her hand in his. Soho is quiet, almost deserted at this time on a Tuesday evening, and he knows it's probably because he's a bit pissed, but he feels a bloom of affection for Karen. This is OK, he thinks, this is enough. It's not Liv, it'll never be Liv, but I've got someone.

He thinks of arriving at Karen's, getting into bed with her and nestling his head into her pillow-soft breasts. Then he thinks of the alternative: going home alone, opening the door to that God-awful silence, broken only by the beep of the smoke alarm that needs its battery replacing, and he thinks, Thank fuck, basically. Thank fuck.

She squeezes his hand. 'I've had such a good time tonight,' she says.

'Me too,' says Fraser, and he means it, he really does.

They walk to the end of Dean Street and around Soho Square, where two wasted homeless people are having a row.

They continue along Oxford Street in a tired silence to the bus stop, and have only been there a few minutes, huddled on the red plastic bench, when a drunken figure seems to loom out of nowhere.

'Karen?' The man is staggering he's so gone. 'What the fuck are you doing here?'

He's got a hard face with a lazy eye – a face Fraser

knows instinctively he would do well not to get on the wrong side of.

'Darren.' Karen lets go of Fraser's hand and, even in that small gesture, Fraser knows this situation has the potential for disaster and bloodshed. That doesn't stop him giggling, however. Fraser has a tendency to laugh at inopportune moments and this is one of them. The 'Darren–Karen' thing has tickled him for some reason, and there's not much he can do about it.

'Is he laughing at me? Why is he laughing at me?'

The smirk is wiped clean off his face, however, when Darren starts jabbing a finger in his direction.

'Sorry, Darren, this is Fraser, Fraser this is Darren,' says Karen.

It doesn't really answer the question and Fraser suspects he and Darren aren't ever going to be on first-name terms, but he holds his hand out anyway. But Darren rejects it so he is left with it sticking out, feeling absurd. He eventually scratches his head for something to do.

'Is this your new boyfriend then?'

Karen sighs and looks the other way.

'Darren, pack it in.'

'What? All I asked was if this was your new boyfriend. Nice trainers anyway, mate,' he says to Fraser. 'I see you really made an effort for a night out in town.'

'Actually we've been to a dance class,' says Fraser, flatly. He's getting a little weary of this pissed, shaggy-haired imbecile intimidating him at a bus stop.

Darren laughs out loud. 'A dance class, eh?'

'Yes,' says Karen, 'a dance class, OK? Fraser and I go to salsa lessons. Now will you leave us alone.'

There it goes again, that shiver of anxiety. It's the way

she says, 'Fraser and I . . .' Like she's boasting. It makes him feel pressurized.

'Go on then,' says Darren. 'Show us yer moves.'

Karen sighs again. 'Sorry about him,' and she gets hold of Fraser's arm. 'Let's move along.'

But Darren's not having any of it.

'Where you going, you wanker?' he shouts after them. 'Where are you going with my fucking girlfriend?'

Fraser sighs and looks skyward. He's knackered; he's used up all the concentration he possesses in the dance class, and now he's a bit drunk and all he wants to do is to get on the bus and to get home and go to sleep, his head resting on those soft, pillowy boobs. But Darren has other ideas.

'Oi. I said, where are you going, dickhead?'

Karen's grip tightens on Fraser. 'Just ignore him,' she whispers, hurrying him along. 'He just can't handle it, he really, really can't.

'You just can't handle it, Daz, can you?' and she turns round and shouts at him. 'I'm with Fraser now, OK? You thought I'd never get a boyfriend again, didn't you? You thought you'd ruined me, scarred me for life, but you were wrong!'

I should be saying something now, thinks Fraser – what should I be saying? He becomes queasily, acutely aware he is saying nothing.

'Whatever, you're still fat!' Darren shouts back. 'You're welcome to her, mate.' And inwardly, Fraser winces, because now he knows he really should be saying something, that there's no call at all for that sort of behaviour.

'I don't think there's any call for that,' he says, turning around. 'You're pissed, mate. Now go home.'

But it seems this is perfect ammunition for Darren, who is not pissed, no he fucking well is not, and he is certainly not going to be told to go home by some Northern wiener in crap trainers.

Fraser isn't prepared for what happens next; all he knows is that he hears the sudden, quickening sound of shoes on the ground and then is wrenched – him letting out a sudden and involuntary sound like he's being choked – by the hood of his top and pulled to the ground. Then he feels a dull ache in the head – no, actually a really, really sharp pain in the head, and can hear Karen screaming, 'Darren get off him! Get off him now!'

Fraser has never been the fighting type – the odd scrap as a teenager but he could never be bothered and, anyway, deep down he knew he had a pathetically low pain threshold, and would he – this is the question – would he be able to stop his eyes watering if it really hurt? But this time, from somewhere deep inside of him, the adrenaline kicks in, the male instinct that he is supposed to make an effort here. He can't shout: 'Ah, you're fucking hurting me and please don't break my nose! It's buggered enough as it is!' So he at least has a go at pushing him off, tries to summon every manly, fearless cell in his body to dodge a punch, even throw a couple back, but he loses out and suddenly his back is against a wall and he hears something crack and feels a stab of pain that gets him right in the throat. There's the familiar trickle at the back of his nose and then splosh, splosh. Fat splashes of vibrant red on the floor.

'Oh, my God, Fraser! Oh, God. You fucking bastard, Daz!'

Then Karen has rushed over to him and is kneeling

down beside him, a look of pure horror on her face, but Fraser is seeing stars, far too dazed to say anything, except eventually, 'Ow. I don't think there was any need for that.'

'No, there was not. There was NOT, Darren. You total fuck-head!'

Karen screams at Darren who is walking off now, swaggering, coolly, not even breaking into a jog, thinks Fraser. That's how menacing I am.

'Fraser, baby, are you all right?' Karen kneels right down beside him and the look on her face just kills him.

'Are you OK, sweetie?' She's brushing the hair from his face.

'Yeah, yeah, just a bit of blood,' says Fraser, sitting up, feeling quite pleased with himself for the phrase 'just a bit of blood', when what he really wants to scream is, FUCK ME THAT FUCKING KILLED!! His top is already covered in the stuff.

'OK, pinch your nose at the bridge and put your head back and I'll clean you up a bit. I once did St John Ambulance, I know what I'm doing . . .' Karen roots in her handbag and comes up with a packet of handy wet wipes. 'Might sting a bit.'

'Thanks, Karen, thanks. I'm sorry about this . . .' says Fraser, practically gurgling on the blood that's now running down his throat.

Karen takes his face in her hands and he tries not to say 'Ow' because his whole head kind of hurts right now. She dabs at him with her wet wipe. 'Now you listen to me, Fraser Morgan, you have nothing to be sorry for. Nothing at all, OK? In fact . . .' She stops.

Oh, God, here it comes again, that look.

'I should be thanking you.'

She looks straight into his eyes

'You know it really meant a lot to me what happened there, it really showed me something, you know?'

'No,' says Fraser. 'No, I don't know.'

'Well, you took a punch for me back there, didn't you? You nearly bloody broke your nose for me! Maybe you have actually broken your nose!'

Fraser smiles, weakly. Great, he thinks. What a hero. 'And I appreciate it, hun, that's all I'm saying. I was touched, Fraser, like, really touched.' She pauses for a minute, for her words to sink in, then she says, 'Right, let's get you home.' And yet another little part of Fraser dies, right there on the pavement, because he realizes he has just spent one of the most humiliating hours of his life (and that was just the dance class) and probably broken his nose, all for someone he really is not sure about. He didn't bargain for this.

SIX

The next morning
Lancaster

Careful to hold in her post-baby belly, Mia rolls off
Eduardo, reaches for the water on her bedside table,
downs the glass and flops back down on the pillow.

'Ow! Cramp!' Then she sits bolt upright, clutching her
right thigh, which has gone into involuntary spasm.

Eduardo laughs his low, maddening laugh.

'You always do this, you always get the cramp,' he
says, yawning, as if it's some sort of personality flaw,
like always picking a fight when drunk.

'That's because I've been straddling you for the last
ten minutes and in case you'd forgotten, I had a baby
nine months ago,' she says, trying desperately to keep an
air of humour. 'My hip flexors aren't what they used to
be, you know.'

He rubs her back, then places a lingering kiss on her
shoulder. 'I'm going for a smoke,' he says, pulling back

the covers, and Mia watches as his tiny, brown Brazilian bum – like a hazelnut she always thinks – disappears around the bedroom door, and she is left clutching her rounded, white one.

The pain eases and she lies back down, feeling that familiar dread wash over her: he will come back up, get dressed, perhaps stay for a polite cup of coffee and then leave, and it will be just her and Billy again, till bedtime. Oh, Lord, roll on bedtime.

It's the second time she and Eduardo have had sex this week and the sixth since Billy was born. Mia knows this because she keeps tabs. It's a bit like notches on the bedpost, although she's painfully aware it doesn't quite hold the same air of bragging arrogance as the teenage version.

This tab – at least at first – was more for herself. Somehow by writing down when they had sex, she could pretend it didn't mean anything, that he was just 'servicing' her – and what woman living in 2008 shouldn't be serviced, if she so desired? It kept things clinical, like a nurse keeping medical notes: frequency of urination, blood pressure, that sort of thing.

Lately, however, there's been a shift. The tab she keeps is no longer so she can tell herself it means nothing, as it means *something*. Twice in one week – this is starting to become a habit – and part of her hopes it will become more than a habit for Eduardo, that he will find it in him to love her, properly, like she deserves to be loved. The other part of her, of course, wishes he'd fuck off and die, and it's a constant source of fascination to Mia how the two can exist in unison.

He is at least starting to make an effort, she thinks.

Historically, he would turn up drunk, at midnight, with no consideration for the fact she had to go to work, or now, get up with *their* son.

Since Liv's birthday reunion, however, and leaving her in the lurch, he has actually turned up at the designated time to have Billy, and last night they had fun – proper, actual fun. They drank wine and talked about movies. She modelled her new Primark sundress for him, then they drank more wine and – when they ran out of that – some more, because woo-hoo! there was someone to go to the off-licence!

Then they snogged and danced to the Buena Vista Social Club in her kitchen, occasionally breaking to smoke out of the window, the view of Lancaster Castle high up on its hill, floodlit, like something out of a child's dream.

Now, of course, hungover and with the prospect of looking after a baby all day, Mia regrets it. In fact she despises him for coming over here on a Tuesday night, taking her away from *Holby City* and a macaroni-cheese-for-one and corrupting her with his heady, Latino ways.

But she also needed it like a person needs air.

Last night, pressed close to him, dancing barefoot in her new summer dress, albeit one probably made in a sweatshop in Latin America, she felt alive; she felt primitive and sexual.

And she needs to feel primitive and sexual, she thinks, looking at their clothes strewn all over her laminated bedroom floor, otherwise she will go mad and life will feel like one big washing machine cycle. She needs to know she can do things with her body other than feeding a child, or hauling him up on her hip a thousand times a day, or if, right now, it is only the often flaky, unreliable father

91

of her child that can give her that, then she is going to take it.

Also, sex with Eduardo is doubly exciting, because it is forbidden, after all. If any of her friends found out, they would go mad – wouldn't they? Now she thinks about it, she wonders if they aren't too wrapped up in their own lives to give a toss about who she's sleeping with these days. Except Liv. Oh, Liv. It makes her suck air through her teeth just thinking about it. 'He wears sunglasses inside, darling, he'll bring you nothing but grief.' And look at her now. Liv would have her guts for garters.

Then there's Fraser . . . he already knows something's afoot; if he knew the whole truth. God. It didn't bear thinking about.

Fraser can't stand Eduardo. He has tolerated him in the past – just, the effort etched on his face, but ever since he walked out when Mia was pregnant, she can't mention his name without Fraser practically spitting on the floor, something she feels is slightly over the top. After all, it's not his life, is it? And anyway, what does he care now since he's seeing 'Karen'? Mia has to try really, really hard not to make a face when she says the word 'Karen'. It's just, even the name has a desperate, over-the-hill air to it, and she suspects Fraser is using Karen as a crutch, that she's not making him happy or vice versa. Which would be a terrible thing to do. Terrible.

She listens to Eduardo clattering around downstairs, probably making the polite coffee that he will drink whilst sitting on the side of the bed, before announcing he is leaving – stuff to do/mates to see/a shift to get ready for. She has no idea what he does with his day and has given up asking – and anyway, even though her friends would be shocked to hear it, deep down she wonders if this whole situation is partly her fault.

She went batty when she was pregnant. Batty. Did she drive Eduardo away? Did her hormones warp everything so that she demonized him, made him out to be worse than he actually is? As she lies in bed listening to the kettle, the clinking of china, the comforting sounds of another body in the house, she gets an image in her head, a memory: her, seven months gone, huge already and haring through Shoreditch on her bicycle at 2 a.m. Ha! What a bloody nutcase! The Wicked Witch of the East End! So fat she could barely turn the pedals for her bump.

She'd become convinced Eduardo was having an affair and decided to catch him out. She knew he'd be at the MOTHER bar – oh, yes, the MOTHER bar – and she burst through those doors, bump first, practically fighting the bouncers to the ground, a force of nature in maternity jeans. She stampeded around, Billy kicking inside her, alarmed at the sudden onslaught of hardcore techno. When she finally located him in a darkened corner, he was topless, wearing sunglasses and writhing around with another man who was also topless.

So he was gay! That was what all this was about. She had almost felt a rush of relief that it wasn't just because he was a complete bastard.

But no, he was not gay, he said; he was just off his face, and apparently this was what one does when off one's face. He was also scared and overwhelmed by the prospect of being a father and he just wanted some fun whilst he still could – was that so bad?

It seemed so at the time, but now she's not sure, and when she pictures that scene now – him, bare-chested in

Ray-Bans, chewing the inside of his cheek whilst she stood before him, a mountain of a woman, bicycle clips around the bottom of her maternity jeans, shouting 'I hate you; I fucking hate your guts!' – she starts to giggle, then really laugh, until she is doubled over in a fit of hysterics.

'What are you laughing at?' Eduardo stands in the doorway of her bedroom, naked, a mug in each hand, laughing at her laughing.

'Oh, nothing, nothing . . . come to bed,' she says, stretching out a hand. He bends down, puts the two mugs on the floor and almost jumps down beside her.

'Eduardo! Bloody hell! About four of the slats in this bed are broken, you'll break it even more if you're not careful.'

'Have you still not got round to getting a new bed?' he says, snuggling up to her.

WELL I WOULD IF I HAD A MAN IN THE HOUSE TO ERECT ONE. She fights the urge to shout, but it's so very hard.

'No, I have still not got a new bed.' She smiles, inhaling his smoky, musky scent. 'But perhaps you could buy one for me. It's the least you could do.'

Eduardo ignores that comment and tidies a strand of hair behind her ear. Here it comes, she thinks, the 'better be going'. But he doesn't. Instead he starts to kiss her tenderly, ever so gently, so she thinks she might cry, and she once more becomes aware of how much she needs this to stay alive, to feel alive. Mia Woodhouse – you're still in there, aren't you?

He softly pushes her hair back. 'Hello, beautiful,' he whispers and she doesn't say anything but she smiles and looks up at him. 'I want to make love again. Can we make love again?' If an English man said that I'd be laughing my head off by now, thinks Mia. But somehow a Brazilian gets away with it. Somehow from him, it's irresistible. It's 6.45 a.m., the early morning sunshine is turning the room golden, and Mia closes her eyes, throws her arms behind her in abandon as Eduardo presses his pelvis down onto hers.

Then 'waaaaaaaahhhhhhh!' Nine months on and it still rips right through her. Still feels like an assault.

'Billy,' she sighs, staring up at the ceiling.

'He'll stop, he'll stop,' says Eduardo, kissing her neck. 'He'll go back to sleep, come on, relaaax.'

She tries, she does, but it's no use.

'No, he won't, unfortunately.' She gently pushes Eduardo off her and drags herself out of the bed. 'Believe me, that's Billy for the day now.'

When Mia comes back from the kitchen where she has been preparing Billy's breakfast, leaving him fastened to the high chair in the lounge, she half expects Eduardo to have gone. It's the sort of shitty thing he does all the time, after all. But as she approaches the lounge door, she can hear talking.

For a moment she's confused – whose is the other adult voice she can hear? – and then she realizes, it's Eduardo's. She freezes, the dish of porridge in her hand. Then, spying through the crack in the door, holding her breath, she watches them.

Eduardo has pulled up a chair and is leaning on the tray of Billy's highchair, playing with his small plastic animals – Billy's all-time favourite toys.

'And this is a sheep,' he's saying. 'In Portuguese we

say "*ovelha*" . . . Can you say "*ovelha*", Billy? That's pretty cool, ha? Which is your favourite, Billy?'

Billy's transfixed: wide-eyed, perfectly still, a string of drool hanging from his mouth, and Mia has to bite her lip to stifle a giggle. Poor baby. Never known a man in the house to talk to him like this, let alone his own father. Well this is a turn-up for the books, she imagines him thinking, I could get used to this.

She could get used to this.

This is how it should be, too. This is how she imagined family life: her wandering about of a morning in Eduardo's shirt, sexy and yet homely at the same time, with tanned bare limbs (in her case, pale ones with a huge bruise up the side where she continually bangs into the coffee table, but never mind), and daddy, handsome and bare-chested, playing with his son, the smell of coffee wafting through the house.

Then her mobile goes on the sofa and she nearly jumps out of her skin.

'Ooh, I'll get that!' she says chirpily, trying to make it look as though she literally arrived at the door just then, that she wasn't spying.

'Hello?'

Eduardo is still playing with the animals – perhaps even more enthusiastically now he knows he's being watched, and Billy has started to do hiccuping giggles.

'Mia, it's me, Fraser.'

'Fraser!' Eduardo turns around and looks at her and she doesn't know why but she smiles and waves at him. 'How are you? OK? Actually you don't sound OK.'

'No, I've been better. I got punched in the face last night.'

96

'What? Why?'

Mia takes herself off into the kitchen to talk.

'Oh, God, long story, involving ex-boyfriends and salsa classes and Karen.'

'My God, Karen didn't punch you, did she?'

'No, no, GOD no . . .'

'Oh.'

She should really try to sound less disappointed to learn that he hasn't been punched by his new girlfriend.

'It was her ex-boyfriend.'

'Really? Gosh. You are quite the threat then?'

She shakes her head. Why did she say that?

Silence. Mia turns round and looks out of her kitchen window.

'Frase, are you OK?'

'Yeah, I'm OK. Just look a bit like an old alky at the moment, bright red, fat nose . . .'

She closes her eyes. Poor Frase.

On the other end of the phone, Fraser is examining his face in Karen's bathroom mirror. He looks dreadful; the bridge of his nose is so swollen that it's closing up his eyes, so they're piss holes in the snow, and he's got a fat top lip.

Karen is at the shop getting milk and more frozen peas. She has taken to her role as Florence Nightingale with gusto and has woken him up several times in the night to check for signs of concussion and to clear his nasal passages of dried blood, so that he is now exhausted, as well as injured.

'I take it Karen is looking after you?' says Mia.

'Oh, yeah, not wanting on that front. Karen is looking after me.'

'Well, that's good, isn't it? That's really, really good. So um, what was the salsa class like?'

'Yeah, great,' says Fraser. 'Well, actually, I made a complete and utter tit of myself, but that's OK, 'coz it's all for Liv.'

She laughs. 'And Olivia wouldn't have it any other way, as we know. In fact she would be disappointed if you *didn't* make a tit of yourself. So come on then, what happened?'

'Well, besides getting my head kicked in at the end of it all, I was an appalling dancer, so bad it wasn't funny.'

'Oh, I bet it was.'

'I assure you it was not, and I wore totally inappropriate footwear, basically my knackered, filthy running trainers, which then deposited little piles of mud all over this pristine white dance floor.'

Mia covers her eyes and smiles. 'Oh, God, Fraser, only you.'

'To top it off, Karen was a brilliant dancer – turns out she was some sort of semi-pro when she was a kid.'

'Oh, come on, I'm sure she wasn't *that* good.'

There was a long pause.

'So listen,' she says, before she can help herself. 'Have you actually told Karen you're doing the salsa class as part of Liv's List? That you're actually doing it for Liv?'

Fraser stands back from the mirror. 'No, course I bloody haven't.'

'Well, don't you think you should? Just out of courtesy? I mean, she's going to find out sometime, Fraser, and then she's going to feel really hurt and really used.'

Fraser frowns; he thinks about this for a minute. Right – so why would he tell her? So she can feel hurt and used now? Did he not have the right to a relationship whilst he was doing the List for Liv? He felt a wave of guilt and panic. She would be back in a second to shower him with unconditional love and frozen peas again. This was twisted; maybe Mia was right, maybe he should just tell her now and get it over and done with. No! No. He couldn't do that to himself or to her, he was giving this a go and that was that. So he says . . .

'Look, I'm not gonna tell her, Mia – is that wrong?' He really didn't know any more. 'Because if I do, it would be the end of us.'

'That is kind of my point. But it's up to you. I just don't think it's fair if you use her, that's all.'

Fraser sighs. 'I'm not using her, I like her.'

'Well, that's OK then.'

The door goes and Eduardo comes in, dishevelled and bare-chested, wearing just his boxer shorts and holding a crying Billy at arm's length. 'He's missing his mama,' he says. 'You've been on that phone for hours.'

For God's sake, would she ever learn? In Karen's bathroom, Fraser shakes his head and tuts. That was definitely Eduardo he just heard in the background. There weren't many people who made Fraser's blood boil, but Eduardo was one of them. Such a spineless, cocky, useless little twat. Fraser had a feeling he was trying to worm his way back into Mia's life and here they were – caught out!

Why would he be there so early if he hadn't stayed over? Mia could be really thick sometimes, not to mention a hypocrite. And there she was on her moral high horse about Karen.

'Is that Eduardo?' he says.

In her kitchen, Mia thinks for a split second about lying – shit – Fraser would really not be impressed; nobody would be impressed, not after everything they'd been through with her on the Eduardo front. But also, her friends weren't on their own with a baby, were they? And Eduardo was making an effort, she should give him a chance. I mean, look at him, he was still here, wasn't he? Standing in her kitchen holding his own son like he was a bomb about to go off?

'Yes,' she says eventually, sheepishly.

'Oh, *Mia*.'

He sounds so disappointed, that's the worst bit.

'What?'

'Mimi, can you get off the phone NOW?'

'Eduardo, don't call me Mimi!' she shouts, suddenly stressed by everything: him being annoying, Billy crying, and now Fraser getting at her. She should go back to bed.

'Look, Frase—' she says.

'Oh, it's *Frase*.' Eduardo rolls his eyes dramatically, Billy's still wailing. 'The handsome Fraser Morgan . . .'

Mia sighs heavily and puts her hand somewhat dramatically on her forehead. She was doing it again; she was acting like a character in *Coronation Street*.

'Oh, God, God, will both of you just bugger off!' she says eventually, more because she doesn't know what else to say than because she doesn't think each of them has a point. 'Fraser, I hope your nose goes down. I'll call you later. I'm going back to bed!'

And she does, and as she draws the cool, white sheets around her, leaving Eduardo to settle Billy without asking her how every five minutes, like he's a new DVD player and only she has the instructions, she thinks just for this, if only for this, it's worth giving him another chance.

Fraser hears the front door go. 'Couldn't get any frozen peas but they did have broad beans so I just got those,' calls Karen down the hall. 'Now are you feeling sick or dizzy at all?'

And Fraser looks at himself. Yes, I am, he thinks, I am feeling sick. It's a type of sickness he's felt before.

SEVEN

Then

December 1996
Lancaster

Fraser sloshed more wine into his glass and leant over the recipe book again: Assemble the Moussaka: Place a layer of potatoes on the bottom, top with a layer of aubergine, add meat sauce on top of aubergine layer and sprinkle with . . .

Bloody hell, this was like something off *The Krypton Factor*. It didn't help that he had now consumed the best part of a bottle of wine and the words were beginning to swim: Potatoes, aubergine, meat. Or was it potatoes, meat, aubergine? He had no idea; all he knew was that she would be here very shortly and he had yet to make something called a béchamel sauce.

He lit a cigarette, wafting the smoke with his hand so that it mixed to form a miasma of Silk Cut, fried mincemeat and Fruits of the Forest, courtesy of the scented candles Melody was constantly buying for the house, because 'candles create atmosphere'. It would seem so. On an average evening, Number 5 South Road could pass for the Sistine Chapel.

He surveyed the kitchen; it looked as if they'd been burgled and he quietly cursed himself for choosing a dish that somehow used up every utensil in the house. Why hadn't he gone for something simple like a chilli or a curry?

Presentation was going to be key. He reached in the cupboard above and got out the big guns: Melody's huge terracotta casserole dish. He set about arranging a layer of aubergine he'd grilled, wishing he'd actually followed the instructions and cut the aubergine lengthways rather than just chopping it into big chunks, which now sat mushy in the middle of the huge expanse of terracotta looking somewhat forlorn, like a mound of cow dung.

He only chose moussaka because moussaka was what Melody cooked for the last dinner party at their house a month ago and that seemed to go down well. (Although he didn't like to think about that night much past the actual dinner stage, when it all sort of degenerated.)

Melody was a worldly, confident girl with an impressive chest, who Fraser thought had some peculiar ideas that didn't seem to sit with her student status, like ordering the Sunday broadsheets to be delivered to their student hovel and having Greek-themed dinner parties where mates from her law course came wearing ball gowns, only to get shit-faced on bottles of cider.

But Melody was also kind and she was capable and at times like this, Fraser was very glad he lived with someone who owned cookery books. Now, though, as he eyed his moussaka and compared it with the one in the picture, he realized he hadn't been aware of the 'layers' component; the layering part was something he had not allowed time for and it was these that were foxing Fraser right now. Far too much to think about for a man who, despite his resolve, was already half cut at barely seven o'clock.

And at nineteen years old, Fraser Morgan was also layered, or at least his mother was always telling him so (such a complicated child, we've no idea where we got him from . . .) and this was how he experienced life: it came in peaks and troughs that he couldn't predict or control very successfully and, in one day alone, he could go from a moment of intense joy – like those few seconds between finishing a gig and the applause; was there a finer moment in life than that? – to bouts of melancholy, which saw him take to his room to strum on his guitar and listen intently to lyrics and maybe to write some. He came up with his best work when in the throes of melancholia.

He doubted he had ever really experienced 'happiness' as such, if happiness was the sort of unquestioning confidence he saw in his peers on his philosophy course. He had chosen philosophy, not because he had done it at A level (he'd done sciences) but because to him, it was the sort of subject you could only do at university.

He was the first of his family to go; most of his mates were staying back in Bury to resit their A levels or get jobs in plumbing or as fitness instructors and he wanted something that sounded impressive and brainy when they asked. 'Computer science' didn't quite cut it, but philosophy? Now that was good.

Fraser loved his mates back home but sometimes he

did yearn for something slightly more than the pub, and hoped that in a philosophy course he'd find that. He imagined it would be full of cool, interesting people who possibly wore scarves and scurried across campus carrying piles of ancient books and having 'ideas'. Fraser very much liked ideas, he saw himself as relatively deep and sensitive. In reality, though, philosophy seemed to be a course chosen by earnest and yet alpha types with whom Fraser had nothing in common, and he felt a bit lost in lectures, scared to participate in case he said something rubbish and sounded too northern.

Those guys seemed to know instinctively what they wanted out of life. Fraser wanted to be in a band: he sang and played guitar and imagined that first album cover where he and Norm (drummer) and the two other members of the Fans (Fraser, Andy, Norm and Si – an acronym of the four members; they thought that was pretty slick) would be photographed in some ironically old-fashioned living room looking moody and emaciated, although he wasn't sure Norm would quite be able to pull off that look at present.

That was it, he didn't have a back-up plan. He had no further plans for life. These people, his peers, seemed to know exactly where they were going, whereas life to Fraser was an ever-unfolding mystery, exhilarating at times, but which all too often disappointed him. This was because he had not yet cultivated the art of making himself happy and still made terrible, often catastrophic choices based on fear, not having any better ideas (the moussaka being one such example) and flattery. This had always definitely been the case with girls.

Fraser was good looking; maybe not everyone's cup

of tea with his unrefined looks but definitely attractive. He was tall, in possession of a good head of hair and (so girls had told him) a pair of 'beautiful, almond-shaped eyes', which was a compliment he wafted away only to go home and peer at them in the mirror from different angles. Were they beautiful? Wasn't that just a cliché handed out by girls when they were drunk and sentimental, which in his experience was pretty much all the time?

Whatever, Fraser Morgan was never short of female attention, never short of girls throwing themselves at him and telling him he was funny, yes, and 'layered', and had lovely eyes.

Although Fraser was bemused by all this attention, he was also flattered, and it seemed ungrateful and downright rude not to take them up on their offers. So far in one and a half years at Lancaster University, he'd been out with a Becca – one of Melody's law-course mates, posh and a little bit terrifying. Being with Becca was like some sort of endurance test for the character and, Fraser had to admit, the challenge gave him a twisted thrill.

After Becca, there was Steph: sweet, clever and thoughtful. She was on his course and was everything Fraser had fantasized that a philosophy student would be like, as in she wore scarves and glasses and sat cross-legged a lot. (Actually this really disturbed him in the end. There is only so long a man can stare at a women's crotch in tights before they just don't find them attractive any more.)

He and Steph had really good 'discussions and debates', which he found genuinely interesting, about education and the rich/poor divide, but ultimately Steph had no sense of humour, and would get really offish when Fraser got drunk and took his clothes off – which was just something he did; it wasn't meant to upset anyone and it certainly wasn't sexual – and in the end he just got sick of her being angry all the time, and him having to constantly apologize.

Steph lasted five months and was followed by several back-to-back flings, the latest being Sara, of moussaka evening fame, who now of course was known as 'Sara Moussaka' and who he'd rather forget (another reason he was now asking himself why the hell he'd decided to make moussaka).

Fraser had started to get himself a reputation that he was a bit of a ladies' man, although he thought this was unfair, he thought he just liked the company of girls. You could talk to girls and, also, he liked how girls did stuff. They went for walks and to restaurants – all the things he hadn't yet had the chance to do in life – and it made him feel alive for a bit, say, after a breathtaking walk in the Lake District. But he'd discovered that feeling would soon fade because the person he was with was not the *right* person. He was finding he needed sparkly lights and a big hill and a beautiful day to enjoy their company. That was, until he met Mia, who frankly he would still love being with if they spent the day in Asda's frozen fish section. Which, actually, they sort of did.

Mia stood in the damp, December evening outside Fraser's front door and took a few deep breaths. She had been looking forward to this moment all week, even counting the sleeps – oh, yes – and yet suddenly she was crapping it, a total nervous wreck.

She had ummed and ahhed about what to wear and had settled on an emerald-green satin top and new (cheap) jeans, which she was now regretting not washing first, since on the half-hour walk from her house to Fraser's (where she'd been wiping her clammy palms on them), they'd turned her hands blue so that she looked as if she'd spent several days in a morgue.

The wardrobe quandary hadn't been helped by the fact that Fraser hadn't given her any clear indication about what 'tonight' actually WAS. When he'd asked her to 'come over', they'd been buying a rotisserie chicken in Asda – hardly the foundations for a meaningful love affair. But then their fortnightly trip to Asda, in itself, was hardly the foundations for a meaningful love affair.

It was just that bulk-buying there was cheaper than shopping at the campus shop, so she and Fraser had started doing that, then sharing a taxi back from town with industrial-sized bags of rice. Dear God, listen to her. Had that actually been her idea? Effectively a Saturday afternoon spent at a cash 'n' carry? No wonder he'd never asked her out before.

Standing there, on the steps of 5 South Road, she still wasn't sure if he had now, either: 'You should come over next week,' was all he said. Would there be other people? Was that him asking her round for dinner? On a date? Mia hoped it was, because she was already falling for Fraser Morgan. She had fallen for him the first moment they'd kissed, or rather the moment she'd pinned him down and suctioned herself onto his face (it still made her cheeks burn and it was over a year ago now), deep under the spell of Shane Parry, Fresher's Week '*Hypnotist Extraordinaire!!*' – and Destroyer of her Undergraduate Love-Life thus far, too, as far as she was concerned. As if putting her into a trance and instructing her to snog members of the audience wasn't humiliating enough, he'd also made her eat an onion as if it were an apple beforehand so, when she kissed them, she must have stank.

Sensibly, she had claimed amnesia ever since.

She breathed out once more and gave the brass knocker two bold strikes. Fraser answered immediately, as if he'd been lurking behind it. He was holding two full bin bags and looked flustered.

'Ah! Out with the old rubbish and in with the new,' she said. Why had she said that? It was idiotic and overly self-deprecating, the sort of thing her housemate Anna always warned her against. (Don't put yourself down, boys hate that kind of shit.)

Fraser laughed. 'Sorry?'

'Nothing,' she said. 'Please ignore that comment.'

He put the bags in the wheelie bins. 'Come in,' he said. 'I've been cooking up a storm.'

'Quite literally, I see,' said Mia as she stepped inside the house.

The first half of the lounge was OK – there was a table set for two for dinner no less (check!), but then, as if there'd been a natural disaster and they'd only got so far with the clean-up effort, the closer she got to the kitchen, the more the debris built, so that the kitchen was almost completely blocked by half-emptied Tesco bags and saucepans 'soaking'.

But he'd cooked! Or at least was still cooking. That had to be a good sign, and there were candles. She bit her lip as she followed him through the lounge; felt a little bubble of excitement rise in her belly. Why would he have gone to the trouble of candles if this were just a mate coming over? Why would he have invited her on her own in the first place?

So she was excited, but also curiously embarrassed too, because now she had evidence that Fraser did have romantic intentions at heart, how was she supposed to behave? Should she have worn something nicer than a pair of jeans? Brought a bottle of fine wine rather than a four-pack and some cheese-and-onion Pringles? Should she be flirting? Right now? Arranging herself on the sofa, a glass of wine in hand?

Obviously, she did none of these things; instead she overcompensated by being larky and matey and totally asexual. Unfortunately, so far in her life, Mia had only been out with cocks. Cocks, as it were, were all she knew. Vain, cockish men were totally unthreatening in their way, after all, since if you didn't actually like someone, there was a limit to the fall-out should it go wrong. And she could flirt with cocks – it was a very simple formula, one she'd seen her mother play out time and time again: laugh at their jokes, flutter the eyelashes, show a bit of cleavage and – hey presto! – you generally got a snog.

With Fraser Morgan, however, she felt curiously out of her depth. For the first time in her life, she actually liked spending time with someone; she had actually found a member of the opposite sex who could make a trip to Asda fun. The amazing thing was, the feeling seemed to be mutual, and it unnerved her – especially now when she appeared to be on a date. She didn't know what to do with herself, so of course she snapped open a can from the four-pack and hid her face in it.

'So, Delia Smith, let's have a look then . . .'

She tried to sidle into the kitchen and have a nosy, but Fraser blocked her, putting his arms out.

'What are you doing?' Mia giggled.

'Er, can you give me a minute? I'm not really finished yet. In fact, if you were to go in there at the moment, you might get the wrong idea.'

Mia frowned. What did that mean? Had her assumptions been wrong? Would she think he was cooking a romantic meal only to discover that he was cooking for his flatmates who were soon to arrive? Which would be fine, of course, absolutely fine.

Actually, what had happened was that he had tried to assemble the moussaka, got the layers in the wrong order, so had disassembled it, putting all the different components – mincemeat, tomato sauce, potato – on any empty surface he could find, but then she'd knocked on the door so he hadn't got any further.

She peered over his shoulder, but he moved, suddenly and comically, to block her view, but not enough to stop her getting an indication of the carnage going on in there.

'Fraser, what are you doing in there? Slaughtering something?'

'You could say that. Actually, it's a sort of work in progress, a culinary collage if you will, but about to be revealed as a work of art.'

'Right.'

He put his hand on her shoulder and Mia tensed, self-conscious. He never touched her, he must be drunk.

'Look, just have a drink, make yourself comfortable, and I'll be right with you, OK?' He ushered her away from the door. 'I'm a bloke. I can't multitask!'

Fraser shut the door and disappeared into the kitchen. Shit, he was drunk. Why had he allowed himself to get quite so drunk? In the ten minutes before Mia had turned up, aside from dismantling the moussaka, he'd decided to have a quick shower to sober himself up, but the water had been far too hot and the cooling-off period far too short, so now he could feel sweat running down the back of his shirt. She looked lovely, though. God, she was lovely. As was the fashion, Mia had her blonde hair cut in what was known as a 'graduate bob', or was it graduated bob? – short, swingy and cut into her neck. It wasn't every girl who could pull this off but Mia, Fraser decided, as he peered at her through the tiny gap in the door, definitely could. She had a beautiful neck and a pretty, sort of pointy nose, so she looked great in profile. She had lovely eyes, too – grey, a bit slanty and wide set, which she enhanced with this smudgy make-up malarky, something she'd informed him once was a 'smoky eye'. It made her look strong, as if she could deal with anything life threw at her and as if she knew stuff, but not like Becca or even Melody knew stuff, but proper stuff – stuff, Fraser knew instinctively, that was worth knowing.

Mia stood in the lounge now, bemused and a little bit excited in equal measure. Clearly he'd gone to some trouble, but she'd never seen her friend like this, flustered and nervous. It made her feel the same.

She looked around the living room. It was way nicer than the student house she shared with Anna and Liv, which required protective footwear to enter the kitchen.

It was tidy, for a start, and had signs of civilization such as a magazine rack, actual lamps (rather than a lava

113

lamp that had died long ago and so now sat in the corner like a fetid pond) and a large cream sofa sporting various tasteful cushions.

'Wow, your house is classy.'

'That's one of the bonuses of living with a couple,' called Fraser from the kitchen. 'Melody and Norm are basically married already. Melody can't leave the house without buying a cushion.'

Mia laughed.

'So where are Melody and Norm tonight?' She squeezed one eye shut, waiting for an answer.

'In Surrey – "Terribly sorry, I'm from Surrey . . .!"' Must stop making shit jokes, he told himself. You're not funny, you're just pissed. 'They've gone to Melody's parents'.'

'Oh, right, nice one,' said Mia, trying to sound nonchalant. 'So, er . . . I won't get to see them tonight, then?'

Mia had met Norm and Melody a few times since meeting Fraser and liked them a lot.

''Fraid not, you're stuck with me.'

He stuck his head around the door.

'Gosh, you're joking,' said Mia, sucking air through her teeth. 'Shall we go out?'

'You're very funny, aren't you, Miss Woodhouse? Now you can put some music on if you like.' He went back into the kitchen to fret over his sorry little mound of moussaka once more. 'The CDs are by the sofa.'

Mia grimaced; this request always made her shudder. She was good at films and books, films and books she could do – but music? She had appalling taste in music. Or rather she didn't have an opinion, something she had so far managed to conceal from Fraser. She wouldn't want him to think she only went to his gigs to see him . . .

She walked over to the CDs.

'So what are the other Witches of Eastwick doing tonight?' asked Fraser, referring to Liv and Anna.

'Liv's gone out with Boring Ben . . .'

Boring Ben was Liv's much older, very patronizing, very boring boyfriend whom she'd had since she was about twelve and who seemed to think she was still that age. Everyone hated him.

'And Anna's gone clubbing to Wigan Pier.'

'And you hit the jackpot by coming round to mine, eh?'

Mia ran her eyes across the CDs, reckoning she knew only about four in the first ten.

There was only one way through this, and that was comedy.

Ba-ba-da-da-ba-daaaaa

A few seconds later came the familiar drum intro to Phil Collins's 'Something in the Air Tonight'.

'Hilarious, Mia. Another totally hilarious gag,' Fraser shouted from the kitchen.

'What?' she said. 'Are you dissing the legend that is Phil Collins? A musical genius of our times – it's you that owns the CD! Although actually, if you really want my favourite, then it's got to be "One More Night". Now that, Fraser, is a tune.'

You sound like you're trying too hard. Stop trying to be funny. Just be yourself.

'Actually, rubbish music aside, his drumming is second to none.' Fraser appeared at the kitchen door. 'Sadly though, my cooking is not.'

'Oh, come on now, you don't have to be modest.' Mia

115

walked towards the kitchen and this time Fraser let her in. 'Are we going to have to get another rotisserie chicken from Asda?'

She eyed the fruits of Fraser's efforts: basically a small mound of mush in the middle of a vast, terracotta pot.

She tried not to laugh.

'Fraser, why did you just not put it in a smaller pot?'

He bit his thumbnail. 'I don't know.'

'Or just make *more* of it.'

'I don't know – it was a spatial awareness problem coupled with time restraints.'

She looked up at him.

'You know how it is.'

'Fraser, are you drunk?' she said.

'Yes, I am,' he said. 'Unfortunately, I am drunk.'

'Out of ten?'

'Not too bad. Six?' His eyes shifted to the side. 'OK, seven.'

She took another look at the very small moussaka.

'We'll have to fill up on Pringles,' she said.

They sat down, ate the miniature moussaka very, very slowly so it would last longer, Phil Collins's *Greatest Hits* in the background. At first, they laughed. How ironic! How amusing they were! But after a while the comedy sort of tapered off, until they realized they were actually sitting listening to love songs in candlelight and for a horrifying fifteen minutes the conversation dried up.

Thankfully, they then got extremely drunk – Mia played catch-up – and eventually they were bantering as they always did.

'Well, I think, fair play to us,' announced Fraser, putting

his knife and fork down. 'I reckon we did a sterling effort in making that moussaka last a whole hour.'

Mia put a hand to her jaw. 'I've got lockjaw now, must have chewed the same mouthful seventy-two times.'

They laughed, and yet, Mia still felt they were sort of avoiding the issue.

But Fraser was actively thinking about the issue. In fact, ever since Mia had walked in tonight looking gorgeous, graduated and downright snoggable, he had wondered how to approach 'the issue'.

Best take the bull by the horns.

'OK, let's go upstairs!' he said, suddenly.

'Gosh, steady on . . .'

He rolled his eyes and tutted. 'To listen to music.'

Of course they were already listening to music, but were also drunk and sufficiently relaxed enough now to ignore this small inconsistency, and so carrying a half-bottle of red wine and both their glasses, she followed him up the stairs to his bedroom.

Both being of the belief that alcohol and musical instruments were a match made in heaven, they banished the stereo and got stuck into their homegrown efforts, Fraser playing 'She's Electric' by Oasis and Mia singing along. It was something she'd done many times for karaoke, with Liv and Anna, in various bars, but alone, in Fraser Morgan's bedroom, it took slightly more doing, and she already knew, as drunk as she was, that she was going to be embarrassed about this the next day. Not that that stopped her: more Oasis, Babybird and a track by Crowded House that she clearly didn't know the words to, so chose to dance to instead, erratically mumbling a lyric or two.

'Right, more wine!' declared Fraser, eventually. 'I reckon we definitely need more booze.'

He sang to himself as he went downstairs and Mia went to the bathroom. Someone had put a notice above the lavatory: PLEASE DO NOT DO BIG SHITS IN THIS TOILET!! Which really tickled her and so she sat there, having a wee on Fraser's loo, snorting to herself with laughter.

So this was going terribly well. Surely she'd be getting in Fraser's pants by the end of this. Let's crank this whole thing up a level from mates! She told herself, drunkenly. Let's get this show on the road!

Maybe I should just hurl myself at him. No, no, look at what happened last time she did that. Precisely nothing. That was the problem. She flushed the chain and pulled up her trousers and it was only as she did so that she noticed the cool blue hue of her legs where the cheap jeans had been. If she ever did make it into Fraser Morgan's bed, she would have to do it with the lights off.

She practically skipped back to his bedroom and it was only as she closed the door that she noticed the obligatory clip-frame of photos on the back of it. How predictable. Every student bedroom in the land must have one of those, but they were also fascinating and Mia couldn't resist. She crouched down on the floor and studied it.

There was one of Fraser and his brother, obviously as a little boy – the same opal eyes and a head of white-blond curls. She looked away before she started imagining their children. There was one of him at school – a *Grange Hill*-style portrait of playground mayhem. Then, Mia felt an unpleasant flip of her stomach – Fraser with a girl.

118

A very pretty girl. It was obviously a party or a sixth-form ball because Fraser was wearing a DJ and dicky bow and she was in a black velvet strapless number. They were on a sofa or chaise longue, the sort you get in the entrance of a hotel, and Fraser was leaning back, knees open, arm around her, brimming with boyish confidence; she was leaning into him, her hand on his chest.

Mia leant in and peered at it, just at the moment that Fraser stumbled drunkenly through the door . . .

'Ow!'

. . . and hit Mia in the face, sending her backwards.

'Oh, God, sorry I'm so sorry!' Fraser put the bottle of wine down, and suddenly he was holding Mia's face. They gazed at each other. 'Are you all right?' She got the chance to look at him properly now, something she'd been dying to do all night. Yep, she still fancied him. Ridiculously, in fact.

Kiss him. Kiss him now . . .

But she seemed suddenly paralysed, suctioned to the carpet.

'Yeah, I'm fine . . .'

And all too soon the moment was over.

'Serves me right for nosying at your photos.'

They both sat up against the wall and Fraser poured more wine.

'So who's that girl?' said Mia. She was drunk now, what the hell?

'Oh, that's Amanda.'

Fraser had only glanced at the photo but clearly he knew who 'that girl' was.

'She's very pretty,' said Mia.

'Pretty mad.'

Mia laughed. 'She doesn't look mad. Was she a serious girlfriend?'

'Oh, yeah, like I say, seriously mad.'

'What do you mean?' Mia huffed and rolled her eyes with pretend annoyance.

'I went out with her for a year and a half and when I dumped her, she used to stalk me, wait outside school, outside football practice, outside my house. I had to threaten her with legal action in the end.'

Mia nudged him in the side. 'Fraser Morgan, you heart-breaker, you.'

He looked at her. 'Hardly, but I can spot a mad one from a mile off now. Now I'd like a sane one, a really down-to-earth one. Someone low-maintenance who you can really have a laugh with, do you know what I mean?'

Close up, she was even prettier, he thought. Her skin was dewy and totally flawless, she had these deep-set, dark, wise sort of eyes. He was laying it on thick now, he knew that, but she didn't seem to notice. She carried on talking.

'So is that you at school?' she said.

'Yeah, worst school in the world. There'd be an article in the paper if someone got an A. Lunch was going halves on a packet of Silk Cut and maybe a bag of scraps from the chippy.'

'Wow. Really?' Mia couldn't imagine a school where everyone was not expected to go to university, where everyone didn't think it was their God-given right.

'Anyway what about you? I bet you went to a dead posh school, you. Everyone who does *meed-yah* studies went to private school.'

Mia gave him a dead arm. 'Fraser! You are such an inverted snob!'

'I'm only kidding.' He laughed. 'I'm only pullin' your leg.'

'Actually I hated it,' she said. 'All those rugger-buggers, those really bitchy girls. I left as soon as I could and went to a normal sixth form.'

'Ah,' he squeezed her hand, 'so that's where you get your down-to-earthiness from then?'

There was a pause, a really long pause, and Mia wracked her brains as to what to fill it with.

'So, er . . . how long have you known Melody and—'

But she couldn't finish her sentence, because Fraser had leant over and was kissing her passionately and fully on the lips. Mia had had many unsatisfactory kisses in her life, especially first ones, but this. *This*. This was exquisite. Soft at first, almost tender bites, then full-on passionate snogging, there was no other word for it. It was neither too fast, nor too slow. His eyes never left hers. Their tongues and lips seemed to work in perfect rhythm, without either of them having to say a thing. They carried on like that for a good five minutes. Mia felt a bloom in her chest, her throat, her lips. She worried the feeling might come out, like she might actually have made a sound. Nothing, ever, in her life had ever felt this good.

'Bloody hell,' she said, when she could finally come up for air. 'Is that to make up for accosting you?'

He got hold of her chin and brought it towards him to kiss her again. 'I thought you said you couldn't remember accosting me.'

'Hello-o!' Ten seconds later the front door suddenly went and they sprang apart.

'Who the fuck is that?' hissed Mia, wiping her mouth.

'Hello-o! It's us. We're back . . .'

'Shit, it's Norm and Melody. I thought they weren't back till tomorrow!

'Fraser?' Mia and Fraser froze in his bedroom. Downstairs they could hear footsteps going into the kitchen. 'Jesus – what a state – and have you been using my terracotta pot without asking?' Melody shouted upstairs.

Mia winced sympathetically at Fraser.

'Actually, also . . .' There was a bit of stomping around now.

'Oh, God,' groaned Fraser, 'we'd better go down.'

'Have you fucking well been helping yourself to my wine – again?'

Fraser stood up and opened his bedroom door. Melody was already at the bottom, Norm standing behind her pretending to slash his throat.

Fraser attempted to look sober.

'Mels, I'm really sorry, we'll tidy up. We only drank one bottle of wine, didn't we?'

'We? Who else is there?'

'Oh, Mia came over for a bit – she's still here, actually, I attempted to make moussaka—'

'I can see that,' said Melody, and her face softened. 'Fraser, why didn't you just call me?'

'Mia came round for a bit.'

That sounded a bit 'matey', Mia thought, standing in Fraser's bedroom. (Mind you, what was he supposed to say? Mia came over, I seduced her and we were snogging each other's faces off, just as you arrived?) And they weren't strangers; she'd met Melody and Norm loads of times before. They knew she and Fraser were mates, so it wasn't beyond the realms of possibility that she should be in his bedroom, but what to do now? Did she go outside and hold his hand? Carry on like nothing happened? Just leave? Either way she had to show her face. She flattened her hair down in Fraser's mirror, just to check she didn't look too bed-head, and opened the door.

'Hi, Melody.' She smiled, apologetically. 'So sorry about the mess and I'm mortified about the wine, I mean obviously we'll replace it, and more . . .'

Melody waved her hands about, embarrassed. Mia was embarrassed. This was so embarrassing.

'So, er . . . right, I need a waz.' Fraser excused himself, and Norm smirked at his friend. He knew that look, the look of a man in deep trouble.

Melody looked at Norm, shame-faced, and stuck her bottom lip out. 'Oh, God, Mia's going to think I'm a dragon now.'

Norm laughed. 'No, she doesn't.'

'No, I don't at all,' said Mia, following them downstairs. 'I'm just mortified about the wine, I didn't know about the wine. I mean, I'm not blaming Fraser as such, but I should have checked . . .'

'Mia, honestly . . .' Melody was in the kitchen now, bottom in air, making a start on the tidying up. 'I wouldn't mind normally, it's just he's not in my good books as it is. I had a dinner party a few weeks ago – I cooked moussaka funnily enough – and Fraser, as well as embarrassing me in front of my mates by taking virtually all his clothes off and dancing around in the kitchen with a colander on his head . . .'

Mia tried not to laugh

'. . . then proceeded to get off with a very good mate

of mine, drink loads of my wine and then chuck her after three dates. She was DEVASTATED.'

'He shagged her in the bath, too,' added Norm, who was sitting quietly in the living room rolling a fag. 'Dirty bugger.'

Mia's stomach plummeted. She didn't know what to say, she knew she just had an overwhelming desire to get the hell out of there.

'So, anyway,' said Melody, turning around, cloth in hand, 'Needless to say, she is now "Sara Moussaka".'

Well, I am not going to be Mia Moussaka, thought Mia. Mia Moussaka I am not.

Fraser came downstairs and grabbed his coat from the banister.

'Right, so shall we go to the offy?' he said, smiling at Mia. 'Get some more wine?'

Why did he have to be so bloody sexy?

'Um, actually, look I've got to go now. . . . It's later than I thought.'

She didn't look up but she thought she heard a short exhalation of disbelief, or was it disappointment?

'I'm already way too drunk. But here, here's some money towards it.'

She reached inside her coat pocket for her purse and handed him a fiver.

'But thanks for the moussaka!' And she made for the door.

EIGHT

May 2008
Venice and Vegas

Venice in May and Mia has never in her life seen anything as jaw-droppingly beautiful. Right at this moment – 10.30 a.m. on a cloudless morning – she, Melody and Anna are reclined on the seats of a gondola, shaded by the crumbling terracotta houses on either side, the water lapping as Lorenzo, their gondolier, navigates the narrow emerald straits of the Grand Canal, which occasionally open up into glittering lagoons.

Mia put a lot of thought into her wardrobe for her first-ever trip away from Billy and now feels a sudden surge of pleasure, so rare these days when it comes to clothes, that what she had in her mind's eye – Italian Riviera, circa 1955 – has actually been realized, and that her ensemble of cropped white trousers, sheer blouse tied at the waist and gold-rimmed Ray-Bans – albeit £4.99 fake ones from Lancaster market – could not be more perfect for the occasion. For the first time in her post-baby life, she has achieved fashion Nirvana.

She slips down further in the gondola, tipping her head towards the fierce blue, Venetian sky, and thinks about Fraser and Norm, wondering if they too are under an unforgiving sky right now, the one that lays bare the Nevada Desert. Mia has never been to the Nevada Desert, but she imagines those two, lost in the middle of a red, dry expanse; sweating, fretful, probably intoxicated, and she smiles to herself.

(Actually, as fate would have it, they're also in a gondola, only theirs is electronic and drifting down a different Grand Canal – the fake one on the second floor of the 'Venetian' Hotel and Casino on the Las Vegas strip, an ostentatious monstrosity where they have spent all evening and most of the afternoon drinking Jack Daniel's because, you know, that's what you do in Vegas, and are now (Mia got this bit right, at least) well on their way to being impressively drunk.)

When Mia pulled Number Eight on Liv's List out of the hat: *Go to Venice, properly this time, and have a bellini at Harry's Bar*, she thought this was one they could all do together, a trip to Venice! Just like old times! All the girls had been in 2001 when they were InterRailing (just saying that word these days made her feel ancient), although 'been' was a loose description by anyone's standards, since they'd got off the train, gone on a gondola, eaten some extortionate spag bol at a place just off St Mark's Square, then got on the train again, considering they'd 'done' Venice, and moved on to Pisa to take pictures of themselves holding up the leaning tower.

Maybe this time they could do it properly, then. Like old times only better. Although, as Anna had pointed out, or rather snapped in front of everyone, nothing would ever be like 'old times', which made Mia blush because she was well aware of this, of course she bloody well was. These were new times, brave (perhaps not-so-brave in her case) post-Liv times. Everything had changed.

'Why do you want the boys to come anyway?' Anna had said with a face like she was sucking on a lemon. 'Can't we do anything on our own any more? Just us girls go on holiday?'

Lately, Anna – beautiful, passionate, reckless Anna – often had a face like she was sucking on a lemon and Mia has begun to wonder if this is about to set, bitter at twenty-nine. 'Course we can,' said Mia, suddenly humiliated, 'it was just an idea.' And so it was decided that they'd go on a girls' weekend to Venice whilst the boys would go to Vegas to fulfil one of the tasks Norm had pulled out (*Vegas, baby!*). For once in his life, Norm had seriously lucked out.

Still, she was determined to enjoy herself, to make this a tribute to Liv. So far, she knew she'd approve: Prosecco for breakfast, on a gondola before midday . . .

'Right, well,' she says, 'all we need now is one Cornetto.'

'Mm, preferably a strawberry one served by him,' says Melody, nodding towards Lorenzo, who has his back to them, and is wearing the obligatory gondolier strip of striped top and straw boater. 'Honestly, will you just look at that sensational butt?'

Mia and Anna both look at one another, Anna from

over the top of her *Buddhism for Life* manual, which she bought at the airport as part of her recently emerged lifelong passion for Buddhism.

Since they arrived, late yesterday evening, Melody has taken to making these bizarre, oversexualized comments using words like 'butt' and 'sensational', as if merely being in the country of romance and love has suddenly turned her into a bitch on heat. Or Joan Rivers.

Mia wouldn't mind – hell, this holiday feels all about reinvention, and if she's going to fancy herself as a 1950s film star, then Melody can be Joan Rivers – but it's just that it's so out of character. Melody has only ever had eyes for Norm, surely, and, as Norm's mate, Mia finds herself wincing, wanting to shout, 'Oi!!' every time Melody comments on some waiter's 'ass'. It makes her sad because it's just another sign, one of many in the last few months, that all is not well between the couple everyone thought were going to be forever together, and if Norm and Melody, college sweethearts, don't make it, what hope is there for everyone else?

Not that Norm's probably giving much thought to his wife, to be fair, since he will probably have bankrupted himself by now or been arrested. She thinks about the boys at the poker table, JD on the rocks, and she looks at them all on their gondola and laughs to herself because it all just seems such a cliché! And who'd have known that the reason they were all where they were was about as far away from a cliché as it was possible to get: that they were not on a hen or stag do, but a 'dead friend' do. But this weekend will be special. She hasn't left her son with his father and spent her savings for it not to be . . .

128

'What do you reckon the boys will be up to now?' she offers, trying to lighten the situation in her own mind.

'Drunk,' says Anna, not looking up from her book.

'Declaring their love for one another in an Elvis suit at the Little Chapel of Love?' adds Mia.

Anna sniggers. 'I can just see Norm in an Elvis suit, especially with his sideburns,' she says. 'Not sure about Fraser though. Not sure he could really pull off white satin flares.' Then they both pause as if expecting Melody to say something comical or affectionate, but all she does is roll her eyes with all the charm of a long-suffering wife and say, 'Andrew' (she's taken to calling him Andrew lately, something she never did, it was always Norm) 'will probably be in bed with heatstroke. I told him he'd never cope with the heat in Las Vegas. He's always been terrible with heat.'

So far, Melody's behaviour suggests she doesn't miss poor Norm at all, that she's glad to be shot of him for a few days.

But perhaps this is just 'transference', Mia thinks. It's a word Valerie once used – Valerie being the therapist she saw after Liv died and then again when Eduardo left her – and one she uses liberally these days because it makes her feel better somehow that there may be a term for it. Because the thing is, she doesn't miss Billy. Not really. And what sort of person, or mother, does that make her?

'Oh, you'll feel dreadful leaving him,' Jo and Tamsin had said to her. Jo and Tamsin are mums from Rock-a-Bye Baby, a mother-and-baby singing class Mia has started to go to – or persevere with might be a better description, since the first time she took Billy he screamed

129

blue murder, and the second he threw a brick at another baby's head.

'I've never left Daisy overnight,' Tamsin added.

Why the hell not? Mia wanted to say. You've got a FREE babysitter living in your house. She never did get this – married mums who never went out and complained continuously about it. If she had another person living in her house – any person; it didn't need to be her husband, just as long as she didn't need to pay them every time she went to the shop for toilet roll – she'd be out every night.

To top it off, her mother had (in that infuriating subtle manner she had) laid the guilt on too. 'Oh, you're not leaving him, are you?' she'd said, in that 'poor-little-mite' voice. It really pissed Mia off – the number of times her mother had left her, sometimes for a fortnight at a time, with grandma or Aunty Gill, so she could bugger off on holiday with whoever she was shagging at the time. The number of weekends Mia had sat outside pubs drinking endless glasses of lemonade and eating packets of crisps as a child, waiting for her mother to take her home.

What was even more galling was that it worked, she did feel guilty; she felt guilty that she didn't feel guilty about leaving Billy, that in fact she couldn't get out of the door fast enough.

Eduardo had looked at her as if she was leaving him at the foot of Mount Everest without supplies, but sod him, if she'd done this for ten months, he could bloody well cope for a weekend. When she finally walked out of her door to catch the airport train, she'd never felt lighter. Buying a coffee and being able to drink it without fear that a small child might knock it down her top, or just being able to sit, for one English hour, without having to read *This Is Not My Tractor*, was nothing short of thrilling.

Of course she did worry if her baby was OK with his feckless father. Would he remember he needed feeding several times a day? Would he realize that that demented cry was because he was tired? But, to be honest, these thoughts are few and far between because she is free! Free for the first time in nearly a year and sitting here with the sun on her face, it feels truly incredible.

And also, this is the test. For the last few months or so, Mia has been giving Eduardo a chance. Deep down she worries this may be the worst idea she has ever had in her life, but so far she is sticking with it because she needs someone, she wants to be a family. She's sick of being a 'single mum' because it's not cool and it's not romantic, it's shit, and maybe she just needs to compromise and accept Eduardo will never be perfect.

Fraser seems to be compromising – heavily as far as Mia is concerned. Every time she's called him in the past month, he's been on his way to a wedding with Karen or just back from salsa class, or driving to godforsaken Milton Keynes with her to pick up something she's bought on eBay. It's insane. God, it's insane! If Liv could see, she'd be flabbergasted, because Karen is about as far from Liv as is humanly possible. For weeks, Mia has had to bite her lip to stop herself saying, 'Are you serious? Karen makes you happy?' She's a forty-two-year-old dolphin enthusiast, for crying out loud. But Fraser has made it clear that Karen is 'a lovely person' and that 'he's just growing up and learning to compromise', and

131

so she's said to herself, Mia, shut up. Shut up and concentrate on your own life, because it really is none of your business. Just as what she and Eduardo are up to is none of *his* business, either. These days, there's quite a lot off limits in terms of the conversations she has with Fraser, much more small talk than there used to be.

Melody leans forward and makes as if to cup Lorenzo's butt cheeks, and Anna tuts, disdainfully. Once upon a time, she would have been the first to be eyeing up gondoliers. Mia watches her. Lately she's been wondering if she really knows her friend any more. Did she ever? They always came as a group, after all, a 'whole' – the six of them. But now Liv has gone, the linchpin, they are fragmented, they're suddenly having to relate to one another as individuals, and Mia isn't sure if she actually *does* relate to Anna as an individual, which makes her feel sad and also a little guilty for some reason.

They've always had fun, of course, you could always count on Anna for fun, an adventure, a story to tell at the end of the night; but in terms of anything deeper? Mia is beginning to wonder if it was only with Liv that Anna shared her innermost thoughts and insecurities. Liv was always close to Anna; she went that extra mile to understand their complex, sometimes infuriating friend. As Liv's best friend, Mia feels she should be the one to take over that role and yet, she doesn't feel able, she's not up to the job. Right now, sitting here, she resolves that she'll try.

'So how's your book, Span?' she says, brightly. 'Maybe you can teach me how to live in the moment.'

'Amazing. Really fascinating. Throws a whole new perspective on life, actually, do you know what I mean?'

Mia didn't really, but she smiled at her friend, immersed in her book.

And she did suppose that this was Anna's MO after all. Spanner is a girl of contrast and extremes, somehow making up for her overindulgence in casual sex and hedonism in all its forms (predictably, nothing had been heard of Ollie since Liv's reunion), by indulgence in health fads such as cupping, flotation tanks or, now, Buddhism. One of the things on the list that Anna pulled out was *Learn how to meditate*, and so, not one to do things by halves, she has started going to a nearby monastery to take part in silent weekends, and hanging around with a meditation guru called Steve – a name that, Mia couldn't help thinking, didn't exactly say 'chakra' to her.

But Mia is glad Anna has some focus in her life. Work doesn't give her much of that, after all: it's a series of temping contracts and career diversions. Anna seems incapable of finding that one thing to set her world on fire (and Anna can't just get a job, it has to be one that 'sets her world on fire'). It's just this new spiritual direction seems too extreme, even for her. What happened to the bolshie Anna of old? The reckless, naughty Anna who would have rolled her eyes at the idea of 'meditating'?

Lorenzo pushes on and Mia marvels at her surroundings, drinking it in like she's been in prison for years and this is her first blast of fresh air: the twinkling jade-green water, the wooden jetties with the gondolas lined up, like rows of Aladdin's shoes; it seems unreal, like a painting. Now and again, she gets a sudden flashback, an image in her head of them all the last time they were here, drifting along in a gondola. It's not so much a whole picture, though, as a feeling or a sense of something: the firmness of her nineteen-year-old thighs in her denim cut-offs; the sound of Liv's cackling laugh, totally un-inhibited; the way Anna would check herself out in the water's reflection and they'd all pretend they hadn't seen – where did that vain Anna go? Mia wants her back.

'Liv would have loved this,' she says, suddenly. Must get a grip, she thinks, must not get too introspective. 'She would have been very impressed with us, girls, I think. Very impressed indeed.' And then, without having to say anything to one another, Anna puts her book down and Melody gets up and moves so she is wedged between the two of them and they hold hands for a few seconds in sombre silence before eventually not being able to take it any more and falling about laughing at nothing in particular.

The afternoon is whiled away pleasantly with a trip to the Guggenheim Museum, where Anna spends hours reading every single word on the information panels and Melody and Mia take themselves off to the gallery shop to buy postcards and browse through the art books.

This is so nice, thinks Mia. When was the last time I did anything vaguely cultural? When was the last time I looked at any book that wasn't waterproof or made noises? She is revelling in this feeling – she can practic-ally feel her mind expanding – when her mobile goes.

She picks up, and all she hears is Billy screaming.

'Eduardo?' Her stomach flips. 'Eduardo? Are you there? What's wrong with Billy?'

There's a crackling sound and then a louder wail and Mia realizes Eduardo has had the phone to Billy's ear.

She takes herself outside the shop, leaving Melody. 'Eduardo. Answer me: why is Billy crying like that?'

There's a long pause as Billy takes a silent breath, which Mia knows is about to be followed by an almighty howl.

'He misses his mama,' says Eduardo.

Mia stands outside the Guggenheim shop and feels the blood rise to her cheeks.

'He misses his mummy, don't you, Billy?'

Mia sighs, infuriated, a horrid mix of guilt and anger and worry rolled into one.

'Eduardo, this is not fair. What am I supposed to do about it here?'

'I don't know,' says Eduardo. 'But he's been like this for hours. I didn't know what to do.'

'*Hours?*' says Mia, alarmed.

The crying goes on and on and she feels a wrenching in her bones, an overwhelming desire to feel her son's springy, smooth skin, to hold him close to her and smell him.

She rubs her forehead.

'Has he had his lunchtime sleep?' she says. 'He's tired, that cry is tired. Or maybe he's not well? Have you felt his head? Feel his head, Eduardo, is it hot?'

Mia has always prided herself on not being an over-protective mum, but then she's never been hundreds of miles away and unable to do anything before.

Billy wails and wails. He's beside himself now, hysterical, and Mia has to hold the phone away from her ear for a second because she can't bear to hear it any more.

'Look, I'm going to have to go,' huffs Eduardo, over

135

the noise, when she puts it back. 'I'll work it out – have a good time, yeah?' And Mia says, 'OK . . .' Then, 'Put him on, Eduardo, put Billy on the phone.'

The crying calms a little as Eduardo puts the phone to his son's ear.

'Hey, Billy, I love you, OK?' she says. Has she ever said that to him? To her baby? Has she ever said it out loud? 'Mummy loves you lots and I'll be back soon, OK?' But Eduardo has already hung up.

'Everything all right?' Melody comes out of the shop and Mia looks away, fighting the almighty lump in her throat.

'Yeah, yeah, everything's fine,' she sniffs. 'I need a drink I think, shall we go and find Anna?'

The three of them walk idly along the cobbled lanes, which open into quaint squares and streets of designer shops, to Corte del Arsenale, where they have lunch alfresco, facing two gigantic stone lions straight out of Narnia in the fading afternoon sun.

And because they are old friends, they don't talk about the big picture, or where their lives are going (although secretly, perhaps, this is exactly what they need to talk about), but instead about their shoes, Davina McCall's exercise DVD and, of course, there's always their shared history: how funny it was when Liv did this; how they all spent their money getting their portraits done in Budapest on that InterRailing holiday and then had to starve. 'Never been thinner though,' said Melody. 'Norm didn't recognize me when I got back.' How Liv got a shocking bout of holiday belly and lost control of her bowels on the ferry to Corfu. They cry with laughter at this one and, for a second, a fleeting second, Mia sees her friends as she used to.

Plans to go back to the hotel to shower and change so they can look their best for Harry's Bar are replaced by ordering more wine. It's what she would have wanted, after all.

'Mmm, I know!' says Melody suddenly, mouth full of wine. 'Let's play, I Have Never . . .'

Mia fills up her glass. Since the call from Eduardo she's struggling to relax and thinks more alcohol might help. 'Is that wise? Haven't played that for years,' she says.

'Me neither.' In contrast, Melody seems to be having no problem at all relaxing and is already tipsy. 'But it was a game Liv made up, wasn't it? It was one of hers so I think it's only right. Spanner, are you in?'

Anna sips her wine.

'Yeah, I'm in.'

'OK, good, I'll start. I have never . . . faked an orgasm.'

Mia puts her glass down. 'You've got to be joking—'

'Just down it, down it!' says Melody, wagging her finger bossily at Mia's drink. 'Don't discuss, just down the hatch if you have done it.'

Mia does as she's told, gagging as the wine hits her throat. 'OK, but I still want this matter cleared up. You mean to say you've never faked an orgasm – IN. YOUR. LIFE?'

'Never,' says Melody.

'Wow,' is all Mia can say. 'If I'd never faked an orgasm with Eduardo before, I'd never have got any sleep. Norm must be incredible.'

And she could see this in a way. Norm wasn't the most

137

conventionally handsome man in the world, but he had something – he was sparkly and optimistic, a constant sunny presence. He could really make you laugh.

Melody throws her wine back and scoffs at this. 'Oh, it's nothing to do with Andrew. I'm just a very orgasmic woman.'

Mia and Anna look at one another. 'She's just a very orgasmic woman,' they say, and promptly piss themselves laughing.

'I am!' protests Melody. Occasionally, especially when drunk, Melody Burgess finds it hard to laugh at herself. 'Norm can't keep up with me; he calls me Melody O.'

Euugh, thinks Mia. Now she's quite drunk.

'So when are we going to see the fruits of all your hard work?' says Anna. 'When are you going to be making a mini-Normanton? We've been waiting long enough.'

Melody fills her and Mia's glasses. 'Oh, God, give over. Not for a long time. Two years at least. Although Norm would have one tomorrow if I let him, he's desperate.'

There's a resounding *ahhh* from the rest of the group. Norm is a natural with babies, one of those men small children gravitate to.

'Seriously, it's really annoying, he's unbelievably broody, but I've told him, two years.'

'But Billy needs a playmate,' protests Mia. 'I'm bored of being the only one with a kid. Get a move on, Burgess. I'm counting on you.'

Melody groans: 'OK, time to change the subject. I gather both of you have faked an orgasm, then . . .?'

Anna says, 'I don't think I've ever had a real one, actually.'

'*What?*' say Mia and Melody.

Anna tuts. 'With another person, *obvs* . . .'

But Mia's still staring at her, utterly stunned. Of all the girls, Anna has always been the most promiscuous, the one you could rely on to come home with sordid stories of drug-fuelled shagathons with nineteen-year-old models, of threesomes, weekend love-ins with millionaires, and mutual shaving with Kiwi art directors (actually, they'd all gagged at that one). And *none* of these had made her orgasm?

The thought translates directly to her mouth. 'So *nobody*, of all the people you have bedded, Anna Frith, has ever made you come?'

Anna shrugs and pops an olive in her mouth. 'As I said: yes, myself. Men haven't got a clue. Far better to accept that nobody can do it better than yourself and just have a laugh with blokes. Use them to get places . . .'

Mia's jaw drops and Anna raises an eyebrow, as if to say that that last bit was a joke, but Mia's not convinced.

'Anyway,' says Melody, slapping the table, 'the fact remains that you have both faked an orgasm, so down your drinks!'

They both do as they are told and Melody refills their glasses.

'Also, I've got another one,' she says. 'A really, really good one. I have never kissed anyone other than Norm. OK, I'll rephrase that: I have never kissed any other bloke in our group – i.e. Fraser or Si or Andy,' (The members of the Fans were still considered 'in the gang' even though they'd all moved to London and got married now and were only ever seen at weddings and christenings.)

There's a long pause. Mia shakes her head and folds her arms.

'Nor have I,' says Anna eventually.

Nope, never, says Mia, 'Well, except when under hypnosis so that doesn't count.'

'No, it doesn't,' agrees Melody. 'Oh, how boring! So, no goss there then.'

But Mia can feel Anna's eyes on her.

'What?'

'Nothing,' says Anna, 'don't look at me.'

'So is that that then?' says Melody, glass in hand, looking slightly disappointed. 'Nobody's got any juicy confessions? No juicy secrets they want to share . . .?'

Another pause. Mia's aware now that there's an atmosphere, a slight frostiness in the air – and she laughs, nervously – or maybe she's just being paranoid? She really needs to hurry up and get drunk. The phone call from Eduardo has set her nerves on end.

'So maybe we should be going to Harry's Bar?' she says, eventually. But Harry's Bar has begun to feel a bit like New Year's Eve now – full of pressure and anticipation and the secret knowledge between them that the law of averages means it's bound not to live up to expectations. It was making her more tense.

Harry's Bar is not what Mia was expecting, she has to admit. She doesn't know what she was expecting – more of a jazz bar, more dingy and buzzy and smoky from the Internet pictures, perhaps, but this is not it. It's small and fairly characterless, with hints at a cruise-liner feel with its panelled walls and marble floor, and pale yellow walls with black-and-white pictures of Italian celebrities – none of whom Mia recognises – who have frequented this Venetian institution. Waiters, stiff-backed in their ivory

DJs and dicky bows, serve the famous bellinis on silver platters to the clientele who are largely locals, it seems: groups of glamorous women, gondoliers who have finished their shift, rotund men, their white hair slicked back, talking loudly and gesticulating in the way only Italians do that makes them seem as if they're permanently having a row.

After wine and the somewhat awkward game of I Have Never, Anna announced she wanted to go and find a church, that she wanted a few moments on her own to meditate and think about Liv and that she'd join them later. This seemed totally random to Mia. (Although of course she and Melody said it was fine. They are all always careful to respect any way their friends care to deal with the event that ripped their twenties apart.)

However, Mia can't relax; she cannot shift this feeling that Anna is in a mood with her and is reminded that travel is all well and good, save for the fact that you have to take yourself, and other people, with you.

She must admit, too, that these famous bellinis are a bit of a disappointment – just a flat, peach-coloured drink served in the tiniest of tumblers. No umbrella, no sparklers. She and Melody order one anyway, setting them back the best part of fifteen pounds.

A couple of Italians across the way meet their eye. Mia watches as they get up and make their way over.

'Oh, shit,' she whispers to Melody.

'What?' says Melody. 'They look nice.'

Melody is drunk; she arranges her hair on her shoulders, lets her spaghetti strap – somewhat underdressed now in a place like this – fall off her shoulder and gives them a wave.

'Hey, Engleesh?' Mia's heart sinks as one of them – tall, suave looking – sits beside her and the other – his much shorter sidekick, but with a sweeter, more attractive face, Mia thinks – takes his place next to Melody.

'You guessed right,' she says, moving along on her seat, aware that his thigh is touching her thigh and that she can smell what he had for lunch on his breath.

Melody leans forward, sunburnt bosom falling out of her top. 'And you're Italians, right?' she says. 'I knew it! I told you so! I mean, I know we're in Italy so that's kind of obvious and everything . . .' She laughs, no, *guffaws*, showing red-wine-stained teeth and most of her tonsils, and Mia cringes; God, she's pissed. 'But only the Italians know how to dress to impress.'

The evening wears on; there's no sign of Anna, and Melody continues to flirt, with Bruno and Patricio from Bologna, embroiling Mia in a very convoluted and complicated drinking game involving trying to guess what number everyone has in their heads between five and ten, displaying the number on your fingers after counting one, two, three, and whoever is furthest off has to down their drink . . . Or something.

But still Mia can't relax; still she has a knot in her stomach and still they haven't raised a toast to Liv, or marked the fact they're here in Harry's, having a bellini – just as she would have wanted. That was the whole point!

Bruno and Patricio go outside for a cigarette and Melody leans in; she puts her arm around her friend. 'Right, Bruno's mine, but you can have Patricio.' She giggles and Mia manages a laugh. (Look drunk, she thinks. At least *look* like you're having fun.) Why isn't she having fun? Why isn't she flirting with Bruno and Patricio? It's not like she's had the chance to flirt in the last few years.

Melody orders another round of bellinis and Mia is reminded of the gaping chasm between her and her friend's income. Bruno and Patricio come back and Melody totters back from the bar, sets the drinks on the table. 'Right, I know another really good drinking game!'

Mia has an overwhelming desire to call Fraser and wonders what time it is in Vegas.

On a pedestrian bridge straddling the Las Vegas strip, Fraser stands, sweating, toxic, his shirt ripped, the blood surging around his body.

It is midday, the blistering Vegas sun high in the sky, and he has one hand gripping the handrail and one holding his mobile phone and he has lost it, he knows this; gone way too far to pull himself back now.

He wants to shout out to whoever is listening down there, among the neon and the palm trees, in the twenty-four-hour party town: 'This is like the good old days! The mad, bad early days when I was proper mental! PROPER mental!'

In some part of his logical, sane mind, the tiny part not drenched with alcohol, cigarettes and God only knows what else, the debris of a three-day bender, he knows this is something he himself has created, something self-inflicted, and he hates himself even more for this. You idiot, Fraser, he thinks. You stupid fucking idiot.

But it's Liv – he knew coming here might do this, he knew a bender was a bad idea – he can't get her out of his mind. Or rather he can't get certain images out of his mind. He leans over the bridge and has to catch his breath because there she is again, lying broken, glassy-eyed on the floor. He's never known if he saw this, or if it's an image he's seen on television and that his mind tortures him with, but in the early days it used to come to him, often in the small hours of the morning, and it's coming to him now, a horrifying, mind-shattering image that makes him sway and gasp for air and cry out – 'Liv! Liv! I'm sorry Liv!' – as the traffic roars beneath him. He grasps onto the handrail tighter and squeezes his eyes shut in an effort to rid the pictures from his mind. There's the ambulance siren, the awful, raspy scream he doesn't know if he heard or he imagined, then the police walkie-talkies, the zip of a body bag. There's the hospital morgue, the smell of it, scratching at the back of his throat. And then, in the middle of it all, the kiss, the most delicious kiss he's ever known; and yet it comes at him like a nightmare because he has no doubt in his mind now that Liv saw it.

And so I get to finish my kiss at last . . .

There they are, standing in the villa kitchen, having to shout over the music – Moby, 'One of These Mornings'. Her with her arms draped around him, him looking into her slate-grey eyes, their pupils huge and black.

I get my kiss with Mia Woodhouse. We never did finish that kiss, did we? Me and you and I never knew why . . .

He can feel the kiss now, the urgency of it, their racing breaths as she almost melted into him. He wants to enjoy this feeling but then he remembers the window, the open window in the villa kitchen, the scent of those

144

huge pink flowers. They were everywhere in Ibiza and he has smelt those flowers in Vegas too, in the Venice Hotel and Casino garden, and he almost retched, because he was right back there, in that kitchen in Ibiza, kissing Mia, and out of the corner of his eye, Liv, standing on the balcony, eyes wide, mouth open, looking straight at him.

He pulls his hands away from the handrail, scrambles down the steps and heads towards the twenty-four-hour bar where he left Norm, or rather lost him an hour or so ago, both of them in too much of a state to keep together. No sleep yet and it's midday.

He walks along the strip. This place isn't helping, he thinks, it's messing with his mind: everywhere he looks, the Eiffel Tower, Venice, Caesars Palace, the buildings seem to loom out of the blinding daylight. But we're not in Paris, he thinks, we're not in fucking Italy! This is fucked! He doesn't know what's real any more. He gets his phone out of his pocket and he dials.

At Harry's Bar, Mia's phone goes in her bag. She scrambles for it: maybe it's Anna, she thinks, come to save the day. When she sees Fraser's name flash up, however, she looks for the exit and goes outside.

'Fraser?' She puts one finger in her ear to cut out the noise from the bar, but all she hears is white noise, the roar of traffic coming from the other end.

'Fraser?' she says again. 'Are you all right?'

'It's fucked!' is all she hears. 'It's fucked, Mia. It's totally fucked!'

She swallows, she suddenly feels sick, and she walks away from the bar towards the canal-side and the flickering lights. 'Fraser, what's fucked? Where are you? Speak to me.'

Fraser is sobbing; she can barely make out the words between breaths but she hears 'Liv' and 'Kiss' and she knows, she knows . . .

'She saw!' he says. 'I know it, she saw! And it's fucked, Mia,' he says again. 'Our lives, her life, everything!'

Mia closes her eyes. On the other end of the phone, she hears her friend's awful wrenching sobs.

'Fraser,' she says calmly. 'I want you to take some deep breaths.'

'She saw, she *saw*, Mia,' is all he says again, and Mia feels suddenly panicked. He's never been this bad before; he's never sounded this out of control.

'You don't know that,' she says, careful to keep her voice low. 'You don't know that, it's just your mind playing tricks on you. Nobody knows exactly what happened that night; we all have to live with that.'

Nothing, just the sound of him sobbing over traffic and, next to her, the gentle lap of water.

'Fraser, listen to me,' she says eventually. 'Where is Norm?'

'I don't know, I lost him ages ago. But it's all fucked, that's all I know, all of it and it's all my fault . . .'

It's at least ten seconds before she speaks again.

'I was there too, Fraser,' she says, but the phone's gone dead.

'Fraser?' she says again, more angry this time. 'Fraser? Speak to me!' But there's nothing, just a single flat tone.

She stands there, staring into the black water below. Her first thought is, 'I've got to call Norm.' The second is the kiss, the kiss . . . he's never said what he thought of the kiss?

When she finally goes back to Harry's Bar, she scans the room, only to see Melody, in the corner, both straps dangling off her shoulders now, arms around Bruno, her face suckered onto his.

NINE

May
Morecambe

Mrs Durham wiped her mouth with her napkin, and inhaled slowly through her nose. 'UHT cream,' she said eventually, with all the graveness of a doctor making a terminal diagnosis ('Tertiary syphilis, I'm afraid; three weeks at the most'). 'Far too much of it on these scones and I can always tell when they use the squirty stuff.'

Mia smiled, politely and somewhat wearily, thinking, I don't doubt that for a second, Maureen. You eat enough of them. In fact, despite 'sky-high' blood pressure, a 'lactose intolerance', not to mention the UHT cream, she'd managed to polish off two in fifteen minutes, a very commendable effort all round.

Now and again, when the weather was nice, Mrs Durham liked Mia to take her down to the Midland Hotel in Morecambe on a Tuesday afternoon, to sit and have a scone in their 'Rotunda Terrace café'. Often they would just enjoy the sea view; occasionally, when she was really on form, they'd have a game of Scrabble, which she loved. *Always* she'd complain about everything, from the hardness of the chairs ('Honestly, it's like sitting on your own gravestone') to the smell of the soap in the Ladies' and, now, the UHT cream.

The Midland had been derelict for years, but had recently been restored to its former glory and was the pride of Morecambe promenade now, a dazzling white ocean liner of a hotel against a seaside-blue sky; a fine example of art-deco architecture with its curves, porthole windows and a grand, sweeping staircase.

Inside, however, they'd gone for a modern approach, with a minimalist 'island' bar, floor-to-ceiling windows and the terrace café, with its huge, purple chandelier in the centre, like a sea anemone dangling above them, where Mrs Durham liked to take her tea and scones.

It was now the sort of place trendy couples who had moved to London came back to get married in a 'I may have turned into a meed-ya type, but I really come from a northern seaside town' kind of a way, and Mia couldn't help thinking there was something incongruous about Mrs D sitting on the hot-pink, leatherette banquettes with her swollen ankles and her Crimplene skirt, but despite many suggestions to the contrary, she insisted.

Mia didn't really mind. After all, on a day like today, and with the tide up, the view was something else: sparkling blue sea for miles, the odd, brightly painted fishing boat bobbing idly, and Grange-over-Sands, green and hilly, across the bay.

'More tea, Mrs D?' Mia was being somewhat over-cheerful, but Mrs Durham had been to a funeral this morning – the third in as many months – and Mia was keen to keep her off the subject, although so far had not had much luck.

For five months now, Mia had been looking after Mrs Durham on a Tuesday for a bit of cash in hand and a break from Billy; in that time she had deduced that funerals for Maureen Durham were a bit like christenings for the single and childless thirty-something: the only real time she got to see her mates these days and occasions she looked forward to, but with a sort of relished martyrdom.

'Would you believe it, Mia, I've another funeral to attend!' – when really she was looking forward to a natter and a subtle bitch (Mrs D was terribly good at a subtle bitch; the archetypal passive-aggressive) and maybe a free slice of Battenberg. She seemed to delight in telling Mia which of her mates had popped their clogs this week – as if to say, 'I'll be next! Mark my words. I told you I was ill!' – and Mia got the impression that attending funerals for Mrs D was just a chance for her to fine-tune plans for her own: didn't think much of the coffin, hymns quite nice, far too much mayonnaise in the egg-mayo baps.

Mrs Durham bowed her head and gave a low, uninhibited belch. 'Well, I suppose that's another one over,' she said, as Mia poured the tea; and Mia wondered whether Mrs Durham meant funeral, or life, so she frowned, hoping this neutral expression might cover them both.

They were the only people in the café now that the lunchtime rush had gone, and they sat for a while in comfortable silence, save for the melancholy whine of the gulls and the odd burp, and watched the tide come in through the curved window.

If she were honest, it was only recently that Mia could look at a sea view at all, without being overcome by a vertiginous, agoraphobic feeling, as if she might be swallowed up by it. All she could see when she looked at any expanse of water for months after Liv died was the view from their villa that summer – the summer of 2006. Ibiza. A glistening band on the horizon. It would have been the last thing Liv saw as she fell, thirty feet to the concrete below, dawn breaking over it. What was she thinking? Had she felt happy that day? Was she scared? Mia hoped she was too drunk to think anything. How sad that this was the only wish she had for her dying friend: no hoping she was with those she loved, or that she got to say all she wanted. Just oblivion, that's all.

It was ironic, really, because Liv loved the sea. She liked nothing better than a day trip to a tacky seaside town – Blackpool, Fleetwood, Southport – as students, they'd done them all. There was something of the old lady about Liv that liked a blanket over her knees when she watched TV, a tea cake and a cuppa at a seaside caff. 'Ooh, this is marvellous, isn't this marvellous?' She was full of comedic, old-fashioned hyperbole. She was good at self-preservation, too, at taking care of herself, as well as other people, of course, which made how she went all the more shocking. And absurd, actually, just ridiculous, Mia couldn't help thinking in her angrier moments. It was almost a comedy death, like being decapitated by a lawnmower.

Although certainly less funny when it actually happened.

Seriously, though, Liv, what were you playing at?

Mia knew this line of thought was futile and damaging, but occasionally, very occasionally, she just couldn't help herself.

I thought I was supposed to be the clumsy one? The one who tripped over things: wine glasses, my own feet, balconies . . . If anyone should have died falling from a balcony, surely it should have been me?

'To tell you the truth, I was surprised to see quite so many people at her funeral in the first place. She was a selfish so-and-so, deep down, although nobody ever says these things once you're six feet under, do they?'

Mia jumped, suddenly roused from her thoughts.

'Who? Who was?'

'*Barbara*, dear.' Mrs Durham leant forward and peered at her, a slight look of irritation in her enormous, varifocal-enlarged eyes, as if to say, 'Keep up! I can't be repeating myself all day long, you know.' She'd reapplied her lipstick in the time that Mia had been lost in thought but had missed, so now had coral grease smeared down her chin, making her look more mad than usual.

She gave a big sniff. 'She never did come to see me, you know. A week in the Infirmary having that camera down my throat, another in the Nuffield having my veins done. Eighteen months and not a whiff or a whistle . . .'

'She did have cancer, Mrs Durham.'

'For three and a half years, Mary! She can't have felt rotten all that time.'

Mia tried not to look too appalled at this – it was a skill she'd had to perfect over the last five months – or to correct Mrs Durham on her name. Again. She'd had Mary, Emma, Meera. She could call her Clive for all she cared now. She really had given up.

'She had a family, a husband and children who could have brought her, you know . . .' (This was fair enough, as far as Mia could gather. Mrs Durham had no family nearby: she'd been married but her husband passed away twenty or so years ago and her only son lived in Australia.)

Mrs Durham gave an offended little bristle of her shoulders.

'I'm sure she was thinking about you.' Mia filled up Mrs Durham's teacup again. 'It's hard to get out and about when you're older, even with the best intentions – you know that.'

Mrs Durham sniffed, unimpressed, and Mia groaned inwardly, wondering if she should order another scone just to make the afternoon go more quickly. Was inducing a sugar-coma abuse of the elderly, she wondered?

Most of the time she could tolerate Mrs D; Mia was robust and patient like that, it was one of her best qualities. Sometimes, she even enjoyed her company – ah, the ever-present smell of cat piss and the threat of death!; the hoarding of rancid food. When Mia had tried to remove blocks of mouldy cheese and bits of ancient cake wrapped in clingfilm from her fridge, Mrs D had accused her of being a glutton. Hardly – she would have died from listeria by now. Mrs D was a fruitcake – that went without saying. But she was also funny and loveable in her own VERY special way; and anyway, it beat CBeebies seven days a week and it kept her on her toes. Sometimes, that two-mile cycle ride to Mrs Durham's was the best part of Mia's week.

Today, however, she was having a bad day. Venice and the phone call from Fraser had set her off. Of course, at the time, she'd been sympathetic; at the time, she'd been worried sick about him, barely able to speak he was in such a state, miles away in Las Vegas, with only Norm to mop things up.

Over the last few days, however, Mia had begun to feel progressively more irritated. She'd begun to see Fraser Morgan in a new, not altogether flattering light. He indulged himself, that's what he did. He gave in to his demons far too easily. It was all right for him: he could get obliterated, wander off, take his shirt off on the highway, stand naked on top of the bonnet of a parked car if he liked – *Fear and Loathing* and all that. In fact, she wouldn't put it past him to have had that film in mind as he raged and ranted. He could be a dramatic little so-and-so when he wanted, complete with victim mentality. It was bloody annoying.

But the fact was, they both had to bear the guilt of that night, of not knowing and of the what-ifs.

The difference was, Mia had to keep it together. As much as she sometimes longed to go out, get drunk and not come home for days, she couldn't. There was a baby to look after, and now, seemingly, a mad old lady. She couldn't give in to the demons inside like Fraser could; she couldn't block out the thoughts with endless booze – although she gave it her best shot on occasions.

And also – unlike Fraser of late – she was making an effort to keep things in perspective, to remember what sort of person her friend actually was.

Bloody hell, even if she had seen them kiss, Liv would have demanded an explanation, not thrown herself off the nearest balcony! She was pragmatic – exactly the reason she was good for Fraser.

She was gone. No amount of sobbing down the phone would bring her back. But still, on these bad, dark days that seemed to make her feel heavy and nonexistent, like she could sink to the bottom of the sea and nobody would notice, it didn't stop Mia being angry and it didn't stop the horrid, gnawing injustice of it all. Sometimes she even felt angry at Liv: – Why did you have to go?

She looked over at Mrs Durham – she wasn't helping with all her talk of death and funerals and decay. And this sea, too: this huge, unfathomable expanse of water. It made her feel lonely and overwhelmed and defeated. Nobody would ever know exactly how Liv had managed to fall off the balcony, because nobody saw her fall – she was on her own – but, Christ, if you could lose your balance and fall off a balcony and die like that, if you just took your eye off the ball for a moment and it cost you your life, what was the effing point? Life was just a drop in the ocean, after all.

God, listen to her, she sounded morbid, not to mention mad.

You loved people and then they died. Billy was no different, one day he'd be gone. Maybe Mrs Durham had the right idea . . .

'You know we were good friends, Barbara and I, you'd never have thought it, would you? Not in the way she treated me these last few years.'

Mia arranged her mouth into a smile and turned to Mrs Durham.

'Now don't be getting yourself all upset, Maureen.' She started to clear up the cutlery. 'Even though she wasn't there in person, doesn't mean she wasn't your friend till the end, now does it? I'm sure she'd be mortified if she heard you talk like that.'

And also, FOR CRYING OUT LOUD, YOU SILLY OLD COW!!!! How can you possibly hold a grudge against someone who's dead? How can you not forgive someone who's dying of cancer? Sometimes Mrs Durham really tested her patience.

Mrs D had had years to say what she wanted to say to Barbara – years to forgive her, to pick up the phone herself. Mia hadn't had the chance to say one thing to her best friend. No goodbyes, no last words. That day, they'd bickered about avocados for an hour – a whole hour! Their finest bickering hour. Mia said they were fattening, it didn't matter if they were 'good fats' or not, calories were calories. Liv said that was the thickest thing she'd ever heard her say: How could something that was healthy possibly be fattening?

They never did get to the bottom of it.

God, she missed her. Often it was not during the big events, the important times that she did, but during odd, seemingly insignificant times, like now, like sitting in a new hotel with a batty old woman who kept belching when the mood took her. Liv would have thought that was hilarious. She wanted to tell Liv about Mrs Durham and her amazing guttural belching. She'd wanted to tell her, the other week, how she'd gone out again wearing odd shoes, or the fact that Billy could point to his nose if you said 'nose' now.

Sometimes, she forgot she was gone at all, only to email her and remember that Olivia.Jenkins@northside. ac.uk didn't exist any more. 'She no longer had an earthly presence' – that's what was said at the funeral. So where was she? Where had she gone? Where was everything she'd said and felt and laughed at?

Mia wondered when she had turned into this person who only looked back. She had read a feature recently, something in one of the Sunday supplements that she made herself read from time to time, just so her brain didn't dissolve. It was an interview with some poet, a female African poet (she'd put a Post-it note on her fridge to remind her to buy her anthology some time), who was saying how she thought that as a young person we look forward, and as an old person we look back – and it's only in middle age that we sort of have peripheral vision. And so, Mia was old already. At twenty-nine, she felt as old as Mrs D.

After they'd finished their tea and scones, Mia put Mrs Durham on the bus and took her home. Then she went to pick up Billy from nursery and she fastened him into his buggy and, as she was walking home with him down the hill, she got that feeling in her stomach again, that terrifying feeling: how easy, how simple it would be just to let go. Everything over. Gone.

TEN

Then

It was at least a month after she'd narrowly escaped taking Sara Moussaka's crown to become Mia Moussaka that Mia saw Fraser again. The Christmas holidays had been and gone and Mia had spent them at home in Chesham, feeling depressed, not to mention mortified.

She'd thought, hoped, it was a date. She'd planned her outfit for *WEEKS* and he'd just seen it as an opportunity to get fresh with his mate?

Good old Mia, up for a laugh, up for a snog. Well, he could bugger off. She was not going to be his shag buddy. Shag buddy had never been on her agenda.

The worst thing was, she couldn't talk to Anna and Liv about it, she was far too embarrassed. They'd already ribbed her incessantly about her and Fraser's little shopping trips to Asda.

'Shopping again? Yeah, *course* you are, Woodhouse. Getting jiggy in George more like, fondling in the freezer aisle, *HEAVY PETTING IN THE POULTRY SECTION?*' Their 'hilarious' puns knew no bounds.

Of course, she'd tut and roll her eyes, but secretly, she'd suspected they had a point. Maybe Fraser did fancy her back? Surely he felt the sexual chemistry too? Jesus Christ, it was electric! Those journeys back in the taxi, the only thing stopping their hands touching being two industrial bags of rice, were becoming more than she could bear.

But whereas she'd dared to dream they might have a future together, that they might have something special, he clearly just saw her as his mate, whom he possibly wouldn't kick out of his bed if they had fallen into it, on occasions (which thankfully they hadn't. At least she had spared herself that humiliation).

The most galling thing was that it had taken them so long to get to this point. Or at least 'the point' at which Mia thought they were. They were now in the second term of the second year. They'd met on day three of the first year, not at some glamorous Fresher's Ball, but when Mia had leapt on him, hypnotized and tasting of raw onion. A baptism of fire, to say the least.

After that, when her friends had taken great delight in pointing out her victim all over campus, she'd been so mortified (she was beginning to see a pattern emerging here) that she'd avoided Fraser for much of the first year. It had become a running joke between her, Liv and Anna . 'Duck, Mia!' They'd laugh. 'There's that bloke you attacked.' Once, their eyes had locked in the queue for the bar in the Student Union and she'd literally blanked him, stared right through him.

He probably thought she was mental.

Mia had lost count of the number of times someone had said to her, 'Aren't you that girl from Fresher's Week who snogged that bloke hypnotized?' She always claimed complete amnesia, but feared she'd never live it down. She was fully prepared to spend her entire undergraduate life avoiding the bloke with the wavy dark hair and the beautiful blue eyes. Then, one day just before the end of the summer term of the first year, they ended up in a lift together. She remembered thinking it was the stuff of romcoms starring Cameron Diaz, except she didn't have legs up to her armpits to compensate for her hilarious, ditsy adorableness. Or even the hilarious, ditsy adorableness. Just a penchant for assaulting strangers.

'Sorry, but aren't you . . .?' Fraser started.

Mia narrowed her eyes at him.

'That girl,' he carried on, encouragingly. He was smiling. A wide, infectious smile and Mia felt a bit better. He can't have been that offended, then.

She still didn't come clean. 'Sorry, what girl?'

'That girl from Fresher's Week,' said Fraser. He *did* have gorgeous eyes; such a beautiful shape. 'You know, the one . . .'

'Nope. Sorry,' she said, slowly shaking her head. This was impressive. Maybe she should have done drama instead of media studies. 'I don't mean to be rude but I've no idea what you're talking about.'

The lift stopped and they'd both got out, Fraser standing with his hands on his hips, surveying her. It made her giggle.

'Fuck,' he said eventually. 'You really were under, weren't you?'

161

Mia left it a good few seconds for the penny to drop, as it were.

'Oh!' she said eventually, slapping a hand to her mouth. 'Oh, God, *SHIT*. You're that bloke . . .!'

'Yes.' She'd been pleased to see that he was still grinning and nodding his head enthusiastically. 'I'm that lucky bloke.'

Had he just said 'lucky'?

The profuse apologies had gone on for some time: she wasn't a complete mentalist, or a man-eater or a bunny-boiler. She'd never done anything like that in her life. In fact, she did, normally, try to strike up a conversation with someone before sticking her tongue down their throat and, God, she didn't even know his name!

'Fraser,' he said.

Fraser. She liked that. Very sort of understatedly cool.

'Well, I'm Mia,' she said.

'Hello, Mia,' he said. 'Normally, I tend to know girls' names before we share saliva but you know, that's fine . . . Er, I don't suppose you fancy going for a coffee?'

Obviously the coffee turned into a beer then into another beer, then into a bus into town where they went to the Sugarhouse to get monumentally lorded and dance up and down to Pulp and the Soup Dragons.

And Mia did feel free. She did feel free to do what she wanted, any old time. This Fraser Morgan character seemed to make her feel like that. She could really be herself with him. He was unaffected and silly and fun but also deep; they could really talk about stuff, which was more than she could say for any other bloke she'd ever met.

So that was that. They became friends. Fraser introduced

Mia to Norm and his girlfriend Melody and Mia introduced Fraser to Anna and Liv.

In the second year, they moved from halls into houses:
Fraser, Norm and Melody into South Road and Liv, Anna
and Mia into Station Road – a stone's throw away from
one another. There were others, of course, including Si
and Andy from the band, but they were the hardcore
six, and gradually, they became inseparable. Mia had
always aspired to be part of a 'gang' and she loved it,
thrived off it. She felt as if she belonged.

And over time, she'd thought she and Fraser had got
something special and that perhaps he thought the same
too. But she'd got that wrong, and now she figured she
could go one of two ways: fall out with him and never
see him again, or suck it up and get on with being mates.

Since she liked hanging around with him – fuck it,
she *loved* hanging around with him – she decided on
the latter. It was a stupid idea to go getting a boyfriend
at university, anyway, as cute as Melody and Norm were
together, one cushion-buying twosome was enough for
any group of friends. No, she should be footloose and
fancy-free. She should experience life.

That way, things would be far simpler. That way she
wouldn't get hurt.

ELEVEN

June
Hampstead Heath, London

Fraser watched on as Norm, fuchsia in the face, grimacing and spluttering, struggled to finish his last set of sit-ups. To be honest, he felt thoroughly uncomfortable. I mean, what was he supposed to do with himself? Cheer him on? That seemed a bit embarrassing. Join in? That was even more so. Instead he took this opportunity to smoke a quick fag, to stand there in his running gear and take in the glorious view over Parliament Hill, as well as a whole lot of carbon monoxide into his lungs.

It had been like this all morning. Fraser had been more than happy to run around Hampstead Heath with Norm – it was something he did on his own, anyway. However, ten minutes in, Norm had suddenly flung himself to the ground and started to incorporate sets of sit-ups, or 'ab crunches' as he now called them, and Fraser felt this was a step too far. He'd seen the groups of Hampstead ladies with their yoga mats of a morning on the Heath and he wanted nothing to do with 'group exercise' in any form. His weekly salsa class was as much as he could take.

Norm had come down from Lancaster to stay with Fraser for the weekend and, although it had never been articulated, they both knew this was a compensatory weekend for the disaster that was Vegas, a sort of second attempt at their light-hearted 'lads on tour' mini-break.

After Fraser had finally found Norm, back at the hotel after that awful, horrible day that saw him lose it in the middle of the Las Vegas strip, he'd completely broken down. Norm had had to basically hold him on the bed in a bear hug to stop him escaping again, and then as good as rock him to sleep. They were best friends; they'd known one another since they were eight years old; they'd been through everything together – heartbreak, disappointment, the band, the break-up of the band, and a funeral they should never have had to go to – and yet there was an unspoken thing between them now, that that day in Vegas was the heaviest things had ever got, that they'd reached an altogether different plane.

So now, they needed to – what was it? – 'regroup', to have 'a laugh'. Yeah, a good old Fraser and Norm knees-up! Bloody hell, thought Fraser as he lay down on the long grass and watched the clouds as they tumbled towards the city down below, am I even capable of that any more? Or have I become one of those sad liabilities of a friend, who can't even have a beer without turning dark and twisted?

He sincerely hoped not, and had planned two days of boozy lunches, possibly a spot of jammin', him on guitar, Norm on drums, like old times back at 5 South

Road – perhaps they could finish that song they'd started. Or even just an afternoon on Super Mario Five because, sod it, they needed to regress. But Norm had other ideas. Fraser should have known the minute he declined a beer on arrival:

'Can't, brother. I'm on a health kick . . .'

Fraser had sniggered. Since when did Norm call him 'brother'? That sounded worryingly like steroid, pumped-up talk to him. But from his straight face, Fraser knew instantly that to Norm this was no laughing matter. He had pulled out 'get a six-pack' from the hat, from Liv's List that day back in March, and he was taking it very seriously. That much was obvious from the second Fraser saw him.

Barely in the door, Fraser had made Norm lift up his T-shirt to confirm what he suspected was indeed a greatly reduced version of the famous Normanton gut, the begin-nings of definition around his normally barrel-like belly.

'Jesus, mate.' He took him by the chin. 'And is that your jaw line I see?'

Norm had promptly slapped him about the head.

They'd gone inside, Norm to grill Fraser on the running routes around Kentish Town and to bang on about his new 'Hunter Gatherer' diet. ('You know, human beings don't need farmed produce, Frase. And that includes legumes. Do you think the cavemen ate anything other than berries and vegetables and meat?')

Fraser tried to muster an appropriately enthusiastic response. 'Dunno,' he said eventually. 'But what's a legume when it's at home?'

He'd ribbed Norm all afternoon but, deep down, he was disappointed that this was not going to be the weekend he'd envisaged. And also, there was something about the way Norm was SO obsessed with getting his six-pack by July, so obsessed by Liv's List, full stop, that was starting to bug him.

'Oh, man.' Fraser stubbed his cigarette out, just at the point that Norm collapsed, panting, clutching his knees to his chest in agony, and gasping, 'That was proper *evil*.'

'Another twenty, son. On yer back!' Fraser joked, lightly kicking his friend in the side.

'You bastard,' said Norm, straightening out as if he was about to start again.

Fraser rolled his eyes 'No, but the thing is, Norm,' he had his hands on his hips and his head cocked to the side in a pseudo-matronly fashion, 'nobody's actually making you. You don't have to do any more sit-ups, or any sit-ups at all for that matter. This is not an army assault course, mate, I thought we were just going for a jog?'

Norm sat up, looked momentarily a bit hurt, then laughed and got up. 'Come on then, let's carry on.'

They ran for a bit; it was gearing up to be another day in what was, so far, a week-long heat wave, and Fraser was sweating profusely already, regretting that mid-run fag now and wishing he'd put some socks on with his trainers.

'I just wanna do it by the book,' said Norm suddenly, as if taking up a conversation they'd started, although Fraser couldn't remember exactly what that conversation was.

'I just want to get a six-pack – if six-pack is what Liv said, do you know what I mean? I wanna do it properly. To make her proud.'

Fraser found himself rolling his eyes again. Norm and

Liv always got on brilliantly. They had a bond over music – the type of music he himelf didn't care for – and a silly, almost surreal sense of humour (for example, they both thought *Shooting Stars* was the funniest thing on TV, while he couldn't stand Vic Reeves). It had never bothered him before but now he felt a little . . . what was it? Jealous? Threatened? That was ridiculous.

Fraser paused. 'Sure,' he said, 'although let's be honest: we both knew Liv and know the chances she'd ever have actually got a six-pack are slim. This is the girl who paid five hundred quid to join a gym, then went once in eighteen months and dropped a dumbbell on her foot.'

Norm burst out laughing. 'Oh, God, I remember that. That was classic. She broke three toes, didn't she? Had to wear that stupid fucking support shoe for weeks – in fact, she came to our wedding in it, remember?'

Fraser did. He remembered everything. He remembered the very morning of Melody and Norm's wedding in Godalming – a belter of a July day. Liv standing in front of the mirror in their B&B, in the pretty summer dress she'd bought, a flip-flop on one foot, the humongus yeti shoe on the other, and almost crying and yet laughing at the same time.

But he didn't say anything; he could feel that familiar tightness in his stomach again – anxiety – like he'd eaten a huge meal he couldn't digest.

'Anyway, I'm just grateful,' said Norm. They were on the last uphill trek before the descent home and Norm was struggling to speak and run at the same time. 'I'm just grateful for the List – well, to Liv, truth be told, 'coz let's face it, me and Livs were similar in that way: a pair of lazy bastards when it came to exercise and I don't think I'd ever have got my act together and got fit and rid of this gut if it wasn't for her, d'you know what I'm saying?'

He looked across at Fraser, Fraser kept running.

'And exercise just makes you feel so much better, doesn't it? So much more alive. God, it makes you feel alive.'

They'd started their descent now, their feet slapping the ground.

Fraser looked skyward for the umpteenth time that weekend. Norm was often like this – evangelical. He was the same when he 'found' golf, when he moved from London to Lancaster ('No sirens, Fraser, NO SIRENS. It's fucking Paradise!') and now Project Six-Pack, the List. Fraser felt irritated and suffocated and he didn't really understand why. It was his girlfriend who wrote the List. Shouldn't he be at the helm of it all? Raring to go? But it was just bringing everything back. Liv's voice in his head, her writing on the page, a life suspended.

The Kiss.

Fraser took a sharp intake of breath.

'Hey, I was thinking, you know, too,' said Norm. They had stopped running and were walking towards the exit now and Fraser could hear the birds, the faint cry of children playing, and something else, he wished he could stop. 'I wanted to talk to you about it this weekend. How do you fancy us doing the biggie on the List? Going to China and doing the Great Wall? We could go this autumn, if we got our act together. I've got time I could take off from work.'

'Can't afford it, mate,' said Fraser, flatly. Best nip this in the bud, he thought; change the subject as quickly as possible. Maybe they should pop into the Bull on the way home and go and see Karen? She'd just be starting her shift now and Karen was very good at talking to new people, even if they didn't always talk back. It was getting a bit intense just the two of them and she would be a good distraction. She would give Norm her 'How to pull the perfect pint of Guinness' talk, that would kill an hour . . .

But again, Norm was persistent. 'Now, I knew you were going to say that.' He put an arm around his friend. 'But Norm's got a bit of spare cash. Mum and Dad cashed in some shares and me and my sister got a couple of grand. It wouldn't pay for everything, but I could pay for the flights . . .'

'I don't know,' said Fraser.

They stopped now – Fraser was bent over his knees, wheezing like an old man, whilst Norm poured an entire bottle of water over his head, a gesture Fraser couldn't help but think was a bit OTT: they'd had a jog around the Heath, not finished the London Marathon. But then Norm was a pro these days, dedicated to his cause: a man on a mission for the six-pack Fraser's girlfriend had apparently dreamt of. It suddenly all seemed a bit sycophantic to Fraser.

'Oh, come on, Frase, it'd be awesome! Just me and you and one of the Wonders of the World. We could do a whistle-stop tour . . . I'm thinking Beijing, Shanghai, gadding about rice paddies wearing one of those cone hats. Mr Wu's all-you-can-eat Chinese buffets every single day . . .'

Mr Wu's all-you-can-eat Chinese buffet had been the height of sophistication at one point in their lives, when they were skint and all living in London.

'. . . Liv would so approve.'

Norm's hair was flat to his head now, making him look ridiculous, and Fraser started to laugh.

'See, what's not to like?' Norm grinned, encouraged, and arranged his hair in an even more ridiculous combover. 'Do you know what I mean?'

After showering and a disgusting egg-white omelette that Norm made them eat, Fraser took Norm down to the Bull after all. He was going to make his best mate have a pint with him if it killed him, and he wanted him to meet Karen – Norm was always so positive and so unjudgemental and it would make him feel better and calmer about things if Norm approved.

There were only about four other people in the pub and Karen was kneeling on the floor, writing the lunch-time menu on a blackboard, her colossal breasts hovering over another very low-cut top. Karen was one of those women who was in love with her breasts, for whom her breasts were a boulder against which the waves of life could crash and she would be protected.

Fraser stood looking at them for a few seconds before coughing to get her attention.

'Karen? This is my mate, Norm. Norm, this is Karen.'

'Oh!' Fraser made Karen jump – she hadn't seen them come in the door; she was now in the bizarre position of kneeling at two men's feet.

'I'm so sorry – you must have been able to see right down my top!'

Norm splayed his hands. 'Hey, don't be sorry . . .' Fraser flashed him a look and Karen stood up.

'Sorry, that came out all wrong, didn't it?' He laughed,

and Karen laughed too, somewhat over-zealously, Fraser thought. 'Oh, I think Norm and I are going to get along,' she said.

And, as Fraser had predicted, given they were two of the most appeasing people he had ever met in his life, Norm and Karen did get on, like a house on fire – which was fine by him. Karen gave Norm the 'How to pull the perfect pint of Guinness' talk before moving on to a tour of the pub (Fraser had had that already) and the cellar, and a full rundown of what it was like to work for a pub – delivery day, changing the barrels, the ethos of a giant of a brewery. Fraser sat at the bar, the June sunshine flooding in through the window, warming his back, and he watched his girlfriend talk animatedly, eyes aglow with a sense of purpose.

This was something he loved – perhaps loved was the wrong word, but admired about Karen – the fact she took such pride in her work, no matter that, essentially, she was a barmaid ('I'm a bartender, Fraser. Barmaid is demeaning to a woman . . .'). How he wished he could muster some pride for his work, too, but so far in life, work had just been something he'd fallen into, that kept him out of trouble during the daytime. Fraser had never been a career man by any stretch of the imagination, but at least he used to have dreams, vague intentions of getting off his backside and 'making his mark' – whatever the fuck that meant. Now, work was drying up, but maybe that was because he was turning it down. In the past month, he'd been offered a gig with *London Tonight*, a prime-ministerial tour of Kenya and two weeks filming polar bears in the Arctic for quite a prestigious production company, but he didn't want to go away, he just didn't have the drive any more.

'So, Karen, your boyfriend and I are going to go to China together.' Norm patted Fraser on the shoulder and he suddenly sat up.

'We are going to walk the Great Wall of China, no less. Me and Morgan on the path of the Gods!'

'Are you now?' said Karen, looking at Fraser, her smile slipping.

'Are we now?' said Fraser, looking at Norm.

'Yeah – 'coz I'm going to pay for it,' he said, banging his fist on the bar, 'and it's going to be awesome, I'm telling you, Karen. It's gonna put a smile on that miserable mug of his.' He got Fraser by the cheeks and Fraser played along, giving his best false grin. 'Beijing, Shanghai, the Great Wall . . .'

Karen wasn't saying anything and Fraser knew this wasn't really the reaction Norm would have been hoping for.

'We'll only be three weeks,' he added, possibly when he realized this wasn't going down too well. 'Do you reckon you can live without him for that long? I mean, I know I'd struggle, him being so devilishly handsome and all . . .'

Norm was stammering now and laughing, nervously. Karen looked at Fraser, mouth open. 'Well, I don't know,' she said, with a shaky smile. 'I mean, yes, I mean, I'm sure . . . but, well, what's brought this on? He's never mentioned anything about China to me.'

Under duress, Norm had sunk a pint of Guinness, which, for a man in his honed and pure condition, had clearly gone straight to his head.

'It's one of the things on the List, you know, on Liv's—'

Fraser could feel his heart thumping. 'Norm and I have a mental list,' he said just in the nick of time. 'A list of things we've always wanted to do, since we were kids, you know, haven't we, Norm?'

'Uh . . .?' Norm turned to Fraser, his face all screwed up, and Fraser kicked him under the bar. It was a childish thing to do but circumstances called for it.

'But anyway, I don't think I'll be going to China.'

Karen stood back. 'Oh, no, but you must, hun,' she said, and she reached out and touched his hand, her nails, newly dolphin-painted, briefly scratching his skin. 'He must, Norm. You must take him. I know how long you two boys have been friends and you don't find mates like that every day, or ever in your life if you're me, actually!' She laughed, and Fraser briefly closed his eyes. She had a knack for this, for breaking his heart in one line, whilst being completely unaware of it.

The pub filled up and Norm and Fraser went to sit down, Fraser with another pint of full-strength lager and Norm with a J20.

'What the fuck was all that about?' hissed Norm

'She doesn't know about the List, does she, dumb-ass? I haven't told her about the List.'

Norm looked alarmed.

'But she knows about Liv, right?'

'Course she knows about Liv.'

'So why haven't you told her about the List?'

Fraser was getting irritated now. Norm was acting like the List was some sort of religious guide, or political manifesto, like everyone in the world should be aware of its power and importance.

He leant forward for extra emphasis. 'Because she's my girlfriend, Norm, you moron, so perhaps she wouldn't be too enthusiastic about me carrying out the wishes of my other, dead girlfriend, you know what I mean?'

Norm looked at his drink. At last! Perhaps he got it.

'But why don't you want to come to China?' (Or perhaps not.) 'It's what Liv would have wanted. Imagine her, looking down on us, as we walked on one of the Wonders of the World. She'd be so chuffed, man. So chuffed we did it for *her* . . .'

Fraser rubbed his head; he felt suddenly exhausted, the knot of anxiety becoming ever tighter.

'Look, Norm. Don't take this the wrong way, but I didn't have that good a time in Vegas.'

'I know, mate, I was the one who practically rocked you to sleep, remember?'

'And I'm not sure doing this List business is really doing me much good.'

'Why?'

'Well, it brings it all back, doesn't it? That I should have done more . . .'

'Now come on,' said Norm. 'We don't want any silly business. We don't want you going down that road again.'

Fraser couldn't help himself. 'But I wasn't there, Norm.'

'Course you weren't. We were having a party, you idiot. None of us were there on that balcony that night.'

'But I was her boyfriend. I should have protected her.'

'How did you know she was going to wander out on a balcony, drunk? How the fuck were you to know that? You can't know what's going on in someone's head, Fraser. Believe me, I know.'

They moved onto something else. Fraser was eager not

to let the mood slip, as it had so disastrously in Vegas, and suspected Norm felt the same. They stayed in the pub until the light faded and their shadows were long on the stripped wooden floor.

It had been another gorgeous day, but a storm was threatening now, the air was warm and soupy, and as they walked across the heath, towards Fraser's flat, the grass was a striking, vivid green against the darkness of the clouds.

'Karen's a great girl,' said Norm. 'I thought she was sound.'

'Really?' said Fraser, encouraged. 'You think so? You don't think—'

'What?'

'I dunno, that it's too soon?'

Although, if he were honest, the matter still occupied his every waking thought. In the last fortnight or so, Fraser had begun to come to terms with the idea of Karen as a steadier presence in his life, even if it was so he didn't have to think about other things. Las Vegas had unsteadied him, deeply. He felt he was walking a tightrope between sanity and unsanity and Karen with her eBay and her rubbish love gifts and her minced-beef dinners was a welcome breath of normality that he was holding onto for dear life. She'd started to plan things way ahead – and that worried him – but, if he were honest, without her, he knew there'd be a big vacuum in his head, that would inevitably be filled with demons and truths he could do without.

Also, the salsa classes had become an unexpected bonus in his life. He never thought he'd ever say this after that terrible first lesson, but he actually looked forward to

Tuesdays. He would never be a natural dancer, but he could put steps together now and lead Karen with some mastery, which gave him a sense of achievement he could never have predicted. Calvin told him weekly how much he'd improved – nobody had ever, in his life, told him he'd improved at anything, except perhaps the guitar, but even that he'd taught himself. No, this was a teacher/pupil relationship he'd never experienced, and he liked it. It was worth staying with Karen a little longer just for that.

Norm turned to him. 'Can I say something, mate? I don't think you should feel guilty about having a relation-ship. Karen's a great girl, she seems to make you relatively happy and Liv would have wanted that – you know that, don't you?'

'Yeah, I guess,' said Fraser, fighting that uncomfortable tightness in his stomach again.

'Also, we all have to move on, don't we? We've been seeing Mia and Eduardo a bit lately, and they seem to be getting on well, seem to be putting their differences behind them.'

Fraser stopped. 'Right, so are they back together then?'

Norm had got his mobile out and was fiddling about, walking on ahead and looking distracted.

'I said, are they back together, Norm?' shouted Fraser, stopping. It came out stronger than he'd planned and his voice echoed over the Heath.

'Well, *I* don't know,' said Norm, bemused, and he went back to his phone. 'You'd have to ask Melody, she's the one who keeps on top of all that.'

TWELVE

Then

Fraser was gutted. Pissed off beyond belief. It had taken him six months to pluck up the courage to ask Mia over and now he'd totally ballsed it up. Or rather, Melody had, albeit unknowingly.

'What the fuck? Why did you tell her that?' Fraser had said to Melody, when Mia had suddenly disappeared out of the door.

He'd wanted to go ballistic at Melody, he'd wanted to blame her, but she was obviously so confused, so clueless . . . 'What you on about?' she'd said, standing there with the dustpan and brush. 'I'm sure Mia wouldn't care, she'd just think it was funny' – that he didn't have the heart, or the balls, come to think of it, to admit what the whole night had been about for him. He'd done such a fine job of pretending he and Mia were just mates that even his housemate believed him. Nice one, Fraser!

He'd gone round to her house two days later and searched all over campus to no avail. Then it was the Christmas holidays and he'd spent the month at home in Bury, fretting, kicking himself, planning what he'd say to her when he finally got a chance to explain.

And now that time had come. Now, he was sitting in the Merchants in the January of 1997 – a brand-new year in which he was determined to get the girl of his dreams – and Mia was having none of it. And also he'd drunk too much to make his point clearly. Why did he always do that?

'Listen, I know you think I'm just this big tart, this big skirt-lifter who can't keep his hands to himself.'

Mia had sniggered at 'skirt-lifter'.

'You make it sound like a hobby, Fraser. Which I think it kind of is, for you.'

Damn it, he'd chosen that word carefully too. He thought it sounded less serious than 'massive shagger', which, for the record, he didn't see himself as either.

'You were different though, Mia.'

She smiled, wearily.

'Yeah, Fraser, course I was.'

'You're my special shopping buddy.'

'Wow. Now I do feel honoured. Now I feel like one of those tartan things you see old ladies pulling along, that you can buy in the back of the *Telegraph* magazine.'

God, she could be annoying.

'But, Mia, seriously, I really like you . . .' he said leaning forward.

'And I really like you too,' she'd said, putting her hand over his. 'But I don't want to spoil what we've got. I don't want it to be weird. I couldn't bear that. Now can you just shut up, go to the bar, and get me another drink, please?'

For a year after that, Fraser intermittently tried his luck with Mia; there were drunken declarations of love, declarations of love on ecstasy, and a truly embarrassing attempt to show her his 'massage skills' he'd picked up on a trip to India with Melody and Norm in the summer of 1997, which ended up with a visit to A&E, when Mia had pulled a muscle in her neck and had to wear a neck brace.

He was obsessed with her. For the first time in his life he knew what love was – at least he thought he did. But it was unrequited, and there was only so long, he figured, you could be in love with someone if they didn't love you back. So eventually, he'd given up. Sod her, he'd thought. I found The One but she didn't want me.

And eventually the pain eased, the wanting waned and Fraser learnt a valuable lesson in life: that no intensity of feeling lasted forever.

And then there was Liv: lovely, no-nonsense, dry-humoured Liv. Of the two boys in the group, it had always been Norm who'd had more of a bond with Liv, them being into the same (dreadful) music, doing the same course and going to gigs. But essentially, Norm was with Melody, and so when Boring Ben dumped Liv, and suddenly, six months after they graduated, she and Fraser found themselves alone, stumbling into their early twenties, scared at what the future might hold, they started to hang out more, just the two of them.

Feelings grew – Fraser had never seen his friend 'like

that', but suddenly he got Olivia Jenkins. She wasn't Mia but she was a beautiful person – kind, funny, someone pragmatic to balance his often emotional and brooding side. He then learned another valuable lesson: that broken hearts do mend, and you can love again.

THIRTEEN

15 July 2008
Lancaster

Mia took another great spoonful of mayonnaise and dolloped it into her mashed egg. Egg-mayonnaise sandwiches – was that just too common? It was a baby's first birthday party, so surely she shouldn't be doing goat's cheese on ciabatta, but still, maybe Jo and Tamsin's kids were allergic to eggs? Or they didn't approve of shop-bought mayonnaise? Maybe she should have bought brown bread?

She spooned some egg mixture onto a corner of white bread and stuffed it in her mouth. Ah, but it was bloody delicious though. And anyway, she told herself, this was *Billy's* first birthday party and Billy loved egg mayonnaise on white bread . . . and cocktail sausages and cheesy Wotsits and, oh, Christ, she'd better do some carrot batons.

She stood at her kitchen sink, in her pyjamas, chopping away manically at a bag of carrots, her worries about the day buzzing about her head. Melody had been so sweet offering to host Billy's first birthday at their house, even if it did mean she could tick one of her tasks off Liv's List:

'Ooh, that fits so well because I pulled out "Have a massive party for my wonderful, wonderful friends. Just because . . ."'

Mia thought about this and found she couldn't help smiling because it wasn't 'just because' at all. In fact, Melody – God love her – had managed to shoe-horn in about five different, entirely self-interested reasons to have this party. Talk about killing two birds with one stone, she could have murdered an aviary.

So there was the List, then there was the fact that it was also her and Norm's wedding anniversary today – their third. Then, Melody had called her to say: 'How thick am I?! This would be the perfect chance to flog some of my Pampered Chef stuff to all your mummy mates!' – as if Mia's 'mummy mates' spent their entire life on a quest to procure more kitchen implements and would be ecstatic to fuse a kid's birthday party with a chance to buy a tomato de-seeder.

Mia sniggered quietly to herself at this, making a mental note to tell Liv all this when she next visited the bench, whilst at the same time fighting another wave of nerves about the day. It wasn't like her to be neurotic, but for some reason this birthday party business had really given her the jitters. There were just so many variable factors and unknown quantities: for example, would Jo, Tamsin and the other mums she'd invited from Rock-a-Bye Baby think she was cheap for having the party at her mate's house? (Not that she had much choice, you couldn't swing a cat in her lounge.) She worried about how her 'mummy friends' would get on with her 'normal friends', or her 'real friends' as Melody 'jokingly' called them, and also how well SHE was going to get on with her real friends. This was the first time she'd seen them all since telling them she and Eduardo were officially back together, after all, and the news hadn't exactly gone down a storm. Also, her mother would be here any minute. God, her head might explode.

Chop, chop, chop, but must keep on with the job in hand, she told herself. Today was not the day for an existential crisis. As if on cue, Billy shuffled across from the other side of the kitchen on his bum, his arms in the air as if to say, 'Up! Up!'

Billy hadn't quite mastered the art of walking as yet, and Mia was quite happy to stave it off for a bit, if not for a few years. Why everyone was so desperate for their baby to walk, she'd never know. Weren't they hard enough work without being mobile?

Having said that, just lately, she was feeling more like it was worth it. When she was pregnant and working at Primal Films, she'd asked her friend Maxine what all the fuss was about, what was so good about having a baby? Maxine had looked at her as if she was mad, and Mia had felt dreadful: clearly she must have no maternal bone in her body. 'You just love them so much,' Maxine had said, misty-eyed. 'And they love you and it's soooo flattering.' Mia had never got that; Billy had never seemed that impressed and even looked mildly relieved when someone else came to look after him. In the past month or so, however, Billy would sometimes cry when she went out of the room, and although Mia would roll her eyes and say, 'Oh, Billy, come on . . .', inside it felt incredible, and, yes, flattering.

She hitched her pyjama bottoms up and picked him up – 'Hello, birthday boy, my little friend – and picked off the bit of egg he had stuck to his lapel. Melody had wanted to buy him a first birthday outfit and, not exactly being flush, Mia wasn't going to say no. However, she now regretted this decision as she regarded her twelve-month-old son in his pinstriped suit and tie.

'What's she done to you, that Aunty Melody, hey?' she said, kissing him on the forehead. 'Made you look like William Hague?'

She screwed her nose up at him and Billy started to giggle as if at her joke, and she got that feeling again, it had been happening more and more lately, as if something was expanding in her chest and her throat and there wasn't enough room. She had to catch her breath.

The doorbell went – her mother – and Mia mentally prepared herself for disappointment (after twenty-eight years, it was better that way).

She padded towards the door in her slipper-socks, carrying Billy, and arranged her features into what she considered to be her best, most serene and coping face.

Lynette Forrest (maiden name, although Mia had lost count she'd changed her surname so many times) was dressed almost head to toe in animal print and had at her feet a gigantic box wrapped in pale blue Cellophane and topped with an equally gigantic blue bow. She'd had her blonde hair blow-dried for the occasion in a smooth, bouffant bob, and Mia cursed herself. Why couldn't she have got it together to at least put some clothes on? Why put herself through this every time?

Lynette put her arms out for Billy.

'And how's my scrummy birthday boy?'

Billy nuzzled coyly into Mia's neck and Mia rolled her eyes as if to say, 'Honestly, so clingy . . .'

'You are going to love your nanna!' said Lynette, pushing Mia to the side with the gigantic box, in a waft of Ysatis. She kissed her grandson, leaving lip gloss on his cheek, and Billy almost recoiled, more due to the wall of overpowering fragrance than any personal aversion to his maternal grandmother, but Mia felt the need to cover for him: 'He's a bit overtired, Mum, you know, his birthday and everything . . .'

Lynette tottered on her zebra-print heels, through the hallway and Mia closed the front door, Billy still in her arms, looking skywards as if for some Divine support.

She followed her mum through to the tiny lounge, most surfaces covered, she now realized, with toys and opened birthday cards.

'Cup of tea, Mum?' she said, as Lynette set the box in the centre of the coffee table and sat, hands clasped, in front of it, as if this was *her* present she was desperate to open.

Lynette smoothed her hair down as if merely being in her daughter's flat made her feel untidy. 'That'd be nice,' she said . . . and then out it came: 'Now I know you're very busy, darling, but it *is* quite a mess in here and I always brought you up to be so clean and tidy . . .'

Wow. That was definitely less than five minutes.

Billy started whimpering and bucking to get down. Then the timer went off on the sausage rolls and Mia put Billy down to go into the kitchen.

'Well, is he going to open his nanna's pressie?' shouted Lynette from the lounge as Mia opened the oven door – Oh, God, oh, surely not – to find she'd put the grill on rather than the oven and the sausage rolls were now like lumps of charcoal, smoke billowing from the oven.

The smoke alarm started going and she swore, loudly, wafting it with a tea towel, wondering why everything would always be going so smoothly until the minute her mother arrived and then all hell would break loose, making it look as though she spent her whole life in her pyjamas setting fire to her kitchen.

'Mia? Are you all right in there? It smells very smoky and Billy's going crazy for this present, aren't you, sweetie-pie? Yes, that's right. Nanna Forrest's big pressie!'

Mia abandoned her efforts to stop the alarm and just took the goddamn batteries out of it instead, gathering herself in the face of what she always forgot was her mother's overwhelming capacity for self-centredness and a total inability to help.

Very attractive in a Hertfordshire, well-put-together way, life for Lynette Forrest was one big, grand gesture without chipping her nail varnish. She had groomed blonde hair, large, expertly made-up blue eyes and a penchant for expensive, diamanté-covered T-shirts with slogans like PARIS, JE T'AIME, even though she'd never been to Paris, and preferred the Canary Islands for its all-year-round sunshine and potential for holiday flings.

Today she had her uplifted breasts (present to herself for her fiftieth, three years ago) poured into said T-shirt, a cream leather, tasselled jacket that obviously cost a fortune but still looked cheap, a lace and leopard-print skirt – probably also cost a fortune from her favourite shop, Karen Millen, and zebra-print stilettos. The look said 'glamorous and expensive' – and also WAG.

Mia was Lynette's only child, the product of a brief fling with a car dealership owner named Ray in the late seventies; after splitting up from him (the relationship had broken down before Mia was born and Mia had never known her father), Lynette had gone straight back to where she'd left off, palming her daughter off to whoever, so she could resume life as a single person and life could be one long shopping trip to Brent Cross.

Of course she'd had copious boyfriends; Mia had lost count of the number of times she'd been introduced to one of her mummy's 'friends', only to find that 'friend' kissing her mother in the kitchen in the morning. They were always rich. Always had big cars and stank of aftershave. She'd married two of them: Barry, who then ran off with a Thai girl he met in a strip bar. He was classy was Barry. And Claud, an American, whom she'd met on a Caribbean cruise and who'd turned out to be a kleptomaniac. Still, she'd got some nice handbags from him. Apart from that, it had been a constant string of vain, younger men who seemed to last as long as her last shade of nail varnish.

Lynette owned a beauty salon – sorry, spa – in a posh Home Counties village near Chesham in Bucks, the town where Mia grew up. To be fair to her, she had made a real success of it and seemed to have an endless flow of cash, which she'd lavished on Mia as a child, in the shape of private schooling and expensive holidays, but which of course never made up for her not actually being there.

When Mia looked back at her childhood, all she remembered of her mother was the lipstick stain she left on her cheek before she went out – then the heady waft of Ysatis as she closed the front door.

Now, it seemed, she wanted to make up for being a shoddy parent by being a good grandparent – which would be great, but sadly this seemed not to consist of actual time or help, but in the ludicrously ostentatious presents she insisted on buying. At Christmas, she'd bought Mia a mother-and-baby photoshoot with make-over, so that Mia had then had to hang hideous soft-tone photos of herself throwing Billy in the air whilst lying on a sheepskin rug, with hair and make-up that made her look like Elaine Page.

After dumping the sausage rolls in the bin – sod it, sausages on sticks it would have to be – Mia went back into the lounge where Billy was pawing unsuccessfully at the tightly wrapped Cellophane. Then got bored halfway through and wandered off.

'Billy, that's not very nice, is it? You've upset Nanna, now,' said Lynette (yes, she was actually trying to emotionally blackmail a one-year-old), as Mia tried to entice Billy back. 'Come on, baby, look at this nice paper. Come and see what Nanna has brought you.'

Eventually, after a rather embarrassing few minutes, she and her mum unwrapped the box themselves

'Ta-dar! Look, Billy, it's a car! Nanna's got you a brand-new car! And not only that, but a Ferrari car!'

They opened the box and Billy looked, unimpressed, at the various bits of metalwork and bags of nuts and bolts.

'Of course, you have to put it together,' Lynette said. 'But Daddy will be able do that and then it's big enough for you to sit in and drive!'

Mia looked at the instruction book, as big as a telephone directory, and her heart sank. Where the hell was she supposed to put this car? And what was the likelihood of Eduardo ever putting it together? In this lifetime?

But of course, being a privately educated, Home Counties girl, she said, 'Wow, thanks, Mum, it's fantastic. What do you say to Nanna Forrest, Billy?'

Billy wandered off to play with his xylophone.

One thing Mia hadn't thought through when she agreed to Melody hosting Billy's party, was that Melody was a domestic freak and that generally, domestic freaks and one-year-olds didn't go together.

Right now, Mia was attempting to hold a conversation with Cameron's mum, Fiona, whilst keeping one nervous eye on Daisy – Tamsin's little girl (not as delicate as her name might suggest, let's say) – as she violently bashed a cheesy Wotsit with a toy hammer into Melody's glass-topped coffee table.

There had already been a leaking nappy incident on the cream sofa and Billy had pulled down a bowl of golden bracken (one of many 'naturalistic' displays in Melody and Norm's house; you couldn't put a glass down for knocking over a collection of sprayed twigs or a stone egg) and Mia felt she had to intervene.

'Daisy, sweetheart, do you want to give me the hammer?' she said, leaning across Tamsin who was chatting to Jo and seemed entirely oblivious to the proceedings. 'Maybe come for a splash with Billy in the paddling pool, outside?'

Tamsin didn't seem to take the hint and simply stopped

mid-conversation to regard her daughter with the same bovine look of adoration she always did.

'Well, she knows what that hammer's for, don't you, Daisy boo? You're making fine work of that Wotsit, missy!'

And Melody's table, thought Mia despairingly. She couldn't bear to watch the ritualistic battering of a cheesy Wotsit any more, so literally climbed over Tamsin (who didn't stop talking), scooped up Daisy, who howled, and took her outside to the paddling pool to join Billy who seemed to be in the midst of a one-man, naked slapstick show for Cameron and another baby, Georgie.

Although this was Melody's house, Mia still felt like the hostess, and hosting was not something that came naturally to her, especially when there were different social groups who didn't know one another.

She looked around her – as she'd feared, it was like a zoo, each species in their different enclosures. For the most part, her 'mummy friends' had monopolized the inside of the house and were all huddled on the cream sofas, some of their offspring at their feet, Melody intermittently attempting to slide a protective towelette or wet wipe into their hand, as she hovered nervously. Her university friends were on one side of the decking outside (Anna and Buddhist Steve, sitting cross-legged alone and in deep conversation); Eduardo and his mates on the other, posing in their sunglasses and drinking expensive bottled beer, as though this was a rooftop party at Pacha.

Neither group was talking to the other and Mia found herself flitting about, unable to have a conversation with anyone, too busy keeping one eye on her mother – who, so far, had spent the afternoon knocking back Pimm's and flirting with Eduardo's friends – and Melody's breakables. She was exhausted already.

There was also the fact that Fraser had not yet turned up.

The last time they'd spoken, they'd had a row, and Mia had told Fraser he was a 'self-indulgent, narcissistic baby' – something she now regretted but, you know, things had escalated. She'd tried to talk to him about the phone call in Venice, how she felt he had to start taking responsibility for his feelings, and he'd said: 'Right. And this is from the woman who's just got back together with the man who left her, at thirty-six weeks' pregnant?' (Were people going to throw this back in her face for the rest of her life?)

'Also, it's all right for you, Mia, you weren't Liv's boyfriend.'

She knew he'd spoken in the heat of the moment – Fraser was very good at flying off the handle – but, FOR GOD'S SAKE, what an arse! She just wanted him to get here now, she thought, mainly so she could stop being annoyed with him. She hated being annoyed with friends, especially Fraser.

She lowered Daisy, who stopped crying immediately, into the paddling pool, only to hear Melody in the midst of trying to sell a vegetable chopper to a bemused-looking Fiona: 'It's amazing, it's changed my life! Chops carrots, nuts – even nuts!'

'And how much is it?' asked Fiona, politely.

'Seventy-two pounds,' said Melody, without flinching. 'But it's an investment piece – will save you oodles of time in the long run.'

Mia looked over at Norm, who was shaking his head. She smiled and went to sit with him.

'You want to get her a job on QVC, she'd be brilliant.'

'It's alarming, frankly,' said Norm, shaking his head. 'Who'd have thought there'd come a day when my wife would think a vegetable chopper was an investment piece?'

'Could be worse. At least it's not a big fat diamond ring, she needs to "invest" in, or a second home in the country . . .'

Norm took a swig of his beer. 'There is that.'

They sat and watched the babies play, Billy holding onto the side of the paddling pool, standing up, then sitting down with a big splash, making the other babies laugh hysterically.

'He's quite the comedian, your son.'

'Oh, yes, his mother's razor-sharp wit. Watch and learn,' said Mia, as Billy did another Norman Wisdom fall to the side.

Mia remembered what Melody had said in Venice and was intrigued – it wasn't often she got to talk to Norm one-to-one these days.

'So what about you, Norm, eh? Pitter-patter of tiny feet?' He rolled his eyes at her. 'Sorry.' She grimaced. 'That's like the male equivalent of "tick-tock, tick-tock", isn't it? Please feel free to punch me, now. Look, right here, punch me in the face.'

Norm laughed. 'You're OK, it's just a bit of a sticky subject at the moment.'

'Really?' Mia resisted the overwhelming urge to make a filthy pun involving the word 'sticky'. 'Because Melody said you were gagging for a baby.'

Norm turned to her, open-mouthed, and Mia had the uncomfortable feeling she might have opened a marital can of worms . . .

'She's the one who wants a bloody baby!' said Norm. 'I can't look at her without her waving an ovulation stick at me. You've got about thirty-six hours, Andrew, to impregnate me! It's like trying to get tickets for the bloody Olympics.'

Mia sniggered but was confused. 'Right, so you don't want a baby, then? So, Melody's made that up?' She looked over at Melody, now cooing at Billy. Good God, it was obvious. Of course it was her who wanted a baby. 'It's just in Venice, she said . . .' She stopped herself before it got any worse.

'Look, I do one day, just *definitely* not yet; but what can you do? I can't have a headache every night of the week, can I? And can I just say, whilst you're here,' he took his bottle of beer back and downed the rest, 'I'm scared shitless about this homemade porn shoot thing. I mean, what if it turns into some twisted baby-making project? Melody with her legs in the air for fifteen minutes after we've done it, me tied to the bed with handcuffs and a gas mask on?'

Mia snorted, then frowned. 'Why would she have to put her legs . . .?'

'So, you know, all the little fishes swim upstream.'

'Ew . . .' The trying-to-get pregnant thing was a mystery to Mia since she'd never had to try. 'You know, you don't actually have to do it, Norm,' she said, as if this option just occurred to her, too. 'I don't think Liv would mind. In fact she'd probably be up there squirming with embarrassment if you did.'

Norm looked at her intently and Mia realized, not for the first time, how seriously he was taking this List business. 'Oh, no, we have to do it,' he said, resolutely. 'It's on the List, Mia. It WILL get done. I'm going to try and get Span to do it anyway,' he said, scanning the garden for Anna. 'What with her drama degree and pool of fuck buddies.'

'You make it sound like a typing pool.'

'It'd come as naturally to her as selling vegetable choppers does to Melody.'

Mia looked over at Anna, who was sitting, cross-legged, eyes locked with Buddhist Steve. They'd not talked to anyone since they got here. Despite Mia's efforts to get closer to Anna – calling her more often, asking after Steve, showing an interest in Buddhism, even though she feared Anna had as good as joined a Buddhist cult, she felt that Anna was growing more isolated, more *odd*. And it unnerved Mia. Anna was the undisputed drama queen of the group and yet, of all of them, she was creating the least drama out of the most dramatic thing that had ever happened to them. She just wasn't herself. 'Actually, I wouldn't be so sure of that,' said Mia, watching her nodding enthusiastically at everything Steve said. 'She's changed. Fraser and I don't think she'll be making any homemade porn vids these days – for herself, or for Liv . . . as selfish as that may be.'

'What, not even if it was with me? Spanner in a foxy police costume, me in a blond moustache.' Mia was just about to slap him when Melody came tottering over on her new wedges, so high they were cutting the circulation off on her toes, turning them a dark shade of purple.

'Two vegetable choppers and a mini-muffin tray!' she

announced, beaming, like she was a midwife and had just delivered triplets. 'I'm doing well, aren't I? Aren't I, Andrew?' She nudged Norm, so the lager he was drinking went up his nose. 'A hundred and fifty pounds already! That's our weekend in the Lakes paid for, sunshine . . .'

Norm was busy wiping the drips of lager off his T-shirt.

'Have you told Mia about our weekend away, darling?'

Mia stared straight ahead so as not to catch Norm's eye.

'Liv's gonna be so proud of us.' She sat down on Norm's lap, Norm making a little grunting noise, as though the weight of her had pushed air out of his mouth. 'And this one's not going to know what's hit him.' She nuzzled her nose close to his; the start, Mia feared, of a long and drawn-out foreplay session, starting now and finishing somewhere on a bed in a Thistle Hotel in Penrith.

Since Venice, no more had been said about the Patricio incident. Melody had simply said at breakfast: 'We shall speak of this never again.' Which was fine by Mia; the whole thing was gruesome.

'So, when do you think we should get the buffet out?' said Melody, and Mia, recognizing a get-out-of-jail opportunity, stood up.

'Soon, I'll make a start,' she said, making towards the kitchen, just in time to hear Melody saying behind her, 'Ooh, Jo! Just the woman I was looking for. Do you have five minutes? I wanted to show you my mini-muffin tray . . .'

The afternoon grew close and hot and Mia stood in Melody's kitchen, arranging the food on plates and

197

cringing as she listened to her mother, drunk by this point and becoming sentimental and inappropriate about other people's children.

'Oh, she's beautiful, isn't she the most beautiful child?' she was gushing to Suzy, mother of India. 'And did you conceive her in India? Is that the idea behind her name?'

Mia was just about to go and physically remove the glass of Pimm's from her mother's hand, and possibly even her mother from the party, when somebody screamed.

Mia flung herself out of the back door, convinced she was about to find a drowning child, not that that was possible in a centimetre of water. Maybe it was the relief, then, that the situation was by no means life-threatening, but when she saw a thin, pale turd floating in the paddling pool and Billy looking wistfully out towards the fields behind the house (if he could have whistled, he would have), she started to snigger.

'Daisy, don't touch it, darling. Daisy, DO NOT TOUCH THE POO!'

Mia could not stop the giggles rising in her throat, so that by the time she'd got a nappy out of her bag, scooped up Billy and slid it under his bottom, she was actually crying tears. Then there was the sight of poor Melody, trying to fish out the turd with the kitchen sieve at the same time as balance on her wedges, shouting, 'I've got it, it's fine. It's ABSOLUTELY FINE!'

Mia couldn't take it any more, and was beside herself, whilst the other mums stared at the paddling pool as if they'd found a dead dog.

'I did suggest she might want to put a swim nappy on him,' she could hear Suzy say as she took a crying Billy upstairs to the bathroom. 'I mean, it's toxic waste, that's the thing.'

She burrowed her face in his hair. 'Don't worry, baby,' she whispered.

This was another thing that was happening a lot of late – she wanted to stick up for her son, even when he defecated in paddling pools. Maybe this was the incredible mother–son bond she'd heard so much about?

'You just shat yourself. I mean, it's not the first time, is it?'

As it happened, he went on to do another, spectacular poo, and Mia had to shower him twice and went through three nappies, until she finally got him clean, got all the dirty nappies bagged up and went downstairs as if she'd just killed and dismembered someone and was disposing of the body. She went outside and handed Billy to Eduardo, giving him her best daggers (God, would he just lift a finger? Just so she wouldn't get her ear bent by her friends, if nothing else), and was just walking around the side of the house to put the bags in a wheelie bin when she saw Fraser getting out of his car outside the house . . .

With Karen.

Of course. Why hadn't she thought he'd bring his girlfriend?

'Fraser!' She looked . . . she didn't really know what she looked, but it wasn't the expression she would have been going for if she'd been forewarned.

Fraser walked down the side path of the house and went as if to kiss her on the cheek, but then thought about it too much before he did so, so that they both panicked, wavered from side to side and finished kissing each other on the lips, instead. It was pretty dreadful, made worse by the fact that Mia was still holding the bags of poo and if she could smell ammonia, she was pretty sure they could too. Mia didn't blush often but she knew she was blushing.

'Um, Mia, this is Karen, Karen this is Mia.'

Somewhere in Mia's peripheral vision, she could see that Karen's hand was clasped firmly in Fraser's.

'Hi, Karen, I think we have sort of met before –' Karen's face was a blank – 'and I would shake your hand now but, as you can see, I've got my hands full, since my son just did the most enormous shit you've ever seen.'

Fraser kicked at a stone and gave an embarrassed little laugh.

'Oh, dear, has he had too many raisins, grapes or anything?' said Karen, earnestly. 'My mum's friend's daughter always swears that fruit gives her baby the trots . . .'

No, he's a baby, babies just shit all over the place whatever they eat, Mia wanted to say, but managed to avoid it.

'Um, anyway, we brought Billy this . . .' and Karen handed Mia a beautifully wrapped present with a card Sellotaped to the top.

We? WE? On joint presents already? It started with this and ended up in a joint grave, thought Mia, particularly darkly.

She arranged her face into a smile.

'Thank you, guys, that's really kind . . . Now, if I can just dispose of these,' and she gestured, holding up the two small bags.

'Oh, hun, look, let me take those. You and Fraser have

a chat,' said Karen unnecessarily, and there followed an awful, five-second tug of war with the bags of baby shit until Mia finally surrendered and let Karen take them, one in each hand, to the bins.

Fraser and Mia stared at one another.

'Well, this is a bag of crap, isn't it?' she said, eventually. It was an awful joke, contrived and inappropriate, and Mia felt herself blush for the second time that day. Thankfully, Fraser saved her.

'Well, we've all done it . . . Got overexcited on our birthday and lost control of our bowels. I know I have . . .'

Mia giggled and he grinned and she grinned back.

'Anyway, how are you?' she said, standing back as if to get a good look at him. 'You look well. All that home-cooked food, the love of a good woman. It suits you, Fraser.'

Dear God, listen to her, she sounded like his middle-aged aunty.

'Thanks,' he said, and he held her gaze until she had to look away. 'Sorry we're late,' he said eventually, 'we had to call in on Karen's relative somewhere in Hertfordshire. You know how these Home Counties types don't half witter on . . .'

Mia pushed his shoulder but it felt fake and awkward.

'Well, as I said, marriage definitely becomes you.'

'Mia, I'm not married . . .'

'And, oh, my God, are those slacks?' she tugged at his trousers in an attempt to be amusing, when really she was genuinely alarmed. He never wore trousers!

'Yeeeess. We got them at Brent Cross last week,' he said, wearily and somewhat provocatively.

'Bloody Nora,' was all she could muster.

'Anyway, where's the birthday boy?' said Fraser, craning his neck.

'Oh, hiding somewhere, keeping a low profile after doing a crap in the paddling pool.'

Fraser burst out laughing. 'No way. Nice one, Billy.'

'Anyway, YOU should go and find your girlfriend,' said Mia. 'She doesn't know anyone. You're not looking after her very well.'

'Yeah, I know.' Fraser put his hand on her waist as he walked off into the party. 'Speak to you, later, OK?'

He turned back, and she was sure she saw him wink at her.

Mia headed inside to wash her hands, her heart hammering horribly inside her chest. God, that was awful. Truly awful. She'd never, in her life, had an awkward conversation with Fraser, and there they were, completely lost for words.

'So *this* is the lovely Karen,' she could hear Melody saying in the garden. 'We've heard so much about you.'

Eduardo sauntered into the kitchen. 'I see Mr Handsome's here with his fat girlfriend.' He came up behind her and wrapped his arms around her waist.

'Oh, Eduardo, for God's sake,' Mia snapped before she could help herself. 'Don't be so bitchy, you're worse than a girl. Now will you help me with this food?' She turned around and took his sunglasses off. 'And take these off. Jesus. Honestly! This isn't the Pacha closing party, you know, it's your son's first birthday.'

'All right, chill out.' It wasn't like Mia to blow up like that these days and Eduardo backed away from her. 'What's wrong with you?'

She rubbed her face. 'Nothing, sorry. Just, you know . . .' and she kissed him, hard on the lips, as if she wanted to bruise him really. 'Just help a bit, that's all, OK?'

'Hey, babe, what do you think I'm here for now?'

The afternoon wore on, the sky turning a more intense blue, so it looked like it might eventually crack. Eduardo reluctantly helped Mia with the buffet, whilst occasionally throwing Billy up into the air when people were looking.

Mia helped Billy work through his mountain of gifts, made an effort to have mummy conversations with the other mums, whilst all the time keeping one eye on Fraser and Karen.

Apart from Liv, she'd never seen Fraser with a girlfriend; she'd only really seen him with girls who were friends, and he always did a lot of talking, crap jokes, getting naked for no apparent reason and arguing (Fraser was very good at arguing) – so she was intrigued to find he'd turned into a mute.

Karen sat on his knee, they held hands – like all five fingers clasped together. Mia even caught them kissing at one point and looked quickly away. They can't have exchanged more than a sentence in an hour, and yet they didn't seem awkward, either. Maybe this is what a contented couple looked like, after all? Maybe muteness was a level a couple could only hope to reach in the higher echelons of loved-up bliss? Let's face it, she and Eduardo were hardly the epitome of contentment, her giving him daggers from the other side of the garden.

'She's lovely, isn't she?'

Then suddenly, Anna was standing right beside her,

leaning into her ear. 'I think her and Fraser are perfect together, don't you?'

Mia started.

'Yes, definitely. Absolutely. They seem to be getting on, anyway. Can't have been easy for him to bring her today, what with us and Liv—'

'Well, I guess life moves on, doesn't it?' said Anna, briskly.

Mia smiled and stared at the floor. She briefly thought of having it out with Anna, of telling her that she was worried they didn't seem to be bonding, how distant Anna seemed, how she really didn't appear to be herself. She opened her mouth, but the moment passed.

'Steve seems nice,' she said eventually. Even though she and Steve hadn't shared two words.

'Yes, he's amazing. He's really changed my life.'

Mia blinked, hard.

'Wow, that's amazing, Span,' she said.

'I know. Also, and don't take this the wrong way, but he doesn't call me that and I'd like it if you lot didn't either, any more. Is that OK?'

If Mia were taken aback, she tried desperately not to show it.

'Sure. No probs. Just Anna from now on.'

'Thanks, and also, Mia . . .' Anna flicked her long red hair behind her and touched Mia's shoulder, as if she was going to tell her a secret. 'You know, I think it's great you and Eduardo are back together. Really, really great.'

Mia screwed her nose up. 'Really? You're not just saying that?'

'No. I mean, people change, don't they? And I've been

chatting to him today and he's really grown up, and also, it's great for you and Billy, isn't it?' She ruffled Billy's hair, but sort of quickly, as if it might contain flammables. 'You can be a proper family now, get on with your life. It always comes right in the end.'

And then she pecked Mia on the cheek before she could say anything and sauntered off in her bottom-skimming sundress, leaving Mia standing there with Billy, feeling, what was it? She wasn't sure, but she couldn't move for a minute or two, she was stuck so fast to the grass.

She took a deep breath. Still, Anna was right, Karen was lovely. She began to feel bad for dissing her now; all that, 'Really, Fraser? A forty-two-year-old dolphin enthusiast?' What a cow she must have sounded.

She must make an effort, so she stood up with Billy, and was just about to go and talk to her, when Karen made towards her, all bouncing smile and bouncing chest. (By God, that was enough to render any man mute.)

'Hi. I thought I'd come and see how it was all going.' Karen was standing beside her now, stroking Billy's cheek. 'Billy's so cute!'

'Thank you. I guess he has his moments. Perhaps not when he's crapping in paddling pools.'

This was met with the same blank face as before and Mia resolved never to bring poo up again – clearly it wasn't something Karen was comfortable with; some people just weren't.

'I'd have loved to have babies,' Karen said suddenly.

Mia smiled sympathetically but she wasn't comfortable with this soft of oversharing, not when she didn't know the person.

'But I couldn't sadly.'

'Oh, I'm sorry.'

She looked at Karen: large, watery eyes, inoffensive features and yet plain in every way – the very opposite of Liv, who was striking and dark.

'It's OK, I've come to terms with it now. You see, I had a blocked Fallopian tube. A cyst on my right ovary to add to that, and then I went through the menopause at thirty-five. I think the universe was trying to tell me something!'

'God, that's terrible,' was all Mia could say, doubly aware of Billy squirming in her arms.

'I know, but the universe repaid me in other ways.'

Mia wondered if the 'universe' was a euphemism for something else, but she couldn't think what so she said, 'I really like your nails.' A desperate attempt to change the subject.

'Oh, thanks, they're actually pictures of dolphins, see?' And she held them up to the light so Mia could see they were indeed pictures of dolphins. 'I have an adopted dolphin in Florida. I call her the baby I never had! I'm mad about dolphins, you see, which is so funny because Fraser is too, as I'm sure you know. He told me about swimming with them in Zanzibar. God, SO jealous!'

Zanzibar? Dolphins? Mia drew a blank.

Mia was glad to see that people were mixing and chatting a little more easily now.

Karen wandered off to take her place next to Fraser again, where she could rub his knee, mutely. Two mutes together.

Mia needed a wee – excellent. Since having a baby,

needing a wee always filled Mia with a frisson of excitement. Twenty seconds alone on the loo! Going for a number two? That was practically a mini-break. She gave Billy to Eduardo again – who promptly threw him in the air – then went inside with her handbag, planning to retouch her make-up.

She flushed the toilet then studied herself in the mirror. The afternoon sun streaming in through the window was unforgiving, and she blew air out through her mouth in dismay. She looked knackered – this year had really aged her. She pulled the corners of her cheeks up, wondering how much a face-lift might set her back, put some Touche Eclat under her eyes, bared her teeth, checking on the encroaching state of yellowness, and made to rejoin the party.

'Oh, there you are . . .'

'Fraser, *Jesus*,' Mia gasped. 'Do you make a habit of stalking people outside toilets?'

'I've been looking for you everywhere. How are you doing?'

'Good – where's Billy?'

'Karen's got him.'

'Oh.' She forced her eyebrows down. 'She's lovely, Fraser. Really, just lovely.'

'Do you think so?' He was sort of screwing his face up.

'Definitely. Really nice.'

They hovered on the stairs saying nothing for too long.

'Well, you and Eduardo seem to be getting on well, too.'

She rolled her eyes 'Like a house on fire . . .'

Fraser laughed through his nose and looked at the floor.

'I saw Karen showing you her dolphin nails,' he said, grimacing.

'And very lovely they were too. Apparently, it's a love you share.'

Fraser looked blank.

'She told me about you swimming with dolphins in Zanzibar.' Then Mia bit her lip and it took him a second, but then he started to laugh, a low chuckle. 'You know, I don't tell you everything I've ever done in my life.'

'No, I suppose not. Anyway, you look happy,' she said, and then she thought about it for a moment, what the heck. '*Are* you happy?' she asked.

'Yes,' said Fraser, but he paused. 'Yes, I think I am.'

There was another, very long pause as Mia searched his face.

'That's good,' she said eventually. 'I'm really pleased for you, Fraser.' She smiled. 'Anyway, I'd better . . .'

'Actually, I just wanted to give you this,' said Fraser, quickly, handing her a small, thick blue envelope that said BILLY on the front.

'But you and Karen gave him a card already?' she said.

'I know, but this one's from me.'

'Oh.' She beamed. 'Shall I open it now?'

'No, no, just open it at home . . . Anyway,' Fraser looked flustered, 'listen, about that phone call last week. I—'

'Oh, look, I'm sorry—'

'No, *I'm* sorry, I was being a twat, I . . .'

'No, honestly . . .'

'Frase? Hun, are you up here?' They both started and turned around to see Karen stomping up the stairs, her chest leading the way. 'They're doing . . .'

And then she stopped mid-stair and, for some bizarre reason, Mia found herself putting the envelope behind her back.

'They're wanting to do the candles and cakes, now.'

'OK, we're coming,' said Mia, brightly.

'Yep, we're coming right now,' said Fraser.

But she'd already gone back downstairs.

'Happy Birthday to you, happy birthday to you, happy birthday dear Billy . . . Happy birthday to you!'

Billy screeched with delight, kicking his legs, and Mia helped him blow out the candles in the low, afternoon sun. 'Make a wish, Billy,' she whispered.

'Him and Daisy forever!!' someone shouted from the back, and everyone laughed and clapped.

'Let's raise a glass to Billy,' said Melody.

'To Billy!' everyone said, chinking their glasses.

Then Norm stood up. 'Um, if you don't mind, I do have one other person to toast . . .'

Oh, Norm, thought Mia. Not here, not now. '. . . and that is our friend Liv. Those here today who knew her, some very closely . . .' Mia looked over at Fraser, their eyes locked for a second and she looked away. '. . . will know that she would have loved to have been here today. She would have been the life and soul.'

'Hear, Hear,' said Mia, almost to herself, and she gave Billy a little squeeze.

'Yes, Olivia was always the last to leave a party,' piped up Melody. She was a little drunk now and stumbled slightly on her wedges. 'In fact, on her List that she left us – well, at least we like to *think* she left us, the list of things she wanted to do before she was thirty, although bless her heart she never saw that birthday . . .' The garden had fallen silent now. People were looking confused. '. . . she actually specifically requested we hold a party, so here we all are!'

There was a ripple of nervous laughter.

'Melody.' Norm silenced his wife with a squeeze of her hand. 'I'd just like us to also raise our glasses to absent friends, that's all,' he said, turning to the crowd, 'and specifically to Liv.'

'To Liv,' everyone said, and there were a couple of seconds' awkward silence as everyone sipped their drinks.

'Oh! And also to Norm and me,' Melody suddenly said, 'for three glorious years of marriage. It's our anniversary today!'

But everyone had started to meander back to what they were doing and her words were soaked up in the chatter.

FOURTEEN

Same day

After the hot, muggy day in Norm and Melody's back garden, the heavens had finally opened, and Mia sat at traffic lights on her way home, windscreen wipers on 'manic', having a row with Eduardo.

'But *why* do you have to go out though? You've been out all day?'

So far, they were trying to keep things tame – Billy was asleep in the back, as was Mia's mum (five long hours hard at it, flirting and drinking Pimm's had finally got to her). But Mia knew this had potential to become an all-out barney and she was quite up for it, actually. She had that sinking, tetchy feeling after the day's events, like coming home from a long holiday to find you've left the freezer door open and everything's defrosted.

'It's my son's first birthday, Mia. A milestone. I just want a celebratory one with the boys. I'll be back for nine p.m.'

Mia actually gasped – she couldn't help it. This was exactly what she meant when she said her relationship with Eduardo held far too much potential for ranting, raving and getting out of moving cars (something she would seriously consider NOW if she wasn't driving herself). Of course it was a bloody milestone! That's why she'd made a cake! And organized a party! (And looked after his son for the past twelve months, but she'd have to overlook that right now, otherwise she might kill him.)

Also—

'That's what you said on his actual *birth*day, remember? That you would be back to see us by nine p.m. after you'd "wet the baby's head". Then I didn't see you for three months, Eduardo. How do I know the same thing isn't going to happen this birthday, too?'

Mia and Eduardo don't talk about him leaving her when she was pregnant, they don't talk about how he missed the birth because he was pissed in a pub in Columbia Road or how he went AWOL, literally uncontactable for three months afterwards, because if they did, Mia wouldn't be able to look at him.

'Now you're just being . . . FACTITIOUS,' he said.

'I think you mean facetious.' Ten years in England and Eduardo still got some words wrong.

'Whatever, a pain in the ass.'

'Oh, that's lovely, that is.'

The lights changed, Mia drove on towards the station. James Brown 'Sex Machine' came on the radio and she had to turn it down in case she laughed, or very possibly cried. They were rowing (again); they had several Tupperware boxes of uneaten egg-mayo sandwiches

212

packed between them, making the car smell of farts. She couldn't feel less of a sex machine if she tried. She felt miserable, really miserable, all of a sudden. She wanted to get home, put her baby to bed and work her way methodically through a four-pack of lager.

'I don't mind you going out, but you've been with your mates all day. You've been drinking beer in a garden *all day*. If anyone should be going out, it should be me!'

'But you don't like going out.'

Oh, this drove her INSANE.

'I don't have anyone to go out with. Or any money. Everyone's in couples, or lives in London. Melody and Norm are going through some marital crisis, all my old friends got bored of asking if I could go out long ago, Anna lives in London and has turned to Buddha, Fraser's got a girlfriend . . .'

She was tired and ranting; she hated it when she got like this.

'And you're jealous.'

'What?'

'Of Fraser's girlfriend. I saw you watching her at the party.'

'Oh, give it up, Eduardo.' Mia leant forward to try to see anything through the lashing rain.

'You love him, I think.'

'He was my best friend's boyfriend, you are being *absurd*.'

'. . . you kissed him once, you told me.'

'Yes, I was hypnotized, I'd just eaten a raw onion and it was more than TEN YEARS AGO. Shut up!'

'Dearie me, what are you two arguing about?'

In the back, Lynette suddenly stirred. She'd had her

eyes open for three seconds and was already applying lip gloss.

'Sorry, Mum,' sighed Mia, bad-temperedly. 'We're almost here now anyway . . .'

Mia drove up the hill and turned right into Lancaster train station – a handsome, sandstone, old-fashioned sort of station, where she would drop off her barely conscious mother, so she could hit the buffet car and start on the mini-bottles of Blossom Hill.

Mia's mother never came to stay the night. Apparently, if she didn't get her full eight hours, she was 'unbearable'.

It didn't bear thinking about.

Mia reached under the front seat to unlock the boot.

'So, come on, what is all the noise about?' said Lynette. 'I'm interested now, you woke me up.'

Eduardo stared out of the window.

'Oh, Eduardo wants to go out,' said Mia. 'Which isn't a big deal. I just thought, since he's been out all day, he might want to stop in, open the rest of Billy's cards and presents together and have a drink, you know, raise a glass to our son.'

Lynette sighed. 'You are hard on him, Mia Saffron.' Mia cringed at the reminder of her awful middle name. 'Children's parties are really quite tiring, you know . . .'

Mia got out of the car before she did something she'd regret.

'OK, Mum, thanks for coming!' She lugged Lynette's pulley case out of her boot, practically steered her mum towards the automatic doors of the station. 'Have a good journey home, OK, Mum? Billy and I will come to see you soon.'

Mia stood under the shelter of the entrance and went to give her mum a peck on the cheek, but Lynette stopped her.

'You know, I do know what it's like, being on your own,' Lynette said suddenly. 'I was on my own when I had you, remember?' Mia couldn't remember her mother being with her on her own, ever, but anyway . . . 'And you know my advice?' her mum said, leaning in so she could whisper in Mia's ear. 'Keep hold of him, because it's so much easier when there's two of you, even if he's a bit of a shit. Money-wise, time-wise. Believe me, I've been there. And he's just a normal bloke, Mia. They're all the same, love.'

And with that, she kissed Mia on top of her head and tottered off on her zebra-print stilettos, slightly wobbly now with a hangover. Mia watched her. 'Mad, mad mother of mine,' she said to herself.

Then she ran through the rain to the car.

'Just go out,' she said, getting in. 'I'll drop you off at Revolution.'

After three trips up and down the stairs to her flat, carrying Billy in one hand and endless boxes of Tupperware and presents in the other, Mia was finally home.

The flat was warm, and like everything in her life of late, smelt faintly of nappy sacs and hard-boiled egg.

She switched on the light and stood there for a second, leaning on the doorframe, getting her breath back.

'What am I doing, Olivia?'

It wasn't often she had the urge just to speak to her like that – unless, of course, she was at the bench. It wasn't as if she felt 'her presence'. Mia wasn't into all that supernatural stuff: that used to be Anna's job; she was always claiming to have had a visit in the night, or to have smelt her perfume. ('Yeah, probably from when she was actually last there,' Fraser would joke, drily. Liv didn't so much put perfume on as jump in the bottle.) So no, Mia wasn't surprised one bit when the curtains didn't flutter, when nothing fell off the shelf and smashed, when nobody replied. It's just sometimes, usually when she was asking herself whether she'd made the right decision, she'd ask Liv – it was as if she were her conscience – and right now, having taken the path of least resistance again, she imagined she'd be none too impressed.

She walked over to the window. The rain had stopped and it had started to brighten up, the castle suddenly backlit, and Mia felt that familiar drag of loneliness take hold of her. It was 6.30 p.m., she had three more hours of daylight – what the hell was she supposed to fill them with?

She used to love summer – a summer bunny, she was, prone to getting people round for barbecues in March, then not putting shoes on until October. These days, however, she dreaded the long summer evenings in her flat, even longer up North than in London, with the sun in July not dipping behind the castle till gone half past nine sometimes. At least in winter you could rack up the central heating, put on a DVD at 5 p.m. and call it a day.

She opened the window further and listened: traffic, the rhythmic rumble of a train making its way towards the Lakes, somewhere too . . . church bells. Evensong. She held Billy and she shuddered, because these sounds, this vivid light, the smell of summer after rain, they all reminded her of exactly this time of day last year, when all her friends would be going to the Water Witch to drink pints by the canal, and she would be here, in this flat, with a tiny, mewing, writhing baby she didn't know.

Four months before giving birth, and in the throes of grief, she and Eduardo had not so much decided to move back to Lancaster as been forced to. Mia had had to give up her beloved job at Primal Films – the long hours just weren't doable pregnant. She had tried. In the last week before she'd finally surrendered, she'd trawled the prop houses of London with her five-month bump, sourcing one hundred and fifty different clocks one day, and a room's supply of mangoes the next. But she was knackered; the prop store managers looked at her as if she were mad. She had no choice but to give up and go on the dole at six months.

London was far too expensive on the dole and she was twenty-seven. Her friends were still happily losing whole weekends clubbing. At least in Lancaster, Melody and Norm were there to help and it was cheap, rent at least a third less than it was in London.

But this was not the same Lancaster she knew as a carefree student, and there had been really dark times, humdingers of bad times, when she doubted she'd get through this alive: the time she got a stomach bug (breast-feeding plus Norovirus, it wasn't a combination she'd like to revisit); the time he'd had a febrile convulsion – a fit because he had a temperature. She'd thought her baby was dying and had been forced to hammer on the door of her neighbours in her nightie. 'He's fine, it's very common,' some young, emotionless male doctor had told her at A&E. She'd wanted to shake him and tell him, 'This has just been the worst night of my life!'

There was the time – Billy must have been six months old – when, after three nights of teething and zero sleep she took him, in utter desperation, in a taxi round to Mrs Durham's.

When she'd got back from the pub, where she'd stopped, only for forty-five minutes, to drink half a lager and try to stop shaking, she'd found Mrs Durham calling him Patrick and showing him her collection of royal memorabilia and Billy, perfectly happy, propped up on cushions. Little bugger. She didn't know who was madder that day, Mrs Durham or herself.

A rainbow arced above the castle. 'Look, Billy,' she said, 'a rainbow. Look at all the lovely colours.' She bent her head and inhaled the baby scent of his hair. 'We've survived, Billy, hey, haven't we? God knows how, but we have.'

She bathed him whilst drinking a can of Carlsberg and listening to the coverage of some festival on the radio. Ah, young people, who had a life! But then she looked at his round little tummy, full of mini-sausages and birthday cake, and the look of concentration on his face as he turned the pages of his waterproof book. 'But I've got you,' she said aloud. Just having the thought surprised her.

He went down at 8 p.m. – miraculous after his sleep in the car – and Mia actually punched the air as she left his room. She opened another can of lager and rolled herself a cigarette – sod it, she deserved it – and leant

218

half her body out of the window to smoke it, watching the post-storm clouds slowly get burnt off by the sun.

The day had left her anxious and empty and she wasn't sure what to do with herself. She wandered from room to room for a while – she'd done this a lot in the beginning – sniffing the crook of her bare arm, like some sort of comfort blanket.

She went into her bedroom, lay on her bed, and absent-mindedly picked up the photo from her bedside table. It was of all of them at Melody and Norm's wedding – three years ago today. How much had changed in that time. She sat up and drank her beer and smiled to herself as she looked at the photo. Melody, a vision in an enormous white tulle dress, all fake-tanned bosom and blonde tendrils and not so much a tiara as a crown. Her, Liv and Anna in their lemon, Empire-line bridesmaid dresses that made them look like Bo Peep. The boys – look at the boys, they all looked so thin! – awkward in their Moss Bros hired suits. Fraser and Liv seemed to be having some sort of joint footwear malfunction, since not only was Liv sporting the yeti-shoe-and-flip-flop combo, but Fraser had forgotten his shoes and so, after a frantic attempt to buy more in the tiny, Surrey village, had had to wear his trainers – Liv had been appalled. But then it didn't matter; they'd all got drunk and it had been a day of unbridled joy and happiness.

The next time she'd seen her friends in their suits, it was Liv's funeral.

So much had changed. Today, she couldn't help remembering, as she had sat next to Norm and seen the look on his face as he'd listened to his wife trying to sell a vegetable chopper to Fiona, of the afternoons Melody and Norm had spent entwined in each other's limbs on the sofa at 5 South Road.

And Fraser, lovely Fraser. Mia was suddenly overcome with a feeling of it all being over. Today, she'd caught him with Billy on his knee, and as he'd talked to Norm, she'd seen him absent-mindedly stroke Billy's leg. Fraser had never been a natural with babies, not like Norm, who had that touch – ironically. But the few times she'd seen him in recent months, she'd caught Fraser interacting with him, almost fascinated but scared, as though he was something precious he didn't want to break.

She knew he wanted kids. They'd never discussed it, but it was there so potently in his body language. And now, if he were to be with Karen, that was never going to happen. Which would be fine, if she were the love of his life, but Mia doubted that were the case. So he might be wasted, and waste was the thing she feared the most for her friends, because whilst they had the time to waste before, she wasn't sure they did any more.

She sat up, determined to stop being so morose, and looked at the clock: 8.30 p.m. Eduardo should be back in half an hour, but experience told her this was unlikely. So she got up, took a pen and paper to write down who had got what, for thank-you notes, and made a start on the unopened cards and presents in the centre of her lounge rug.

There was a lovely card from Aunty Gill and Uncle Dave.

'Dear William (she'd told them a hundred times he was just plain Billy but they wouldn't have it), We hope you have a lovely birthday with Mummy and Daddy, and lots of cake and treats. Aunty G-G and Uncle David xxx'

There was a present from Anna (surprising in itself since she didn't get anything when he was born): a cute handmade wooden clock in the shape of the Hungry Caterpillar. 'Dearest Billy, may your day be filled with all good vibes. Hugs and peace, Anna and Steve x x'

Bloody hell, thought Mia, standing it up on the shelf: that was a bit scary.

There was one from Mrs Durham. NOW YOU'RE 2! it said on the front, and Mia chuckled aloud to herself. How much had she gone on to that woman about Billy's FIRST birthday? Clearly, she was more senile than she thought.

She opened present after present, watching the clock, but there was no sign of Eduardo – it was now 9.16 p.m.

A present from his parents, though, Valeria and José Luiz were truly lovely people but utterly clueless about their son. They'd come to visit early this year, when Billy was six months old, and Eduardo had 'borrowed' his son, spent the weekend with them, taking him to farms and all manner of other places, as if he did this all the time. Then, Mia hadn't heard from him for three weeks.

She took the next card from the pile. It was the thick blue card that Fraser had given her, with BILLY written on the front in Fraser's almost illegible scrawl.

She opened it, there was a card – a Quentin Blake illustrated card.

'Keep it real today, Billy. And eat cake till you're sick. Love, Big Fraser xxx'

Mia smiled. Sometimes she called Fraser 'big Fraser', since there was another, much younger Fraser, who Billy knew from down the park. She held it in her hand and was just about to throw the envelope away, when she realized there was something else inside. It was a folded piece of A4 ruled paper, a handwritten letter of some sort. She unfolded it, and began to read, sitting in a puddle of light, cross-legged in her living room.

Dear Mia,

Right, so you know I'm not that good at expressing my emotions, only of course, when it concerns myself. (What is it you called me on the phone the other day? 'A self-indulgent narcissistic baby'? Yep, I'd say that was a high point in our friendship.)

Anyway, just so you don't think I'm being indulgent (I'm joking, I'm joking, can't help myself, can I?), I'll keep this short. I just wanted to say, as your old friend, I'm really proud of you. REALLY proud of you.

I can't believe it's a year since you brought Billy home from hospital with a look on your face like all your family had been wiped out in a car crash, and look at you now!

Seriously, you're an amazing mum, Mia. A-MAZING. And I know I say that with no authority or knowledge whatsoever about parenting and maybe you lock him in a cupboard at home and feed him gravel, but from what I see of you, I'm very impressed. I know you don't believe this sometimes, but he's lucky, that boy, damn lucky to have you.

It's been a shitter of a year for all of us. I'm sure we'll look back on this time and think, that was the most dire year of our lives, but you've had more to deal with than anyone of us and have probably been the most upbeat. I know I've been a tit a lot of the time recently, but I'm working on it, and I'm not promising I will suddenly stop freaking out, or that I can really control that stuff when it comes to bite me on the bum, but you made me think.

So thanks for that, thanks for being honest, for being a top friend, and a very, very old, wise (OK, less of the old, but definitely very wise . . . OK, I'm signing off now before I get myself in trouble . . .) OWL, is all I wanted to say. A top girl.

I'm well proud of you, that's all, really. We all are.

Love [the L had been tampered with and Mia guessed he had maybe originally gone to put 'all my'],

Fraser.

There was no kiss.

Mia held the letter in one hand and bit her thumbnail. Should she call him now? She picked up her phone. Then she looked at the time – 9.25 p.m. They wouldn't be home yet. She imagined him and Karen driving down the M6 together, the window open and the radio blaring and she changed her mind. Instead, she sat there, in her flat, and she opened all the cards and presents, till a deep orange glow finally flooded the carpet and then the sky turned violet.

Actually, in the middle lane of the M6, just past Coventry, Fraser sits in a traffic jam in a hired Vauxhall Astra, jiggling his knees, fighting an attack of claustrophobia.

223

It's hot, they haven't moved for sixteen minutes, the car has one of those pine air fresheners, which is making him feel a bit sick, and he's needed a wee since Preston.

The other thing that's curbing his enjoyment of this epic journey from Lancaster to London is that he has felt a row brewing, pretty much since they set off from Melody's.

He wasn't in the best mood with Karen as it was, ever since she made them spend a hundred and fifty quid on hiring a car, because she didn't trust his (perfectly adequate) car to make the long journey up North (something about being scarred for life after her clutch went once on her way up to Hull). This is something he's finding lately – Karen's initial, perpetual cheeriness, is giving way to neurotic, subtly controlling behaviour, which somehow makes him spend money he hasn't got and agree to things months in advance. Apparently, they're going to see *Billy Elliot* at the theatre in two months. He hates fucking musicals! How did that happen?

And now she's started on about other, more worrying things.

'So, nothing has ever happened between you and Mia then?'

Fraser sighs and looks at her.

'What? I'm not being awkward. I'm just asking, that's all. I just want to know.'

'And as I've already said, no, nothing's ever happened.'

Karen looks out of the window and sniffs. 'OK,' she says; and then in the next breath, 'What, not even a kiss?'

Just that word does funny things to Fraser's stomach these days. It's like that feeling when you wake up after a drunken night out and the slow realization of what

224

you did last night dawns on you, only it happens to him every time someone says the word 'kiss'.

It's the reason there was that dreadful, awkward, non-kiss the minute he arrived at Melody and Norm's. He doesn't know what's done it – maybe the drugs he took in Vegas released something in his head – but it's like the slab of concrete that's been pressing down on him since Liv's death, the grief that meant he could think of nothing but the tragic details of that night, has been dislodged, and there's a crack of sunlight there now, and that sunbeam is that kiss.

He opens the window for some air. He thinks, if he gives her something it will lighten the load.

'Look. If I tell you something, will you just leave it? Will you promise you won't bring this up again?'

'OK.'

'I kissed her once, all right? But it was really her kissing me and it was totally meaningless. It was Fresher's Week and a hypnotist guy came to uni and he hypnotized Mia and he made her eat an onion – telling her it was an apple, which she did, so she was really under, you know? She really didn't have a clue what she was doing. Anyway, he then told her to get up and kiss anyone she wanted in the audience and she ran over and she practically fucking jumped on me!' And he laughs now, really laughs with the ridiculousness of it all.

Karen doesn't.

'And?'

'And what?'

'Well, was it nice, Fraser? Did you enjoy it?'

'Oh, for God's sake.' He's pleased with how this comes out – the *disdain*.

225

They've started moving now and he revs the engine for extra 'disdainful' effect.

'No, of course I didn't enjoy it,' he says.

'Well, I don't know, do I? I mean a kiss is a kiss, hypnotized or not.'

Fraser rolls his eyes. He thinks, that is fucking ridiculous, but then he also knows, if he starts on that one, he may not be too convincing; no, better take the path of least resistance.

He puts his hand on her thigh.

'It meant nothing, OK? I wish I hadn't told you now. Honestly, Jesus, she wasn't even conscious.'

'So since then you've just been friends?'

'YES, Yes! Of course we've just been friends and I take the piss out of her all the time for that night she stuck her tongue down my throat and she tasted grim – of raw onion!'

Karen shuts up and Fraser thinks maybe that was a step too far, an embellishment that didn't go entirely in his favour. She says, 'OK, it's just today, there were a couple of things, Fraser, a couple of things that didn't quite add up.'

'Like?'

'Well, for example, when we arrived, the way you were looking at her, almost staring at her. I thought there's something simmering there, something unresolved . . .'

'She was carrying two bags of shit, Karen.'

'But I could *tell*.' She was leaning forward now, her hand to her chest to stress her point. 'I'm not totally stupid, you know. I know I'm only a "barmaid" –' she puts this in inverted commas – 'but I'm perceptive, too. Very perceptive. Remember, I see romance playing out

226

before my very eyes, night, after night in the Bull. I see the way people look at one another.'

Shit, thinks Fraser, you're telling me, all that Tarot card reading – maybe she did have special powers, after all.

'And also, when I came looking for you to do the candles on the cake and I caught you on the stairs, and well, if I'm honest . . .'

Fraser runs a hand through his hair, frustrated.

'I felt like I'd *interrupted* something.'

The traffic has slowed down again now, and Fraser really wishes he didn't need a wee quite so much, then he might be able to really think about this.

She looks at him with those big, pale brown eyes, those eyes that were pretty, actually, but held absolutely no mystique for him.

'We were talking, that's all,' he says.

'So, what about?' says Karen. 'Because I saw that letter, that letter in her hand.'

Fraser takes a deep breath through his nose. He's annoyed now. How dare she grill him, in the car, when she knows he can't get away?

'Look, Karen, it was a private letter. A letter which had nothing to do with you, actually, about Billy and Mia and the fact that today was a pretty big day for them. Mia's been through a lot this year, after Liv and everything. She was her best friend, you know, and I—'

'I know. God, I'm sorry.'

She puts her face in her hands and Fraser has a rush of empathy for Karen – or is it pity? He's not sure. It can't be easy for her – Rebecca syndrome and all that – trying to take the place of a dead girlfriend. And she's good about it, very good, actually. She asks him often, whilst stroking his hair in bed, what Liv was like, does he want to talk about it? But Fraser doesn't want to talk about it and he feels doubly guilty because he knows – because Karen's shown him – that there are women prepared to take on his baggage, but also, in this case, that that is not enough.

When they get home, at gone 11 p.m. that night, and he is lying next to Karen, blinking into the darkness, she strokes his hair away from his face and for the very first time, says, 'I love you.' Then she mumbles into the dark, half asleep, 'What was that thing that Norm was going on about, anyway, something about her List?'

FIFTEEN

Late July
London

Inside the Last Word café, situated in the vast, red-tiled piazza that leads to the British Library in London's King's Cross, Fraser sits on a window-facing stool, waiting for Anna.

Uncharacteristically, he got here forty minutes early and has already used this time to acclimatize to his surroundings – mooching round an exhibition about science fiction, which posed the questions, What does it mean to be human? Are we alone in the universe? Before moving – brain-fried – to another gallery, where he happened upon some completely awesome, original manuscripts of the Beatles' lyrics.

Fraser has relished this time alone. He enjoys culture, although at twenty-nine is still unsure of what form this 'culture' should take, and has often suggested to Karen that they should go to an exhibition or to the National

229

Film Theatre to see something that doesn't star Sandra Bullock, only to be shouted down with, 'But it'll be out on DVD in three months', and then somehow spending his Saturday afternoon in Matalan.

Today then, it's been a real treat to be left alone to feed his mind with things that interest him, and although Fraser doesn't see himself as an 'intellectual' by any stretch of the imagination, just being in these cerebral surroundings gives him a kick: he likes the echoey air of the place, the sense of purpose and the loftiness of the entrance hall with THE WORLD'S KNOWLEDGE written across it, like just being here might spark an idea for a ground-breaking invention or an original philosophical thought. If all else fails, he's discovered they do a mighty fine millionaire's shortbread in the caff on the first floor.

Now, though, as he drains the last dregs of his double espresso, he detects a slight slump in mood. He knows as soon as Anna arrives, that that will be the end of his 'me' time. Also, just a few minutes ago, he was standing in the queue of the library shop, buying a nice notebook and some pens, when he was informed by some pompous American – or was he Canadian? – that, 'You can't use pens in the Reading Room, if that's what you're buying it for . . .' He felt like saying, 'No, I'm buying it so I can crack on with my graffiti all over the toilets, you IDIOT.'

It's really got to him: how dare some random stranger patronize him? Did he look like a vandal? He was already thinking he would rather look at the exhibits and the manuscripts than sit in a stuffy reading room learning Wordsworth poetry off by heart, and now he's convinced of this fact, but Anna was very insistent.

'Come on, Morgan, you're my only close friend who lives in London, and anyway, it's for the LIST, after all, *your* girlfriend's List.'

Fraser really wishes people would stop saying this. It makes him feel more responsible than he is comfortable with – and he hates to be pedantic but wasn't the List Mia's idea? Let's face it, too, so far it's like the List is doomed: Vegas, even Billy's birthday to some extent, which wasn't exactly the 'massive party for my wonderful, wonderful friends' Liv would have wanted, more an endurance test: two hundred and fifty miles down the motorway with a moody girlfriend; having to watch as Eduardo threw Billy up in the air when people were watching. Twat. He was really hoping Billy would throw up on him. *Go on, Billy, chuck up those Wotsits all over yer dad's Ray-Bans . . . I dare you!*

If he's honest, though, he's already losing sight of what Liv would have wanted, full stop. Sometimes he feels that doing the List makes him feel further away from her, rather than closer. Did she really want to learn the works of William Wordsworth off by heart? As much as she loved her English degree, as much as she probably had a lot of time for the works of William Wordsworth? Wasn't that just written on a whim, and probably when drunk? Wouldn't she be laughing her head off now if she could see him, moody and awkward, knowing he'd rather saw off his arm than spend his Saturday learning poetry?

Also, Fraser has had to tell Karen some pretty extravagant lies to get here in the first place – something about helping Anna with a job application. He certainly couldn't say anything about the List, and she wouldn't have

231

believed he genuinely wanted to spend his afternoon in the British Library, even though he genuinely did. That was the point.

Karen hasn't mentioned the List since bringing it up, half asleep, after Billy's party three weeks ago, and he wants to keep it that way, but Fraser's conscience is alive and kicking as ever and it's getting harder to keep the truth from her.

Just the other day, he came back from town with a roll of material from Laura Ashley – spotty and a bit twee – but it might as well have been a wedding ring to see the look on her face.

'I fancy making a Roman blind,' he announced, as easily as that, as easily as, 'I fancy watching the match this afternoon.' Karen had barely been able to contain herself. He was 'nesting', she announced. Fraser is not stupid, he knows this is woman talk for 'committing', and he'd thought how scary it was, how fast things could escalate in a woman's mind. One mention of a Roman blind and they were moving in together. This was all made far worse by the fact that, of course, he had no idea how to make the Roman blind and so Karen had to help him and he had somehow found himself spending an entire Sunday afternoon cutting and drilling and putting a blind up and, damn it, if he had been Karen, he'd have thought he wanted to move in together too.

He wouldn't mind but since his run-in with Anna in the Merchants back in March, at Liv's birthday reunion, things have been lukewarm between them to say the least. They'd had one or two excruciatingly awkward phone calls, and the only words she'd spoken to him at Billy's birthday were mirroring Steve's epic monologues spouting spiritual shit – why did she want to spend the afternoon with him, anyway? It all seemed a bit forced.

Still, here she is now, flicking her hair and skipping down the steps towards him in that coquettish way she has. Never mind dance like someone's watching, Anna lives her life like someone is watching, with every movement, Fraser suspects, practised in a mirror. Today, she's wearing a knee-length pleated skirt, brogues, a truly awful cardigan. Even at the best of times, there's something about Anna Frith that looks like it needs a good scrub, and this ensemble isn't helping. She really was going in for this granny look of late, and Fraser doesn't get it at all. Also, what's with the Woody Allen specs? Spanner didn't wear glasses, did she? He watches her and feels a little stab of shame nonetheless. He really went for her, that night in the Merchants; he slagged off her squeeze in front of her and lashed out when really, the anger he felt was towards himself. He must try to be nice to her today.

So he smiles and waves, slowly, and goes outside to meet her and they have one of those dreadful faux-hugs where neither person actually touches the other.

Fraser steps back. 'Have those got lenses in them?' he says.

'No,' says Anna, defensively. 'It's called fashion, Fraser. Ever heard of that? No, I didn't think so.'

Fraser nods, resignedly. After ten years, he's used to her brittleness on occasions, especially when she feels silly; especially, perhaps, when she feels a little hurt. 'Oh, OK, so they're just for effect, then? Part of this whole intellectual look you've got going on. I like it, though, Anna.' He smiles, a little naughtily, giving her the once-over. 'Very appropriate.'

Anna huffs and tosses her hair. 'Very wearing, Fraser, that's what you are,' she says, and she nudges him with her shoulder towards the entrance and he nudges her back. 'Really fucking tiresome, actually . . .'

They have to get a Reader pass in order to use the Reading Room and there's a very 'tiresome' ten-minute wait at the registration desk where Fraser tries to ignore the frosty awkwardness between them. Clearly, she hadn't quite forgiven him.

He stands in the queue, which snakes out of the registration room, staring at Anna's back and feeling unnerved. He's always known where he was with all the girls: Liv and Mia obviously and, despite having his fair share of showdowns with her in his time, also with Melody. At least Melody was consistent with her keeping up with the Joneses; she made no bones about having moved seamlessly from student into middle age, about liking *Songs of Praise* and having kitchenware parties. Anna, on the other hand, could be a much more unpredictable and furtive creature, all bravado and defensiveness, especially today, and Fraser can't work her out. Also, there's something about the way she's backcombed her mane of red-dyed hair to make it look like a bird's nest that says potential 'loose canon' to Fraser, and he's not messing with that, no way. No, he shall just continue mildly irritating her; it seems to be the way they roll.

He leans over and whispers in her ear: 'So what poems do you know, then, apart from the Daffodils one?'

Anna shakes her head, as if to shake away this imbe-cilic comment and looks around to check nobody heard. 'It's "I wandered lonely as a cloud", even though everyone calls it "that Daffoldils poem", and I know *loads* more, I did a degree in English Literature, Fraser. That's how I met Liv, remember? We both did literature of the 1790s as a specialist module.'

Fraser inhales through his nose and nods to himself, momentarily impressed.

'Go on then, what other poems should I have heard of?'

'Well, *The Prelude*, that's really famous. Surely, you've heard of that?'

Fraser sticks his bottom lip out. 'Nope, but it sounds like a good one to start with.'

Anna rolls her eyes

'There's *Lyrical Ballads* – he and Coleridge, as in Samuel Taylor Coleridge, who wrote "The Rime of the Ancient Mariner" . . .?'

'All right, I'm not a *total* philistine.'

'Well, they worked on that one together. Changed the face of English poetry with that collaboration.'

'Cool. Is that a bit like me and Norm changing the face of music with our collaborative album for the Fans?'

'Er, no,' says Anna. 'Not really.'

Fraser tuts, mildly irritated by Anna's pomposity on the matter. OK, so she did a degree in English Literature, but it's not like she ever used it and, anyway, he seems to remember Liv complaining that she had to help her with her Wordsworth dissertation, that she practically wrote half of it. Since graduating, Anna has had an array of temp jobs: marketing, advertising, event organization (currently she was doing some work experience at a fashion house as well as concentrating on her Buddhism, which didn't seem an obvious union). She once did a course in counselling, too, which everyone was *stunned* by. But none of these have secured her interest for long and Fraser strongly suspects this is because Anna Frith thinks she's above actual work and should simply sit in cafés wearing fake glasses and mingling with 'interesting people' for a living. At least Liv taught English to secondary school students; at least she was genuinely interested in literature.

They'd once gone, come to think of it, to visit Wordsworth's home, Dove Cottage in the Lake District; it was one of the best places Fraser ever went with Liv – being a city kid from the outskirts of Manchester – and he remembers being amazed, *awestruck*, by the scenery – how ridiculously idyllic it was, like nothing he'd ever seen – so much so that he was moved to put down some lyrics in a fit of inspiration.

Ah, that was the Fraser Morgan of old, he thinks, ruefully, as he stands in the queue. The one who was inspired, occasionally, who had the peace of mind to *think* about stuff.

Anna seems to insist on having her back to him, and Fraser has no option than to amuse himself by people-watching. He is transfixed by the students – they are everywhere: sitting on the marble steps with a pile of books, working on their laptops in the armchairs up on the first floor. How come they look so *young*? It's offensive. They don't look more than twelve, any of them. Mind you, he must have looked like that one day, before the fags and the booze and the worry set in. What had he thought of people pushing thirty, back then? Old, that's what – what was the point of life past thirty?

They register at the computers. 'Now what is your purpose for study, today?' asks the woman at the desk: quite pretty, save for an unbecoming bowl-cut.

Fraser blows air out through his mouth. Oh, my dead girlfriend's wishes, he thinks. And he gets that knotted feeling in his stomach again. It feels like hypocrisy.

Still, he is here now and he must concentrate on the job in hand. He remembers the note he wrote to Mia: how he would try not to make any of this about him, by which really he meant about their kiss that neither of them will ever know for sure if Liv saw. 'Guilt,' someone once told him, 'is a selfish, useless emotion.' No, this was for Olivia, for the things she didn't get to do and the life she didn't get to live.

Eventually, after what seems like an hour of the sort of security procedures that wouldn't look out of place at a Category A prison, they make it to the Humanities Reading Room on the first floor. Fraser is carrying only the designated plastic bag allowed; with pencils, laptop, mobile phone turned on silent and a notebook. He is still reeling from being told that he won't be allowed to take in even a bottle of water, in case, you know, he tears a page of *War and Peace* into tiny pieces and makes a snow-shaker out of it, so he intends to be taking a coffee break, very soon.

'Right, so are we decided, then?' whispers Anna, as she holds the door of the Reading Room open.

Fraser narrows his eyes at her.

'You look at *The Prelude*, OK? I'll look at *Lyrical Ballads*, because I love *Tintern Abbey* – Liv and I both loved that poem – then we'll read them, make a few notes, go and discuss somewhere and learn say, ten lines off by heart?'

Fraser pauses then bursts out laughing – he doesn't know why, it's just Anna's serious face and those fake glasses and the fact he suddenly feels like he's joined an intensely intellectual poetry book club. But Anna's face falls; she looks hurt and, without thinking, Fraser throws his arms around her. She cares about the List, she cares about Liv; she has a good heart underneath it all, does Spanner. It was a shame she had to be such a pain in the arse sometimes.

The Reading Room is huge and pretty darn impressive. Fraser has never seen this sort of studiousness en masse, except perhaps in *Dead Poets Society*, and he is surprised to find himself feeling intimidated. Anna goes to the help desk to request some books and he stands there for a second, leaning back on his heels before righting himself again, unsteady with a sudden fit of vertigo. The room is vast, with a high, vaulted ceiling. At row upon row of long wooden desks, people are heads down, over books and laptops, their faces illuminated by the study lamps. Some of these dudes look as though they've been in here for *weeks*. The walls of books, so many old books! It fries his head to think of the people who have passed through here, the scholars who have sat in these seats. It is silent, save for the odd cough or rustle of paper, which echo and reverberate around the cavernous space.

They are given a shelf number for the books they need, by a woman so mousy and librarian-looking that Fraser wonders how she copes in the outside world.

He finds *The Prelude* nestling among the Coleridge

and Byron and the Keats. It is an unimaginably old book, with THE BRITISH LIBRARY stamped on its brown leather front – a proper book, as books should be. He smells it, that fusty, leathery, charity-shop smell, and has an immediate olfactory-induced memory: him, in the May of 2000, revising for his finals in Lancaster Library – a somewhat less inspiring, low-ceilinged building, eventually losing his fight to stay awake and dribbling over Plato's *Symposium*. Ah, happy days . . .

'OK, let's sit here,' whispers Anna, and she takes her place at one of the benches, switches on her reading lamp, opens her copy of *Lyrical Ballads*, seemingly exactly where she needs to, and starts reading. Fraser stands there for a moment. Wasn't she going to tell him which part of *The Prelude* to start with? It looks bloody lengthy, that's for sure – if this is *The Prelude*, he dreads to think how long the main poem is.

He looks around him for a few seconds, as if checking nobody is watching, then he slides his plastic bag containing all his belongings onto the desk next to Anna and sits down, slowly, trying not to make a sound.

There is a woman next to him, obviously with a cold or a chronic case of hay fever because she is surrounded, on all sides, by balled-up, snotty tissues, forming a sort of paper-and-snot barricade. She blows her nose, for a long time and very loudly, and Fraser uses these few seconds to get everything out of his rustling plastic bag and arranged on the desk in front of him, before leaning purposefully to the left to see what she's reading: *The Odyssey* – Now, there's a book! he thinks. By her side are reams and reams of elaborate, pencil-written notes on yellow A4, like the scribblings of a serial killer.

Fraser gives a short, sharp cough as if he means business, and turns on his laptop, but he's forgotten to put that on silent so it chimes, excruciatingly loudly, as it starts up, and he squeezes his eyes shut, silently cursing, waiting for it to stop. '*For God's sake, Fraser*,' hisses Anna, and then she tosses her hair dramatically, swiping Fraser in the eye so that it starts watering and he has to hold his hand over it for a good few seconds.

Eventually, after at least ten minutes of doing everything possible to put off the inevitable, he opens his copy of *The Prelude*. This poem is so long it is split into separate books, for crying out loud – wasn't the whole point of being a poet that you didn't have to write so much? He decides to start with the Preface, which gave an overview of Wordsworth's life. Yes, the best way to understand poetry was definitely to start with the poet. To say that this guy was fond of nature and the Lake District was something of an understatement. Liv loved the Lakes too and was often arranging mini-breaks and camping trips with everyone. Fraser has one particular fond memory of a rainy afternoon in Bowness, buying camping equipment whilst drunk on Bluebird bitter.

He reads on; he imagines old Willy Wordsworth in his ruffled shirt and his britches, awestruck by the host of golden daffodils.

'"I wandered lonely" is a poem about nature and memory", he reads, "Unity between man and nature. Daffodils are personified, the speaker is part of the scene, wandering lonely as a cloud . . ."'

There seems to be a lot about this concept of 'a unity between man and nature', and about the 'sublime', and Fraser, a philosophy graduate, after all, is quite taken with this. It sounds transcendental and psychedelic, possibly a drug-induced state. Weren't they all on drugs, these Romantic poets? Off their tits on opium?

He looks up 'sublime' on *Wikipedia*:

'A form of expression in literature where author refers to things in nature which affect the mind with a sense of overwhelming grandeur . . .'

Mmm. Sounded a bit vague.

He leans over to Anna. 'Hey, what's this sublime business I keep reading about? . . . It sounds, well, *sublime*!'

Anna looks at him blankly; across the bench, someone tuts. Then, Anna leans in, adjusts her glasses, as if about to impart ground-breaking, intellectual wisdom.

'I think it just describes a state when he was really, really happy,' she says, looking intently into Fraser's eyes. 'You know that feeling when you see something really beautiful, when everything just feels really right and good in the world, and words can't really describe it?'

Fraser is impressed. Perhaps he spoke too soon when he assumed Anna didn't know anything about Wordsworth, because he gets that, he really does. He can remember being rendered speechless by the scenery up there in the Lakes; it's just he can't remember the last time he actually felt like *that*, like everything was right and good. Has he ever?

'Look,' whispers Anna, sliding her book across the desk. 'This poem is famous for explaining the whole "sublime" thing.'

Fraser takes the book, 'Tintern Abbey, Lines composed a few miles above, on revisiting the banks of the Wye during a tour,' it reads. (Ten out of ten for a catchy title . . .)

'It's this line.' She points to it. 'Read this, this is what he meant.'

'. . . *of aspect more sublime; that blessed mood/In which the burden of the mystery/In which the heavy and weary weight/Of all this intelligible world/Is lightened*.'

Contentment, perhaps? It sounds pretty nice whatever it is, thinks Fraser. I'll have some of that. He is just about to say as much to Anna when his mobile phone (at least this is on silent) starts to vibrate. Fraser looks at the number. KAREN flashes up in capital letters and at first he ignores it, but then twenty seconds later, she rings again. Fraser looks around him. He could walk outside, but they are at the far side of the library, as far away from the exit as it is possible to be and he doesn't know, maybe it's important – freak accidents do happen after all – and it would be just his luck that the day he decides to ignore her call is the day she gets mugged or run over by a bus.

So he picks up, cupping his hand around the phone and cowering beneath the desk in an effort to be as quiet as possible. 'I'm in the British Library, Karen, is it important?'

'Yer in a LIBRARY?!' It always surprises Fraser, how northern, how 'from *Hull*', Karen sounds on the phone. 'What the monkies are you doing in a library, hun?'

'Helping Anna. Anyway, can I call you back? I'll call you back. OK, OK, gotta go,' and then he hangs up before waiting for her to do the same since, clearly, Karen Palmer is alive and well.

He puts his phone on the desk and is aware of Anna's disapproval next to him, as well as that of the woman reading *The Odyssey* – not that she can talk with her constant farmyard snuffling – and he is just about to settle back to *The Prelude* when he hears a familiar American drawl:

'Excuse me, you are not allowed to use your mo-bil phone in the library . . .'

It booms and reverberates and Fraser looks up to see the man from the shop queue standing up, a smug look slapped all over his annoying moon face. What was wrong with this idiot? Lurking all over the library, suddenly showing up to tell him off like a child? Fraser can deal with the likes of Darren – mindless scrapping doesn't really rile him, it's just inconvenient and unnecessary – but authority or, worse, this sort of misplaced authority from a pompous goon with a fucking anorak on. Nah, he's not letting this one go.

'Look, I had it on silent, mate, OK? But I thought it might be an important call and I was too far from the exit to take it outside. *Jesus.*'

Fraser goes back to his book, head dramatically in hands, but can feel the man glaring at him.

'Shut up,' Anna hisses, but no, why should he shut up? This man has humiliated him in front of a whole reading room, when all he's done is whisper, for all of four seconds.

'You are SO selfish,' snarls the man.

'Selfish?' Fraser laughs. 'I think you're the selfish one, don't you? Embarrassing me in front of everyone, for no good reason?'

And with that, Fraser switches his lamp on studiously because, as far as he's concerned, this matter is closed. Anna gives a short, humourless laugh of disbelief and the woman reading *The Odyssey* has her face in a tissue, embarrassed, or possibly not in any fit state of health to deal with a revolt in the British Library of a Saturday afternoon.

Anna nudges him, hard.

'What?'

'For fuck's sake, Fraser. You're going to get us thrown out.'

'Oh, shut up, Anna.' Fraser is irritated now, that double espresso kicking in, making him feel agitated. Where was the backing up? The support? Liv would have backed him up – and Mia? Yeah, well, she would have joined in.

American anorak in London stands up.

'You are unbelievable,' he spits. 'This is the British Library!'

So pompous! So. Fucking. Pompous.

Fraser gets up, and then, very calmly, walks around to his side of the desk and leans in – in a possibly intimidating fashion – right up to his big moon face, which looks as if it's been punched in the middle already.

'You're acting like I committed a crime,' he breathes in his face. 'You just cannot help yourself, can you? Just *cannot* get enough of your own pompous voice?'

'Excuse me?' drawls the man, with the sort of shaking, barely concealed rage that tells Fraser he now means WAR.

But Fraser shows no signs of leaving the man's side of the desk. Across the way, Anna is panicking, shoving her stuff into her bag.

'Right, we are going,' she says, red-faced, through clenched jaw. 'Fraser, get your stuff.'

He doesn't know if it's the caffeine or he just hasn't grown out of the attitude problem he had when he was thirteen, but he says, 'No, we're not going. Why the fuck should we go anywhere?'

Then the man huffs and puffs, before stuffing his things into a laptop bag dramatically and flouncing out like a scorned lover.

'HAPPY?' says Anna, and Fraser looks around to see that at least three wooden benches' worth of students are now staring at them. 'No, really, we are going this time, Fraser.' She chivvies him along like a naughty child. 'Come on. Out, NOW.'

They're sitting on the piazza, just outside the entrance now, trying to ignore the rain that's just begun to spot.

'God, I feel like we've been chucked out of a club,' says Fraser, before stubbing out his cigarette and hugging his knees as he exhales his last lungful of smoke.

Anna scoffs, unamused.

'YOU feel like that, I feel like I've been caught smoking when heavily pregnant – ashamed and humiliated, Fraser. That's what I feel.'

'Oh . . . chill out.'

'Well, what do you think Liv would think if she could have seen you in there?'

'She would have applauded me.'

'She would *not*.'

'She would! She was my girlfriend, as everyone keeps telling me. I knew her better than anyone else and I can categorically say that actually she would.'

Anna puts her head on her knees and looks at him, side on. There's a long pause.

'But did you *really* know her?' she says.

'What the hell's that supposed to mean?'

245

'Nothing, just how well does anyone know anyone? How can you know anyone completely, know what's going on in someone's head? That's all.'

Fraser gives a nervous laugh. 'You're freaking me out now. Basically, all I'm saying is that that man in there was a cock. Anyone could see that. What have I ever done to him – a perfect stranger, lest we not forget – to warrant him telling me off, not once but twice, in a public place?'

'Karma.'

'*What?*'

'Karma.' Anna shrugs. 'What goes around, comes around, what comes around, goes around . . .'

'OK, now you sound mad, Anna. Now you sound like Mystic Meg. Explain,' demands Fraser. 'What do you mean?'

'I mean, things come back to bite you on the bum, that's all. Everything happens for a reason, doesn't it? Life has a habit of . . . evening things out.'

Fraser rolls his eyes, but inside he feels that familiar tightening. Ever since she's been seeing Buddhist Steve – who, in Fraser's opinion, likes the sound of his own voice rather a lot – she's been like this, bandying around words like 'karma', throwing heavy philosophical questions into perfectly normal conversation. It's really beginning to get on his tits.

'*You* need to stop seeing Steve,' says Fraser. 'Next, you'll be telling me I'm coming back as a widow spider – one shag and I'm dead – and that'll teach me.'

Anna sighs, wearily, stands up on her long, skinny stalk legs, straightening her skirt.

'Steve talks a lot of sense, actually. It's just sense he talks Fraser, nothing more weird than that.'

'Really? Well, I'm going to the pub – there's some sense for you – and you can come too if you promise not to mention karma, or to tell me I'm about to face some terrible fate for having a couple of pints.'

He starts to walk, but she doesn't follow him.

'Agreed?' he says, turning back.

'Yes, OK,' but Anna is arranging her hair about her shoulders, still thinking.

'Thank God for that,' says Fraser, and he starts to walk across the piazza.

But halfway across he hears Anna shout, 'Look, Fraser,' and he turns around. 'It's not just you I'm talking about, OK? It's me too.'

They end up in an old pub, a proper boozer, just off the Euston Road.

At first, Fraser finds he is rather enjoying himself. He can't remember ever being out on a one-to-one with Anna before and she's good company when she gets a drink inside her: girlish and giggly and – now she's taken those bloody silly glasses off – much more the Anna of university days.

They talk about her job at the fashion house, her mad boss who starts drinking at 4 p.m., then insists Anna sit in her office, to look at pictures of her dog on her computer.

Fraser tells Anna about his job, too, about misery guts Declan, the veteran of sound recordists, who constantly bangs on about how it was 'not like this in his day', and letchy John who spends his days putting cameras down ladies' tops. 'Trust me, I'm a sound recordist.'

He confesses how he's coasting, really, hasn't taken on

any big jobs in ages, but that this suits him at the moment because, almost two years on, he still has too much to think about outside of work.

And this is where it goes wrong. Or perhaps it's just that Anna's drunk now, several rum and cokes inside her, but the conversation takes a much more intense turn.

She leans in, across the table.

'I enjoyed today. It brought back some nice memories. Some *really* nice memories.'

'Really? Like what?' says Fraser, hiding his face in his pint glass. He's not sure he likes the way this conversation is going already.

'Like reading Wordsworth again. When do I, or you, for that matter, get to read Wordsworth poetry without feeling like a dick?'

'Oh, no, I did feel like a dick,' says Fraser. 'Let's make no bones about that.'

Anna laughs, a coquettish laugh, but then her smile fades, her face is serious and Fraser gets that feeling again, like he wants to get the hell out of here as quickly as possible.

She tosses her hair, lowers her eyes at him. 'I didn't tell you this, because you'd probably think I was being silly – these days you seem to think quite a lot of the things I say are silly, Fraser, to tell you the truth.'

Fraser doesn't say anything. He smells conflict now and, for once, he's not getting involved.

'But I just had this amazing image in my head, when I was sitting in that reading room. The sunlight was coming through the windows, straight onto my desk; it was almost like Liv was there with us, you know?'

'Really?'

'Definitely. And I just remembered her then, those times at university, that time we went camping in the Lakes. Do you remember how much she loved water of any kind? Any expanse of water? How she used to just disappear off and we'd find her swimming in Windermere or whatever? You used to joke: "Don't let Liv smell the water!"'

Fraser does remember that. He has a picture, in fact, of waking up, unzipping his tent, to see Liv's dark head in the middle of Ullswater, surrounded by sun-dappled rings. 'Come in!' It was so cold she was gasping between words. 'It's tropical in here!'

But he doesn't want to talk about Liv right now. He doesn't want to think about her.

'Fraser, you know the thing that really gets to me, that I think of when I go to bed at night?' She's staring at him intensely now, her blue eyes positively glinting; it's freaking Fraser out. 'I think, was she happy when she died? Do you ever wonder whether she was happy when she died?'

Fraser feels the muscles of his face tighten.

'Well, I guess we'll never know that, will we?'

Anna pauses.

'But does that ever worry you, Fraser?'

He blows air through his nose; he can't believe this. It was like she could read his mind, like she'd found the most tender spot and wanted to stick the knife in. Of course he fucking worried if she was happy when she died. That's all he worried about. What sort of question was that for his friend, Liv's friend, to be asking?

He shifts uncomfortably in his chair and then he thinks about it: Why shouldn't she ask? She didn't know the demons playing in his mind; she doesn't know about what happened that night: the kiss, Mia. They were drunk, all of them.

He has played that night and the day before, over and over in his head, examining every little detail, forensically. They'd got up late, as they had every day of the two-week holiday, and he, Mia and Liv had played rummy on the veranda, hung over and in their sunglasses. They'd gone to the beach; just an ordinary day on the beach. Liv had been reading a recipe book – Gary Rhodes and something about a Mediterranean adventure – and they'd all taken the piss out of her mercilessly, because only Liv could bring a recipe book as a beach read.

It was the penultimate night that night, and they'd all discussed how they wanted to save themselves for the last night and had planned a quiet night in, a barbecue at the villa.

Of course, that didn't happen. They went straight from the beach to a bar. Liv was wearing a white, strappy sundress over her bikini, gorgeous against her two-week tan. They went straight from the bar to a beach-side club. The DJ was playing old skool, 90s tunes. Hands-in-the-air stuff, perfect for their holiday mood.

They were all going for it. The doors of the bar were open, the heady scent of those flowers drifting in. Everything felt good.

He remembers Liv shouting in his ear:

'I'm going off to swim in Lake Me!' It was their little joke. 'Can't resist that sea a minute longer. Look at it, Frase,' she'd said, turning towards the beach, 'isn't it beautiful?'

And Fraser had turned around too, putting his arm around her to look at the sea, which was almost dancing too, revelling in the moonlight.

Then she'd gone and he hadn't thought much of it, he'd carried on dancing. The next thing he knew, they were all back at the villa, worse for wear, loud music; they'd brought at least eight randoms with them back from the bar. He has a vague memory of Liv, sopping wet hair plastered to her head, opening the fridge to get a beer out, a puddle of sea water around her feet.

And then of course, hours later, she was gone. That puddle of sea water by the fridge remained. Was she happy? He has no idea. Did she see the kiss? He is almost certain of this.

He says, 'Look Anna, I don't know. All I know is that doing this List' (he was about to lie; he was feeling increasingly more uncomfortable about doing the damned List) 'is a way of doing the things that *would* have made her happy, and that's all we can do now. I think it was a brilliant idea of Mia's, actually. A really thoughtful idea of hers.'

Anna gives a humourless laugh.

'Yeah, well, you would think that, wouldn't you?'

Fraser feels the hairs on his skin stand up.

'What the fuck is that supposed to mean? Why do you keep coming out with this shit?'

'Well, you know, you and Mia, you seem very close.'

She was very drunk now. Her eyes were swimming.

'Always having little convos together, hatching your little plans, all that time you hung out after Liv died. You even came to the funeral together.'

Anna was becoming ugly now – why turn against Mia? He didn't understand.

'She was Liv's best friend! My friend. OUR friend.' His heart was pounding in his chest because he knew no matter how much all these things were true that, in some way, she had betrayed Liv. *They* had betrayed Liv. 'Why are you being . . . you've gone mental.'

Anna downs her drink in one go, dramatically, affectedly, as though she's in a film.

Did she order doubles? thinks Fraser. Triples? They've only had three drinks and she's off her head.

He stands up. 'Look, I'm going. Karen will be wondering where I am and I'm just not up for an argument, Anna. Whereas, I think you might be. I'll see you soon though, yeah? We'll meet for a coffee, maybe back here and we can go through the ten lines we've learnt then, OK?'

She doesn't speak, she just sits there, on her stool, swaying slightly, so he pecks her on the cheek and leaves. It's raining now, a torrential summer downpour, and Fraser stands under the door of the pub, his heart pounding, pulling his jacket over his head.

Just then, Anna comes out.

'Fraser.'

'Here,' he says, 'stand under here. It's pissing it down.'

But she doesn't stand next to him, instead she comes round to face him and, before he can say anything else, she leans in and she kisses him, hard and long on the mouth, so he's rooted to the spot, he can't get away.

'Anna, what the *fuck*?' He pulls back, wiping his mouth with the back of his hand and she wobbles, slightly loses her footing on the step and staggers back. She gives him a stunned look, as if she had no idea that was going to happen either, the rain now coming so hard it's bouncing off the floor. Then, without saying anything, she runs off, down the lamp-lit street, leaving Fraser standing in the rain, wondering what the hell that was all about.

SIXTEEN

SIXTEEN

August
Lancaster

'Espero que todos tenham tido uma boa aula e desejo-lhes um bom fun de semana. O que vocês planejaram?

Translation from Portuguese to English: 'I hope you all had a good class and I wish you a great weekend. What are you all doing this weekend?'

In a stuffy back room of Lancaster Library, Emilia Neves, six feet plus of Amazonian pedigree – burnished skin, wild green eyes and a cascade of caramel hair – stands in front of her mute class of seven and thinks, How long? How long before I lose my fucking mind with this bunch of imbeciles?

In the corner, Mia sits gnawing on a nail, cringing on Emilia's behalf, simultaneously regarding her in wonderment. The girl was amazing. She had the patience of a saint. Emilia speaks six languages – Mia knows this because she and Emilia have struck up a rapport, being the only two women in a class of nine. (Perhaps word had got out among the single fifty-something males of Lancaster that a Giselle lookalike was about to take residency in the library.) Her father is one of the richest men in Brazil, and yet she swapped Rio – beautiful Rio, the City of Carnivals and feather headdresses – for this: spending her Friday mornings in an unventilated, provincial library in northwest England, teaching Portuguese to a bunch of middle-aged blokes. Gutted. She must be absolutely gutted. And yet there she is, beaming away, the very picture of sunny, patient encouragement.

Mia has been coming to Portuguese classes for four weeks now. Learn a foreign language is one of her tasks from Liv's List and it made sense to finally get down to mastering her son's second language; it's made her focus. And for the most part, she loves it. She relishes this chance to use her brain again. It's just watching Emilia go through this, week in week out, trying to get even the most simple sentence into the thick heads of this lot, so stupefied by her beauty that they can't absorb a word – it's killing her.

Emilia asks the question again and, this time, as she does every week, Mia puts her hand up.

'Yes, Mia?' Emilia's face is awash with relief.

'Espero ir às compras no sábado e depois aos amigos para o almoço no domingo. Possivelmente, também no parque.'

('I'm hoping to go shopping on Saturday and then to friends for lunch on Sunday. Possibly, also the park.')

'Thank you, Mia. Beautiful use of verbs,' replies Emilia, and they exchange their little eyebrow raise, their mutual understanding. Mia was never a swot at school but now she's wondering why. It could be very satisfying.

'Now, can anyone tell me what Mia has planned this weekend?'

Again, silence . . . just a phlegmy cough from Gerry: 61, retired truck driver; just met a Brazilian on the Internet.

The lesson eventually finishes. An excruciating hour of pain and torture – and that's just me, thinks Mia. She makes her way to the door. Emilia is crouching on the floor, putting her things in her bag, her honey-toned hair covering her face. Mia hovers, deciding whether to say something or not.

'Um, Emilia?'

Emilia is startled, she throws her hair back from her face in one dramatic sweep.

'Yeah?'

'I just wondered, you know, if you're OK?'

Emilia stands up, dwarfing Mia with her six-foot frame. 'Sure.' She smiles. 'You saved me, as usual. Thanks.'

Mia smiles shyly, and tries to ignore the fact that she only comes up to Emilia's chest. A perfect 32C, in a white crocheted top that shows off a stomach, sleek and walnut-brown, like a beautiful violin.

'So, what are YOU doing this weekend?' she says, brightly. 'Let someone ask you a question for a change. You must have a boyfriend? Beating them off with a stick, I imagine!'

Mia laughs but Emilia frowns. Must not use colloquialisms, she tells herself. Or sound like someone's great aunty. 'Not much.' Emilia shrugs, fixing her with her languorous green eyes. 'I mean, I know you live here, so

I don't want to sound rude, but what the fuck is there to do in this mother-fucking town?'

Mia snorts. It makes her laugh when Eduardo uses inappropriate idiomatic English too. Using 'cunt' when really 'slighty irritating' would do.

'I've been here three months and I don't have any friends, Mia. These English girls, all they want to do is get drunk, so drunk they look . . . they look, like this . . .'

And she puts her hands up like paws, flops her head back and mimics frothing at the mouth. It's the first time Mia has seen her look ugly and she's transfixed, before laughing. Emilia laughs too; a relieved, wide-mouthed laugh full of white, bright teeth.

'Well, listen, if you want to hang out with me and my friends some time . . . we're not wildly exciting. I have a baby, so I don't get out that often . . .'

Emilia gasps. 'You have a baby? I love babies!'

'Brilliant. Well, that's my sitter sorted then.'

Emilia's face falls.

'Oh, God, I'm joking . . . Look, let's swap numbers.' Mia roots in her bag for her phone. 'And then next time I'm doing something vaguely exciting, I'll invite you along, OK?'

'Cool, thanks,' says Emilia, getting out her phone.

'It could be some time,' says Mia, before being met by a very blank look and deciding that perhaps sarcasm, at this point, was wasted on Emilia.

Mia undoes her bike from its lock and makes her way across Market Square, towards Moor Lane and Williamson's Park. It's a clear, bright morning, but like all provincial towns on a week day, the only inhabitants seem to be OAPs – rotund ladies with their tartan shoppers – and students. Oh, and pigeons, so many bloody pigeons! Mia flaps them away with her hand.

The date is 20 August 2008. Two years since Liv died, and Mia considers she has done well so far today. Not stopping to get maudlin, or tearful, or asking herself huge questions about the meaning of life and death – because, quite frankly, that way madness lies, and she doesn't want to end up like Mrs Durham.

Last year – the first year – everyone made a pilgrimage to Peterborough to visit Liv's grave before calling in on Liv's parents the day after to pay their respects, which by all accounts was a bad idea. At that point, Liv's mum, Ann, in particular, found it very hard to see all her friends and, even though it was never said, there was the feeling that she blamed them in some way, or resented them at least. After all, they were alive, her daughter wasn't.

Mia couldn't go – Billy was only six weeks old – and she spent possibly the worst twelve hours of her life that night, alone, weeping catastrophically, the reality of everything that had happened coming down on her all at once in a wall of darkness. She'd never been more pleased in her life to see the sun rise the next day.

So she was determined that this year would not be like that: it would be business as usual and a personal, quiet celebration of Liv's life, remembering the quite brilliant friend and woman she was.

They have all called each other this morning, of course, just to check in, to check nobody has descended into a black hole or is drinking alone and, so far, they seem to be dealing with things admirably: Anna was about to go off on one of her 'silent weekends' with Steve to a Buddhist monastery; Norm . . . well, it wasn't altogether clear what Norm was doing, but Melody called up this morning, saying she was going to be alone for the day and could she join Mia at Liv's bench in Williamson's Park? Where she's heading now, picnic supplies in her rucksack; And Fraser? Ah, Fraser. He sounded odd when she finally caught up with him, just before she went to Portuguese. Not down exactly, but stressy and clipped, as if he was desperate to get off the phone. But then Mia is getting used to Fraser's erratic behaviour and today, anything goes . . . Probably just holding hands with Karen on the sofa. Being mute.

So here she is, cycling through the streets, the sun bouncing off the sandstone buildings, a golden city; full of memories. She feels in her top pocket for the folded-up piece of notepaper, soft and dog-eared now from six weeks of being carried around. Mia's noticed a shift in herself of late; she's come over all self-confident and feisty and she suspects Fraser's letter has something to do with it. No, she *knows* Fraser's letter has *everything* to do with it.

He said she was an 'amazing mum'; nobody has ever said she was an 'amazing mum', or even a 'good mum', come to think of it. She's never had feedback of any kind and it's given her a boost and made her see things differently. OK, so sometimes she has to lock herself in a room for a few seconds, just so she can swear at the wall, but she's doing her best and if she is a good mum, then she deserves better from Eduardo. She doesn't want to be like *her* mum, settling for this idea that all men are shits so you may as well get used to it. And so, for the first time in their relationship, she has laid down some rules for Eduardo; she is getting tough:

1) He will look after Billy at set times in the week rather than when the mood takes him. So far, one weekend night, one night in the week and, now, Friday until 2 p.m., so she can go to Portuguese lessons, then have a little 'me' time.

2) He will give her £30 a week for Billy – it's less than the CSA requirement of fifteen per cent of his salary, so Mia considers she's being generous as it is.

3) He will be generally more considerate, cleaning up after himself if he looks after Billy at hers, replacing toilet roll, buying milk, noticing when he is wearing 3–6 months' clothes and buying some new ones. He isn't Billy's childminder and you can't 'babysit your own son'.

This is her new mantra and she's very proud of it. She doesn't know why she hasn't thought of it before.

The thing is, Eduardo doesn't disagree. So far, he seems to be playing by the rules, and it's freaking her out.

She freewheels down Cheapside, the warm breeze enveloping her, reading in her head the words from Fraser's letter that she knows off by heart now.

There's no doubt it's been the catalyst for changes going on, but it's also probably the first nice, deep thing he's ever said (or written) to her in his life. Fraser has said many nice things over the years, but always drunk and she could never take him seriously.

But this, this was genuine, from the heart, and she's been treasuring it.

Before Karen, before this year, in the immediate aftermath of Liv's death, she and Fraser spent lots of time together, lots of time, just the two of them and Billy, and she misses him; she misses that closeness, and perhaps the letter is compensation for that. It's like a little bit of her friend, on her person at all times, which she can get out when she feels shaky, like a bottle of Rescue Remedy.

But there's something else, she thinks, as she crosses at the traffic lights, something she is less easy with, that's been playing on her mind since Billy's birthday. Everything was fine when Fraser was being an idiot, when Fraser was calling her up from Vegas, hysterical, swearing at her down the phone and being a 'narcissistic baby'. She knew what to do with that, she could come over all parental and self-righteous – babysitting him meant she was distracted from her own feelings. But now he's started to be reasonable, get on with life and take responsibility for his feelings, and there's a vacuum – a very definite blank space – where she is forced to confront her own emotions and ask herself what she feels.

She pushes her sunglasses up onto her head as if this might give her more clarity. She felt jealous. No, not jealous exactly – YES, jealous exactly! – when she saw him and Karen together at the barbecue. It came as a shock, a thump in the chest: the way their hand-holding made her feel, that kiss she witnessed, the way Fraser had tenderly got an eyelash out of Karen's eye; her whispering in his ear – their secrets. She realized something had grown between her and Fraser since losing Liv – perhaps something that's always been there, deep down.

Mia is trying not to hark back to the past, obsessively – the present is hard enough to navigate. But lately, she's been thinking back to when they met, when they used to hang out together as students in Asda, before Moussaka Night; before it all sort of went wrong before it got a chance to start. There was something special then between them, at least she thought so. Did that ever go away? Or has she just buried feelings for him because Liv was with him? But then, she and Fraser had been friends for ages before he eventually got together with Liv, a year after they graduated in the autumn of 1999. If they'd been destined to be together, they would have, surely? No, he was with Olivia and that was just the way it was.

But now Fraser has Karen's shoulder to cry on, now he sits with her at parties and spends the day with her on Liv's anniversary, she feels . . . well, bereft if she's honest. The letter has taken on more meaning than just a friend's kind words. She knows it off by heart, for goodness' sakes. And now she's on her way to talk to Liv, her best friend, Fraser's girlfriend.

Oh, God. She cycles faster.

'Mr Mor-gan?'

It takes Fraser at least five seconds of staring blankly at Demetrius, leaning across the counter, enormous, hairy arms bulging from his T-shirt, to remember why he's here.

'Oh, right, yes, sorry, Demetrius; away with the fairies. I'll have some ciabatta, some of the Parma ham, a small tub of the anchovy-stuffed olives and, er . . .' He stares at the cheese but he's not registering the cheese.

'Some of the usual? The manchego?'

Fraser blinks, slowly.

'Yes. Sorry. A lump of that.'

Fraser pays. 'Get some sleep, my man,' says Demetrius, patting him on the shoulder as he ushers him out of the deli with a ring of the shop bell.

Fraser stands on the street, plastic bag hanging from his hand, aware he doesn't want to go home.

He was determined today was going to go well. He was going to show Mia and Karen that he had come a long way from the wreck who sat sobbing at the bar this time last year. He was going to show Anna that none of her weird talk of karma, or messing with his head, was going to get to him.

Fraser had waited a few days before calling Anna after that truly bizarre evening when she launched at him, partly because he was so shocked – she'd never said anything about fancying him before! And also, wasn't she with Steve? Like, obsessed with Steve? However, she'd cut him dead before he could even open his mouth: 'Forget it, Fraser. I was shit-faced. I had no idea what I was doing.'

It didn't take away from the fact she'd been bonkers that day, mad as a bag of snakes with her karma and her intense questions about Liv and whether she was happy the day she died. Even so, she'd got under Fraser's skin. This morning, when he'd woken up, he'd promised himself he wasn't going to let it get to him, but right now, he is wondering if that's possible.

Karen was ridiculously sweet this morning, which, of course, is part of the problem. When he opened his eyes, she was already looking at him. Already smoothing the hair from his face as if he was a child with a fever.

264

'It's all about you, this morning, sweetheart. Whatever you need to do, wherever you need to go . . .'

And Fraser thought, Drink. In the pub, which didn't bode well.

Then she instructed him to sit up whilst she massaged the knots from his neck to the soundtrack of the washing machine going mad.

'If you wanna look at photos of Liv, or go for a walk, or be alone . . .'

(Or at work? Why the fuck had he taken the morning off work?)

Then she went into the lounge and came back, grinning and carrying a pink bag with the word FREED written on it and Fraser's heart dropped through his feet.

'For you, from me. Just to make today easier,' she'd said, perching on the side of the bed.

Fraser slowly took the box from the bag and slid off the lid as if he were uncovering a dead rodent, to find the very thing he was dreading: a pair of men's dance shoes with a Cuban heel. A Cuban fucking heel . . .

'I know how much you're enjoying salsa these days,' she'd said, 'and I wanted you to have the proper shoes – his and her dance shoes. You can wear them tonight, they'll give you something to look forward to . . .'

Fraser *was* still enjoying salsa. It had definitely not turned out to be the condemnation to torture he had feared when he first arrived (except for Joshi: talking to Joshi was still torture). Now he could perform a whole routine without looking as though he had a neurological disorder, which if Liv were alive, she'd think was a miracle, so he considered he'd done his job. But he didn't 'love' it, and no way did he intend to carry on when the term they'd signed up for came to an end. But now Karen had bought him these shoes, and the guilt was becoming unbearable. The worst thing was, Mia called literally the nanosecond after he opened them and Karen stood there, turning one shoe over in her hand like a gun. He didn't even mention them.

It was all too much, and so he sneaked out for some time alone, on the proviso of getting a 'special' breakfast for them both. But he doesn't want anything about today to be special; he wishes he'd just gone to work. At the moment, he's on a three-day corporate job, shooting a promo for the Tena Lady website (the UK's No. 1 bladder weakness and incontinence expert, no less); holding a microphone up over some woman in a leotard, as she demonstrates exercises to stop you weeing yourself when you sneeze. Yesterday, he asked Brett, the director, if he could come in at lunchtime instead, on the grounds of compassionate leave. But now he wishes he hadn't; now he wishes he was putting a mic down someone's Lycra tights. At least it would take his mind off things.

He takes a deep breath and begins the short walk home, the plastic bag, full of breakfast things he has no memory of buying, banging against his shin. When he gets there, Karen is sitting at the kitchen table, picking at her lip, the phone in front of her, like the clichéd tableau of a wife who has just discovered a mistress. For a second, Fraser wonders if this actually could be the case. Whole events, relationships seem to happen in his life, after all, that he has no recollection of starting.

'What's this about a list?' she says. Her tone is more worried than accusatory.

Fraser freezes.

'What list?' he says, idiotically.

'A list. Anna just called. She said, "Can you ask Fraser to call me back about Wordsworth and the List? He'll know what I'm talking about" – and I remembered Norm said something about a list at Billy's birthday, too, and I just wondered, what is it?'

Fraser's instinct is to lie. Lie, lie, lie. But then it dawns on him, why should he? If he played this coolly, there was no reason to and so he says:

'Look,' and he sets the bag down and sits down opposite her for extra 'cool' effect. It's a list for Liv, or rather, a list that Liv wrote – things she wanted to do before she was thirty. Norm found it in an old coat of his. She must have left it there one day . . .'

Karen's eyes shift from side to side as she tries to compute this. 'Right, and?'

'And so we decided we'd do the things on the List – us lot, I mean: me, Mia, Norm, Anna and Melody. We decided it would be a nice tribute if we all split the things and tried to do them, before she's thirty. Before next March.'

'Okaaay . . . And is there any particular reason why you didn't tell me about this List? 'Coz, hun, honest, I think it's a lovely idea . . .' She reaches out and takes Fraser's hand and he is once more overcome with how it is possible for someone to be so lovely, SO lovely, and yet not the right sort of lovely for him.

She waits.

'What? No! Course not. There is no "particular reason",' he says, slightly overzealously. 'I just thought, it's no big deal, just a thing between us. Why would you really *care*, you know?'

267

'Well, of course I *care*, sweetie. But, yes, yes.' Fraser can see the cogs of Karen's mind whirring. Karen often needs time to 'get' concepts like this: that's what scares him, you never know what's coming. 'I can see it's personal, just a private thing between you and your mates.'

'Exactly,' says Fraser. 'Exactly that . . .'

She looks at him. Fraser thinks he sees a flicker of something like fear in her eyes.

'OK. So what's *on* the List?'

Fraser wasn't expecting this and he needs to get his story straight, he needs to tread carefully.

'Well, Vegas, for example,' he says, assuming the tone of a man who has nothing to hide. Going to Vegas was one of the things on the list. But, obviously, I'd only just started seeing you then.'

Karen frowns and Fraser keeps on before she starts talking details or dates.

'And, what else? Well, silly things, like learn how to use chopsticks, learn how to meditate . . . Anna's doing that one, that's probably why she's really into this Steve bloke. You know, gone all "Om" on us, spending all weekend in silence. I mean, Jesus, she wouldn't have been able to keep her gob shut for ten seconds six months ago!'

And he laughs, and Karen laughs too and he thinks, Phew! Jesus Christ. That was close. But then her smile fades, her pale brown eyes cloud with worry.

'So, is that it?'

'Er . . . pretty much. There's a few other odds and sods (odds and sods? He made it sound like a car boot sale). Mia's learning a foreign language. I think I have to use up all the letters in Scrabble in one go at some point, and there's the Great Wall of China thing – you know, that

268

Norm was banging on about in the pub that time? But I'm not going to go on that, can't afford it . . .'

Shut up. Shut up now. Quit while you're ahead.

'So, yes, that's it.'

SHUT. UP.

But he's about to start talking again, because he's afraid of what might happen if he stops, but then she sighs. 'Do you know what?' she says. 'Come here . . .' and she gets up, goes round to the other side of the table and wraps her arms around him.

'You are SO sweet, do you know that?'

And she squeezes him with her short, stocky little pint-pulling arms.

'You're so deep and sentimental . . . I love that about you, I really do.'

Fraser wonders how long till he can leave for work.

Mia arrives early at the park. Melody won't be here for fifteen minutes, so, still breathless from the uphill cycle, she leans her bike against Liv's bench and takes off her rucksack. It's hazy now, a band of sun-infused cloud hovering above the horizon and, behind that, darker blue clouds gather, spelling imminent rain.

'Hi, Liv, wow, look at me, eh? The peak of physical fitness. I brought you this,' she says out loud, rummaging in her rucksack for her 'offering' – she's not sure what else to call it – which she bought from Homebase, yesterday: a square, ceramic pot filled with stones and foliage.

She sets it down on the floor.

'Don't ask.' The woman in the shop said it was an 'autumnal collage'.

269

'Wow, a year, hey?' she says, sitting down. 'And so much to tell! Firstly, the List is going well. Well, sort of. I also brought this . . .' and she takes out the photo of them all in Melody's back garden on Billy's first birthday. 'As you will see, my muffin top is very evident, but as I keep saying to people, "I've just had a baby." I wonder if I'll get away with that when he's seven, what do you think?'

Mia looks at the photo. There's someone missing and it takes her a few seconds to realize that that someone is Liv. This still happens to her from time to time – the realization that this is forever, that it just has to be managed, like a hole in your heart. She swallows. 'And how's the gang?' Like someone visiting their old, infirm mother, she likes to 'go round the family', as it were, when she comes up to the bench. 'Well, Anna is learning to meditate, as per your List, but we're a bit worried, because she's getting rather carried away. She's met this bloke called Steve, who's filling her head with bollocks about karma and reincarnation and the like and she's just, well, turned into a bit of an odd-bod to be honest. Take today for instance: obviously it's a tough day, but she's taken herself off with Steve, or Buddhist Steve as we now call him, to a monastery for a silent weekend where you can't talk for forty-eight hours! Can you imagine? Spanner with her mouth shut for FORTY-EIGHT HOURS? I'd have been less worried if she'd decided to abseil naked down the Gherkin.' She laughs, somewhat pointlessly to herself, then she tips her head back and looks at the clouds, sailing across the sky. She sighs. This is what she really wants to tell Liv:

So, basically, Anna and I aren't that close any more

270

and it makes me sad, because I know you two were really close, I thought we were *all* really close but, without you, I'm not that sure it works, Liv. I'm not really sure there is an 'us' without you. I've tried to 'get' Anna, but I can't – not like you did. I feel bad about that.

'She misses you so much, I think. More than she lets on. So yeah, if you've got any tips on understanding Spanner – on carrying on your good work, you SAINT! – do pass on, won't you? Send me some guidance.'

She leans forward, takes a bottle of Lucozade out of her bag, unscrews the cap with a fizz and takes a big glug.

'So, now, Melody,' she says, screwing the top back on. 'OK, here goes, how long have you got?'

She tells Liv all about the party, how Melody didn't have one 'just because' but for several reasons, and how their former friend – indie kid, militant lefty – was now becoming Hyacinth Bouquet before her very eyes. She wanders off on a tangent with the story about the poo in the paddling pool, the Portuguese lessons taken by a Giselle lookalike and how, last week, Mrs Durham had belched at full volume in the big-print section of Lancaster Library, and she'd been so embarrassed that she'd had to walk away from the wheelchair as Mrs D rattled on, barely noticing.

Norm?

'Well, I'm afraid to say, it's not exactly happy campers at the moment where Norm and Melody are concerned, but we're hoping that's going to change because this weekend . . . *ta-dar!* . . . they're going to make a home-made porn vid. Oh, yes! That was your idea, Olivia, in case you've forgotten. Two nights in a Lakeside hideaway with "props". The potential for disaster is palpable. In fact,' she laughs quietly to herself, 'me and Frase . . .'

She wants to tell her about all the names she and Fraser have been discussing for Norm and Melody's film, the time they've actually given over to this, whole evenings spent on the phone, sniggering over spoof porn-film names: *Honey, I Blew Everybody*, *Throbin Hood* . . . but she stops. It doesn't feel right to talk about Fraser.

She crosses her legs and leans back. 'So . . . Me. I'm fine. Billy is walking now and he's lovely – my little friend. It used to annoy me when people said that. I used to think if you call a pint-size who you can't even go to the pub with your friend, then you seriously need to get some. But he is, at least, my ally these days, rather than a dictator.

'I have other news, too,' and even though she is perfectly alone, she winces. 'Eduardo and I are back together. But! Before you say anything, there are rules, Liv. Lots and lots of rules. I am laying down the law. No more chilled-out Mia, no more path of least resistance, it's all R.E.S.P.E.C.T. in my house. I know you'd approve. The thing is, it seems to be working, which has scuppered things slightly. I'm really not used to it.'

She pauses, for a long time; she knows there's still one person she's avoiding and the more she thinks about this, the more uncomfortable she feels, until she finds she's actually squirming, on Liv's bench.

Thankfully then, from somewhere down the hill, she hears a familiar voice, like a foghorn.

'WOODHOUSE!'

She turns around to see Melody striding, cleavage first, up the hill.

'The first sign of madness is talking to oneself, you know.'

Mia squints at her friend.

And the second is wearing what looks like a bridesmaid dress to the park.

Mia stands up and starts walking.

'Hey, gorgeous,' gushes Melody when she gets to her, doing this strange hug involving no skin-to-skin contact.

'Spray tan!' she squeals. 'No skin contact for an hour, they said. I just had it done in town. I'll have to picnic standing up.'

'You're joking.'

'No, I'm perfectly serious.'

'So I've bought mini Scotch eggs that I now have to feed you by hand? Standing up?'

'Well, no, I can use my hands. Look, palms all clear!' and she waves her hands. 'I just can't sit down. I'll probably already have it all over the dress, anyway, good job it's a similar colour – do you like it?'

Lately, Melody's eccentricities have been coming to the fore. There's surfaced a new passion for 'facial yoga', for example – all the celebrities are doing it, apparently. Just last week, Mia had spent ten minutes trying to keep a straight face, as Melody had demonstrated what looked like her repertoire for the World Gurning Championships. 'You'll be laughing on the other side of your wrinkly face,' she'd said, 'when I still have cheekbones you could slice ham off at sixty.' There're all sorts of strange diets, raw food, no food, Pampered bloody Chef parties and now turning up for a picnic in a peach satin mini and a spray tan. Mia wonders what happened to her friend who only wore black jumpers.

'Wow, darling, you look, you look . . .'

'Go on, what size?'

This is dangerous ground indeed, thinks Mia.

'Dunno, a Twelve?'

'Fourteen, but it's gaping at the back . . . Look! I could fit my whole arm in there!'

And she turns around so Mia can see for herself that she can fit her whole arm in there.

'It's OK,' she says, 'I believe you.'

'Bit OTT for the park – not to mention court this morning – but I thought, Sod it, I've lost some weight and it's a special occasion and I knew Livs would approve.' She smiles, sadly, at Mia. 'How is she, do you think?' She walks over to the bench and pats it. 'Oh, fuck the spray tan, come on, let's sit on over here. Come and give us a hug. I've got something to show you.'

Ten minutes later, after mini Scotch eggs and ham sandwiches, Mia doubts this picnic can get any more bizarre, when Melody pulls an Ann Summers plastic bag from her handbag and says, 'So, listen, I've been shopping. For mine and Norm's porn weekend.'

Mia covers her eyes.

'Oh, God, if it's anal beads, I'm not looking. Anything with anal in the title, I say, "No. No, you can shove it up your arse."'

Melody sniggers.

'It's not anal beads, you fool. I do have some taste. No, look, isn't it beautiful?'

And she pulls out a slender, sleek, gold vibrator.

Mia has never been into sex toys. Ever since she was a runner for a documentary about Swingers, sex toys bring up for her visions of fat ladies poured into PVC catsuits who have given over entire rooms to fluffy hand-cuffs, lubes (could that possibly be the most disgusting word in the world?), vibrators . . . It turns her stomach.

She looks through her fingers. 'Beautiful is not the word I would use. Terrfiying is probably more like it.'

'You're such a prude! Talk to it,' says Melody.

'*What?*'

'Say something: faster, faster, or slower, slower . . .'

'Ugh! No!'

'Oh, for God's sake, faster, faster,' says Melody and suddenly the vibrator starts twisting and vibrating.

'Jesus, it's like *The Exorcist*! Put it away, it's foul, Melody, proper foul.'

'It's a voice-activated vibrator.'

'It's disgusting, that's what it is,' says Mia, horrified.

Melody giggles, unperturbed.

'And I got this,' and she pulls out a red-and-black basque.

'Now that's more like it. I can imagine you'll look like a burlesque dancer in that.'

'And this,' and she pulls out some pink furry handcuffs.

Mia laughs, not really feeling qualified to say the right thing. 'Wow, you've really gone for it. It's like you're actually, properly, making a porn video.'

Melody sighs, her round face serious all of a sudden.

'I just want it to work out, Mia. I just want . . . For Norm to fancy me – is that so ridiculous?'

She looks at her friend.

'No, it's not ridiculous at all.'

'I just want this weekend to be really special. I've lost eight pounds, you know.'

'You look great,' says Mia.

'And I've planned it all, right down to the last detail.'

There's a pause. They look up over the city, the river. Mia sighs and nudges her friend mischievously.

'Hey, do you remember Five South Road days?'

'What do you mean?'

'I mean, you two, shaggers extraordinaire, at it constantly. The three-hour sessions to Sade – I knew the words to "Your Love Is King" off by heart and I didn't even live with you. The chocolate ice-cream massages, the strawberries in the *shower*, young lady.'

Melody laughs. 'Bloody hell, how did you know about that?'

'I have my sources.'

'Fraser?'

'I'm not telling.'

In a studio near Old Street in London, Fraser holds a microphone over Tracey, their 'Tena Lady' model for the day, as she lies on her back in a leotard and tights and demonstrates pelvic-floor exercises.

'When you going to show us yer salsa moves then, Fraser? Your warm-up exercises?' whispers Declan, senior sound recordist and all-round pain in the arse, as far as Fraser is concerned. 'It's got to be more interesting than these exercises. I think I'd rather piss myself when I laughed.'

He has a point, thinks Fraser, Tracey doesn't seem to be actually moving at all. It's just, he's getting a bit sick of Declan and John ribbing him about salsa lessons. The joke's wearing thin.

'The fantastic thing about pelvic-floor exercises,' says

Tracey, 'is that nobody need know you're doing them. You can do them whilst sitting at your desk, doing the washing-up, you can even do them at the bus stop.'

Fraser doesn't think he will ever look at a woman at a bus stop in the same way ever again.

'They should have got you to do the advert, Declan,' says Fraser. He's been working with Declan on and off for around three months now and, despite his best efforts, has decided he doesn't like him. He was a snidey, miserable old sod with short-man syndrome. 'You're about the right age, aren't you? For weak bladder control? Prostate problems?'

'And you're a cheeky little fucker,' Declan hisses in his ear. 'When I was your age, I was following Gorbachev around the globe, travelling to Angola to do documentaries for *Panorama*—'

'I know,' says Fraser. 'You've told me several times.'

'Right, Sound, we're ready to go! One last time. Fraser, my man, can you just make sure that mic is really inside the bust . . . yeah?' says Brett.

This is the part of the job Fraser hates the most, attaching mikes down strangers' tops. Especially strangers like this – the model, or 'artist', as she likes to be known, is a wiry, bony-faced South African who looks like she's not had sex in years. But he warms his hands and goes to thread the wire down nonetheless.

'S'alright, I've got it.' But John has got there before him, hand right down that Lycra front. Such a perv, thinks Fraser. SUCH A PERV!

The shoot drags on and on, not wrapping until gone seven, and Fraser knows he's cutting it fine to get to his salsa lesson by half past. After shoving all his equipment in his car, he sprints to the Tube, takes the stairs three at a time and then sprints down Oxford Street, but still only manages to burst through the class-room doors, looking as if he's just committed a hit-and-run, by 7.40 p.m.: too late, it turns out, to stop Karen in her tracks.

So now, he's standing in a cubicle, in the salsa-me-happy toilets – dank, freezing, pistachio-green bogs, which remind him of the ones at his primary school – with his head in his hands.

There's a bang on the door.

'Fraser?' Karen shouts.

He backs closer to the wall.

'Fraser? Come on. Open the door.'

That'll teach him to be late. In just ten minutes of tardiness, Karen has not only booked them for another term of lessons, but a convention. A fucking salsa convention. Two weeks, dancing day and night, in a Marriott hotel in Nottingham.

'I thought you'd like it,' she says through the door; her voice is shaky. 'I was going to pay for it, for you and me – it would be like a dirty weekend but with a difference: you and me, dancing the night away. Come on, Frase,' she says, sounding slightly pitiful now. 'Open the door.'

He unlocks the door.

He knows he has to face the music, as it were. Locking himself in the bogs was never really a mature response, it was just a response to the guilt that's now consuming him, engulfing him. Enough's enough with the salsa. Karen is getting serious. He has to come clean.

Tonight. He has to do it tonight.

He slowly opens the door. Karen is crying. She doesn't know what she's done wrong and he feels utterly wretched.

They end up going to Ed's Diner: burger and chips in a red leatherette booth, on the corner of Old Compton Street. Karen got a two-for-one voucher from one of the many websites she subscribes to.

He watches as Karen picks at her fries, a look of baffled annoyance on her face.

'But why don't you want to carry on with the lessons?' she says, in a hushed voice. 'I don't understand, I thought you enjoyed them.'

'I do enjoy them.'

'I bought you the shoes, too – not cheap, those weren't, Fraser. Mind you, I s'pose I can put them on eBay. And you'd improved so much. Calvin was just saying before you got there tonight, how much you'd improved.'

Fraser sighs and looks out of the window. He feels like an eight-year-old who's just announced to his mum that he doesn't want to carry on with violin lessons.

'Well?' she says, when he doesn't say anything.

'I just, I've had enough.' He shrugs. 'I can dance the salsa now, can't I? I've no interest in becoming World Leader of Salsa, Global Guru, Latin American Champion of the World.' He was being facetious now and hated himself for it.

Karen puts down her fork.

'Like Joshi, you mean? Is that what this is about?'

'God, no.'

'Are you jealous, Fraser? Because nothing's—'

'No. It's nothing to do with Joshi.'

279

And in his agitation and self-loathing at not being able to just cut to the chase, he slams down his glass.

They continue eating in silence. Next to them – and isn't it always the case? – a couple kiss passionately, mercilessly, clutching at each other's hands across the table.

Karen puts her cutlery down, very slowly, very calmly. She says, 'Oh, my God.'

'What?' says Fraser.

'Oh, my God, I've worked it out.'

Fraser has always thought it a cliché when people have said, '. . . and then I saw the colour drain from his face,' but thinks that when she repeats this story to her friends she will say just that because that's what it feels like.

'The salsa lessons. Learn to dance, it was on Liv's List. It was on the List, wasn't it?'

Fraser's silence says everything.

'So, what? What else was on the List? Our whole relationship? Go out with a barmaid?' Her eyes are full with tears now. Fraser rubs his face.

'No. God, no, Karen. Not at all. You've got it wrong.'

'Have I? What else was on the List? Shag a woman in her forties? Was our whole relationship just one big bet, Fraser?'

'No, course it wasn't . . . Why on earth would Liv have that on her List!'

'Because if it was, and you don't tell me, I will be so bloody angry, Fraser. I will never forgive you.'

Fraser has never seen Karen like this. Frankly, it's frightening.

He looks her straight in the eye and then, very quietly,

280

very quickly, he says, 'Make a Roman blind,' but he has hardly got the words out before she stands up, throws her lemonade all over him and without looking back, walks out.

He is left, lemonade dripping from his hair.

'Ooh, in trouble mate?' says the man from the couple opposite.

It takes all of Fraser's strength not to punch him.

SEVENTEEN

September
Lancaster and the Lake District

'What's that, Norm? I can't hear you, mate.'

'I said . . . I said . . . *Fraser?*'

Norm sounds desperate now and Fraser swears, loudly, and slams the steering wheel, as the line goes crackly again.

'I'm here, Norm.' He fiddles futilely with the volume on the hands-free, whilst still trying to keep an eye on the road. 'Norm, answer me if you can still hear me. Norm? Woah, shit!!' He swerves violently as a sports car tries to overtake him on the inside and plunges, car horns letting rip around him, into the slow lane.

Thank Christ, there's nothing there, and Fraser cruises for a good few minutes before realizing his speedometer says 52 m.p.h., he is gripping the steering wheel so hard his knuckles have gone white and a car pulling a caravan behind him is flashing its lights.

He eventually calms down enough to pull into the middle lane, thinking, how ironic, how dark it would be, that in the pursuit of doing this List, which seems increasingly to be cursed, they should lose another life, and that life should be his. If truth be known, Fraser hates driving, especially on the motorway. It stems from his poverty-stricken childhood where the family car was always a clapped-out joke with no MOT, and the humiliation that caused – in particular, the time his dad picked him and some mates up from Scout Camp in the Pennines and their Peugeot blew up on the hard shoulder.

If he never drove again he'd be quite happy, but he's doing this for his best friend; he is pumped up with a martyred sense of duty as he gets up to a steady seventy-five miles per hour in the middle lane and manages to regulate his breathing. After the awful drive home from Billy's birthday, it would have been too soon if he had never seen the M6 North again, but an hour ago, Norm rang him from the middle of the Lake District, where he and Melody were supposed to be on their dirty weekend, making their porn vid, to tell him that things weren't going to plan. After a huge barney, Melody had wandered off into the Cumbrian night.

Norm sounded deranged, definitely drunk:

'She could be fucking anywhere, Frase. She could be fucking drowned in the bottom of Grasmere for all I know . . . And we haven't even done the bloody porn video. We haven't done the TASK. When are we going to complete the task, now?'

In between some pretty dramatic shouting and the line cutting out because, as Norm kept reminding him, he was 'IN THE ARSE-END OF NOWHERE', Fraser tried to get a few facts straight.

Was she drunk?

Yes, very.

Was she wearing any warm clothes? Because it was September now, any balminess in the air had disappeared with August.

No, she was 'in a basque, suspenders and a Chinese silky fucking dressing gown'.

Fraser tried not to laugh.

Had he tried her mobile phone?

Course, but there was no signal, because there were 'just sheep and mountains and lakes, because they were in the arse-end of nowhere!'

So now, Fraser is on his way to the arse-end of nowhere to help his friend find his wife, with the distinct feeling in the pit of his stomach that he might have bitten off more than he can chew. Even in his inebriation and panic, Norm told him not to come. But Fraser believes this was false protestation, and he, after two years of grief-stricken misery, recognizes – more than anyone – false protestation when he sees it: *No, don't come and pick me up from outside my house where I am sitting in a pool of my own vomit having lost my house keys*; or . . . *rescue me from my house at 8 a.m. where I am a jabbering, drug-fuelled wreck*. Norm has picked him up and put him together again countless times, and now it's his turn to be the big man, to be the saviour. He's almost glad of the opportunity.

It's also, if he's honest, a chance to get away from his parents' house in Bury where he has been staying this past week. Since it ended with Karen, four weeks ago, those old feelings of loneliness have come back to haunt him, and he has spent as little time as possible at home, even taking the train all the way to Lancaster for the weekend a fortnight ago to see Mia (and stay with Norm and Melody, when they were still speaking, that is), where it was such a relief to see real, close friends. They'd gone to Williamson's Park, for beers and a picnic, like old times, and he'd met Emilia – Mia's Portuguese teacher – who, as well as being about six feet tall, played rounders in a pair of tiny shorts that went right up her bum and told Mia she thought Fraser was 'beautiful'. Which was all a bonus, and a much-needed confidence boost.

Alas, after that it was straight back home, and he has even started to take on jobs that go on late, just to avoid that awful stretch from 4 p.m. till bedtime. Last week, when he could take no more, he turned up unannounced at his parents' neat ex-council house in Bury. On Monday, Fraser's thirtieth birthday went past without so much as a drink with friends. There were, of course, many people not happy about this, not least Mia.

'Pull yourself together, Fraser. Billy and I will come down and see you. We can just go to all-you-can-eat at Mr Wu's like old times.'

But Fraser wasn't interested. There didn't seem anything to celebrate about being thirty. He was single, living off Uncle Ben's Savoury Rice and forced to take jobs making promo videos for children's entertainers for pennies. So he went out for a Chinese with his parents instead – tragic enough, and made worse by the fact that his brother, Shaun, insisted on paying.

Since then, he's mainly watched TV with his parents and been grilled by his mother:

286

'What happened to that nice girl, Karen? I can't believe you let that one go. There's not every girl who would take on someone with baggage like you've got.'

If he has to hear that one more time, he swears, he will scream. Will he always be the bloke whose girlfriend died?

He tries Norm's mobile again, with no luck, and drives on into the darkening evening. As the built-up sprawl of the outskirts of Manchester gives way to the fields of Lancashire, the motorway empties, as if leaving the sad stragglers of the party, and Fraser begins to feel more alone, like it's just him and the sweeping, cloud-whipped sky. He's not wanted to turn the radio on, for fear he might miss Norm's call, but he does, just for company now, and his whole body jolts when the song that's playing transports him instantly and with no warning to the summer of 2006. This has happened several times since Liv died, and every time he immediately turns off the radio for fear of what it might unlock. But this time he dares to hear it out and finds he remembers not the sirens, or the balcony, or the revolving beam of the ambulance light, or even the kiss, but before that, the penultimate night at the beach bar. The six of them dancing, happy, freshly tanned. When it was just the beginning.

And now he can see Liv's face. The cats' eyes of the motorway dance off his windscreen like he remembers the swirling disco lights dancing off her sun-kissed skin.

He remembers her making a beeline for him from across the dance floor, then her warm, sweet breath in his ear: 'I'm going down to the beach, going to swim in Lake Me! Look at the sea, Fraser, isn't it beautiful?'

287

It strikes him, as the last chords of the song fade and the presenter starts talking, in a mellow, drive-time voice, that this is the last thing he can remember her saying to him, and then she's gone. Whoosh. And when Fraser blinks again, all he can see is the endless stretch of motorway shimmering through the film of his tears.

He comes off at the next exit – Preston – and pulls into a layby. He opens the car door and sits, smoking a cigarette, his first in five days, blowing the smoke up into the cool, damp air, not really aware of the tears still falling down his cheeks, just thinking the only person in the world he wants to see right now is Mia and – possibly, just possibly – could he ring her again? She's only two junctions away, would she come with him?

He stubs his cigarette out on the floor, and scrolls down to her name before he thinks about it too much.

'Mia, it's Fraser. *Again*,' Eduardo yells from the lounge.

In the bathroom, Mia pretends to bang her head on the side of the bath in despair, making Billy chuckle.

'OK,' she hollers. 'Can you come and watch Billy?'

There's an exaggerated sigh and then exaggerated slaps on the laminated hallway as Eduardo drags his feet from the lounge with the phone. It's the third time Fraser has called this evening, updating her on the Norm and Melody fiasco, and Eduardo is not impressed. Tonight he is conjuring one of his rare, grand gesture dinners with his new culinary toy, and the world must come to a standstill in the face of the pasta-maker.

He appears at the bathroom door, tea towel slung over a naked shoulder, holding the phone out with one hand.

Mia takes it. 'Thank you,' she says, with a sarcastic smile. 'Now,' she whispers in his ear, 'I cannot help when my friends decide to have a marital breakdown, OK? So do try and wipe that grimace off your face. The amount of shit I put up with from your friends.'

Then she saunters through to the kitchen, turning back to narrow her eyes at him.

'Hello?'

'Hi, it's me again with an update.'

Fraser sounds nervous to be calling back again and Mia smiles, she finds this endearing.

'Hello, me again with an update, any news?'

'Norm rang again – about fifteen minutes ago. He still can't get through to Melody.'

'Oh, OK.' Mia wonders if this could be classed as an update.

'. . . and now it's practically dark, so he's really shitting it.'

'Fuck.'

'I know, fuck.'

'What shall we do?'

'I don't know.'

'Did he say anything else?' asks Mia.

'Just that she was really drunk, they'd drunk a bottle of Bollinger apparently, oysters on ice from room service. I mean, the waste is just tragic . . .' He stops as if he's holding something back.

'And?'

'She's only wearing a basque and suspenders.'

'What?' Mia stands up.' Is that ALL?'

'And one of those Chinese silky dressing gowns.'

'Oh, well, that's all right then!'

'I'm not saying it's all right, I'm just giving you the facts to work with.'

Down the phone, Mia can hear Fraser sucking eagerly on a cigarette.

'How did Norm sound?'

'Drunk, incoherent, dramatic, you know how Norm gets.'

Mia smiles and resists the urge to make any comparisons. 'She's probably in the hotel bar and he's walked straight past her,' she says.

'That did occur to me. The problem is, I can't get a signal. I'm hoping the closer I get up North, the better it will be.'

'And where are you now?'

'Galgate, just fifteen minutes from you.'

There's a rather long pause, Mia looks at her reflection in the kitchen window, the alabaster complexion of the tired, harassed mother.

'Oh, great, so you'll be there in an hour . . .'

'Actually, I was—'

'Mia! Can you get in here, please? I want to show you something.' Mia walks into the hallway and cranes her neck to see what all the fuss is in the bathroom.

'OK, Fraser . . .?' she says.

'MIA – NOW!'

'EDUARDO YOU ARE SO RUDE. I'M TALKING TO FRASER! YOU'LL HAVE TO WAIT'

'THIS IS IMPORTANT!'

Honestly, what was he like?

'OK, Frase, I have to go, something with Billy.' Mia sighs, making her way to the bathroom. 'I'll call you back in a min, OK?'

When she gets to the bathroom, Eduardo is sitting with a naked Billy on his lap, dripping wet from the bath.

'What's this?' says Eduardo, accusingly.

'What's what? Aren't you going to put a towel on him, Eduardo, he's going to get cold.'

'I wanted you to see this first,' and he points to a few tiny speckles on his thighs, so small Mia has to strain to see.

'Have you been giving him strawberries? Because you know he's allergic to strawberries.'

Mia blinks hard, lets out an incredulous blast of air and walks into the lounge so she doesn't bloody well throw Eduardo in the bath and DROWN HIM. How dare he tell her what her son is allergic to?

'Well?' yells Eduardo from the bathroom.

'Oh, yes, I forgot about the cream tea we had yesterday,' Mia yells back, 'and the two punnets of strawberries I force-fed him yesterday after his strawberry yoghurt, which preceded a strawberry MOUSSE.'

She stops. She didn't know she had this facetiousness in her.

'I'm just asking, Mia,' says Eduardo. 'I am allowed to ask, you know. He is . . .'

And Mia mouths it, she knows what's coming. '. . . my son after all.'

Oh, GOD. It drives her crazy.

And this is what domestic life is like for Mia these days – an exhausting round of accusations and sancti-monious declaration. She can't cook, she doesn't know what to feed her son. He told her off for the way she was ironing the other day. This is from the man who has not – to her knowledge – picked up an iron in his life. She knows why it is: Eduardo feels 'frustrated' and 'insulted' in his role as head waiter at Bella Italia and, therefore, clearly, it's all her fault.

In his mind, he should be head designer at a design studio by now – this is what he was studying at Goldsmiths when Mia met him. The problem is, Eduardo has always been of the mind that someone would hand him this incredible job, without him actually having to do anything as humiliating as work for it. He would never lower himself to do work experience like she had, hours and hours of working for free, sixteen-hour shoots in the freezing cold, just to get a runner job – then have a baby and watch it all turn to mush.

So, Eduardo's ego is suffering and he is sinking to new lows to get his boosts, even arguing with her in Portuguese: 'Seven weeks of Portuguese and you *still* can't understand a word I'm saying!'

If he were still turning up at all hours, letting her down where Billy is concerned, she would end it now, course she would. But he is playing just closely enough to the rules to make this impossible.

Mia has what she's nagged for over months: commitment. And perhaps Eduardo loves her, in his own way – she's pretty sure he does. It's just, has she ever stopped to ask herself if she loves him back?

Eduardo moodily hands Mia their son, now smelling sweetly and ready for bed, and goes back to the kitchen to continue with his masterpiece.

Mia gives Billy his bottle and puts him to bed; all the time, Eduardo chopping things as if he's dismembering someone in the kitchen.

She wanders, exhausted, into the lounge, flops down on the sofa, flipping open a magazine, and eventually he speaks.

'What did *Frase* want?' he jeers. Eduardo can't say 'Fraser' in a normal fashion, but then he never has. Eduardo has never liked Fraser and this was made far worse last week when he found his letter in Mia's shirt pocket: dog-eared, treasured. Clearly read a thousand times.

When Mia came back from town he was standing with it in his hand:

'What's this?'

'A letter from Fraser, why?'

'It's very . . . slushy . . .'

'Oh, don't be ridiculous, Eduardo.' How dare he rifle through her shirt pockets? And why the sudden possessiveness after years of ambivalence?

'But why did he give it to you?'

'I don't know – ask him – because he's proud of me? Because he thinks I'm a good mum? It's more than you've ever said.'

Eduardo snarled, unable to come up with an answer to this.

'So why are you carrying it around in your pocket, like a locket or a fucking lock of hair?'

Mia is thinking about this conversation as she looks at him now, bent over, the heels of his hands pushed dramatically into his eyes, smarting from the onions, and feels a weariness wash over her.

'He's worried, actually,' she says, calmly, 'about Melody, about our friend. She and Norm have had a massive row, and now she's lost in the middle of the

293

Lake District – could be drowned in a lake for all we know.' (On reflection this was slightly overdramatic.)

Eduardo stood up and gave a sarcastic little laugh.

Just then, the phone rang again.

Twenty minutes later, Fraser sat with the engine running, waiting for Mia in the car park of her block of flats, feeling like a disapproving father. He had already had a run-in with the boyfriend; something, if he's completely honest, he had half engineered. Whilst she was sorting herself out, he couldn't resist knocking on the door to ask how long she'd be. Eduardo had answered but, rather than invite him in, he'd then stood, intimidatingly, in the doorway, his underarm hair in Fraser's face. 'When you have located your friends,' he said, menacingly, 'just bring her back, OK?'

Fraser wanted to say something clever and sarcastic – or alternatively punch him in the face – but his mind had gone blank and all he'd managed was, 'I'll be in the car,' something he was now kicking himself for. He revved his engine, loudly, to compensate, and a few seconds later, Mia appeared at the door. He watched with interest through the wing mirror as she kissed Eduardo goodbye – he could have sworn he saw her wince. Finally, she got in the car.

'Any danger?' said Fraser. It was something he used to say as a joke when Liv or any of the girls took ages to get ready. 'Are we ready to pick up our friends from their porn video gone wrong in the Lake District?' he added, putting his arm behind her and looking behind him to reverse out of the car park.

Mia gave a half-hearted laugh.

'God, our lives are a joke, aren't they?' She sighed, flopping her head to the side and looking at Fraser. He looked tired and pale.

'It's all just a joke,' said Fraser. 'That's what I've worked out.'

They drove through Lancaster's one-way system and out towards Carnforth and the North. It was almost 8 p.m. now and, as they crossed the Greyhound Bridge, the last of the day's sun was reflected in the low tide of the River Lune, turning the high sandbanks a deep, burnt orange.

In the passenger seat, Mia looked out of the window, watched as the familiar urban landscape turned into fields and sheep and villages, and smiled to herself. She knew it was not vital for her to accompany Fraser on this mission to find Melody and that – if they were honest – they were camping up the probability of her being drowned in Lake Windermere or stranded on top of a mountain somewhere (she was far too sensible, too 'daughter of an army major' for that sort of behaviour), possibly to facilitate their going in the first place, and that she was probably fine.

Of course she was concerned, up to a point, but she knew Fraser was more than capable of going to help Norm himself. But no, he had gone twenty minutes out of his way to pick her up from her door and, right now, she couldn't think of anywhere else she'd rather be than in a car with Fraser Morgan.

They finally got back on the motorway, the sun just red, smoky wisps on the horizon. Mia tried to get comfy but was struggling to move her feet among the Coke cans, the empty crisp packets, the landfill that was Fraser's car.

'I see you've kept the Elegance in good shape,' she said.

The 'Elegance' was the model name, streaked in Eighties Flashdance font on the side of Fraser's Vauxhall Corsa, a car he'd bought shortly after Liv died. They had derived great amusement from this name when they had gone together to pick it up from some redneck in Tottenham Hale.

'Do not knock the Elegance: she will take you in five-star comfort wherever you want to go.'

They drove on.

'So, anyway, how did the Latino Stallion take it then?' said Fraser.

Mia frowned. 'Take what?'

'Eduardo, how did he take it you coming with me tonight? You know how Eduardo loves me.' He knew he was fishing dangerously, but he didn't really care.

Mia badly wanted to tell him the truth; she wanted to spew her metaphorical guts. She wanted to tell him how Eduardo was patronizing and cantankerous, how he sloped about HER flat telling her how to live her life and feed her son but gave her hardly any money for the privilege. She wanted to tell him how, when she'd told him Fraser was coming to pick her up, he'd practically spat in his pasta, accusing her of dropping everything if Fraser called.

However, she had had months of listening to the details of Fraser's boring cohabitation: the weddings and the travelling the length and breadth of the country to make eBay collections and the times he had to go from their phone calls because they were 'cooking together'. She was damned if she wasn't going to have at least a short period of smugness.

'Actually, he was really good about it.'

Fraser blew air sharply through his nostrils, knowing, categorically, this not to be the case.

'Really?'

'Yeah, he knew this was about Melody and Norm, about my friends, about the List.'

In truth, Eduardo despises the List. Eduardo thinks the List is just a schoolboy construct by Fraser; an excuse for all her little cronies – 'Liv's Disciples' – to spend yet more clique time together.

'I felt a bit sorry for him actually,' said Mia, laying it on possibly a little too thick. 'He'd just made me this beautiful meal of homemade pasta; then you rang, the minute it was ready to be served. *Honestly!*'

She looked at him and smiled.

'Ah, domestic cohabiting bliss,' he said.

'Oh, now, how the tables have turned!' said Mia. She was being ungenerous but she didn't really care. 'How *is* single life treating you, Fraser?'

Fraser thought about this. He could tell her the truth; he could tell her how he hates it, how he is back living with the awful empty feeling as soon as he puts the key in the door. He could tell her how in the last few weeks, he was still occasionally sleeping with Karen when she turned up at his door, lonely and with wine, because he is weak and because she insists she maybe overreacted about the List and that she's cool 'with them having no labels', which Fraser knows to be bollocks, deep down.

He could tell Mia how, despite his letter and good intentions, he still feels guilty about that night and the kiss. He still feels guilty about pretty much everything in his life, but that there is a growing realization that

297

he's sitting with the right person, right now, and that there's nobody else he loves just being in a car with, and how his mood lifted, instantly, the second she got in next to him, but that he is too scared to ever take that plunge and that, left to him, he will eternally wuss out.

'Do you know what? Actually, I love it,' he says.

Mia laughed once. 'Oh?'

'I think it's good for me.'

'Really? Is that so?'

'Yeah, you know, time on my own, not having to listen to the sound of industrial tape being torn next door, not having to go and meet her boring friends all the time, propping the bar up at the Bull, being able to listen to music I like now, not Enya. Fucking Enya. God, if I ever have to listen to Enya again, I will combust,' and he laughs, somewhat hysterically.

Mia laughs too. 'Well, she did, you know, have dolphins painted on her fingernails, Fraser; what do you expect?'

That's enough, don't go too far, she thinks to herself, but she can't seem to help it.

'And you didn't seem to talk to one another much – at Billy's birthday, for example?'

Fraser looks at her, amused. 'Were you watching us?'

'No!'

He raises his eyebrows at her in the wing mirror.

'Are you *jealous*, Mia Woodhouse?'

Mia did her best outraged laugh. 'Don't be bloody ridiculous.'

'Because it sounds like the green-eyed monster to me . . .'

She punched him on the leg. 'I am very happy with Eduardo, thanks very much.'

'Well, that's good then.'

'Yes, it is.'

'Good for you.'

She huffs, looks out of the window. 'Yes, good for me.'

It was a blessed relief when Fraser's phone went and they both leapt to it.

'I'll get it,' said Mia. 'You're driving. Hello? Norm?'

'It's not Norm, it's me, Melody.'

'Melody, thank God! Where are you?'

Melody sounded eerily composed.

'I'm OK. It's stunning here, actually. I'm sitting by Rydal Water. I'm perfectly fine. I just don't know how to get back, that's all.'

She was right about one thing, it was utterly stunning. When they finally found her, after a hair-raising 60 m.p.h. drive through higgledly-piggeldy lanes in the pitch-black, she was sitting on a rock, shivering uncontrollably in the Chinese dressing gown, before a mirror-still lake, the mountains reflected into it, huge and black.

Fraser stayed in the car and Mia walked, her feet crunching across stones, towards her friend.

'Melody, shit, we were worried about you.' Her voice echoed in the open space. 'We thought you would be back at the hotel.'

Melody looked up and smiled, whimsically, at her. 'I was just enjoying the view,' she said. 'Isn't it wonderful?'

Mia sat down beside her, took off her coat and wrapped it around her friend's shoulders. There was the smell of burning wood and fresh water and she thought, how did it come to this? How did it come to her friend, shivering, alone in the middle of the Lake District?

'What's going on, Melody?' she said.

Melody lay her head on Mia's shoulder. There was a long pause.

'You know, I was just thinking,' she said, eventually, 'just reminiscing before you got here.' Mia saw that Melody had an open bottle of wine in her hand; she took it and took a slug. 'I was thinking of what you said when we met in the park the other day, about me and Norm and the South Road days. It was funny, because I'd forgotten about all that, about the strawberries in the shower and Sade – "Your love is king . . ."' She began to sing, drunkenly swaying, her breath smoking in the air. '"Drowning in my heart . . ."'

'"Your wish is here",' Mia joined in. '"Ruler of my heart!"' Until they both petered out with nervous laughter.

They were silent for a while. It was so quiet, they could hear when a fish came up for air, see the rings of water it made. In the distance, Mia could just make out cars on the road that ran round the base of the mountains, so small, they looked like toys.

'Norm was my first true love,' said Melody, finally, her voice cracking. 'I didn't realize how lucky I was, how intense it was. I just assumed everyone's relationship was like that. But it wasn't.'

'No,' says Mia, putting her arm around her. 'It wasn't. You're dead right there.'

'I never worried about the future, about growing older or things changing, I just thought it would be like that forever. That he was the one.'

'Everyone thought that,' said Mia. 'You were the It couple.'

300

Melody smiled, took the bottle of wine from Mia and took a big gulp.

'You know, the day I married him was the best day of my life.' She laughed, quietly. 'I know everyone says that, but it absolutely was. I thought that was it, I'd never have to worry about anything. It would be me and Norm forever, and we'd have a couple of kids, live in our lovely house in Lancaster and everything would be sorted. And we were good, you know, we were OK. And then Liv died.'

She looked at Mia. Her eyes large and tear-filled.

'And?'

'And then everything changed.'

'What do you mean?'

'I haven't told anyone this,' she continued, 'but Norm has been sad ever since; so sad, Mia, he distanced himself from me from that day.' She started to cry. 'Did you know he has practically a shrine to her in our house?'

Mia frowned. 'Really, what do you mean?'

'In the corner of our loft room, he has a little area with photos and trinkets, tickets from the Green Day concerts they went to together, this photo of a day out in Heysham they went on together, I don't think I even remember them going. Of course, I accepted it. She was my friend too and I loved her, I *still* love her, I miss her so much, but Norm never seemed to recover. He went further and further away from me. We haven't had sex in six months. I just didn't feel he wanted me any more, that he didn't even love me any more and I want a baby, Mia. I'm thirty next year. We've been married three years and he won't even talk about it. I thought this weekend we could, you know . . . it's such a beautiful setting . . .'

Remembering what Norm said to her, Mia bit her lip.

'I thought . . . Oh, God . . .' And she sobbed into Mia's shoulder.

'Promise you won't tell anyone? Anna or Fraser?'

'No, no, darling.' Mia stroked the hair away from her face. 'Of course I won't tell anyone.'

'Good, because I feel so stupid, but basically, the reason I booked this weekend so far in advance was because I was ovulating. God! It sounds insane when I say it out loud like that, doesn't it?'

'I hardly think you'd be the first woman in the world to book a romantic weekend away at a time when you thought you could get pregnant.'

Melody laughed. 'I know, but it wasn't a romantic weekend away, was it? It was supposed to be a sexy weekend away and there was I, after we'd done it, lying with my legs in the air.'

Mia swallowed.

Christ, Norm had predicted everything.

'He came out of the toilet, and he asked me what I was doing. His face was horrified; he was actually *horrified* at the prospect of us having a child together. It all came out, the fact I'd come off the pill, I was trying to 'trick' him, apparently.

Mia couldn't help but think that that *was* perhaps tricking him a little, but then she couldn't talk, she was the scarlet woman of Lancaster, reckless and up the duff by the man who, really, was just her summer fling.

'We had the most almighty row. I mean astronomical. I chucked all the bedding out of the window, Mia. I chucked a lamp at him, cut his head! I mean, God knows what the other guests must have thought, they must have heard it all.'

Mia didn't know what to say. All these young couples in their twenties and their thirties, in their cosy flats and their boutique hotel rooms – were *any* of them having any fun?

Melody gave a huge sob.

'Sssh,' said Mia, rubbing her back, 'come on, it's not that bad.'

'And do you know the worst thing?' said Melody. 'My voice-activated vibrator ran out of batteries, started making this whirring noise, like there was someone dying in our room. A fucking death rattle, in our room!'

There was nothing they could do but laugh.

After much persuasion, Mia eventually got Melody to walk back to Fraser's car and back to the hotel, where Norm was waiting, Fraser having told him the news that Melody had been found alive and well.

Norm was sitting in front of the fire in the hotel lounge, turning a single malt whisky round in his hands, every inch the cross, righteous Victorian husband with the mad, hysterical wife who had just wasted an evening of his life. There was an awful pause, during which Mia and Fraser looked at one another, willing Norm to at least get up and give Melody a hug, but he didn't move. Eventually, Melody gave him a cursory peck on the cheek. 'I'm exhausted,' she said, 'and I'm going to bed.'

People watched as she walked through the lounge in the dressing gown and Norm's trainers.

'I think I'll follow her,' said Norm getting up. The

atmosphere, thought Mia, was one of a party gone terribly wrong. Then he embraced both of them so that their heads were touching. 'Thanks for being my best friends in the world,' he said, choking on his words, drunk and overly sentimental. 'But you can't save this one . . .' And then he kissed them both lightly on the head, turned and left for bed.

They both stood in the middle of the hotel lounge, a chintzy drawing-room affair with thick floral curtains and an open fire, and realized suddenly that the only sound was the crackling of burning wood. Everyone seemed to have their head buried in a book or a newspaper, trying desperately not to look at the two new arrivals, associates, no doubt, of this weekend's hell-raisers.

'Is it me, or do you feel like you are the police?' said Mia, quietly. 'That you have just completed a successful car chase and brought them back in for questioning.'

'No, I feel like a very stern father,' said Fraser, 'who's just dragged my errant teen back into the house after they broke their grounding rule.'

'Remind me never to have children with you, if that's the normal sort of thing they get up to. Pornography, smashing the place up, inebriated.'

Fraser sighed. 'Shall we go and get a drink?'

'Yes, why are you whispering?'

'I don't know, I feel a bit like this is an old people's home.'

'You know, we could always get a room,' Fraser said, grinning, when they were sitting at the bar: an unforgiving, overlit 'hotel' bar, manned by one po-faced man in a dicky bow.

'You're a bit ahead of the game, aren't you?'

Fraser rolled his eyes. 'Separate ones, thank you. Eduardo would never forgive me.'

'No, he would slay you.'

Mia thought how much she'd love to get a room – even a separate one; how nice it would be to have breakfast in a hotel, with Fraser, looking out over the view of Bowness behind them. She briefly worked out how this could work in her head, and then dismissed it as ridiculous and fanciful. She hadn't told Billy for a start, and Billy would wonder where she was in the morning.

'I can't,' she said, 'I have to get back. You could stay though and I could get a taxi.'

'Yeah,' said Fraser, 'because that would be a lovely relaxing breakfast, those two sitting on either side of the room and me, in the middle, ducking as they chucked croissants at one another.'

'It's such a long drive home to Bury, though, I'm worried about you. You could stay at mine.'

'Yes, because that would also be a nice breakfast,' he said, and they smiled shyly at one another.

They had a coffee together; then, because it was late and Fraser had a long way to go, decided to just get in the car and drive.

Mia sat in the passenger seat. It was pitch-black outside, the sort of unfathomable darkness one only gets in the countryside; the only decipherable contrasts in colour were between the sky and the mountains, which seemed like mysterious sleeping giants that would only stir when the sun came up. Mia looked up at them; they seemed to hug them on either side, making her feel content and

305

cocooned. They sat in perfectly comfortable silence for five minutes or so, the road winding, the headlights once catching a rabbit, making them both jump.

Mia felt safe and relaxed, as if she could say anything.

'So what happened between Karen and you, then?' she said.

'Oh, nothing much,' said Fraser, keen to avoid the subject, since they sometimes still slept together. 'She just wasn't right, that's all, she just wasn't The One, I guess.' Mia looked at him. 'Or even "A" One, come to that. But she was nice.'

'Relationships are impossible, aren't they?' She sighed. 'Even when you marry the one you think is The One, they turn out not to be.'

'I s'pose that's just life, just growing up,' said Fraser.

'I know, but I still feel a bit sad,' she said, suddenly.

'Really? Why?'

'Well, because it's like an era is over, isn't it? That time of Norm and Melody, Melody and Norm . . .'

'Nothing stays the same.' Fraser shrugged. 'You never know what's around the corner – we both know that more than anyone.'

Mia turned to look at him in the darkness. She could just make out the shadow of his face in the light of the headlamps, when he turned and smiled at her, the lovely shape of his eyes.

'Do you ever wonder?' she said.

'About what?'

'About where we'd be if Liv hadn't died?'

He was quiet, then he said, 'Course, all the time, what do you mean?'

'Well, would Norm and Melody still have broken up?

306

Would you and Liv have a baby by now? Would I not have a baby?'

If he knew what she was getting at, he didn't show it; he just frowned and carried on driving.

'I s'pose life's just what it is, isn't it?' he said eventually, after a long pause. 'Life is basically what happens to us, we can't then spend it wondering what would have happened if *other things* had happened to us.'

Mia looked out of the window, the view suddenly clouded.

'Do you think so?' she said. 'Because I wonder that all the time.'

When she looked straight ahead again, she could feel Fraser's eyes burning into her.

EIGHTEEN

October
Lancaster

'I'm past my sell-by date, that's the truth of it.'

Mia tried to stop her eyes from rolling as she passed Mrs Durham a glass of water and two paracetamols. 'I should have been killed off years ago.'

Mia stood with her hands on her hips, sucking her cheeks in, not sure whether to laugh or cry. 'Now, Mrs D—'

'I'm only being honest,' she said, grumpily, knocking back the pills. 'Only saying what we're all thinking, sitting in our armchairs all day, bored witless, wondering how long we have to carry on this charade for . . .' Morecambe, of Morecambe and Wise, the most humourless of Mrs Durham's two humourless cats, leapt languidly off her lap, as if to say, 'Give me strength,' and wandered out of the room.

'I'm half blind, I'm deaf, this shoulder is giving me no end of nonsense.' Mrs Durham wagged her glass of water in Mia's face, not so much as a sign of an arthritic shoulder. 'I say this to you, dear: make the most of your time now, because past fifty, all you've got to look forward to is pain and death.'

Mia rubbed hard at her forehead. 'And that's if you're lucky, I imagine, Mrs D.' Unable to bear it any longer, she got up and went out of the room.

She stood with her back against the kitchen wall. 'I don't think I'll bother cleaning the fridge this week. I've checked and it doesn't seem to need it,' she shouted. Then, she waited.

'No, give it a wipe-down, please!' Yes, as she strongly suspected, the only hearing problems Mrs Durham was suffering from were selective. 'And a cup of tea would be nice. You could die of thirst in this house.'

Mia went over to Mrs Durham's old-fashioned kitchen sink, so old-fashioned, in fact, with its fabric curtain wrapped underneath, that it was now back in fashion, if certain vintage-style interior magazines were anything to go by. She filled up the kettle, looking out at the row of enormous knickers hanging from the washing line.

Christ, she felt like Cinderella.

'There's a perfectly good kettle in here. You don't have to hide yourself away in there, you know,' shouted Mrs Durham.

'Maybe I want to hide myself away in here,' Mia muttered as she waited for the kettle to boil and rummaged around in Mrs Durham's cupboards for some biscuits.

She'd been visiting Mrs Durham for almost a year now and was just about used to her eccentricities. In fact, rather alarmingly, it felt almost normal to find custard creams and other food items in amongst old plugs, packets of hosiery and tubs of Bisto granules that had gone out of date in 1987. Mia had tried countless times to organize Mrs Durham's cupboards, at least into perishable and non-perishable, but had always been caught in the act: 'Are you meddling with my things, again?' she'd shout from her armchair. 'Well, don't, please. I won't be able to find a thing.' So Mia was left trying to extract packets of biscuits from underneath electrical appliances; tins of cat food from drawers of clothes. There was still an inexplicable number of bits of off cake, wrapped in tinfoil, dotted around the house.

Perhaps she could understand there not being any individual cupboards as such, if there were individual rooms, but Mrs Durham had just gradually moved various bits of other rooms into the front room where she spent most of her time, so that she might as well be living in a bedsit.

As well as the armchair – a sort of fur-ball in furniture form – where she sat, clutching Morecambe and Wise to her chest all day, as if the RSPCA were circling in a heli- copter overhead and might swoop at any time, there was now her single bed ('made my life so much easier, it means I've barely any reason to go upstairs at all . . .'), a two- ring hob where she heated up insipid soup, a kettle, a chest of drawers where she kept her clothes and in which Morecambe and Wise occasionally went to the toilet, and various other bits of junk. Come rain or shine, the gas fire was always set on 'sweltering', threatening to melt her collection of royal memorabilia, which surrounded the hearth. There were also some Christmas decorations: tinsel strung across the window and door and five glass snowmen in ascending size on the mantelpiece.

'Don't you think you ought to take those down?' Mia had said, many a time, as she'd been doing the polishing.

'Whatever for? I'll only have to put them up again in a few months' time.'

This was what she was dealing with.

Still, most of the time, Mia looked forward to her visits to Mrs Durham. Yes, she could be a difficult battle-axe with little regard for personal hygiene or manners, but she could also make Mia laugh out loud (largely unintentionally, but still), and she could be fascinating. Mia loved to hear, again and again, the story of how her husband, Reg, proposed on the top deck of a London bus, with only three days to go of his leave from his job in the mines, and so they'd decided to get hitched that afternoon, Mrs D wearing the bridesmaid dress that she'd worn for her sister's wedding, because there was no time to get anything else.

Just lately, however, and especially today, she had been extremely difficult. There didn't even seem to be much in the way of inappropriate emissions of gas to keep Mia amused. If she wasn't banging on about her various ailments, she was counting down the days till death, or counting her dead friends. Poor Barbara had been dead several months and she still hadn't forgiven her for not visiting her enough, whilst suffering from terminal cancer.

Morecambe sauntered into the kitchen and swished his tail, firing Mia a dirty look. Mia stuck her tongue out at him and opened the fridge, taking out a half-open tin of cat food. She thought it quite unsavoury to keep cat food in the same place as human food, for the simple reason that Mrs D's eyesight being what it was, she feared

312

it was only a matter of time before she arrived to find her digging into a tin of Sheba, thinking it was one of her rancid tins of Batchelors Steak – not that there was much difference when you put it like that.

She spooned the food into a bowl and pushed it with her foot towards Morecambe, who gave her a look as if to say, 'I may depend on you now, but I shall get you back in another life.'

Then she made a cup of tea, stirred in the obligatory three sugars, placed it on a tray with the biscuits and went back into the front room.

Mrs Durham looked listlessly towards the plate.

'You can take the biscuits away,' she said. 'I've no appetite, Mary, no appetite at all.'

Mia took one of the biscuits and stuffed it in her mouth, finding too late that it was far too big, so she had to turn away to take it out again and bite it in two.

'Right,' she said eventually, brushing crumbs from her jeans, 'I'm going to ring Dr Yelland, to see if he can do something about this shoulder and possibly your lack of appetite.'

She went towards the phone.

'You're wasting your time,' Mrs Durham said in that infuriatingly self-satisfied way she had of late, 'it's a waste of his time and resources and he'll only say the same thing: "Wear and tear, Mrs Durham, wear and tear."'

Mia felt she might tear her hair out.

'Look, let me just call him. At least he might be able to prescribe you something stronger than paracetamol.'

Mia heard Mrs Durham take a long breath in through her nose, and when she spoke, it was in an exasperatingly mournful tone.

'I think I'm further down the line than that, dear. I don't think pills can save me now . . .'

Mia hung up the phone. 'Well, what about alternative therapies, have you thought about that? They say hypnotherapy is very good for arthritis. Aromatherapy?'

'Roaming therapy? I can barely walk down the street, dear. Be reasonable.'

Mrs Durham had a recorded episode of *Cash in the Attic* on – her favourite programme. She turned the TV up louder, and slurped her tea.

Mia sighed.

'What about a little walk then? Get some fresh air? It's a lovely day.'

'I think I'll just sit here, thank you. I like *Cash in the Attic.*'

Mia stood in a shaft of autumnal sunshine at the window, the phone in her hand, looking out at the crisp, blue-skied day, and felt a sudden wave of depression. Here she was – they were – in a boiling hot front room that smelt of custard creams and cat wee, whilst a beautiful October day went on outside. Well, she wasn't having it any more. Quite simply, what Liv would have given to see another year of her life, never mind the seventy-eight Mrs Durham had had. She could have another ten, possibly even twenty years left too, if God were feeling cruel, and yet she seemed intent on sitting in her smelly little front room and rotting. No, she was not having it.

She walked over to the TV and switched it off.

'Now put that back on! I was watching that.'

'Yes, well, I want to talk to you,' said Mia.

Mrs Durham switched it on again. Christ, this was

like minding a child. Mia went over, snatched the remote from her armrest and switched it off again.

'Mrs Durham,' she started. Now she had, her heart was going ten to the dozen. 'I'm going to say this for your own good. With all due respect, I'm getting a little tired of your attitude. I want to help you but you resist every offer of help I give you. You don't want to see a doctor about the pain, you don't want to go out and yet, just days ago, you went to a funeral and seemed happy as Larry, actually. Up and about.' This was true, she had received the call about the funeral on the Monday evening (someone she'd worked with back in the seventies) and then, quite miraculously, like a leper healed at Lourdes, had got up and dressed the next day, taken the bus to Heysham and walked to the funeral with just her stick.

When Mia had picked her up, she was tipsy, if not actually pissed, happily shoving down an enormous slice of black forest gateau, cream all over her face, and now, a week later, she was immobile, unable to eat – it was bollocks, thought Mia. Utter tosh.

Mia took a deep breath. Lectures of any kind didn't really come naturally, but she was all fired up now and raring to go. Mrs Durham looked at her grumpily and slurped her tea. 'Now, I know you are in some pain,' she continued, 'that your sight's not what it used to be and that sometimes it's hard, but you are only seventy-eight, which means you may have ten years, who knows, possibly twenty left . . .'

Mrs Durham closed her eyes and pressed her hands together, as if in prayer. 'Dear Lord in heaven, please let someone shoot me before then.'

'Well, no, that's the point!' said Mia, growing more

irate. 'Nobody is going to shoot you before that' (she hoped, anyway, it was getting harder to resist) 'so the only thing you can do is make the best of life. I come here every week and sometimes it's fun, but recently you have been a real misery guts, Mrs Durham. You're being . . .' She faltered. 'You're behaving like a child, wasting your life, and it's not doing you any good. Now come on –' she took three big strides towards her – the sun is shining, let's get you up for a stroll, or we can go in the chair. It's only quarter past two, we could make it to the Midland, have one of those lovely scones, a game of Scrabble – I bet you fancy that—'

Mrs Durham banged her fists on the table and stood up, making Mia jump. 'I don't want to go to the Midland, Mary! I don't want to go for a walk or eat a blasted scone, with that dreadful UHT cream. I just want to sit here, I'm quite happy here.'

'Yes, well, I'm not, I'm sorry . . .' Mia was shocked by her own outburst; it was as though she suddenly felt choked with claustrophobia, hot and stuffy in this sweltering sitting room. It reminded her of being a child, of when her mum would spend hours entertaining men downstairs, whilst she had to stay in her bedroom and entertain herself. She felt another hot flush come over her and went over to turn the gas fire down. 'It's . . . it's sweltering in here. Christ, I feel like I'm going through early menopause. I feel like . . .' She started taking down the tinsel from the window. 'I feel like time is standing still in this place. Please, at least, open a window . . .'

Mrs Durham got up and stomped towards the window, momentarily cured of her crippling legs, taking one end of the tinsel in her hand and pulling it. Brilliant, thought

Mia, is this what life has come to? Playing tug-of-war with an old lady?

'Put that down,' said Mrs Durham, grumpily.

'No, we are putting it away. It's three months until Christmas: stop wishing time away. And open this window. It smells in here, it smells . . . it smells of death!' Mia knew she had lost it now, gone too far, that she sounded unhinged, but she didn't care.

'DEATH?' said Mrs Durham. Her eyes were wide and giddy. It was almost as if she savoured the word, the woman was obsessed.

'Yes, DEATH,' said Mia, yanking the tinsel from her and tying it manically in a knot. She seemed to be suffering from temporary insanity. Maybe it was catching. 'But you're not dead yet, Mrs Durham, you are not actually dead and I really think, if you just . . .' Mia went on and on, she didn't seem to be able to stop.

She didn't think, when she had answered the ad in the newsagent's window, that she would ever have opinions about how this old woman spent her days, that she would ever really care. She would come here, do some housework, clean up, possibly listen to stories about the war and go home, considering she had done her job. But now, she found herself livid, LIVID about how this woman was squandering her life. She felt hemmed in enough in her own house, her visits to Mrs Durham had always been her light relief, even if it was a game of Scrabble or a visit to the Midland Hotel, and now she felt thoroughly depressed by it all.

Mrs Durham shook her fists by her side. Mia felt a bit scared. 'Now, you listen here, young lady. You listen to me. I didn't ask you to come here, did I? I didn't choose you; you chose me, remember? You answered that advert and decided to accept the job. Nobody made you; it's you who needed me. Morecambe and Wise and I were quite happy before you turned up, so don't think you can just swan in here, turning over all my things, trying to tell me how to be . . .'

She was breathing in short sharp bursts now, and Mia had the sudden, dreadful thought that she might have a heart attack – that her prophecy might actually come true and that she would drop down dead, right now on the living-room carpet. Mrs Durham,' she said. 'Mrs Durham. Please calm down. I'm sorry . . . I didn't mean to . . .'

Mrs Durham shuffled out towards the kitchen.

'So you can get your things and go, Mary.'

She sounded icily calm.

'But, Mrs D . . .' Mia tried to follow her into the kitchen, but Mrs Durham swung around, sweeping up Wise in her arms as she did. Wise hissed at Mia in protective scorn.

'I SAID, you can leave me be. I shall cope. I can feed myself, clean up for myself. I'm getting quite sick of people telling me what to do. I haven't lived through a war, lost a husband, undergone three major operations, lived on my own practically all my life, to be told what to do by a young girl like you who knows nothing about life.'

Mia stood in the hallway, dumbstruck, a mixture of fury and disbelief and, for some reason, overwhelming sadness. She felt hot tears filling her eyes; she had only wanted to help. Was she now being sacked?

She stood there for a few moments – the house was

silent. Then she took her coat off the banister, picked up her bag and walked slowly into the kitchen. Mrs Durham was sitting at the kitchen table now, stroking Wise on her knee, a calm smile spread across her face.

'I'm sorry, Mrs Durham,' Mia said, quietly. 'I didn't mean to upset you. I just . . .' And then, to her horror, she burst into tears; she stood, in the tiny, old-fashioned kitchen, and sobbed like a child.

Mrs Durham watched her, saying nothing. There was just the sound of Wise purring on her knee, the drip of the kitchen tap, the sound of footsteps on the next-door neighbour's garden path. Mia felt suddenly like she was in a parallel universe, that what was going on in this house was not the same life that was going on around them.

Mrs Durham was looking at her now, blinking. Mia found herself hiccupping, actually hiccupping with tears – how utterly embarrassing – and yet she couldn't stop. She waved her hands about her face.

'I'm sorry, I'm sorry . . .'

'It's all right, dear, you have a good cry. You wail like a Hindu at a funeral if you need to. Knock yourself out.'

And even though tears were dripping off her nose, Mia burst out laughing; she wasn't sure whether at the first bit or the 'knock yourself out' bit, a saying she had taught Mrs Durham.

When Mia looked up, Mrs Durham was laughing too, a self-conscious, childlike chuckle, as if to say, 'Did I get that right?'

The two women remained like that for a while, giggling like a pair of schoolchildren. Eventually, their laughter turned into one long 'Aahhhhh . . .'

Mrs Durham rummaged in a drawer and handed Mia a hankie that smelt suspiciously of Parmesan cheese, but she wiped her face with it anyway.

'Feel better? You jolly well needed that, didn't you, dear?'

Mia nodded, and smiled. She felt completely exposed, standing there, weeping copiously. What on earth had brought all that on?

Mrs Durham walked around from the kitchen table and gave Mia a hug, which only made Mia cry more.

'You see, I may be past my sell-by date, but I've not lost all my marbles, not just yet,' she said, patting her back. 'And I can see that I'm not the only one who's been a bit down in the dumps, am I?'

Mia was trying desperately to take control of her chin, which was wobbling all over the place. 'No,' she said, 'I suppose not.'

'You don't seem *that* happy, dear, if I'm allowed to say that,' she said, taking her by the arms and looking at her now. 'You've never seemed that happy, ever since you started. You have a lovely baby, Milly, to love . . .'

Mia smiled, amused. The wrong name was one thing, the gender was quite another.

'. . . which would be quite enough for some people, it was quite enough for me. I wish I could have had more, because it's over so quick. Sooo quick, dear. When you look back on your life at my age, you will realize that this time you had with your baby that seemed so hard, was a mere blink of an eye and you will want it all over again.' Mia smiled, and wiped her nose with her hand. '*And* you've got a bonny one. My word, you've a bonny one. Those girls aren't going to know what hit them,' she said. 'Milly and I got on like a house on fire when you brought him here. That was the best day I've had in a long while, did you know that?'

Mia thought back to that day, that dreadful day, when she'd been so desperate she'd brought Billy over to Mrs Durham's. She'd come to pick him up, seen him perfectly content, propped up on cushions, and felt a total failure: even the woman she was visiting could look after her baby better than she could.

Mia dabbed at her eyes with the handkerchief.

'But it's not enough, is it?' said Mrs Durham, peering at her. 'Mmm? Not enough. And you don't love that boyfriend you're with – mind you, I can't blame you, he's a waste of space by all accounts. You've never said one good word about him in all the time we've known one another.'

Mia swallowed. Had she not? Had she not said one good word about Eduardo?

'But you still stick with him, don't you? And I don't see any signs of you wanting to marry him. I'd been married nine years by your age. So who's wasting their days now, mmm?' She looked at Mia through the glasses that made her eyes look so enormous. 'Who is the misery guts now? Come on!' she said, as if it had been her idea all along. 'Let's go into the garden.'

They wrapped up – Mrs Durham insisted on Mia borrowing one of her hats: a green, knitted, tea-cosy affair that Mia rather liked herself in – and went out the back. Mrs Durham's garden was a simple square of lawn, with border flowers and a small shed at the bottom, tended fortnightly by a gardener. They sat on the bench, which backed onto the kitchen, Mrs D's pants blowing in the breeze, the sun warm on their faces.

'Mrs Durham,' said Mia. She suddenly wondered why on earth she'd never told her. 'There's something I should tell you. Something that might explain if I've seemed a bit sad sometimes. Two years ago, my best friend Olivia died.'

Mrs Durham looked at her, her huge blue eyes filling with tears.

'But why didn't you tell me, dear?' she said, eventually. 'I thought you and I were friends.'

They chatted till the sun was low in the sky and it grew chilly, at which point Mrs D brought out the brandy.

Mia told her how she and Liv had met in halls in the first year, how they'd shared a toilet; one toilet between their tiny rooms with a shower head above it. 'Shit and shower partners, we called each other,' she said, a tiny bit tipsy and uninhibited now.

'Shit and shower partners? Well, I never,' said Mrs D, biting her lips. Mia told her her favourite memories: the camping in the Lakes, the times they'd abandon revision to go and sit in the Water Witch on the canal and sup pints till they were talking nonsense, the trips they made to the seaside resorts of the northwest, the stupid arguments about nothing at all.

And, as she talked, Mia realized that she hadn't really talked about Liv to anyone, apart from her own friends, who knew and loved her as much as she did, and strangely that Mrs Durham was now closer to her than her own mum.

Then, Mrs Durham started to talk.

'I had a best friend,' she said, excitedly. 'A best friend just like Liv. We were best friends from our very first day at secondary school, when we were eleven.'

'Really?' said Mia. 'My goodness, how wonderful.'

'We went on holiday together, too, went to dances with our husbands. And then when we were old buggers –' Mrs Durham chuckled, and Mia did too – 'we used to play Scrabble; every week together, without fail, we'd have a game of Scrabble and a brandy.'

'So who was this friend?' said Mia. 'She sounds great, I like the sound of her.'

Mrs Durham put her hand on Mia's knee.

'Barbara, dear,' she said, as if this was the most obvious thing in the world. 'Barbara was the best friend I ever had in my life.'

NINETEEN

November
London

On a freezing cold night in early November, Fraser finds himself in Soho, sitting in a freezing cold bar, sipping on a freezing cold bottle of Smirnoff Ice. Not that he's complaining – as Wham! once sang, 'the drinks are free'; Smirnoff are launching their new caffeine-infused line this evening. It's just, Club Tropicana this is not, the Arctic tundra is more like it. The bar has been converted into an igloo with ice sculptures and ice pops and bar staff with blue lips and white-sprayed hair, as if they've come straight from the set of *Narnia*. If 'ice' is the theme, then the organizers have surpassed themselves. It's just . . . he's freezing. Absolutely fucking freezing. Sod Smirnoff, where's Norm? So they can go to a proper, *warm* pub and he can have a pint next to a roaring fire?

Fraser stands up, pulling his faux bearskin around him – another 'freebie' handed out by promotional staff at the door – and scans the room for his friend. It shouldn't be too difficult to find him. The new Norm has a brand-new hairstyle: a trendy, side-flick thing that Fraser thinks makes him look like he did when he was twelve – but the place is shrouded in dry ice and heaving with similarly coiffed trendies; hordes of twenty-something media types, the guest-listed 'opinion-formers' of London, out for another night on the freebie party circuit, and everyone seems to be melding into one.

He pushes on through the crowds, holding his fourth bottle of Smirnoff Ice above his head and pulling the cape that keeps slipping off his shoulders – did these things only come in one size?

Out of the dry ice emerges a waitress with white, false ice lashes, like icicles, wearing a tiny fur-trimmed dress and balancing a tray of more drinks on her slender fingers.

'Hey . . .'

She leans in and says something but Fraser can't hear over the strains of 'Ice Ice Baby', which has been playing on a loop for the past hour.

'Sorry, what was that?'

She pouts, coyly, and flutters her white lashes at him.

'I said, hey, don't be frosty, have a free Smirnoff – the perfect ice-breaker!'

Ah, the slick lines of the promotion girls, Fraser's getting to know them well.

He takes one, no two – 'Cheers, I'll probably be needing these' – then he walks off, pulling the bearskin over his shoulders, with all the dynamism of a victim of man-flu shuffling bravely to the toilet wrapped in his duvet.

During the last month or so, this is becoming a normal midweek night for Fraser – maybe not the bearskin and

326

the igloo bar – but the free drinks he doesn't really want and definitely the AWOL friend.

After the hideous homemade-porn-vid-gone-wrong, there was a vague attempt by Melody and Norm to make it work – a dinner party to show they were 'united', which ended dreadfully with Melody drunkenly trying to start a debate about whether it was 'morbid' that Norm insisted on photos of Liv all over the house – but everyone knew it was over and, a fortnight ago, like a royal couple, they ended weeks of speculation with a formal announcement that they were divorcing.

Norm came to stay with Fraser almost immediately, and there was a week of tears and beers and pizza deliveries and Fraser getting home from work to find Norm still with the curtains shut playing Call of Duty. And although it wasn't nice, wasn't nice at all, to see his friend in pieces, Fraser quite enjoyed that bonding bit; he enjoyed the responsibility of being the 'carer'. God knows, it was about time. But now the initial shock has worn off, Norm is reborn, and Fraser's not sure he's liking this bit half as much.

In under a fortnight, Norm has quit his job back in Lancaster, moved to London for good (only staying at Fraser's till he finds place to rent), and started temping at the *Metro* newspaper where, as the newbie, he is getting first option on all invites to launches and promo nights, which nobody else can go to because they have wives and families.

'It's gonna be wicked, Frase . . . free booze all night . . . pretty ladies . . . What's not to like?' he said, when he came home waving the Smirnoff invite in Fraser's face, the second party of the week and it's only Wednesday.

Ah, yes, the joys of the newly single best friend. This is a whole new world for Fraser, full of crippling midweek hangovers, strange, shame-faced women in his kitchen of a morning and nights 'on the pull'. Fraser hasn't had nights on the pull with Norm since they were about seventeen and feels, perhaps, it is something best kept to one's twenties. But as Norm keeps telling him, they didn't get to do this in their twenties; he is *reclaiming* his twenties!

You're not wrong there, thinks Fraser, when he finally locates him, gyrating against a wired-looking redhead on the dance floor.

Fraser stands, the hand that's wrapped around his bottle of Smirnoff slowly going numb with cold, watching his friend dance, and feels a chasm open up within him. He suspects it's because deep down, despite the new haircut and the new life in London and the rack of girls he's had in Fraser's spare bed this month – a Poppy and a Kate and a truly mental Dutch girl who left in a rage at 3 a.m. and slashed the next-door neighbour's tyres – that Norm is hurting, his friend's grieving.

In typical, brush-it-under-the-carpet fashion, Norm hadn't really gone into detail about what went on in that bedroom that fated night in the Lakes back in September, but there was talk of a voice-activated vibrator and 'ovulation' and that was more than enough detail for Fraser.

Basically, Norm had fallen out of love with Melody. Melody the girlfriend was a cider-loving, fun-loving, down-to-earth girl.

('This is the girl I went travelling with, Fraser. The one who didn't bat an eyelid when I had dysentery.')

'Wow,' Fraser had agreed, 'now, that *is* a woman.' He hoped one day to also meet someone who didn't bat an eyelid at his dysentery.

The wife Norm ended up with was his mother – just with spikier heels and a Laura Ashley store card.

'I just knew I didn't want kids with her,' he said. 'I loved her – she was twelve years of my life – but I wasn't in love with her any more.'

So here he is, 'reclaiming his twenties', doing what he 'should' have been doing when he was too busy being dragged around Ikea, and Fraser doesn't know for sure, but he suspects it still hurts like hell. The future you thought was yours now gone, leaving a gigantic 'now what?' – he recognizes it in the way Norm staggers around the dance floor, the self-conscious, silly dancing, the recklessness.

He knows, because he's been there.

And if he's honest, Fraser's sad about the divorce too – they all are – and he and Mia have had endless phone conversations about it, which has been a consolation, he supposes. But the bottom line is, THE couple, the couple all other couples (including Liv and Fraser) have always measured themselves against, are not going to be forever after all, and what, Fraser wonders, does that say about anything? Was anything for keeps? Anything at all?

He elbows his way through the dance floor, craning his neck, hoping to catch Norm's eye. He should be the sensible one here, the leveller. He is suddenly quite taken with this sense of responsibility.

'NORM!' he shouts. 'Normanton? Do you wanna go soon? I'm freezing my tits off in here.'

Norm waves his bottle at him and pouts – the

self-aware pout of a man under the influence of something illegal. Fraser groans, inwardly. So, clearly, he's not going anywhere for a good few hours.

'Norm!' he shouts again. 'Let's go somewhere else. Somewhere we can get a pint . . .'

Norm pulls a face like a child who's been told he has to go in for tea, then flashes all fingers up twice, to indicate twenty minutes more.

Fraser shakes his head and laughs quietly to himself. Ah, yes, and there's another thing about this grieving period: there's nobody can tell you when it should start and when it should end. It just has to be gone through, like labour.

He goes to stand by the bar, watching Norm now – with his tongue down the redhead's throat – with a mixture of mild embarrassment and awe. Fraser got the drinking bit, the wanting to obliterate yourself, but the pulling? How on earth did he do it? Move seamlessly from married to gigolo in a matter of weeks? Fraser has been technically single (although Karen still turns up on his doorstep now and again, and he's not proud of this, but those boobs are hard to resist) for three months now, and he can't muster any enthusiasm for pulling anyone. This getting off with girls required so much effort: all that flirting, all that making conversation. He looks around him and blows air through his mouth. Nobody takes his fancy. There was a time, perhaps, where girls would approach him, tell him he had 'beautiful opal eyes', but they didn't do that any more. Maybe he was just getting old.

Just then, Norm careers off the dance floor, pulling the redhead behind him, laughing, fizzing, to Jimmy

Somerville's 'You Make Me Feel (Mighty Real)'. She's wearing very high heels, a ra-ra skirt and a grey, cropped, retro T-shirt with the words FUN, FUN, FUN . . . IN THE SUN emblazoned on it. She also has enormous, googly eyes that are slightly too close together. She reminds him of one of the royal family. Princess someone – Beatrice, was it?

Norm drapes his arm drunkenly around his friend.

'Fern, let me introduce you to Fraser Morgan. A lovely, lovely man – "*My best pal*",' and Norm does his best speaking-through-the-side-of-his-mouth Taggart accent, one of a repertoire he's been pulling off for the ladies lately. Fraser downs the rest of his Smirnoff and starts on the next. 'And this,' he says to Fraser, 'gorgeous young vision you see before you, is Fern . . .' He breaks off, he turns to her, assuming an expression of enormous shock. 'Actually, I don't know your surname. Oh, my God. How fucking RUDE am I?' And he laughs like this is the funniest, most interesting thing he's ever said in his life.

'Rude!' agrees Fern. 'Rude-erama!' and she bats him on the bottom with her handbag.

'So, Fern,' Fraser tries, stupidly, to make normal conversation. 'That's an unusual name. Is that as in Fearne Cotton?'

She bats Fraser on the bottom too and chews the inside of her cheek. This gorgeous vision he sees before him also seems to be off her face.

'Er, *no*.'

'Fern Britton?'

'Now, that is also rude. She's like fifty years old!'

'Fern . . .' Nope, he can't think of anything remotely funny to follow that.

'Na, you don't get it,' says Norm, taking hold of the bottom of Fern's T-shirt and pulling it out to the side. 'She's Fern, as in Fern, Fern, Fern . . . in the sun!'

Fern throws her head back as if to screech with mirth, but her jaw doesn't seem relaxed enough and so she just ends up doing a strange faux-laugh, a ghoulish, horsey guffaw.

'He's hilaaaaarious. I totally heart him,' she says, taking Norm's face in hers and kissing him. 'Everyone in the office totally hearts Andrew.'

Andrew. Who the fuck was Andrew? And what about me? thinks Fraser. Does nobody heart me? This sudden, juvenile line of thought, shocks even him – Why aren't girls flocking to me like they seem to be flocking to Norm? Why is nobody snogging me on the dance floor?

'Fern's an intern in the fashion department at the *Metro*,' says Norm.

'I see, so you're Fashion Fern?' says Fraser.

'Yeah, why, are you Fashion Fraser?' she asks coyly, and he watches as she gives him the once-over. 'Do you work in fashion?'

'No, I'm a sound recordist.'

'Cool-erama. Does that mean, like, you're a singer? A pop star?'

Fraser laughs. 'No, that's a recording artist.'

'Oh.'

Fern's huge googly eyes seem to cloud with disappointment for a second.

'Oh, I know. You, like, hold one of those big fluffy microphones for a living! Hilaaaarious!'

'Yeah, I do that sometimes.'

'So, do you work backstage for bands and stuff?'

Fern is clearly a budding fashion journalist because she asks a lot of questions. The problem is, she seems to get bored by the time the answer comes.

'Not exactly.'

'Na, he does adverts for stuff like Tena Lady,' pipes up Norm, suddenly bursting into one of his schoolboy chuckles. Fraser frowns at him. He could do this sometimes, Norm, make jokes at other people's expense just to keep hold of the comedy baton, as it were, to keep people's attention. It wasn't one of his better qualities, but Fraser knew it was rooted in insecurity.

'Noooo . . .' says Fern, swinging her bag back and forth.

'Yes, unfortunately,' says Fraser, flatly.

'Oh, my God, is that like incontinence pads?'

'It's not like incontinence pads, it is incontinence pads.'

'Oh, my God,' says Fern, for want of something better to say. 'My cat's incontinent, it's hilarious.'

'Wow, that er . . . doesn't sound hilarious,' says Fraser, and he knocks back at least half of his second bottle of Smirnoff.

'Yeah, I went away on holiday, right? And when I came back she'd weed all over these new shoes I'd bought?'

'Really? Hilarious.'

Fern gives three short snorts of disbelief. 'Duderama, it was not. They were Louboutins. They cost four hundred English pounds!'

And with that, she downs the rest of her Smirnoff and slaps the bottle back on the bar.

'Anyway,' she says, 'just popping to the loo,' and then she kisses Norm on the lips, a long, at least ten-second snog with tongues. Fraser looks away.

333

'She's nice, isn't she?' says Norm, as she stomps off to the Ladies' in her ridiculously high shoes and her ra-ra skirt. 'A stone cold fox.'

Fraser smiles. This is another thing he has observed about his friend of late, he's started talking as if he was in an indie American stoner movie. Like he was Jack Black or Bill or Ted in their excellent adventure.

'Look, can we go now?' says Fraser. 'I really think we should go now, Norm.'

'Oh, come on.' Norm slips a hand in his pocket and takes a tiny parcel from it and slips it into Fraser's, with a wink. 'A few lines of your finest devil's dandruff in there. Go on, just save one for me.'

Fraser looks at his friend and Norm grins, then purses his lips, then grins again, then purses his lips. Oh, Jesus. A whole night of this?

Fraser puts his hands on top of his head, as if in preparation for surrender.

'Mate, I'm trying to be good. You know what happened in Vegas.'

'Yes!' says Norm, grabbing him by the cheeks. 'You fucking freaked out – we didn't get our boys' weekend because you were too busy being a mental case.'

'Ah, but then you came to see me in London and you were too busy on your "Hunter Gatherer" diet and your six-pack to drink anything, you mental case!'

'So, this is it,' says Norm, not really getting the point. 'This is it, Frase. Tonight's the night. Come oooon . . . When do we ever get to go out, just me and you, hey? When is it ever the boys storming it any more? Like old times? When was the last time I had my best mate in the whole world, on form, all to myself?'

'Last night?'

'Oh, come on, that was a mere aperitif compared with tonight.'

They'd met after work in the Angel and drunk solidly until closing time.

'I'm tired, Norm.'

'You're boring more like.'

'I've got a sore throat.'

Norm covers his face with his hands in despair.

'I'll give you sore fucking balls in a minute, now stop being such a penis.'

And then Norm starts to laugh, and Fraser can't help but laugh and then he's walking to the Gents', the tiny parcel in his pocket.

Fraser kneels, hunched over the toilet basin, cringing at what he can hear outside, in the full knowledge that, if he were to go mad tonight, which he does NOT intend to, he could well be spouting similarly coked-up drivel in a while.

A man – he says a man, he looks twenty-two at the most: Pete Docherty trilby, some sort of ridiculous jumpsuit, a pale, baby face covered in a sheen of narcotic-induced sweat – is quizzing everyone about their toilet habits.

'Sir – wee or a number two?' he asks, with the ceremonious wrist action of a circus master, as soon as someone enters.

'Now that would be telling,' is the usual answer – slightly squiffy people humouring the absolutely fucked bloke. Oh, God, thinks Fraser, does it get any worse than this? 'Why do you ask?'

'Because I'm starting a crusade!' he announces. 'Stop the poo taboo! Why does nobody ever admit to doing a number two?'

There follows a mumble of embarrassed amusement from the queue of people in the Gents'. 'Isn't going for a dump one of life's simple pleasures? What do you think, sir, yes, you looking shifty?' Fraser hears the humiliated mumble of someone who just came in for a wee and is now probably deeply regretting it. 'If you could give it up, like never do a number two ever again, would you? Or would you miss it? Don't you think it's one of the most satisfying things in the world?'

Oh, the rambling, attention-seeking monologue of the man who has lost the plot and all inhibitions. Even as Fraser snorts the line, he's cringing.

He goes outside to wash his hands, then, like someone going to the toilet during a comedy gig, tries to sidle out without being heckled.

He isn't successful.

'And what about you, sir? Number one or number two?'

Fraser surreptitiously checks his nostrils for any telltale signs of white powder. 'Now that would be telling,' he says, tapping the side of his nose and going out to find Norm.

Five minutes later and this is all so much better. SO much better. A little pick-me-up. Just what the doctor ordered.

'You see, Normanton knows best!' He and Norm congratulate themselves on their fantastic, genius plan as they gyrate, stupidly, to Hot Chocolate's 'You Sexy Thing'.

'It's just the Norm. It's all the Norm!' Fraser grins, nodding wisely at his friend – it's a hilarious little joke they used to share way back in the day. And then there's some dancing and some pouting, a LOT of dancing and pouting, and some pointing come to think of it, and it does feel like back in the day, like the Paradise Factory, Manchester circa 1991, Wigan Pier, Ibiza . . . before, well . . . before stuff got heavy. And suddenly Fashion Fern is not so annoying as Fern, Fern, Fern, and actually her mate's not bad either – a dark-haired girl called Holly, and of course they have a lot of fun with that; what are her other mates called? Ivy?

'You've got lovely eyes,' says Holly, dancing up close to him. 'Has anyone ever told you that? They're a nice shape – very almond-shaped. And you've got really long eyelashes. Close your eyes.' Fraser does as he is told.

'Wow, look, Fern,' and she gets Fern over to look at this amazing specimen with camel-like eyelashes. 'Hasn't he got the longest eyelashes?' And Fraser flutters them and does some more pouting. I have eyelashes like a camel, he thinks, and really nice eyes and I've still got it. It's just all about what you project.

He does another line, takes another Smirnoff from the girl with the icicle eyelashes, this time engaging her in conversation. Fascinating conversation.

'I like your eyelashes,' he shouts in her ear, dancing up and down. 'Are they all your own?'

'No, and you just dripped Smirnoff all down my top . . . however, these *are* all my own,' and she thrusts her breasts in his face.

'I can see that,' says Fraser, still swaying his hips to

337

the music. 'Anyway, I've just been told I have eyelashes like a camel,' he says, throwing more Smirnoff down his throat and a little more down her front. 'Hey, maybe we could have an eyelash-off later – hey? What you think? Shall I come and find you?'

But then she wanders off, leaving Fraser a little bemused and alone, and so he goes to dance with Holly and Fern, his new friends, and tries to take his top off at one point, before Norm stops him in his tracks: 'No Frase. No. Here is not the place to take ones clothes off.' Then suddenly, it's later, and where are Holly and Fern? Where's Norm, come to think of that? Where the hell has he gone?

Fraser stands in the middle of the dance floor, looking, but the room's kind of spinning now, just a mass of sweaty bodies, jumping up and down to '*jump around, jump around. Jump up, jump up and get down!*', great billows of dry ice gusting in from the sides. The smell reminds him of the discos at the holiday camps he used to go to as a kid.

He'll phone Norm, that's what he'll do, so he gets out his mobile phone but it doesn't seem to be working, some sort of message keeps coming up – it takes him at least two minutes to register that there's no reception. He'll have to go outside, but he's definitely going to be needing more booze to make that sort of expedition, so he finds Miss Icicle Lashes, takes another bottle and staggers towards the exit.

'Sorry, no drinks outside.' The bouncer on the door has shoulders like a bison.

'But I just want to call my friend and then I'm going back inside.'

'I think you look like you've had enough, mate. So just give me the bottle and make your way outside please . . .'

Fraser thinks about arguing but he can't seem to speak correctly, his jaw feels rigid, his mouth won't make the words. So he hands over the bottle to the bouncer and now he's standing in the middle of Poland Street, a high-pitched ringing in his ears, the sweat on his back icing over, like on a windscreen.

His phone beeps, and he sways as he tries to decipher two texts, both from Norm.

The first:

Where r u?

Then:

Me and Fern gone bk – got my keys. Where u go? You fckd off! Top nite tho. Cuddles and Kisses, Norm xxx

Fraser walks up the street, the November wind whistling around his ears, and blows air through his mouth, very slowly. He can feel the drugs wearing off now, the slow regaining of straightness: still high, but not accompanied by any sort of pleasure, just a gnawing, craving, anxious feeling, like something terrible's about to happen.

Beer. He needs more beer. So he walks up to Broadwick Street and then onto Wardour, but it's like a race against time: what will get there first? The beer or the emptiness?

He finds a big, warm, characterless chain pub and instantly feels better, but as he walks into the bar, most people are walking out. It's Wednesday night, after all, not really the night for taking class As and flirting with girls in fur-trimmed skirts. He goes up to order, watching the mass exodus – was it something he said? – couples going home together after dinner or the theatre to go to bed, then get up, get on the Tube to work and resume their routine.

What Fraser would give right now to have a routine. What he would give tonight to be going home with someone. As the drugs retreat and the lukewarm beer takes over, a wave of lucidity washes over him – as if the beer is actually sobering him up. He's thirty, he doesn't want this any more: losing his friends, being alone in a pub. He thinks of going back home now, but it would only be to hear those two at it through the wall and then tomorrow, the awful, sheepish cup of tea in the kitchen before Fashion Fern makes an exit, never to be seen again.

He doesn't want this any more, this feeling like life – and not just his, but all of their lives – is one big messy blip. He wants to feel whole and calm and right. And he suddenly thinks of the word 'sublime', and that strange conversation about Wordsworth he had with Spanner in the silent Reading Room of the British Library: that feeling like everything is good and right. '. . . *of aspect more sublime; that blessed mood/In which the burden of the mystery/In which the heavy and weary weight/Of all this intelligible world/Is lightened.*'

And he gets that, he really does, because he felt it just last month, driving up to the Lake District, the mountains looming out of the dark either side of him, the trees that made a tunnel, the glassy expanse of Bowness, and Mia sitting next to him. Everything was right and good.

He needs to speak to her. He needs to tell her all about this whole feeling. Yes. This is the most right anything has ever felt since Liv died.

But he looks at his watch: 10.55 p.m. She's probably in bed with Eduardo, but maybe Eduardo was at work tonight? It was worth the risk.

He steps outside, scrolls down to Woodhouse on his phone and presses CALL.

Three rings and she answers: 'Fraser?' The calm, measured voice of a sober person. In the background, he can hear the TV. 'To what do I owe this honour?'

Fraser clears his throat. He's suddenly not sure how he's going to go about this; he may just try opening his mouth and hoping for the best.

'Well,' he starts, 'I was just in Soho . . . and it's not late, Mia, not late at all . . .'

'It's eleven p.m., Fraser. I'm normally an hour into my REMs by this point.'

'R.E.M.? Since when did you like R.E.M.?'

There's a sudden snort of laughter. 'No, REM as in rapid eye movements, as in the middle stage of sleep, you goon, not the band.'

'Is Eduardo at work?' he asks; he says a little prayer.

'Yes, he's doing a stocktake, not back till gone midnight.'

'Ah, so you're alone!'

There's a pause.

'Fraser, are you drunk?'

'What? God, no. No. What do you take me for?'

'I'll take that as a "yes" then.'

Fraser grimaces. How come you never know how drunk you are until you try to speak?

'Where are you?' she says.

341

'I am currently outside a fine establishment known as the Slug and Lettuce.'

'Classy, Frase. Did you have some Scampi Fries with your pint? God, I could murder a bag of Scampi Fries . . . Who are you out with?'

'Well, Andrew Normanton, but he buggered off home.'

'What, on his own?'

'Yes, of course on his own.'

'I'll take that as a "no" then. Jesus, just don't tell Melody. So what have you been up to this evening?'

'Mmm, mainly sitting in a freezing cold bar, sipping a freezing cold Smirnoff Ice – free ones, mind, it was another of Norm's promotional evenings. What about you?'

'Very nice.' She sighs. 'Well, talking of freezing, I just batch-froze some cauliflower cheese – it's all very cutting edge. Anyone would think I worked for an airline I spend so much time putting food in and out of small plastic containers.'

Fraser laughs.

There's another, much longer pause.

'It's nice to hear from you,' she says, and even in his state of drunkenness, he thinks he can hear her smile. 'Even though we haven't really got to the bottom of why you are calling . . .'

'Calling? Why I'm calling? I'm calling to harass you, of course.'

'Aw, Frase. You're so sweet.'

He walks along the road, scuffing the remains of the leaves at his feet, looking up at the stars. *Say it. Say how you feel!*

'Listen, I just called to say—'

'I love you? Aw, Lionel you shouldn't have . . .'

And Fraser stops in the street and sort of growls down the phone, frustrated like a child.

'Stop it,' he says, 'stop taking the piss, because actually, yes, I am.' He stands still and bites his lip, it's out now. 'I *am* calling to say that I love you.'

There's a nervous little exhalation of breath down the phone.

'And I love you, too, Fraser,' she says.

Silence at the other end of the phone.

'Well, that's good then,' says Fraser and, even in his drunken state, he's not sure this was how it was supposed to pan out, the big declaration, so he says, 'I had a lovely time driving to the Lake District with you. It was nice, you know, just you and me and the open road.'

'Hey, we were like a Renault Megane advert in motion out there.'

'I'm being serious!'

Unfortunately, he slurs the word 'serious'.

Mia sighs. 'Fraser, you're very sweet but you're drunk.'

'I'm not, well, I am, but I mean it, I loved being with you that night. I love . . .' He suddenly pulls himself together, suddenly becomes hyper-aware that he's drunk and she's sober.

'I'm just saying, you're great company.'

'Thank you,' she says.

'And you're great looking, too, with gorgeous eyes.'

'Oh, Jesus, OK, now I know you're definitely drunk.'

'You've got lovely hair too.'

'OK, Fraser, I'm going now, I was watching a really good documentary, you interrupted me . . .'

Fraser stands in the middle of the street and imagines her, curled up, concentrating on the television, in her pyjamas. Hair tied up. She looks so pretty with her hair tied up.

'OK, beautiful. Sexy . . .'

'Fraser, if you've got the horn, why don't you go and call on Karen?'

'I love you, Mia Woodhouse!'

But she's already hung up.

Fraser stops in the street now, swaying slightly, the phone in his hand. Well, that went well. That went extremely well. So well, he thinks, that he will just compose a little text message to her. Just so she has it for keeps. He closes one eye as he texts and punches the words in with his thumb.

I meant it, he texts. *I love you, Mia. I think you are GORGEOUS. I always have!!!*

He presses CONTACT to send it, and gets as far as finding the W for Woodhouse, but his concentration fades halfway through and he eventually finds himself at the bus stop, thinking he really doesn't want to go home.

'Go to Karen's.' Now that was an idea. Karen's nice, warm house suddenly sounds like a lovely idea – just a glass of wine with a nice girl, just to finish the evening off nicely, no funny business. Well, maybe just falling asleep on those boobs.

Before he sobers up and thinks about this too much, he flags down a taxi instead and asks the driver to stop off at a twenty-four-hour off-licence he knows and grabs a bottle of wine.

'Kentish Town,' he says, 'Leighton Road.'

He has opened the wine in the taxi and had a little swig, so that by the time he is standing on Karen's front doorstep, he is still drunk enough not to have to engage his brain. He is living in the moment.

She seems to take ages to answer the door, so he presses on the bell, leaving his finger on it, just in case she's asleep or got the TV on loud.

Eventually, the door swings open.

'Surprise!' says Fraser, walking straight in. 'Late-night caller! Wine delivery . . . I thought the night is yet young, so we could have a little drink together.'

He takes off his jacket, letting it drop to the floor.

'How are you, darlin'?' he says. 'Give us a kiss.' He moves in to kiss her but Karen remains stiff against the wall, still holding the door open.

'Um . . . Fraser.' She takes one of Fraser's hands, then the other, and places them next to his side.

'Oh, hello . . .'

Just then Fraser turns to see Joshi standing in the hallway, wearing only socks, high-cut chinos and a jumper around his shoulders, like he lives there, like he's fucking *moved in*.

He steps forward, touching Fraser patronizingly on the arm.

'How are you, buddy? Wow, you look like you've had a good night. Cup of tea? Karen, shall I put the kettle on?'

Fraser feels himself sober up in a flash. 'No, thanks. Gosh, sorry I-I didn't know you had someone here,' he says, retreating out of the door, stopping just in time to pick his jacket up off the floor.

'That's OK, buddy,' says Joshi, practically closing the door in his face. Fraser looks, just in time, to see Karen standing behind him, her hands over her mouth.

* * *

As Fraser walks back down Karen's lamp-lit street he is already sober enough to be cringing. To make matters worse, it's started to rain now – no, actually, it's fucking hailing: small, hard balls of ice needling his head.

Suddenly he hears footsteps behind him, growing louder, faster. He turns around . . .

'Fraser!'

. . . to see Karen standing there in her big red coat, high-heeled boots, her hair a slightly frizzy halo under the streetlamp, holding something in her hand.

'You left your phone,' she says, breathlessly. 'It fell on the floor when you took your jacket off.'

'Oh, cheers,' says Fraser, and he takes it from her, almost gingerly, like it might electrocute him or something. 'Look, I'm sorry, I didn't mean to . . .'

Karen shakes her head. 'It doesn't matter,' she says. 'Joshi's just a friend, really, at the moment – we might go to the convention as partners; although I think he'd like to be more, which feels nice, Fraser, to be honest. To feel really wanted.'

Fraser smiles. 'That's good,' he says, and he means it, even if it comes out lamely. 'I'm still sorry, just turning up like that. I should have called.'

She shrugs.

'Well, I've done it to you,' she says, 'so don't worry. Although that's different.'

'Yeah, I know,' says Fraser.

The hailstorm comes to a sudden end, so that they are now standing in silence, in the dark street.

Karen says, 'Fraser, I read your text.'

'What text?'

'The one you wrote to Mia. I'm sorry, it was on your phone when I picked it up, I couldn't really help it.'

He looks at her blankly.

'The one saying you love her? That you always have.'

Fuck, did he send it?

'Fraser, can you do one thing for me? Can you make me one promise?'

Fraser nods slowly. He's wary of making any promises right now.

'I accept that you don't love me, that you'll never love me. I accept that you love Mia, probably. But, don't mess her about, OK? You did it to me, don't do it to her . . .'

'What do you mean?'

'I mean, look at you, hun. You're a state, you're drunk, you take no control of your life or your actions. Mia has a baby and a boyfriend – don't go calling her up and telling her you love her. Don't mess with her life, whilst yours is still a mess.'

Fraser looks at the ground. Shit, was it really that obvious?

'Sort yourself out, that's all I'm saying. Take control of your own life, before you get involved in anyone else's.'

'OK,' says Fraser, looking up at her.

'OK, good,' she says. 'Goodbye, Fraser.'

''Bye, Karen.'

'See you around.'

And then she turns, and she goes. Fraser looks at his message log.

He didn't send it. Thank *fuck*, he didn't send it. He clutches the phone to his chest. 'Thank you, God.'

TWENTY

December
Lancaster

The nineteenth of December 2008, a week before
Christmas, and for the first time in recent history it was
a 'white' birthday for Mia – her twenty-ninth birthday
– and already this morning, in the car park of her block
of flats, she'd made Eduardo and any passer-by who was
willing take pictures of her, then her and Billy, then her
and Billy and Eduardo; with snowman, without snowman
– just to record this amazing event.

Billy, look! Mummy's got a white birthday!

Billy seemed very much to get the momentousness of
this, squealing with glee as he picked up handfuls of
powder in his little fat mittens and chucked it at his dad,
who was not amused. No, Eduardo was officially 'Not
Amused' by the snow. It was 'cold and wet', apparently,
and made the restaurant floor dirty.

It was true that the beginning of December had brought

349

with it record levels of snow in Lancashire, and it just kept falling, in great drifts, closing schools, freezing pipes, bringing the roads to a standstill. Every evening, *Look Northwest* brought only bleak reports of motorway pile-ups, children fallen through frozen lakes, OAPs shovelling snow from their doors. But the city of Lancaster was beautiful, silent and white; the River Lune a frozen, murky slab like months-old chocolate. Few cars were on the roads and, for days now, as she pushed Billy up and down the eerily muffled streets, her moon boots crunching, her parka hood up, Mia had felt as though she was in one of those art-house films by a Scandinavian director, where nothing happens, except a lot of walking in snow.

'The coldest December so far in the history of the world ever!' all the papers said: THE BIG FREEZE CONTINUES, MORE SNOW TO COME!

Mia sat in Lancaster Station waiting room, nose in the *Lancaster Guardian*, scanning the apocalyptic headlines whilst Billy intermittently lurched for the paper, making a rustling racket and shoving it in her face. She managed to wrestle it from him again, this time tearing several pages in the process, making the rest of the waiting room turn and stare. She gave up, abandoning the whole paper to him, which he took with a victorious smile, promptly ripping it to shreds while she scanned the Arrivals board nervously. Fraser's train from London had already been delayed; she feared 'cancelled' was coming next.

Please don't be cancelled.

The birthday plan was this: Fraser would have lunch with her at the Sunbury Café, then he would mind Billy whilst she had her hair done and bought something to wear with a voucher her mum had sent her for her birthday (because really, one couldn't go to one of Lancaster's most romantic restaurants in a pair of New Look leggings). Then she was going for dinner with Eduardo (Melody was babysitting), whilst *Fraser*, young Fraser Morgan, was going to spend the evening with Mrs Durham because he had a very special task from the List to complete:

Use up all seven Scrabble letters in one fell swoop . . .

Fraser, not really a natural word-game player, or a rule-follower, more a lyrics man, was going to need some help.

It was a plan hatched in a moment of genius. After Mia had had her heart-to-heart with Mrs Durham, she'd wracked her brains for how to find her a new Barbara, someone she could play Scrabble with. And then Google had turned up a gem: Lancaster Scrabble Club, the *'Lune-ey Scrabblers'* – who'd have known it! *Ten members meet every week at someone's house, more word-crazy members wanted . . .!'*

Jean Harp – the social secretary – sounded lovely on the phone.

'We're quite an old lot already, so we don't let anyone in without medication!' she'd joked, before letting out the most joyous, naughty cackle. 'We can't have anyone dropping dead.'

Mia knew this was just the place for Mrs D.

And now she was hooked, militant about The Rules (try to get forbidden words past Mrs D at your peril!). This was her new religion and she'd taken to carrying around her copy of *The Official Scrabble Players' Dictionary*, memorizing the five thousand 'sevens and eights' as she called them at every possible occasion.

She and Jean Harp got on like a house on fire too, chatting on the phone daily, comparing personal best scores, gossiping about rule breakers. 'Apparently, there's a woman been banned from Heysham Scrabblers,' she'd heard her say to Jean on the phone the other day, 'for learning to read the letters whilst still in the bag. Like braille, Jean. Yes, I know. Unbelievable.' Mia would listen to these conversations on the phone and smile to herself. What a pair.

Mrs D had only been attending Lune-y Scrabblers for five weeks, but had already taken on the overconfident air of a veteran, which Mia thought was unbelievably sweet.

'All seven letters in one go?' she'd said, sucking in her breath, when Mia had told her about Fraser's challenge and asked her if she could help. 'Is that it? Jean and I would be disappointed if we didn't get at least one of those per club night.'

So Fraser was going to the Lune-y Scrabblers tonight – he imagined ten over-60s in someone's semi and a Fox's Luxury Biscuit Collection. Mia thought of her evening ahead – three hours in an Italian restaurant with Eduardo – and she had to admit she was a bit jealous. She just wished she felt more excited about spending the evening with Eduardo. But then perhaps this was what it was like with a baby? Perhaps she was expecting too much? Mia had spent much of her childhood yearning for a normal adult life: kids, a husband, the low-level bickering (although of course the low-level bickering hadn't really featured in the dream), and here she was. She had arrived! ````Or was this just what she told herself to make herself feel better? Sometimes, when she lay awake at night, which

352

was becoming more often these days, she thought about what Mrs Durham had said back in October: 'You don't love that boyfriend of yours, you've never said one nice word about him . . . who's wasting their days now, eh?' It rang horribly true. Mrs Durham had turned things around – with her help, admittedly – but at seventy-eight she had a whole new life! New friends. And what was *she* doing? Opting out. Sticking her head in the sand. Perhaps if there was just herself to think about, she would have skedaddled by now. But there was Billy and all she'd ever wanted for Billy was a normal family life. Everything she'd never had. That was the way it was meant to be. She at least owed it to him to try a bit longer.

Just then, there was an announcement on the Tannoy.

'The next train to arrive at Platform Four is the delayed, eight-fifteen a.m. train from London Euston.'

Mia felt a churning sensation in her stomach and, for a fleeting and unnerving second, thought, No, *this* is the way it's supposed to be.

She quickly gave herself a talking-to. They were friends, nothing more than that. Fraser's behaviour after the drunken phone call from Soho had made this quite clear. For starters, she hadn't heard from him for a fortnight; then, when she did, pretty much the first thing he said to her was: 'Right, now, about this sleeping with an exotic foreigner thing . . . So does Emilia really want a date with me? Have you spoken to her yet?'

Yes, Emilia *desperately* wanted a date with him – she wouldn't bloody shut up about it. 'I adore British men!' she'd purred. 'They are the very reason I left Rio!' As well as, of course, to improve her English – and, no, she hadn't spoken to her yet.

Mia fastened Billy into his buggy. 'Shall we go and find Big Fraser? He's going to look after you today – aren't you a lucky boy?'

Then she wheeled him out onto the slush-washed platform, just as everyone was piling out of the train, their breath smoking skywards in the icy air. And she saw him now, for the first time since their SOS trip to the Lake District.

He looked healthier and was wearing his parka – Liv had bought him that parka – and a huge smile, and Mia was suddenly overcome with nerves. She didn't know what to do with her face.

'Jesus Christ, it's cold up North.'

Suddenly he was standing in front of her, his hands tucked under his arms, jiggling from one foot to the other.

'Yes, at least five degrees colder than London. I know, I live here. Anyway, you're a true northerner, you were born in the North, what's with this southern ponce behaviour—' But she was stopped, mid-sentence, as he embraced her, for a very long time.

Mia closed her eyes and buried her face in his coat.

'OK, Fraser, I think I may need to breathe now. Have you given up smoking again? You smell very fresh.'

'Smoking gave up on me, I'm afraid. Apparently, I just blew hot and cold,' said Fraser, and Mia rolled her eyes at another of Fraser's crap jokes, at the same time as being aware of not being able to fight the smile stretching at her face.

He crouched down on the floor, the snow sticking to his hair and the fur on his hood. 'Hello, Billy. Have you been nice to your mum so far on her birthday? Got her anything nice? A pot plant, some potpourri? She loves a bit of potpourri, your mum, which is lucky, 'coz that's what Big Frase has got her. A lifetime's supply of your finest orange-peel potpourri.' He whispered in his ear. 'She is gonna be *ecstatic*.'

'God, Fraser, shut up!' Mia laughed.

Fraser stood up. 'Happy birthday.' He grinned, and he took her face in his hands now and kissed her on the lips, just once, very hard. There was an awkward pause. Things had been said when he called from Soho that night, things Fraser had never said before, even if he was drunk.

'So, is this for me?' she said, quickly changing the subject, gesturing to the big box by Fraser's feet. 'Fraser, I told you, no gifts, just donations to my personal charity: Young Mothers on the Edge.'

'Actually, it's from Norm,' said Fraser.

'Really?'

'Yes. He says he's sorry he's not going to see you on your birthday but he's been very preoccupied with the next thing on the List. For a change. Come here . . .' And Fraser ushered her into the warmth of the waiting room, put down the white box and took off the lid. It was a sugar-iced birthday cake. FOR MIA, it said in blue icing, FROM LIV AND ALL OF US.

With no warning at all – she never seemed to be able to make it through her birthday without crying, but still, at barely 11 a.m., this was early – Mia burst into tears.

'Mia!' said Fraser, alarmed. 'It's supposed to make you happy, not blub.'

'I am happy,' she said. 'I'm really, really happy. A Victoria sponge.' She looked at Fraser through tear-filled eyes. 'The

355

perfect Victoria sponge . . .' He wrapped his arms around her. 'Wow, you really are a young mother on the edge, aren't you? And also I'll have you know that that Victoria sponge is the result of about three weeks' practice by Andrew Normanton. If I ever have to eat another piece of fucking Victoria sponge in my life, it will be too soon and all your fault.' She laughed into his chest and he held her closer and they stayed like that possibly longer than they should have in the waiting room of Lancaster Station.

They walked through town towards the café. The snow had started again, soft, thick flakes that drifted silently, sitting forever on their hair and their coats. Lancaster looked like a ski resort: moon boots and Uggs had replaced normal shoes; people had adopted funny walks in their multiple layers.

Fraser was pushing the buggy. Mia kept looking over at him, thinking how sweet he looked, like he was concentrating very hard.

'Fraser, it's not a shopping trolley, you know, it does sort of go the way you push it.'

'I know, I know,' he said. 'I've got it. Anyway, is Anna meeting us there?' Melody was still too busy sorting out the aftermath of the divorce and not in a head space to socialize, she said, so had offered to babysit. Anna was supposed to be joining them.

'No,' said Mia. 'In fact I wanted to talk to you about that. True to form, she was very odd on the phone this morning. She wished me happy birthday, but as if someone were holding her at gunpoint; then when I said you were coming up, she suddenly went really weird and said she'd changed her mind about lunch, something about how this was her only day to Christmas shop – which was a little insulting, I have to say . . .'

Fraser was very quiet.

'Frase? Has something gone on with you two?'

He gave her a double take, as if he hadn't heard her the first time around, but she knew he had.

'What? *No*. Not that I know of anyway . . .' He paused. 'However, who knows what goes on in the mind of that woman. She's totally bonkers most of the time.'

Mia briefly wondered if now was a good time to share with Fraser her worries about how she felt Anna was growing more distant from her; then remembered just in time that – like soft furnishings – this was one of those conversation topics that were essentially incomprehensible to the male species.

They carried on into town, their faces growing numb with cold, deciding to call into Marks & Sparks for Fraser to get supplies for Scrabble night.

He stood in the biscuit aisle examining a packet of luxury chocolate-chip cookies.

'So, apparently, I've got to go round to a woman called Jean Harp's house tonight, to play Scrabble with a bunch of old dears,' he said, as if saying it aloud might make it more normal.

'Think yourself lucky. I've got to go and sit in a really posh restaurant with my boyfriend for three hours. I'm sick with jealousy. What I'd do for a game of Scrabble and a luxury Belgian cookie.'

If Fraser was pleased by Mia's hint at a lack of enthusiasm, he was trying very hard not to show it in his voice.

'You make it sound like community service. You're

lucky: candlelight, the tinkling of a piano, crying into your gazpacho.'

She wacked him on the arm with a packet of bourbons.

'I'm joking,' he said. 'It's going to be lovely.'

'It is,' said Mia, determinedly. 'It's going to be very, VERY lovely.'

Although the longer she spent with Fraser, the more she wished she could just hang out with him, here in Marks & Spencer's food hall. It would be like old times, except they'd graduated from Asda to M&S.

Fraser stood at the cash desk, balancing the biscuits plus some cheese straws and, because he'd heard these Scrabble players could get pretty wild, some pink fizz.

'You know, I think I'm quite looking forward to the Lune-y Scrabblers now,' he said. Mia looked at him. He seemed happier, somehow – more level than in recent times. 'I'm glad I'm going, although I'm still worried we're not going to get the List done by March.'

'Do you know what *I'm* worried about?' said Mia. 'The fact it's December now, there are three inches of snow, and I'm supposed to be swimming naked in the sea at dawn.'

By her own admission, Mia had put off this task for weeks and weeks. If she could have sold it off, she would have done, but the rules of the List were vigorous. No passing up the tasks you pulled out of the bag.

'I'm not one for getting my kit off at the best of times, let alone in bleakest midwinter. But then I suppose,' she nudged in closer to Fraser, 'if you did it, wouldn't your bits shrivel right up?'

Two women in the queue turned around.

'Do you want to say that any louder?' said Fraser. 'Anyway, think yourself lucky, I've still got to sleep with an exotic foreigner.'

There he went again; anyone would think he actually wanted to sleep with Emilia.

'What about Karen?' said Mia. 'Is she foreign in any way? She fosters a dolphin in Florida, or is it adopted?'

Fraser kicked her in the shin. 'Ow! That hurt.'

Seven hours later and Mia was standing before the full-length mirror in her bedroom, trying to be positive. She had gone the full whack at the hairdresser's, having her hair cut, highlighted and blow-dried and – because it was her birthday and there was an offer on – her make-up done. She'd also bought herself a new dress – 'a cocoon-shaped, hound-tooth', apparently to go with a pair of 'bondage' heels that she'd bought in five minutes in Top Shop, several weeks ago, whilst Billy bucked in his buggy, shouting, 'OUT! OUT!' at the top of his lungs. The sales assistant had told her they were 'bang on trend' but, what with the make-up and the hair, a bob blown bouffant-style, because hairdressers seemed incapable of understanding the word 'flat', and her old fake-fur jacket, two words came to mind, and those were Barbara and Cartland.

She hadn't had her hair highlighted since Billy was born, simply because she never had four hours to spare, and, she had to say, the whole thing had been mildly depressing.

'So, doing anything nice for Christmas?' the stylist had asked her, numbly.

'Well, my mum will be coming up from Buckinghamshire,'

she'd said, although she doubted that counted as 'nice'. The thought of cooking Christmas dinner whilst her mother got slowly pissed and flirted with Eduardo filled her with dread. Then came the next question.

'So, what do you do?'

It had become her worst-ever question, right up with, 'So, what does your husband do?'

'Well, I look after my little boy at the moment, but I used to work in films and TV.' Yes, she'd become one of those women – at thirty, not forty, as she was sure it was supposed to be – who talked about what they 'used' to do.

'*Wow, really?*' said the stylist. No other questions as she very, very slowly pasted Mia's hair in bleach and wrapped it up in foil.

Billy was now eighteen months old, and the question of work was beginning to press on her mind. She couldn't go back to films and TV – that would mean moving to London and she couldn't do that, but with Eduardo's measly salary – £350 a week at the most, of which only £30 went to her – she had to do something. Plus, she didn't want to be on the rock and roll forever. She'd never dreamt she'd *ever* be on the dole in her life. The question was, what else could she do? What job was out there that would be worth the childcare?

Right now, the question made her want to open her mouth and pour an entire bottle of white wine down her throat in one go. No, for a little while longer yet, she would put it to the back of her mind. Maybe she would call Fraser to see how it had gone with Billy, but she'd already called Fraser several times this afternoon to see how he was doing with Billy, and they were fine, having a whale of a time – it seemed her services were no longer required. No, she was going to go out and she was going to have FUN. It was her birthday, after all. 'Eduardo?' She got up and called downstairs. 'We should go now or we're going to be late.'

Across town, on the Scotforth Road, Fraser sat on another bus with his brand-new Scrabble board and a Marks & Spencer's bag between his knees. Half an hour ago, he'd dropped Billy off at Melody's. It was the first time he'd been since she and Norm had split up, and he'd tried to act thoroughly normal even though it was thoroughly weird. The house had been so still, so quiet. He'd felt as if he was visiting someone who'd been recently bereaved.

At least they'd had Billy to distract them. Fraser caught his own reflection in the bus window and almost flinched to see himself smiling at the thought of him. Fraser had never thought of himself as a natural with children – they made him a bit nervous and could be very unpredictable, a bit like horses. But even he had to admit that he and Billy got on well and, considering there was a good twenty-eight years between them, they even seemed to laugh at the same things, namely people skidding on the icy streets. Fraser had always been afflicted with a tendency to laugh when he shouldn't and it seemed Billy shared this.

They'd had a great day: After lunch at the Sunbury Café and saying goodbye to Mia (there's a manual with a number you can call in the bottom of the buggy if you get stuck, she'd said. Fraser was ashamed to say, he'd actually looked), they'd walked along the frozen canal,

Fraser throwing stones and Billy watching, transfixed, when they made cracks in the ice.

They'd had a snowball fight – Fraser perhaps at an unfair advantage, but Billy seemed to take the blows like a man, laughing his head off every time Fraser chucked a handful and, when it got dark, they'd popped into the Water Witch, where Fraser had had a pint and Billy a packet of Mini Cheddars.

Fraser had thoroughly enjoyed himself and he'd been surprised how satisfied he'd felt when Billy slept at the right time, or had given him a big grin for no particular reason he could decipher.

They rolled down Scotforth Road and on through the city. Fraser had never seen Lancaster look so still, so beautiful, and it made him nostalgic for student winters, the six of them trying to keep their house warm and themselves in beer. He passed the Greaves Park Hotel, picturing many a hungover Sunday lunch in front of the fire, the snow-covered lawn in front of it glistening in the moonlight. They went around the roundabout, the bus wheezing and bending, and there it was, 5 South Road. Fraser looked inside – probably vacant now that it was Christmas holidays – and, as he did, he saw him and Mia, eating a very small moussaka on a very small table, listening to Phil Collins, everything to play for . . .

And now they were friends and that was fine. Mia Woodhouse and Fraser Morgan were just good friends. Karen was right – what had he been thinking of, calling her up pissed and amorous when she had a baby and a boyfriend? Thank God for Karen. Looking back, Karen had made him see many things, and now he was getting clean and wholesome. He was doing the right thing, and that felt good.

He reckoned a day looking after a baby followed by a game of Scrabble was a good way to start.

In Franco's, 'Lancaster's most romantic restaurant', an intimate, rustic affair, with traditional red-and-white-checked tablecloths, and olive branches hanging from the ceiling, Mia sat alone at a table looking out of the frosted windows onto the white world outside. Eduardo had gone outside for a cigarette for the third time that evening: she didn't know if he was bored, or nervous, or intent on freezing to death; but whatever it was, it was starting to piss Mia off. Their night wasn't exactly going well. Without the TV and a baby to distract them, it seemed they had little to talk about, and their conversation had now turned to polite chitchat, i.e. they had to be polite in front of the other clientele, since chucking tea towels and secretly flashing Vs at one another, like they did at home, might just be plain rude in a restaurant. They'd covered the food, the ambience, and even had a discussion about how nice the cutlery was, but Mia knew there was something hanging in the air.

Eduardo came back, bringing with him a gust of icy air and the whiff of fags. He sat down, cleared his throat, pressed his palms together, placing his fingers on his lips: 'So,' he said, 'I've got something to tell you.'

'I just want to go for a walk,' Mia said outside the restaurant, her breathing still shaky. 'I just want to be on my own for a while.' It sounded dramatic, the sort of thing they said in TV dramas, but she meant it. Plus, if she had to look at him for five more seconds, she might punch him, then leave him for dead in the snow.

She couldn't believe it. She COULD NOT BELIEVE IT. Was it possible for anyone to be more selfish?

'I can't do it any more,' he'd said. 'I can't wait tables any more. It's crushing my soul!' God, she'd wanted to hurl her penne al forno over the table. 'I need to develop myself as an artist. I have a creative soul, Mia, I can't just deny that. I want to go back and do an MA. I want to do Fine Art.'

Right, and what did he think she'd been doing for the past two years if it wasn't putting a lid on her creative soul and looking after their baby? She adored Billy, but didn't he think she rather fancied going back to uni? Doing an art course? Any course? Something that might give Mia her identity back?

Also, now he had not just given his notice in at Bella Italia, but walked out in a hot-headed, self-important strop, what the fuck did he expect them to live on? Thin air? She already had barely enough money for a pint of milk at the end of the week, when all the friends she'd left at Primal Films were spending a tenner on a latte and a Pret A Manger sandwich every day, without even thinking about it. She tried not to be bitter, but sometimes when she was looking down the back of the sofa for 20p it was hard.

'But think about the long term,' Eduardo had said. 'Think about when I get a better job with more prospects.'

She'd cried tears of frustration, right there and then at the table, then slapped down her napkin and walked out herself. God, they were such a cliché.

And now she was standing outside the restaurant,

freezing and mascara-streaked, a week before Christmas and about to go for a walk on her own. Another bloody cliché.

Eduardo had nodded solemnly. 'OK,' he'd said, 'if that's what you want.' No fight, she'd noticed. No, 'But my darling girlfriend, you can't wander the streets alone at night.' That's because, she knew as she watched him walk away and reach inside the pocket of his coat, he couldn't wait to call his mates, find out where they were, and stay out getting smashed till the sun came up.

Well, sod him. She didn't care. The thought of going home with him filled her with dread. Billy wasn't even there, his room would be empty, and it struck her that a home without her baby didn't feel like a home at all. That the thought of just those two being there in the morning made her feel horribly anxious, and that couldn't be right.

So, she wandered the snow-covered streets for a while, not really knowing what to do with herself. Today, Friday the nineteenth, was the day many people had finished work for Christmas, and she suddenly found herself in the midst of festive-season anarchy. The all-day drinkers in their Santa hats, careering across the road, people snogging in public. There was a man sitting on the steps of the library in Market Square being sick between his knees.

Merry Christmas . . .

She walked past the John O'Gaunt pub, one of Lancaster's best live music venues, warm and fairy-lit tonight and, as she did, she thought she could hear the opening riffs of 'Stella', one of the Fans' best songs, Fraser's voice, soulful and breaking. Norm on the drums and all four girls: her, Liv, Melody and Anna, knowing every lyric of every song. So proud.

She fast-forwarded to now: a death, a divorce – how differently would life be lived if we knew what lay in store for us, she wondered? Impossible to live at all, presumably, and, anyway, if she thought about it too much, she knew she'd weep.

Just then, a group of girls wearing reindeer hats and a lot of sequins piled out of the pub.

'Merry Crimbo, love!' one shouted at her, in a thick Lancastrian accent. 'Why you on yer own? Come and 'ave a drink wi' us!'

Paralytic with a group of strangers: for an alarming second, this sounded like the best idea in the world. Then, Mia came to her senses. 'Thanks, but no, but have one for me! And Merry Christmas to you too!' she shouted.

Merry Christmas to you.

She walked to Dalton Square, where she sat on a bench till her bum went numb. She pulled her fur jacket tighter and leant back her head. The sky was still snow-filled; it reminded her of the colour of damson skins and, through the silhouettes of the stark, bare trees, the clock face of the town hall glowed, ghostly and yellow, like the moon. From one of the surrounding pubs, she heard Slade announce, 'It's Christmaaaaaassss!'

She felt a sudden pang for Billy, to kiss his sleep-smelling face, squished against his pillow. For a second, she thought of going over to Melody's and doing just that, but stopped herself just in time. Melody had been through enough recently; she was taking the divorce very hard. The last thing she'd want would be Mia turning up, an emotional wreck on her doorstep. Plus, if she really thought about it,

Billy was the last person she wanted to see, just thinking of him, so sweet in his pyjamas, made her stomach churn with guilt, because what if she couldn't give him what she'd always wanted for him?

Just a mum and a dad in the same house – everything she'd never had; a feeling of belonging and security? She'd tried, she really had but she had pretty much come to the conclusion tonight, that she just couldn't do it anymore, even if – as her mum kept telling her – it was easier, more practical. It wasn't in her heart. She knew now, she was never going to fall in love with Eduardo, perhaps, amongst many other factors, because she was already in love with somebody else.

It was bloody Christmas, too. Weren't people supposed to be with those they loved – at least *liked* – at Christmas? She looked at the clock: 9.10 p.m. – it was still early. She had an idea, and before she talked herself out of it, she picked up her coat and started walking.

TWENTY-ONE

Jean Harp's home, a neat council house, tucked into a cul-de-sac on the outskirts of town, was not hard to find since it had a flashing Santa sleigh in the front garden, three illuminated snowmen leading up the garden path and, just in case you were still having trouble locating it, a giant inflatable Santa Claus yelling, 'Over here!' from the chimney.

Mia stood in front of it, blinded by the flashing lights, feeling as if she should put her hands up in surrender. It occurred to her that this feeling was quite fitting, that as she swept the inch of snow from the top of Jean Harp's garden gate and undid the latch, that the game – whatever the hell that was – was indeed up.

The air rang with the cold and it was snowing so hard that it was difficult to see more than a few metres in front of her. Mia pulled her coat tighter around her and started up the path. It had come to her attention, some time ago in town, when her efforts to catch a bus had failed and she'd begun the twenty-minute hike up to the

Bowerham estate, that the bondage heels, even with thick tights, were not the most sensible footwear choice for blizzard conditions. Her toes were sodden, two packs of ice.

She stepped, knees up like a flamingo, making deep imprints in the fresh snow.

It was a traditional, pebble-dashed, square-fronted house, the sort of house a child might draw, with a red front door and four windows, glowing with inviting light. Mia's insides jittered with nerves. Was this a terrible idea? To turn up in the midst of Fraser's task? Maybe he'd be in the middle of monk-like silence and concentration?

Shielding her eyes from the dancing Christmas lights that emanated from inside, she peered into one of the bottom windows. The glass was decorated with stencils of snowflakes and Mia pressed her nose up against the gap between them, a smile spreading across her face. The sly devils: this wasn't a staid Scrabble tournament; this was a bloody Christmas party!

In Mrs Harp's downstairs, two rooms knocked through with an arch in the middle from which reams of paper chains hung, the furniture had been pushed to the side and two large tables had been set up; round each, four players sat huddled over a Scrabble board.

Everyone was wearing party hats, each table glowed with candlelight, festive tipples glimmered in cut glass and there was music, muffled, but *surely* not . . . Mia cupped her ear and moved in closer to confirm that, yes, indeed, a group of OAPs were nodding their heads, tapping their feet to Beyoncé.

'If you liked it, then you shoulda put a ring on it . . .

If you liked it, then you shoulda put a ring on it. Uh-uh-oh . . .'

Then she spied a woman – could this be the legendary Jean Harp? With grey spiky hair and gigantic bauble earrings, she was shimmying between the tables, a tray of drinks in her hand.

There was the sound of laughter, of festivity, and Mia had to turn away so she could have a snigger to herself.

Turning back, she scanned the room for Fraser, but there was a huge Christmas tree in the corner and, through the snow and the kaleidoscope of bauble lights, she could only make out a sea of silver-haired, party-hatted heads. She shielded her eyes with her hands and there, sitting below the Christmas tree, was Mrs D. Oh, my days, thought Mia. Would you just *look* at her.

She was wearing a Santa hat, cock-eyed on her head, and what looked like elf slippers on her feet. Actually, now she looked carefully, all of them were wearing elf slippers on their feet. Never mind a Scrabble tournament, this was some sort of elf convention. Mrs D's cheeks were flushed with alcohol, or happiness, or both, her eyes animated, as she leant in and whispered something to the woman next to her. The woman turned, her mouth an O, and then she was laughing, bent over, and Mrs D was laughing too, and Mia realized in that moment that all this time she had thought Mrs Durham was a morbid, miserable old bat, when really all she'd ever needed were some friends.

Mrs Durham had her hands pressed together at her lips now, staring at the Scrabble board, as if in antici-pation of something; in fact the whole room seemed to be arrested in anticipation. Nobody moved, everybody stared at the boards. The decorations hanging from the arch in the centre of the room seemed to flutter like tumbleweed.

Then suddenly, there was a muffled cheer, a man shot up from his chair, throwing his arms in the air. Everyone was clapping. The man was jumping up and down now, and as he turned around, his mouth open, grinning and pumping his arms up and down, Mia caught his eye and realized it was Fraser.

His eyes and mouth grew wider.

'Mia?'

Two seconds later, he had flung the front door open, his face obscured by the swirling snow. 'What the hell are you doing here? I just did it! I just used up all my seven letters in one go.'

'I know.' He looked so *chuffed*, so easily pleased, like a boy on Christmas Day, so different from the man she'd just left at a restaurant, that Mia wanted to kiss the living daylights out of him right there and then.

'You do?'

'I just saw you through the window. You're so clever. How bloody clever are you?'

He paused, grinning at her. He seemed to be searching her face.

'*Come in.* It's fucking freezing out there. Did you walk here? Are you all right?'

'I've probably got frostbite and shall have to have my feet amputated but, apart from that, I think I'm OK,' she said, hobbling somewhat dramatically to prove her point.

Mia stepped into the warmth of the hallway. The scent of Christmas flooded her nostrils: orange peel and cinnamon and sherry and happiness.

He was smiling at her intently, but then the smile suddenly fell from his face.

'Oh, God,' he said. 'Birthday dinner. Not good?'

Mia smiled so she wouldn't cry. Then she made two big steps towards him and threw her arms around his neck.

'I don't want to talk about it tonight,' she whispered in his ear. 'I just want to come in and play. Can I?'

'Course,' he said, somewhat bemused, as she lay her head on his chest, felt the warmth of his body. 'Course you can.'

'Also, I'm just wondering . . .' Mia looked up at him. 'Beyoncé? *Really?*'

Fraser clicked his tongue. 'My iPod shuffle,' he said. 'It's my party mix, they can't get enough of it.'

'Mary, is that you? I *thought* it was you.' Just then, Mrs Durham appeared in the hallway, wearing the Santa hat and a violent-green jumper with a snowflake on. They sprang apart. 'My dear Mary,' she said, shuffling towards her with open arms and a brandy in one hand.

They hugged. She smelt of mince pies and booze. 'Well, Mrs D –' Mia did her best to conceal the wobble in her voice – 'so this is what you get up to at your Scrabble nights. And there was me, thinking it was all fuddy-duddies with their heads in a dictionary.'

Mrs Durham chuckled, naughtily. 'I've knocked myself out, dear,' she said. Mia doubted she was ever quite going to get the hang of how to use that phrase. 'I'm knocking myself out with this Scrabble, you know. And this man –' she hobbled forward in her elf slippers and got hold of Fraser's cheeks – 'is a born Scrabbler.'

'She plays a mean game,' said Fraser. 'Whooped my ass.

Thrashed me in the first two games. Sixty-three points on a treble word score. End-game word of twenty-one.'

'Ah, but this one got seven letters in one go and it's only his first time,' said Mrs Durham, eyes alight.

Treble word score, seven letters, end-game? Mia felt as though she'd walked into a cult, a particularly jolly cult.

'So what was the word?' said Mia.

Fraser beckoned her inside. 'You'll laugh at this,' he said. 'Should bring back memories.'

Mia followed Fraser and Mrs Durham inside. Beyoncé had turned into Bruce Springsteen, 'Dancing in the Dark', and the woman with the grey spiky hair was refilling everyone's glasses.

Mrs Durham took Mia by the hand. 'Mary,' and she put Mia's hand into the woman with spiky hair's soft one, 'I want you to meet my very good friend Jane Harp. Jane, this is my very good friend Mary.'

'Mia,' corrected Mia.

Jean leant in. 'Jeane It's OK, she's always calling me Jane.'

Jean had shrewd brown eyes and an elegant Roman nose. Mia guessed she'd have cut a striking figure in her day. In her bright red woollen dress, quite risqué and figure-hugging for an OAP, she still did.

'Now, will you have a tipple, Mary?' and she winked and filled Mia's glass up without her answering.

'And you MUST slip into something more comfortable. Please,' and she gestured to Mia's shoes. 'You look absolutely perished. Here, put on some elf slippers, they are compulsory.'

She took a pair from the collection under the tree and handed them to Mia.

'One size, one quid each from Poundstretcher – aren't

they wonderful?' She chuckled, as Mia sunk her freezing cold feet into their furry warmth.

'Oh, God,' she said. 'They are just heavenly.'

She and Fraser looked at each other, then at their feet and started sniggering. 'You think that's funny, come and look at my seven-letter word.'

And then he took her by the hand and took her to his table.

He pointed at the Scrabble board.

M.O.U.S.S.A.K.A, it said, right across the centre.

'Technically, eight of course, but the "M" was already there.'

Mia slapped a hand to her mouth. 'Ah, the mini moussaka,' she said, shaking her head. 'Happy days,' and then she raised an eyebrow at Fraser.

'You've never forgotten, have you?' he said.

'Never forgotten? Never forgiven, more like.'

'Forty-two points, too. Triple word score. Forget Eureka, darlin', said Fraser. 'This was my Moussaka Moment. I've coined a new phrase!'

Despite her protests, Mia was cajoled into a game of Scrabble. She was terrified as on her table, as well as Fraser and Mrs Durham, were Olwen ('Holder of the highest-scoring word 1983 and 1984, Glamorgan Scrabble Championships,' she informed her; and 'Jukebox on a treble word score, then bettered it by one point with Squeezy the following year'), and Reg, whose Scrabble board it was.

'It's revolving,' he said, showing Mia how it did, indeed, revolve. 'Deluxe,' he added, savouring the word in his mouth. 'Just like my wife, Joyce. Died four years ago last

March, in my arms.' His eyes filled with tears. 'She was a veteran of this club; we used to come together every week. She may have just been Joyce to the rest of them, but to me, she was perfect in every way.'

Mia found herself holding Reg's hand.

The music was turned down for maximum concentration. Mia looked over at Fraser and narrowed her eyes, jokingly, as they all pulled their seven tiles each from the bag. Then they pulled out the 'decider', the tile to decide who goes first. Since Mia got a 'C', the closest letter to an 'A', it was her.

She didn't do too badly with GEEKS, then Reg played a corker with KIKOI (using the 'K' of GEEKS and a blank tile – genius), which Mia had never heard of, but which was apparently some sort of African cloth – one of those sacred words only hardcore Scrabblers knew. Fraser got twenty-two points for ZITS – there was a sharp intake of breath and some leafing through the *Official Players' Dictionary*. Mia couldn't believe how seriously everyone was taking it. This was word war.

The break brought mince pies, more sherry and, because it was Christmas, some dancing. 'Wouldn't be Christmas without dancing,' said Olwen.

Mrs Harp turned off Fraser's iPod, pulled out an ancient-looking 1980s ghetto blaster, took forever to rewind a tape, then led whoever was capable in a round of line dancing, them all dozy-doeing and side-stepping into each other, until they all collapsed with laughter on the various sofas and poufs.

Then it was Fraser's turn: encouraged by the audience (Mia suspected that the old ladies had taken quite a shine to Fraser and he was *lapping* it up) and an old

376

ballroom-dancing tape that Mrs Harp rooted out, Fraser handed his glass of Bristol Cream sherry to Mrs Durham, took Mia by the hand and, despite her cries of, 'No! I'll fall over my own feet!', took her into the middle of the dance floor – well, a six-by-six-foot rug – and led her around it, masterfully, a salsa-dancing pro.

Mia couldn't believe it.

'Bloody hell, when the hell did you learn to do that?' she said, still reeling, the music still playing, as he kissed her gently on the cheek and took another partner to the floor.

'Salsa lessons, baby,' he said, licking his finger and holding it up to the air. Calvin taught me all I know.'

Mia could only stand and stare, she was so amazed. And this was the same man who, at Melody and Norm's wedding, cleared the floor of all self-conscious teenagers, none of whom wanted to be associated with his *break-dancing*?

Mia stood at the edge of the room and clapped as cardigans came off, glasses were removed, and Fraser took one dance partner after another, the ladies shrieking with delight.

'So what's a lovely young lady like you doing without her husband with her?' one lady called over to Mia from the sidelines. 'And no children to look after? When I was your age, I had three children, one attached to each nipple!' she said, and they all roared with laughter.

'We've a few good years in us yet,' she heard Mrs Durham saying to Olwen. 'We can still make like Ginger Rogers when we want. Try and stop us,' and she threw her arms in the air to prove her point.

Mia looked around her. If anyone had ever told her

that on her twenty-ninth birthday, she'd be dancing the salsa in some OAP's front room in a pair of elf slippers, and not only that but having the time of her life, she'd never have believed them. But you can't choose the good times, she thought. The trick is just to take them when they come. She only had to look at Mrs Durham to realize that. Only weeks ago, she'd been miserable, ready for the grave, but given half the chance to be happy, she'd taken it by the horns.

Maybe she should do the same?

They went back to finish the game. Reg played first, then Olwen, then Fraser with REJOIN, which was total, jammy genius and got him twenty-four points. Then it was Mia's turn – she had some shocking letters, all 'N's and 'R's, which she had no idea what to do with.

But one word stood out for her. It wasn't a big earner but it was perfect.

She looked at Fraser over her tiles.

'I think I'm just about to have my Moussaka Moment,' she said. Then very slowly, one by one, she laid out three letters under the 'O' of Fraser's REJOIN.

O.V.E.R. it said.

Fraser's eyes grew wide.

'Is that a definite?' he said.

'Yes,' she said. 'I'm definitely going with that.'

Eventually, at past midnight, the last stragglers of the party left and it was just Mia, Mrs Durham and Fraser waiting for the cab to arrive. Mrs Durham was still chatting to Jean, inside. Something about Eunice Perkins – 'She had a Scrabble board with *pink* tiles? Well I never . . .'

Fraser and Mia stood in the porch, shivering, next to

one another. In front of them, the snow continued to fall in thick, silent flakes onto Mrs Harp's lawn.

Fraser spoke first.

'I had a really brilliant night tonight.'

'Me too,' said Mia. 'Rescued my birthday! Thanks for letting me crash your first Scrabblers' party.'

'The pleasure's all mine,' said Fraser. 'Those Scrabblers are wild.'

'Lethal,' said Mia. 'Jean Harp must have had five large brandys.'

Fraser smirked, there was a long pause, just the hum of the night air and, somewhere on the street, the banging of a car door, giggly goodbyes. Revellers making their way home after a friend's festive knees up. Mia was aware it was Christmas next week: Fraser would be going to Bury, she would be staying here; then it would be New Year, January; there were no more fixed plans.

'So when will I see you next?' she said, nudging him casually. 'Are you coming up for New Year's Eve? I may get a pass out. You never know your luck.'

He looked at her, thinking how lovely she looked when she was cold: bright-eyed, flushed-cheeked.

'I'm not sure,' he said, and he hesitated . . . 'But I've got my hot date with Emilia on the third, so mustn't forget that.'

Mia felt her stomach dissolve. 'No, that's for the List,' she said. 'Mustn't forget that.'

Then she looked the other way down the street, pretending to look for the taxi, so he couldn't see her eyes fill with tears.

TWENTY-TWO

January 2009
Lancaster

1. Sleep with an exotic foreigner – (in an ideal world, Javier Bardem). Night of heady, all-consuming passion: getting lost, snogging amongst lemon groves and being drunk on something thick and hugely alcoholic that I can't pronounce. (*Do this without becoming completely neurotic about what it's supposed to 'mean'.)

Wearing just a towel, Fraser paced Melody's palatial spare room reading Number One on Liv's List over and over again.

He should concentrate on the last bit, he told himself. 'Do this without becoming completely neurotic about what it's supposed to mean.'

And it didn't mean anything, did it? It was just a drink with an attractive girl. And Emilia was attractive. *Stupidly* attractive. He'd seen that when he met her first time around, playing rounders in what were basically her knickers, and then again four days ago on New Year's Eve when she'd cornered him in Mia's kitchen: 'So, I hear you're a free man now, Fraser? Does that mean I get a New Year's Eve kiss?' He'd backed against the sink as she'd pawed his chest, and said something about having a cold sore.

He shook his head at the memory and thought of the conversation he'd had with Norm that morning.

'Right, so you've got a date with the hottest girl I've ever seen in my life, and you don't even seem to want to go. You need help, dude. You need serious help.'

Although Fraser suspected he was coming to the end of it, Norm was still in Renaissance Man mode, and all opportunities for sex had to be grabbed with both hands, as it were.

Of course, Emilia didn't know about the List, but then she didn't need to, since she was the one who'd engineered the date (at least that wasn't on his conscience, this wasn't another salsa class scenario that came with guaranteed tears. He doubted Emilia was the crying sort. She'd probably never shed a tear in her life.)

OK, Mia didn't exactly discourage her (come to think of it, *why* hadn't she discouraged her?) But she certainly hadn't been 'set up' – Emilia was well up for it, anyone could see that.

But all this had started back in August and circumstances had changed drastically since then. Fraser was actually single now, for a start, which made the whole situation significantly more complicated. After all, the attentions of an Amazonian superbabe were one thing. The actual potential for sex, for them eating you alive, was quite another. Also, Mia was now single, which had really thrown an unexpected spanner in the works. He couldn't help feeling this was a betrayal – and he didn't want and didn't need to feel this was a betrayal. Also, who was he betraying? Mia? Himself? Liv? Fuck, he had absolutely no idea any more.

He picked up the shirt he was going to wear – an olive-green one from French Connection that Karen had bought him. Very nice, too – one of the few purchases she'd made that hadn't been sent back. He laid it on the ironing board and wondered what Karen would say if she could see him now? He thought back to that night back in November, when she'd stood in her street and given him the sagest piece of advice she'd ever given him: 'Don't mess her about, OK? You did it to me, don't do it to her . . . Sort yourself out first.'

And now look at him, about to go on a date with a twenty-three-year-old Brazilian, a virtual stranger. He doubted that was really what Karen had had in mind, when she'd told him to 'sort himself out'.

But then this was a TASK and he couldn't help it if it was him who pulled *Sleep with an exotic foreigner* out of the hat, could he? The Rules were the Rules. They'd all gone round to Mia's flat on New Year's Eve (everyone but Norm that was, who had gone skiing with some 'new mates' from the *Metro*) and made a pact – 'renewed their vows', for want of a better phrase; clearly they were all pissed and emotional and missing Liv like crazy because it was New Year's Eve – that they would carry on with the List, come hell or high water.

It was January now, only two months to what would have been Liv's thirtieth birthday, and they owed it to her to at least try to finish what they'd started; even if, as far as Fraser was concerned, they weren't really sure why they were doing it any more.

He picked up his wallet from the side and took out the photo of Liv. He smiled at it: Liv in her kinky little maid outfit winked back at him:

This is all your doing, you know. You and your secret sexual fantasies with Javier bloody whatsisface.

Bastard.

You kept that one quiet, didn't you?

So now he was forced, entirely against his will, to have a night of snogging and full-on passion with an exotic foreigner. He put back the photo and sprayed himself liberally with aftershave, wondering – in the absence of lemon groves, in Lancaster, in January – what the equivalent might be: getting lost at the back of Brook's Nightclub and snogging amongst empty glasses? He shuddered at the thought.

No, he must take this like a man, a true, red-blooded man. He turned up the radio while Katy Perry sang, 'I kissed a girl and I liked it . . .' And he would like it too. He would fucking well like it if it killed him. It wasn't every day a man had an opportunity like this. He stood in front of Melody's mirror, dropped his towel and considered his manly form. He wasn't bad, naked. Good legs, could do with a bit more definition up top, but it was only 3 January, plenty of time for health resolutions yet, and there were no nasty surprises – no hairy back, pot belly, inverted nipples, that sort of thing. No, he was nothing ground-breaking, but he was a man at home in his own skin. As Katy Perry sang on, Fraser cracked open a beer and got a bit carried away. He flexed his biceps, turned at his waist, this way and that.

'Oh, yeah, Gun show of the Gods,' he said out loud. It was a jokey thing he and Norm used to say when they were kids, sixteen-year-olds about to hit Mad-chester.

Then he heard Melody shout, 'Fraser, any danger?' and nearly jumped out of his skin.

He heard her thumping up the stairs and picked up his towel, but not fast enough to avoid her flinging the door open mid-bend-down, which can't have been pretty.

'Oh, for fuck's sake, Fraser!'

She slapped her hand across her eyes and slammed the door shut again.

'Sorry. There's no lock on the door.'

'Well, that's because I don't really expect you to be parading around, butt-naked, or to walk in on you with your arse in the air!'

Fraser put his towel on and opened the door. They were both smirking.

'Well, this is like old times, isn't it, Fraser Morgan?' she said, wielding a bottle of Baileys. 'This is back to 5 South Road days. Us getting ready to go out, you going on a hot date with another lady, me walking in on you naked. You were *always* naked. Jesus, I must have seen your bits as much as Liv did.'

Fraser grinned and felt a rush of affection for his old mate, Melody Burgess, and her mothering, nagging ways. The divorce was going through and she seemed more sane. The house was on the market, she was going to buy herself a 'fuck-off bachelorette pad and a new soft-top Beetle', apparently. Credit to her and Norm, they'd sorted everything out amicably and she was feeling sociable again, and was about to go out tonight with the girls, like old times.

He got her in a headlock.

'Come here, me old mucker,' he said. 'I love you, Burgess, I proper do.'

Melody wriggled.

'Ow, get off, you freak. And you've got far too much aftershave on. Honestly, did you jump in the bottle?'

He let her go, she sighed, smoothed down her hair and held the bottle of Baileys out.

'Now, left over from Christmas,' she said. 'Bit of Dutch courage?'

It wasn't hard to pronounce but it was thick and it was very alcoholic and, right now, he needed all the help he could get.

The first week of January, and Lancaster was a graveyard, the only people out being those with unfortunate birthdays or, in Mia's case, selfish exes who refused to even entertain the idea of giving up their New Year's Eve, and instead offered the brilliant alternative of 3 January.

Christmas had been surprisingly OK. Eduardo had moved out into a flat-share and the only emotion Mia felt was relief. It was as though they'd spent two years dragging out the remnants of a relationship that had never got off the ground in the first place.

He wouldn't be able to have Billy overnight, but he would have him every Sunday, and whenever else he wanted, as long as Mia had some notice. He'd come over for Christmas dinner, too, which Mia was glad of, since it made it less intense with her mum and, miraculously, perhaps now that they weren't together any more and he was 'observing boundaries', he'd even refrained from flirting with Lynette.

Sadly, the snow had not lasted till Christmas; now it was just freezing and wet and, as Mia stood at the bar in the Merchants, looking at the decorations that seemed to be hanging on till the bitter end, she tried desperately to fight it, but she could feel her mood descend. She felt on edge. Drink more. That was the answer.

She leant across the bar. 'Actually, can I have three tequilas with that?' she asked the barman on a whim.

The barman raised his eyebrows. 'No January detoxing for you then, I see?'

'Lord, no,' said Mia. 'January detoxes are the work of the devil, to be eyed with nothing but suspicion and loathing.'

The barman laughed. 'My kind of client.' He nodded, impressed, putting the drinks on a tray with salt and lemon.

Mia carried them back to her table where Melody and Anna waited, their faces aghast.

'Good work,' said Melody, rubbing her hands together as Mia plonked the drinks on the table. 'I like your style.'

Anna was not so enthusiastic.

'No. Bloody. Way. I'm meant to be detoxing, it's January.'

Mia rolled her eyes, downed her drink and then Anna's, trying very hard not to visibly wince.

'Happy?' she said. Anna and Melody looked at one another, incredulous. 'All sorted. That was easy.'

She sat down. Behave yourself, she told herself, just behave yourself, Mia, and grow up. It's just, try as she might, she couldn't get them out of her mind. Where were they now? Were they having fun? Were they snogging?

Every time she thought of them, all she could picture was Emilia fixing Fraser with her hypnotic green eyes. And it didn't take much to hypnotize Fraser. Let's face it, a dumpy, dolphin-obsessed, forty-something had done the trick, she was pretty sure a six-foot Brazilian would manage it.

And she'd half engineered this – was she actually insane? She was beginning to bitterly regret that she'd ever introduced them in the first place, that she'd ever invited Fraser to that fated picnic in the park where Emilia gadded about practically naked.

After all, there was a perfectly nice, very exotic, perfectly rotund Hungarian who lived two flats up. This could have been all so different.

'So, what did Fraser wear in the end?' she asked Melody, very casually, she thought, as she sipped on her wine chaser. They'd already been for a Chinese, a rather depressing start to the evening, since nobody could afford it (Anna had insisted, as she had to complete her 'Learn to use chopsticks' task), and there'd been someone celebrating their birthday in there, which made Mia really sad, when, after they'd sung 'Happy Birthday', they'd all buggered off before 9 p.m. Skint, out-partied. She vowed never to get pregnant in May.

She'd done very well to manage not to ask any questions at all about Fraser and Emilia whilst she was there, but now she could no longer hold out.

'Oh, it was hilarious,' said Melody. 'He was in the spare room getting ready and I walked in on him, butt-naked . . .'

Anna grimaced. 'I bet that was nice for you.'

'He was checking himself out in the mirror, the little

poser. He must have been because he was standing right in front of it!'

Checking himself out in the mirror, eh? Why did he feel the need to check himself out in the mirror?

Anna and Melody were laughing. Mia was too, but only on her face.

'So, um, what did he wear in the end?' she tried again. Both of them looked at her and she suddenly felt self-conscious. 'You know, when he *finally* stopped parading around and actually put some clothes on?'

Melody frowned, looking slightly baffled. Mia shifted in her seat.

'Um, he was wearing that olive-green shirt and a nice coat, the one he got for Christmas,' she said eventually. 'He looked hot, actually. If I didn't know him better, I could have rather fancied him myself.'

This was torture, thought Mia, absolute torture. The olive-green shirt. Why the olive-green shirt?! He looked gorgeous in the bloody olive-green shirt!

'Where were they going? Do you know?' she asked. She was pissed now, shameless, these questions were just toppling out of her mouth.

'The Borough, I think.' Melody shrugged. 'God knows, I didn't really quiz him. Too busy recovering from seeing his bare arse.'

Melody and Anna carried on laughing and drinking. Mia could hear the two of them talking but didn't seem to be able to contribute to the conversation, her mind constantly assaulted by images of what he might be up to. In the past month, her feelings for Fraser had become more urgent, much harder to conceal, and the thing was, she didn't want to conceal them any more. Yesterday, she'd been to see Mrs Durham, and Mrs D had said, quite matter-of-factly as she'd poured the tea:

'So how long have you been in love with Fraser? I have to say, he's much better than that awful foreign one you had.'

She'd spent so many months battling with her feelings, actually trying to extinguish them, and she was knackered! Exhausted! It was out of her control. It had been manageable, just, when he was seeing Karen, but only because Karen was no real threat; but now, knowing he was going to be out with Emilia, almost certainly going to have sex with a gorgeous young woman, and more than that, possibly enjoy it? It had given rise to feelings of jealousy, debilitating jealousy that she had never known in her life, that she never even knew she was capable of. These were bad enough on their own. The fact she didn't seem to be allowed to have them made it even worse.

Melody had gone to the toilet, so now it was just Mia and Anna. Mia could feel Anna's eyes boring into her. She looked away just as Anna gave an exaggerated sigh.

'So, Mia,' she said. Her voice was cold; it was freaking Mia out. 'What's going on? Because anyone would think you were actually jealous of Fraser and Emilia going on a date. You seem to be asking a lot of questions.'

Mia shifted uneasily on her chair.

'I'm just interested,' she said. 'She is my Portuguese teacher, I do sort of have a vested interest.'

Anna gave a little snort.

Mia became alarmingly aware of the fact that she was very drunk, Anna was not, and of the potential for trouble that this spelt.

Anna leant forward, so close that Mia could feel her breath on her face. Her eyes looked enormous in her tiny little face. She looked like a mad, fragile bird. Mia didn't know if she was going to cry or hit her.

'You're in love with him, aren't you?' she said. 'You're in love with Fraser.'

Christ, she had some nerve, confronting her like this.

'I'm not in *love* with Fraser,' said Mia but, even as the words left her mouth, she was aware of how unconvincing she sounded. 'What on earth are you talking about?'

Anna blew air out through her lips. 'I think the least you can do is be honest,' she said. 'Don't you think you owe it to Liv to be honest, Mia?' Anna's lip had started to tremble now.

Didn't Liv already know? thought Mia.

Mia could feel hot tears threatening. She fought furiously to stop them. A million different emotions seemed to collide in her head – overwhelming sadness, regret: how could she and Anna have come to this? How could losing their best friend have opened an ocean between them? Not brought them closer?

And then, literally in a second, these feelings cleared to reveal startling clarity.

It didn't matter what anyone said or thought. She loved him. She could not help herself. She loved him with every molecule in her body. If anything was to come of this night with Emilia, she would never forgive herself.

Melody came back from the toilet.

'Right, so, shall we get another round in?' she said, brightly. 'One more tequila?'

Mia slowly shook her head.

391

'Actually, no, I think I'll go home,' she said, knowing perfectly well she was about to do nothing of the sort.

Deep down, in some tiny corner of her still-sober consciousness, she knew what she was about to do was a bad idea. In most of her drink-fuelled one, however, this was the best idea she'd ever had in her life. But first, she needed to do something else.

In a candlelit corner of the Borough pub, Emilia leant over the table and stared into Fraser's eyes. 'Do you know what, Fraser?' she said, rolling the *r* of Fraser, which terrified him slighty. 'I think you have something dark about you, something mysterious.'

'Really?' he said. Actually, he just felt stuffed and exhausted. Exhausted from all this intensity, and stuffed after a Portuguese meal of meat, and more meat. He'd never seen a girl eat so much meat.

Emilia gathered her hair and cocked her head to the side. 'Yes,' she purred, 'I think you're fascinating, actually.'

Under the table, he swore he could feel Emilia's foot circle his.

Fraser flinched slightly. He was aware that the more intimate Emilia's body language was becoming, the more closed his got. Christ, he was sitting with his arms, legs and feet crossed now, and she still found some naked part of him to rub her foot up against. The woman was a fiend.

She sighed deeply, taking a sip of her wine.

'I also think you have a lot of potential,' she said, and she tapped her head. 'In here. I think you have a LOT of potential.'

'Thank you,' said Fraser, whilst inwardly crying for help.

They'd been on a date for almost three hours now; during that time, Fraser had deduced that Emilia didn't really have much in the way of conversation. He'd tried to talk to her about Brazil, about what she thought of England, but she always brought it back to these strange, intense statements that Fraser had no idea how to respond to. He felt like a specimen in an art gallery or museum.

He looked at her now, her eyes positively smouldering in the low light. There was no mistaking she was a beautiful woman. Long, honey-coloured hair, the most incredible green eyes he'd ever seen. Gravity-defying breasts that, when she leant forward, he could see were held in a leather bra, which perturbed him a little, it had to be said.

She was a stunner, there was no mistaking it. But she initiated no desire whatsoever in him. He just did not fancy her. In fact, he had no desire to go to bed with her – he didn't even want to kiss her.

All he could think of, when he looked at her minute, hard waist, was Mia's soft one, the way it rolled – just ever so slightly – over her jeans. When he looked at her red-painted mouth, he could only think of Mia's mouth, wide and full, which always looked so kissable, as if she put strawberries and cream on it – or something like that, anyway – not bright red war paint.

Every time Emilia got up to go to the bar, he looked at her endless, slim, Amazonian legs and only craved Mia's sweet, slightly full ones, with their cyclists' thighs (her description, not his).

He thought back to how beautiful she'd looked when she'd turned up at the Scrabble night. How glamorous. Even though she said she looked like Barbara Cartland.

It was no good, his heart just wasn't in this – it felt like a betrayal, which was inconvenient but there it was. And yet, the more the evening went on, the more obvious it was becoming that Emilia was up for it. Not just up for it, but that this was the reason she'd come. Why else would you wear a leather bra, for crying out loud?

The question was, how was he going to get out of this? He knew right now, he couldn't go through with it.

'Shall we go to another bar?' he said, hoping for somewhere noisier. 'Or maybe dancing? Do you like dancing?'

She reached out, caressing the side of his face, and curled her foot around his again. 'Shall we just go back to your friend's place?' she said, through her canopied eyelashes.

Fraser's throat seemed to constrict a little.

'Right,' he said, 'sure.'

Mia sat in the back of a taxi, feeling powerful and almost possessed. She was utterly resolute that this was the right thing to do. This didn't happen very often – utter confidence in her decisions – and she was revelling in the feeling, the sheer novelty factor, spurring her on.

This is what they did in novels and films, wasn't it? Mad dashes to airports to stop the objects of their desire in their foolish tracks? Except she wasn't going to the airport, she was going to a pub, drunk, probably mad, and before that she had somewhere else to go, something else she had to do.

'Will you wait for me?' said Mia as they rolled up outside Williamson's Park. 'I just need to do something, I won't be long.'

The taxi driver nodded, reluctantly. 'Cost yer,' he said. 'I don't sit here for nothing, you know.'

Mia got out of the taxi and ran towards the gates. They were locked – of course, it was 9 p.m. – she'd have to climb over. So she chucked her bag over, hitched her skirt up, prayed that this little decision of hers wouldn't leave her impaled on a fence, because that would teach her to take control of her life, and jumped.

It was a bigger drop than she'd envisaged, and she landed painfully on her ankle. 'Fuck ow!' her voice echoed in the empty park. And then she was half limping, half jogging in the cool, dark stillness, the only sound, the wind rushing through the trees.

She arrived at the bench panting, and wasted no time.

'Liv it's me!' she shouted from the bench on its place on top of the hill. Behind her, Ashton Memorial cast a pearly glow on the lawn in front.

The park was deserted now; she could talk as loudly as she wanted.

'Listen, I'm going to say this now and I'm drunk, but as we always said, that is never an excuse, alcohol is never an excuse, and anyway, you know all my secrets, so it doesn't matter.'

She suddenly had an image of herself in her fur coat, alone in a park, slurring slightly, talking aloud. This would possibly have been better if she'd been sober, but she'd started now, so she'd have to go on.

'Liv, I love Fraser!' She paused, then she shouted it out again, louder this time: 'I LOVE FRASER! But you know that anyway, so I don't know why I'm telling you.

'There doesn't seem to be anything I can do about this – I didn't want to fall in love with your boyfriend,

I really, truly did not. But it's happened now and what I would love most in the world is your blessing. Just a sign, Livs. Your permission that I can do this, because I'll take such good care of him. I'll love and treasure him, I promise, I won't let you down.'

She waited. Nothing.

'Liv?' she said again. 'What do you think?'

What did she expect? Something to fall from a tree? An owl to swoop? A crash of lightning?

She waited and waited, but still there was nothing.

She sat down on the bench and smiled, quietly to herself. *You moron, Mia.*

She knew what Liv would say. She knew what Liv would do.

She waited a few more minutes, gathering her thoughts. Then she got up, picked her bag up, ran to the gates, scrambled over the fence, feeling sure she'd ripped a hole in her jeans, and got back in the cab.

'The Borough pub, please,' she shouted through the screen. 'And can you wait outside there too?'

Once there, she slammed the taxi door shut and ran in, straight up to the bar.

'Have you seen a tall, dark guy with a drop-dead gorgeous girl in here?' she asked the barman.

His face lit up. 'Oh, yeah, right stunner, she was. He'd lucked out, he had. Dead ringer for that model, Giselle.

Mia closed her eyes for a second.

'Went ages ago,' said the barman. 'Let's just say he looked like he was in for a fun night.'

Mia covered her face with her hands. 'OK, thank you. Thanks for that.'

She got back in the cab. Fuck it. FUCK IT. They must

have gone back to Melody's already. The thought entered her head for a second: you're drunk, you've gone slightly batty, go home and sober up . . . But she was sick of being reasonable, she was sick of being mature. This was her *Fear and Loathing* moment. She was taking charge of her life, because nobody else seemed to be doing it for her.

The taxi pulled into Melody's quiet cul-de-sac and outside Melody's huge house and, this time, she paid the driver and told him to go.

She hammered on the door. 'Fraser, it's Mia. I know you're in there! I know you're in there, let me in.'

There was no answer so she just lifted up the letter-box flap and hollered inside.

'FRASER! It's me, Mia! Listen, you must *not* go through with it, you must *not* sleep with Emilia. I've been doing some thinking . . .' Her knees hurt with the bending down and she had to stand up to flex them. 'You do not have to do this for the List. I'm sick of the stupid List. I'm sick of everyone telling me who I should love, who I shouldn't love, all this feeling guilty, and you should be sick of it too. It is what it is, Fraser, and I can't help it, I can't help the way I feel. I thought I could control it but I can't and also . . .' She hesitated for a second: once this was out it was out. 'I'm jealous –' she was almost spitting the words – 'like insanely, psychopathically jealous . . .'

Just then the door flew open. Fraser was standing in his dressing gown.

'*Mia.*'

'Who the fuck is that?' someone called. 'Oh . . .'

Then Emilia appeared at the top of the stairs, wearing nothing but her underwear.

Mia stood there for a second, unable to move. Thinking only that legs that long were not natural.

'Shit,' was all she said eventually. She looked at Fraser's face. For a second, everything seemed to slow, everything seemed to stop. Then she turned and she ran.

Behind her she could hear Fraser, standing in the street, calling her name.

TWENTY-THREE

6 March 2009

They were all to meet in Departures at London Heathrow Terminal One at 10.00 a.m. It had been a dawn start for most of them: Mia and Melody because they'd had to catch the 6.00 a.m. train from Lancaster, when it was still dark and Lancaster was just a collage of orange squares against a black sky, and Fraser, because he'd woken up at 4.38 a.m. which, when he'd looked at his alarm clock, blinking in the darkness, he'd remembered was the exact time they'd pronounced Liv dead.

He remembered he'd also done this on the very first anniversary of her birthday and, just like on that one and this one and the other anniversaries of her death and her funeral, from the moment he'd opened his eyes this morning, the world felt different. The air had changed.

It felt as if she was everywhere. He'd heard someone laugh like her on the bus on the way to the Tube this morning, seen the way she used to look when she was interested in something, in a face in the reflection of the window of the Heathrow Express, as the city flew by, beneath a bruised, dawn sky.

Her voice had seemed to whisper through the trees when he went jogging with Norm on the Heath first thing, Parliament Hill pushing a huge red sun high into the sky.

And now they were in the vast, white, strip-lit cavern of the Departures hall at Terminal One of Heathrow Airport, and she was even in the rumble of their suitcase wheels, her face flickered on the Departures board.

Today, on her thirtieth birthday, she was coming with them.

But where?

Where *were* they going, asked the assistant on the help desk, a meek-looking Asian girl with a severe parting and a strong Geordie accent who, to Fraser's dismay, had the word TRAINEE on her lapel.

'We don't know yet, that's what I'm trying to say,' he said again.

They all stood behind him, craning their necks, resisting the temptation to take over. All except Anna, who – true to form – had not yet shown up.

'We won't know where we're going until we pull one of the destinations out of a hat.'

A look of utter blankness met him and Fraser grew even more convinced they would be spending Liv's thirtieth right here, at the Terminal One information desk.

The girl tapped a few keys on her keyboard, Fraser suspected just to look as if she was busy. 'So, you haven't booked anything, sir?' she said eventually, very quietly.

'No' (finally, *finally* she got this much) 'we haven't booked anything.'

'But you'd like to book something?'

'Yes, we'd like to book flights, but only when we know where we're going, which will be . . . drum roll . . .' he gestured to Mia, who held up her floppy, purple woollen hat, and smiled, an encouraging children's TV presenter smile, 'when we've pulled it out of there!'

Fraser felt a wave of annoyance and guilt all rolled into one, when a look of panic crossed her dainty, heart-shaped face once more.

Melody shouldered her way to the front and Fraser thought how great it was, sometimes, to have a lawyer as a very close friend.

'Basically, what we want to know is, can we get stand-by seats? Because we haven't booked anything but we want to fly today.'

The girl's face lit up.

'Ah! You want to go on stand-by?'

'YES!' they all chorused.

She was suddenly animated. Clearly 'stand-by' was something she had covered on her training, whereas pulling stuff from woolly hats probably wasn't.

'Oh, yous shoulda said before,' she said, in her thick northeastern tones. 'I didn't understand yous wanted stand-by. Right, no problem, so let me see. OK, where is it you want to go again?'

In the end, in order to explain the whole concept (that they'd put several destinations into a hat and were about to pull one out – did all flights this morning have a good chance of stand-by seats?), they'd just told her about Liv. And she'd cried; she'd actually shed tears. 'Wow, she was so, so lucky to have friends like you.' They'd all practically climbed over the desk to hug her. 'If I died, my mates'd *never* do this for me. My mates are shit, man. They're all soddin' off on bloody 'oliday to Lanzarote this week, leaving me in this shit-hole, because I can't afford it.'

If they could have, they would have taken her with them.

But where were they going?

'Well, we can't pull anything out of the hat until Spanner gets here,' said Fraser.

He was already angry and generally disappointed with Anna for a whole catalogue of reasons, including the fact that she'd been supposed to meet him and Norm at Paddington to get the Heathrow Express this morning and she hadn't shown up, no phone call, nothing.

'She doesn't like to be called that any more,' said Mia.

'Well, I can think of far worse things to call her. Where the fuck is she? It's nearly half past ten.'

They stood in the middle of Departures, with the hat. The airport still had that morning feel to it: children dragged from their beds in the middle of the night, pale-faced and clinging to their parents; couples, already staring into space, secretly wondering if two weeks alone with their spouse was actually a good idea after all. A baby screamed blue murder in its buggy. 'Childcare with the sun,' Mia had once described the prospect of a sun 'n' sea holiday with Billy, and that phrase came to Fraser's mind now – he could see where she was coming from.

But look around and there was also the lovely stuff, too, the stuff that made Fraser stand and stare: life's mini-joys and -heartbreaks, all under one roof. Man, if he wasn't so knackered, he would write a song. There was a group of foreign teenagers hugging their hosts goodbye – connections made for life, perhaps? A trip they'd remember forever? In the queue for the BA134 flight to Rome, a woman was kissing a baby goodbye, her son having obviously married some beautiful but insistent Italian, whose family she probably envied more than life itself.

In the middle of the concourse, a couple who couldn't be more than twenty embraced, kissing passionately, the man wiping the girl's copious tears with his thumbs; an aching departure.

Fraser watched them. The man, tall, scruffy and passionate, reminded him of himself at that age and, as he looked away, he saw that Mia had been watching them too.

They caught each other's eyes for a second. After the Emilia incident at the beginning of January, they had eventually spoken on the phone, but Fraser didn't really know where it left them. It was almost as if, if ever there had been a moment (and Fraser suspected there'd been far too many), it was now gone. Over.

Mia had been mortified; something that was obvious from her silence. Fraser had tried to ring her several times, desperate to tell her, 'I didn't do it! I couldn't do it! I couldn't do it, because I love YOU, because I'm still screwed up, because I have so many emotions, I can't decipher one from the other any more . . .' But she never picked up and he felt a text didn't quite cut it.

Eventually she had rung, one Wednesday, but it had all spilled out in the wrong order; he'd actually sounded as if he was lying and Mia had laughed as he'd stumbled over his words.

'Frase, shut up. Let's talk about something else, shall we? For starters, we need to discuss Liv's birthday.'

And so here they were.

Fraser looked at her, talking to Norm. Last time he'd seen her, she'd been standing on Melody's front step, drunk, raw, mascara down her face. This time she was composed, wearing a neat, nautical-type jumper, her blonde hair tied back. She was back in control and she looked determined. The thing was, determination only made Mia Woodhouse even more beautiful.

'Sorry, I'm here! I'm here!'

Suddenly a familiar voice echoed around the concourse, and they all looked around to see Anna, dressed in shades and a huge Afghan coat, like a member of the Russian super-rich, dragging her suitcase across the concourse at top speed.

'I'm sorry I'm late,' she panted, pausing to tie her hair in a knot on top of her head. 'I totally overslept. Fucking alarm clock didn't go off.'

Everyone looked at her and there was a moment's accusatory silence.

Anna gave a short grunt of disbelief. 'I overslept, *OK*?'

Mia put her arm around her. 'OK, nobody's getting at you. Nobody's having a go.' After the last time they met, Mia was keen to keep things convivial with Anna. After all, this trip was about Liv. She wanted it to be nice. 'We don't even know where we're going yet, do we?'

'Hey, what's that, Span?' Norm asked, somewhat tensely, eyeing up a huge Tupperware box tied to the top of her suitcase.

'It's a cake, why?' said Anna.

Norm cleared his throat.

'Oh, because I've made a cake, that's all. I made Liv's birthday cake.'

'*You* made a cake?' said Melody, looking at him.

'Yes, I made a cake,' said Norm. 'I'm very good at it now, actually, thanks very much.'

There was an awkward silence. Anna looked at everyone looking at her.

'Right, so can't she have two cakes?' she said. 'Does it really matter?'

'Well, no, NO, of course it doesn't matter, it's just . . .' Norm squirmed, a man under threat, and Fraser felt a smile curling at his lips. 'What sort of cake is yours, anyway?'

'Triple chocolate, why? What sort of cake is yours?'

'Victoria sponge,' said Norm. 'Which I think, actually, was Liv's favourite ca—'

'Oh, for fuck's sake,' said Fraser. 'She's not even here to fucking well eat it!'

There was a horrid silence.

'Well she's not, is she?' he said, matter-of-factly. 'So, you know, let's not have a cake war, please.'

Norm and Anna glared moodily at the floor like two scolded children.

'Let's just go and sit down and find out where we're going today, shall we?'

They all gathered in Costa Coffee on an elevated level of Terminal One Departures. It seemed a bit soulless for something so significant. Fraser had imagined doing it with a glass of champagne in one hand, watching the planes take off from a floor-to-ceiling window that didn't seem to exist.

They bought hot chocolates and coffees and huddled around a tiny table.

'Well, who's going to choose, then?' said Anna. She hadn't yet taken the shades off.

Due to finances and time restrictions, mainly UK destinations had been put in the hat: Cork, Glasgow, Leeds, Galway, Newcastle, Edinburgh, Belfast and – just to add a little excitement – Paris because, fuck it, they'd find the money from somewhere. Melody had joked that she could take it from her and Norm's divorce settlement.

Nobody said anything.

'I think Fraser should do it,' said Mia.

'I think Norm should,' said Melody, staring at Norm. Everyone sort of frowned. 'You know, just an idea.'

'Well, I'm cool with that.' Fraser shrugged. 'I don't want the responsibility. Liv would have forgiven you for choosing a crap place, whereas me, I'd have got a right bollocking.'

They all laughed.

'All right,' said Norm. 'All agreed?'

At the other end of the table, Anna gave a big sigh.

'As long as you're all OK with that, it'd be an honour to choose Liv's thirtieth birthday destination. I mean, I feel a *bit* greedy since I was also official cake baker . . .'

He winked at Anna but she was too busy hiding behind her shades.

'Andrew, just get on with it.' Melody laughed.

He dug deep in the hat.

Silent anticipation while, out of the speaker in the corner, Gloria Estefan sang out some soppy, whiny ballad.

Norm pulled out a piece of paper and kissed it.

'Come on, Livs,' he said, lips tight, clutching his fists. 'Come on, you beauty, let's be 'aving Paris.'

There was an intake of breath as he unfolded the paper. Fraser couldn't bear to look and covered his eyes.

'Well, come on, Norm,' said Mia. 'The suspense is killing me. What's it say?'

He looked up, his face utterly crestfallen.

'Leeds,' he said.

They arrived at gone 4 p.m., already feeling like they'd been up an age.

The flight had been a short but rather tense affair, with them all hovering in the aisle before take-off, deliberating about who should sit where, but none of them able to admit the truth, which Mia deduced to be that Melody and Norm didn't want to sit next to each other, Fraser and Anna didn't want to sit next to each other, and Mia was desperate to sit next to Fraser, but would rather sit in the toilet than own up to that fact.

In the end, Mia had flounced down on the nearest spare seat, next to a morbidly obese man, and spent the rest of the flight asphyxiated by his shoulder fat and feeling rather sad that the last time they'd all got on a plane together to go on holiday to Ibiza, it had all been so different.

Still, in the way that die-hard campers refuse to stop enjoying themselves, even when Force Nine gales hit, despite the stresses and strains that bubbled away underneath, and the toll the last year had taken, they all faced this break with a gritty determination. After all, this was Liv's thirtieth birthday. And, as Norm announced as they all gathered outside Leeds/Bradford Airport, they would 'bloody well do her proud if it killed them', which was followed by a very long silence and then much nervous laughter, which was a welcome release.

They had a nice hotel, anyway. Miraculously with six rooms spare. 42 The Calls – where Melody had apparently once attended a hen do – was a converted mill on the Liverpool Canal, the water lapping right up against its red-brick façade. It was nestled in between many other converted mills and warehouses in Leeds' trendy Brewery Wharf district, a place that, judging by the old photos all over the hotel, had once seen men in flat caps and braces heaving great sacks of corn about, but now saw architects and graphic designers poring over plans amid loud music and exposed white brickwork.

The hotel, which itself had exposed white brickwork, also sported exposed pipes and stable doors in some of the rooms, which looked out over the water. Mia had one of these rooms and the officious manager, a small, moustached man, spent quite some time explaining how it was through these doors that, once upon a time, the bales of hay were offloaded from the boats, ready to be milled using the vast, iron machinery, the remains of which Mia *also* had in her room.

She was all for authentic surroundings, but as she lay on her vast double bed staring at the huge iron wheel that jutted out of her ceiling, she grew mildly anxious: what if it fell down in the night and crushed her to death? A more ridiculous and unbelievable death, even than Olivia's? It also occurred to her that this was all quite mental. So they had got up, gone to an airport not knowing where they were going, and flown to Leeds. And now she was lying in a hotel room, predicting her own gory death, suddenly missing Billy, all because of the List.

Just then, there was a knock at the door.

'Are you naked?' came the Kenneth Williams-esque nasal voice from the door.

Fraser. Mia smiled.

'No, I am *nude*' (she and Fraser had decided long ago that 'nude' was one of the funniest words in the English dictionary) 'but do please enter nonetheless.'

He put his head around the door. 'What, no foreplay? You're rather forward.' And, despite trying really hard not to, Mia couldn't help but laugh.

He strode towards the window.

'Gawd, check out your room, you jammy sod. You've got a canal view and a wheel. Check out that wheel!'

'Actually, I was just worrying about it crashing down and crushing me in the night. Slicing me clean in two, so you will find one leg here and one on the floor.'

'Nice. Like a Sindy doll,' said Fraser. 'I worry about your mind, sometimes, you know. The twisted things it's capable of—'

'Yes, I may look blonde and harmless, but actually I'm black and rotting inside. Gnarled and twisted like an ancient tree.'

Fraser laughed and sat down on the bed. He prodded her leg annoyingly.

'Anyway, I just came to see how you are. You were a bit quiet at the airport. Is everything OK?'

Mia shrugged. 'Yeah, everything's OK.'

'Are we OK?'

Mia rolled her eyes. 'Yeees, we're OK.'

Fraser pulled at a thread on the bed cover. 'Good, because I just wanted to let you know, that, you know—'

'No, what Fraser?'

'That I didn't do it, did I?' He shrugged, unconvincingly, like a child who doth protest too much.

Mia groaned and rolled to face him.

'Frase, give it up. It doesn't matter. It was two months ago now.'

'She was terrifying. She wore a leather bra and only ate meat.'

'Wow, she sounds like Wilma Flintstone.'

'She was! She was like a cavewoman: primal, like raaaAAAA!'

'Like what?' Mia laughed.

'Like raaaa! Frightened the life out of me.'

Mia smiled and picked at the same thread.

'Did you carry on the Portuguese lessons?' he said, eventually.

'Are you mad? I was mortified. Could never show my face there again.'

He put his hand on her leg.

'I've missed talking to you, you know?'

'And I've missed talking to you,' she said. 'Very much.'

So, SO much.

'How are things with you and Billy, anyway?'

'Oh, good, great. He's the only man in my life right now and that is how I like it. He's very low maintenance, you know; likes to get a movie out, go for walks, chill on the sofa, that sort of thing . . .'

'Is he as happy staying in with a DVD and a nice bottle of wine as he is going out and hitting the town?' said Fraser, referring sarcastically to the dating sites they'd once looked at together for a laugh, the ones Mia had threatened to join. He didn't dare ask if she had.

'I miss him too,' said Fraser, and for a second Mia didn't know who he was talking about. 'I loved our little afternoon together, our pint and a packet of Cheddars in the pub.'

'You gave him Cheddars?' said Mia. 'Outrageous. He didn't tell me that.'

'I'd like to do it again some time, you know, if you could ever find it in yourself to trust me?'

'Course I trust you,' said Mia. 'He'd like that. I'd like that. Very much.'

These days it was like a love affair between Mia and Billy. Although he saw his father regularly, something both she *and* Eduardo were grateful for (Eduardo especially, since he'd finally realized that Billy was all he had), it felt as if it was just the two of them again, against the world.

They spent mornings in bed together, sometimes on a boring afternoon they'd just lie in the middle of the carpet in the sun, Billy on top of her, falling asleep like a little sloth bear.

She'd never admit this to anyone, but sometimes when she watched him sleeping, marvelled at his exquisite mouth, the way his lashes fell on his cheeks, she doubted there would ever be a man in the world so beautiful, and she would think to herself, if ever anyone dared hurt him, she would personally rip their heart out.

Then she'd come to her senses, remind herself not to drink in the evening because it made her sentimental, go downstairs and watch *Coronation Street*.

They sat saying nothing for a while. In the bars outside, they could hear the first of the post-work drinkers arrive.

Eventually, Fraser said, 'Anyway, see you downstairs. We've got someone's birthday to celebrate.'

Then he got up and walked out of the room, closing the door softly behind him, and Mia curled up on the bed and, for ten minutes, fell asleep, thinking as soon as she woke up, that she would call her boy.

Back in his room, Fraser now sits at the dressing table in the hotel's fluffy robe, listening to the water gush and tumble into the roll-top bath next door. He's had fun examining all the free potions in their mini-bottles, going for a use-all approach, and the room fills with a heady, lemony scent now, the steam from the bath filling the room, creeping across the mirror like a ghost.

He lets it almost conceal his face, then he leans forward and wipes it clean.

Not bad, he thinks, examining himself. A nine o'clock shadow that he intends to address in the bath, pouches under his eyes that don't go any more, even after a good night's sleep. Definitely not the face of a man in the flush of youth, the one who actually *believed* he could be a rock star, but it's a face he likes better, somehow. One he is less angry with, less often; one that he trusts, that feels like his friend. Most of the time.

He gets up, opens the wardrobe, and lays out his clothes for this evening: a suit, tobacco brown, slim-fit legs, two-button jacket. He hasn't worn a suit since Liv's funeral and, if he's honest, that's probably why. Almost like the reverse of a happily married woman who likes to take her wedding dress out of the wardrobe just so

412

she can play back the memories of that perfect day, every time Fraser catches sight of the black Next suit hanging there, his stomach rolls, he can smell only the fustiness of a hymn book, feel only the weight of her coffin on his shoulders.

So he's thrown it out and this is a brand-new suit. 'A birthday suit, Liv,' he says quietly. Three hundred quid from Hugo Boss, no less. It was in the sale, but still it's the most expensive item he's ever bought in his life. He smooths it out on the bed, slips off the towelling robe and stands in front of the mirror, naked. It feels as if they've waited an age for today; that it's been ten years, not a year, since the anniversary of her last birthday and the decision to do the List. In the reflection of the mirror, he can see the bare March trees outside, black against the night sky. They remind him of the same time last year – that grim day after her birthday, after both birthdays, when he felt he might cave in and never recover. However, he looks at himself now, in all his bare glory, and he can feel in his bones the premature relief that he won't feel like that tomorrow, or perhaps ever again.

The hotel lounge bar was a small, elevated room off the lobby, with more white-painted brick and several tastefully upholstered chairs around cocktail tables. Mia walked in at 6 p.m., as arranged, self-conscious in an already seen outfit, the hound-tooth dress she'd worn on her birthday. Melody was also in a dress, and the boys in suits.

They both looked so handsome in suits, she thought: Fraser tall and distinguished – elegant even; Norm, twinkly eyed, with a neatly trimmed beard. For a split second, when she came out of the lift and saw them, the image that came to mind was of them standing in Liv's parents' tasteful lounge in a pool of August sun, talking to her father at the wake.

Time to stop this.

They raised a toast. 'Well, to Liv, I guess,' said Norm. (Fraser said he wasn't drunk enough to do this particular toast.) 'Happy birthday. We fucking miss you, man,' and it was only as they chinked their glasses, and drank silently, tears in their eyes, that Melody suddenly said, 'Wait, where's Anna?'

They looked at one another.

'Oh, I'm fucking sick of this.' Fraser slammed his drink on the table and went towards the stairs. 'I'm not having this any more, I'm going up.'

Mia went after him. For some reason, she felt as though Anna's mood, the potential she seemed to hold for ruining everything lately, fell on her shoulders, and she didn't want Fraser to bear the brunt.

'Wait,' she said, tugging at his suit jacket, 'I'll go and get her. You stay here.'

She took the lift to the second floor and knocked softly on door 220.

'Anna, it's me. We're all waiting downstairs. Are you going to be long?'

She could hear faint talking, faint music. Ten seconds later, she knocked again.

'Anna?' she said, louder this time. 'Open the door, it's me, Mia.'

There was the click of a phone, the soft pad of footsteps. Eventually, Anna opened the door, still in her dressing gown, a glass in her hand. She looked as if she'd been crying.

'Oh, Anna,' said Mia.

'Oh, what?' she shrugged.'

'Can I come in?'

Anna walked back inside the room, leaving the door open, so Mia followed her in. There were candles lit, four empty mini-bottles of vodka on the dressing table. Anna was midway through her own private party.

'Would you like a drink?' she said, going to the mini-bar. 'I've got vodka, gin. I can open a bottle of wine, if you like?'

'No, I don't want a drink,' said Mia. 'I just want to know what's wrong. I just want to know what's going on with you.'

Anna knocked back her drink. 'I think you know what's going on with me, Mia.' She smiled, her lip trembling. 'I haven't forgotten our conversation in January. I don't know about you.'

Mia gave a quick, nervous laugh. 'But, Anna, it's irrelevant.'

'What's irrelevant, Mia? That you're in love with Fraser? You think that's irrelevant?'

Mia swallowed. 'I'm not in love with Fraser,' she said. 'I don't know, maybe I was at one point.' She paused. 'OK, who knows, maybe I still am. But, Anna, so what? Do you know what I mean?'

Anna fixed her with fierce blue eyes.

'Why do you care? I don't mean that horribly – but exactly what can either of us do about it?'

And as Mia said the words, they made total sense. Even if this was a cop-out – what *could* she do about it?

'Today is not about me, or Fraser, or Norm, or you,' Mia carried on. 'It's not about any of us, it's about Liv. It's about making tonight good for Liv.'

Anna smiled and went over to the dressing table. 'That's the very reason why it *is* about everyone else,' she said, refilling her glass. 'Why it is about you and Fraser . . .' She hovered over the words, Mia shifted nervously.

She passed Mia something, a photo. 'Remember this?' she said.

It was of them all in Ibiza. It was evening, but they were still in bikinis and shorts, their tans deep in the moonlight, the picture of health and youth. They were outside the beach bar on the night Liv died, arms slung around one another, drinks held in the air, mouths open, laughing. Their faces said: this is the time of our lives and we know it.

'Remember that night?' said Anna.

'Course,' said Mia. 'How could I ever forget?'

'Well, yeah. How could you ever forget?'

What did that mean? Anna was freaking her out now.

'That was the best holiday of my life – until what happened, happened, obviously . . . I've never had such a good time since,' Anna said. 'Never had friends like I did then.'

'But we're still friends,' said Mia, feeling tearful and anxious now. 'I know this year's been tough, I know none of us are a replacement for Liv, I know you miss her so much, darling, but we're still friends. I'm still your friend,' and she reached out and squeezed Anna's hand.

'Friends tell the truth,' said Anna, moving her hand away.

416

'About what? About Fraser? But I've told you the truth. I've told you I had feelings for him.'

Suddenly there was a banging on the door. 'Ladies, we're leaving for the restaurant now,' Fraser shouted. Mia jolted and pulled her hand away. 'So if you're coming, Anna, then you have to come now.'

Anna turned to Mia, her eyes full of tears. 'I'm not coming,' she said.

'But, Anna, why not?' Mia suddenly felt panicked. 'It won't be the same without you. It won't be the five of us.'

Anna stared into her drink. 'It's already not the five of us,' she said, as one single tear rolled down her cheek. 'It hasn't been the five of us for a long time.'

They'd taken a punt on the restaurant, like they'd had to take a punt on the hotel, choosing it because – on their brief walk around town on arrival – it looked the most obvious: a modern, cavernous establishment imaginatively named the Restaurant, Bar and Grill, slap-bang in City Square in what was apparently the old Post Office.

They'd all looked inside as if they were eyeing up a wedding venue. Uh-huh, big (probably meant it had tables available), chic, high ceilings, glass-backed cocktail bar, black-and-white photos of movie stars. It had something of an old-style glamour to it, and Liv loved old-style glamour.

'Well, clearly, she did go for Leeds, so sod her,' Melody said sardonically, as they went to reception to make a reservation for that evening. 'If we all get food poisoning, or it's rubbish, then on her head be it,' and she threw an arm around Norm and pulled him close and they all smiled because they knew that Norm felt wretched about pulling Leeds out of the hat; and also it was just nice to see them getting on. Almost six months after they'd separated, Norm and Melody had gone full circle. It was like they were friends again, being 'larky and matey' (rather than 'arsey and hatey', as Norm had put it.)

They had a drink in the main restaurant first. Behind it, Leeds Station was just visible, the curve of the train tracks making their way out of the city, the distinctive black-and-white taxis rolling up in front. Mia had thought they were police cars when she'd first arrived: even she'd had to laugh at how clueless she could be sometimes.

The private dining room they'd booked was on a mezzanine level, above the main restaurant. It was self-contained and almost soundproof, with a long glass table and swanky, tan leather, high-backed seats. Although it was smart it lacked any of the character of the main restaurant. Mia couldn't help feeling she was attending an AGM.

'So, just wondering, did any of you bring your lists?' asked Norm, rubbing his hands together. Mia looked at Fraser at the other end of the table and wondered whether he was having similar thoughts.

Clearly, he was: 'This isn't a business meeting, mate.'

'I have to agree,' said Mia. 'We're ordering dinner, aren't we? Not coffee and biscuits.'

Norm looked a bit hurt. 'Hey, I'm just doing things properly,' he said, splaying his palms defensively. 'I do feel a bit of a twat for us being in Leeds in the first place, do you know what I mean?' He adjusted his tie. 'I just want to do her proud. In case you'd all forgotten, we were all meant to have completed the List by now, which we haven't. I just thought we could see where we were.'

'OK, later, Norm,' said Melody softly, touching his arm. 'Don't get your knickers in a twist, we'll do it later.'

They ordered food: rock oysters because Melody insisted (her treat), even though Mia wasn't even sure she liked oysters and wondered if she might have a life-threatening allergy to them: death by rock-oyster-induced anaphylactic shock – what was it with her and her morbid fascination today? It was supposed to be a happy day.

But of course it wasn't a happy day, not really. It wasn't a happy day because it wasn't Liv's birthday. She didn't make it to her thirtieth birthday.

The rock oysters came – shiny and, Mia couldn't help thinking, the consistency of huge gobs of phlegm. She ate a couple anyway, felt them slide down her throat, vinegary and lemony. 'Well, this is proper romantic, this is,' Fraser said, and they all laughed – it felt like something of a release. Then he told some hideous, out-of-both-ends story regarding him and Liv and a mutual food-poisoning encounter with oysters. Mia wondered if he'd embellished it a little, just to get things going, to lighten the mood.

They ordered wine, or rather Melody tried to order wine – a £57 bottle of Burgundy. Fraser, seeing Mia's face (£57 was pretty much what she had to spend on living per week), overruled with house white.

It's what Liv would have wanted.

But would she have wanted any of this? Mia was beginning to wonder. Every time she and Fraser exchanged looks, she suspected he was thinking the same.

They chatted and laughed; they talked about Anna and about what could possibly be her problem, Fraser becoming more bolshie the drunker he got: 'Fuck her. She's just attention seeking. She's probably having a Buddhist ceremony in her room, chanting at the walls or something. She'll be happy as Larry.' But it was definitely tense, a birthday celebration without a birthday, after all.

Mia looked around the table at her friends, Anna's words reverberating in her head: She was right. They weren't the five of them any more, not the same five they'd been back in Ibiza, anyway, not even the same five they had been this time last year.

She watched Fraser as he laughed and joked. He was so much more confident than the man who'd sat on her sofa a year ago tomorrow and cried like a baby, and yet he looked older – unmistakably handsome but definitely older. She'd never looked at one of her friends and thought they'd aged before, but now she did.

Norm and Melody were divorced now, too, and yet Melody had sat on the front steps of her marital home just days ago, before she started the task of sorting through her and Norm's stuff, and said she hadn't felt happier in a long time.

It was because things were changing – Mia had said as much to her; things were evolving. Mia couldn't help feeling suddenly so sad that Liv would never evolve.

She would never know what it was to be divorced, or even married; her face would never age. Mrs Durham joked these days, 'See these wrinkles? All paid for, Mary! Life's rich tapestry, etched on my face.' It was a privilege to age, thought Mia, but Liv was robbed of that. Her life was interrupted and the List was just a concrete reminder of that fact. Literally a life suspended, dreams frozen in time.

It had been Mia's idea to do it. It had to be her idea to stop.

TWENTY-FOUR

The main courses came and went, then Norm got a piece of paper out of his jacket and rustled it, officiously.

'Right, so, what have we got left on the List to do? Because there were twenty things on there and I swear we've not done all of them.'

Mia reluctantly got her copy of the List out of her bag. It was agreed that the following were outstanding:

9. French kiss in Central Park. 'Well, that's not going to happen, is it, Andrew?' said Melody. She was pissed now and any efforts to be sensitive had gone with the last bottle of wine.

Thankfully, Norm saw the funny side: 'I'm sure we French-kissed in Williamson's Park at some point in our relationship?' he said. 'Thorpe Park? Chessington World of Adventures?'

Melody sniggered, laying her head on her arms in surrender. Norm could still make her laugh.

12. Live in Paris. That was Anna's, and so far they'd heard nothing about Paris.

10. Climb Great Wall of China. 'Well, actually,' announced Norm, 'I'm going to do that this summer.'

And they all *oooh*ed and *aaaah*ed whilst looking at him as if to say, 'Course you are, Norm.'

14. Swim naked in the sea at dawn. (Oh, God), Mia fake-coughed and looked out of the window

'Woodhouse!' They all pointed at her. 'You said you were going to do that in the summer!'

'This summer,' she cowered. 'This summer I shall swim naked, constantly. Try and stop me! Every single day I shall be in Morecambe Bay.'

But really, she couldn't bear it any longer. Just as the idea for the List had hammered insistently at her mind a year ago, now it seemed to curdle in there and she needed to be the one to say something.

She spoke suddenly.

'Just out of interest, has anyone actually ever made one of these Lists?'

They all looked at her blankly.

'One of these "Things to Do Before I Am Thirty" lists? Because Fraser's already thirty and the rest of us turn thirty this year.'

Across the table, she caught Fraser's face. She could have sworn she saw a smile curl at his lips.

'No, I didn't make a list,' he said, palms pressed together, not taking his eyes off her. 'And I don't intend to make a list. Ever, actually.'

He looked at her so long that she had to look away.

'What about anyone else?' she said.

Silence; they all looked at one another.

'I haven't got time to complete my shopping list,' said Melody. 'Never mind anything else.'

'Well, I have,' announced Norm, suddenly sticking his hand up. 'I wrote a list of things to do before I'm thirty.'

'You didn't tell me,' said Melody. But then you don't tell me everything. I've realized that about you.'

Norm laughed through his nose. 'What's that supposed to mean?'

'So what's on this list?' said Fraser. 'Come on, I'm interested now.'

'Learn to dive,' said Norm. 'Finish that song we started, do a stand-up comedy gig, loads of things . . .'

Mia leant back in her chair and folded her arms.

'And have you actually done any of those things?' she said. 'I mean, with all due respect, Norm, you're six months off thirty, and have you actually done any of the things from your list?'

Norm coughed.

'Well, no, I haven't *yet*.'

Mia downed her wine. Speeches weren't really her thing, but she felt compelled now. This was down to her.

'Well, I rest my case,' she said, flopping back in her seat.

'Your case for what?' said Melody. 'Aren't I supposed to be doing the cases for things?'

'Do we really feel,' she said, and, as she spoke, she was aware her heart was thumping; that this felt more controversial, more scary than it had in her head, 'that if Liv had survived, she'd have done the things on the List, anyway? Gone to Vegas, learnt a language? That she'd even remember she wrote it?'

The room fell silent.

'She wrote this List a year before she died, and to my knowledge she didn't do one thing on it. Would anyone like to contest that fact? Does anyone know if she did even one of the tasks?'

They all looked at one another.

'Because please speak up if you do.'

She was met with only silence.

They walked back towards the hotel, arm in arm along the moonlit streets, busy now with weekend revellers, lots of men with paunches and striped shirts who looked as if they played a lot of golf. And girls with pulled-back black hair and not much in the way of clothes.

The plan was to go to the wharf and light the birthday cakes at a bar on the waterfront.

Mia was linking arms with Melody, Fraser with Norm: 'You love each other, you do,' said Melody, walking behind them. 'You should get it together – just the right heights, too.' Their laughter echoed in the mild night air.

Mia felt bonded and close and secure. The wine helped, but also her point about the List. They'd all been quick to say how nutty Anna had got this year, how the List had fucked her up, but when they'd looked at it, they were screwed too. Nobody had come away unscathed, but then perhaps it was just that they needed to do the List to see their lives were pretty screwed in the first place.

If Liv had survived, chances are she wouldn't have bothered going to Venice because, let's face it, she would have been far too busy living her life. And they'd all made a pact inside that soulless, odd, business-like dining room, that that's what they'd do too from now on.

'Don't you think we should call Anna? Tell her that we're doing the candles and her cake?' said Mia, as they stood in front of the hotel.

They all tried her mobile but she didn't answer.

'Ah, leave her,' said Fraser. 'She's probably drunk, or asleep. We'll light a candle for her.'

So they walked down the passageway at the side of the hotel and crossed the mini-suspension bridge to the other side of the canal. There they found a modern, dome-shaped bar, right on the waterfront, with bright orange chairs, aqua leather sofas and lots of white chiffon.

'A little Ibiza in Leeds,' said Fraser, and it was as if it was OK to say it now, that her death was not the only memory they'd ever share.

They got drinks at the bar – pints of lager for Mia and Fraser, cider for Melody and Norm – and huddled together under the heaters on the wicker furniture outside, the lights from the buildings opposite glowing in the dark.

Fraser took the cakes and candles out of the bags he'd been carrying and set them on the table in front of them. 'Right, who's got a lighter?' he said, and it was only then that they realized that none of them smoked any more.

They got matches from the barman, and Melody lined up the candles. One, two, three boxes were opened; she counted them out on the table and began to put them on the cakes.

'How many are you putting on?' said Mia.

'Well, thirty,' said Melody. 'Is that OK?'

Mia looked at Fraser – he spoke before she did: 'Don't put thirty on,' he said, quietly. 'Just put a random number . . . eight, five whatever.'

'Okaaay . . .' Melody frowned, taking them off.

'Well, it's morbid, isn't it?' said Fraser. 'Because she didn't make it to thirty. She wouldn't want that.'

427

Melody nodded slowly in silent agreement. 'OK, I'll do six,' she said. 'Five of us, one for Liv.'

Slowly, she placed three on Norm's cake and three on Anna's, then she struck the match. It smelled delicious, thought Fraser, like Bonfire Night in the winter air.

There was a moment's silence. Singing 'Happy Birthday' was out of the question now, and everything else seemed to have been said.

'Well, make a wish, I guess,' said Fraser, eventually, and they all closed their eyes and blew the candles out.

They sat there, watching the lights flicker on the water, one of them occasionally saying something, the rest of the time suspended in the sort of silence that only very old friends find comfortable. Eventually, Melody and Norm went back inside to get more drinks. Fraser and Mia remained sitting outside.

Neither of them said anything for a while. Fraser idly struck a match and relit some of the candles, and they sat like that, watching the flames.

Then Fraser spoke.

'Thank you, Mia,' he said.

'For what?' she said, genuinely confused.

'For what you said in the restaurant; for putting an end to the List, basically. I've been thinking the same too, for a long time now. I just didn't have the guts to say so.'

Mia gave a little shiver; she had glittery make-up on and it shimmered in the candlelight. Fraser thought she looked ridiculously pretty.

Mia took a match and lit another candle.

'You should have more confidence,' she said. 'Trust your instincts.'

428

'I do, I have,' said Fraser. 'Look . . .'

And just then, maybe because everything seemed perfect – the candlelight, the water, Fraser *knew* he had to get this right. For once in his life, he could not fuck this up.

'. . . whatever you think about what happened with Emilia—'

Mia put a finger to her lips. 'Shh,' she said.

'No, honestly, let me finish.'

Fraser brought his chair closer, leant around the candles and took one of her hands in his.

'I didn't sleep with her,' he said. 'And I never would have done. Not because she was scary or wore leather underwear . . .'

Nope, he couldn't do it without joking – just a little.

'But because of where my head was.' He paused. '*Is* . . .'

Mia took a deep breath in and smiled at him.

'And where *is* your head, Fraser?'

He took her hand, put it to his mouth and kissed it. 'Well, it's—'

'Jesus, can you two smell smoke?' Just at that moment, Melody and Norm appeared, holding drinks. 'Is the cake on fire?' said Norm. 'Something's burning . . .'

And it was only then that they turned, to see great clouds of smoke billowing from a building opposite.

Fraser stood to his feet. 'The fucking hotel's on fire,' he said, calmly at first and then much louder. 'OUR HOTEL'S ON FIRE!'

And then it was as if they all had the same hideous thought at the same time. Oh, God. Not again.

'Jesus Christ, *Anna* . . .'

They all ran like lightning across the suspension bridge, just as the fire alarm started wailing. They could hear the shocked cries and *ooh*s and *ahh*s of people from the other bars around them. Guests were already being evacuated from the hotel, scores of alarmed, bemused, irritated faces, people in pyjamas and dressing gowns, people dressed for dinner.

They all squeezed into the small revolving doors of the entrance, getting stuck in one compartment, swearing, panicking.

The officious manager was in the lobby, a voice of calm, the face of barely concealed panic.

'Everyone out, please, everyone stay calm,' he was saying, ushering people with an officious hand. 'Everyone stay calm, the fire brigade are on their way.'

Fraser grabbed his arm. 'Where's the fire? Where's the fire coming from? You have to tell me where the fire's coming from.'

'The second floor,' said the man, without even looking at him.

'Fuck, Anna's on the second floor. Our friend's on the second floor!'

The man continued ushering people out with his arm, but Fraser was running around now, hands on his head in panic. 'Anna!' he was shouting, his mouth dry, his heart threatening to leap out of his chest. 'Anna, Jesus Christ, where are you?'

The girls – Melody and Mia – were frantically trying to call her mobile. Norm was talking to people outside.

'Yeah, I think she was drunk,' Fraser could hear him saying. 'Yeah. she would definitely have been drunk, she's got long reddish hair, very slim, tall . . .'

It was all coming back to him, the frenzy, the nightmare.

Not again, he thought. Please, God, not again.

Fraser ran up to the manager. 'I need to go up,' he pleaded. 'We think our friend's on the second floor, we can't see her down here.'

Everyone stood behind him. 'Fraser,' Norm pleaded, a hand on his shoulder. Fraser shrugged it off. 'Don't go, mate. Please. It's dangerous. Wait for the fire brigade.'

Fraser shrugged it off again, more aggressively this time.

'NO. I wasn't there for Liv. I'm not letting another one go.'

The man put his hand out to stop him. 'Nobody is to go inside,' he said. 'Nobody is to go upstairs. Wait until the fire brigade get here, health and safety, I'm afraid, health and safety.'

Fraser saw red.

'I don't give a fuck about your health and safety,' he said, grabbing the guy by the arm and practically dragging him to the side. 'My friend's up there.'

Smoke was already drifting above the corridor when Fraser got to the second floor. He couldn't remember which room Anna was in. Why hadn't he asked what room she was in? He hammered on every door. 'Anna! Anna!'

The fumes were really getting to him now, at the back of his nose and his throat, making him cough.

He covered his mouth with his sleeve, stopping for a second to recover himself. Outside he could hear sirens wailing. They made his blood run cold.

Then he saw her, or rather heard her; she was backed

431

into a corner of the corridor, a tiny figure, crouched down on the floor, the phone in her hand.

'Anna, *Jesus* . . .'

He scrambled towards her, pulling her up by her arms, like a rag doll. She was as light as one and shaking uncontrollably.

'My room's on fire,' was all she could say, clinging to him, clawing him. 'My room's on fire, Fraser. My room's on fire!'

There were two fire engines and two ambulances in all. Fraser joked it was hardly *Holby City*. Anna sat in the back of one of them now, wrapped in a blanket, hyperventilating and hysterical.

She'd been very lucky, the paramedics said. If Fraser hadn't got her when he did, there might not have been 'the same happy outcome', and they all knew what that meant.

She'd got drunk and fallen asleep, the window had been left open and the wind had caught the flame of a candle, setting the curtains on fire.

Thankfully, the smoke alarm had roused her and she'd got out of the room before the fire spread but if she'd been left much longer . . .

Only two people were allowed in the ambulance with her, so Fraser and Mia sat with her while the other two huddled outside.

Anna was crying, rocking backwards and forwards, her breathing fast and short. 'I'm sorry,' she kept saying. 'I'm so sorry.'

'She's just in shock,' said the paramedic, attaching something to her finger, apparently to test her heart rate.

'She's having a little panic attack, aren't you, Anna? Come on, now, you're all right.' She had a seen-it-all-before approach and a strong Yorkshire accent. 'Deep breaths. Good girl.'

'Deep breaths,' they all said. Even Norm and Melody outside. 'Deep breaths, Span. We're all here.'

What went unsaid, though, was that they knew instinctively that this was an Anna-created drama, a drama to block out what was really going on; it's just that nobody could fathom exactly what that was.

Fraser squeezed Anna's hand and looked around him. Something told him people weren't supposed to go through this twice in their lives. That just doing *this* twice – the ambulances, the sirens, the flashing blue, revolving lights – was more than enough for one lifetime.

He looked at his friend: a little smoke inhalation but *here*, not even having to go to hospital, and for a terrifying millisecond the 'what-ifs' seemed to grab him by the throat, before retreating and leaving a wave of gratitude, so big that he had to put his face to the window, so nobody saw him cry.

Anna was ridiculously drunk; more drunk than Fraser had ever seen her. More drunk than vain, confident Anna usually allowed herself to get. But then this wasn't vain, confident Anna. This was scared Anna, this was Anna at crisis point; her own, self-made crisis, perhaps, but in crisis all the time.

She started talking: 'I saw it,' she kept saying, but she was crying and shaking so much that for the first few times nobody took much notice.

'I saw you,' she said now, louder and more urgently this time.

433

It was Fraser who eventually said, 'You saw what, Anna? Who? What are you on about?'

'You kiss. I saw you kiss. The night Liv died, I saw you kiss Mia. I was standing on the balcony and I saw you, in the villa kitchen.'

Nobody said anything, except Norm who said, 'Yer *what*?' as if this was actually pretty ridiculous.

Fraser and Mia exchanged glances.

'Why didn't you say anything?' said Fraser quietly.

'Yes,' said Mia, 'why didn't you just say?'

'Because I couldn't, could I?' Anna said to Fraser. 'Because your *girlfriend* had just died. I didn't want to make you feel any worse or any guiltier. I know I can be a pain sometimes, but I'm not that bad, am I?'

'You're not "bad" at all,' said Fraser. 'We love you, you idiot.'

'I didn't even think about it for ages,' she went on. 'I was too much of a mess. But then, as time went on, it was like this thing I saw, this kiss, became this huge thing in my head. I felt like I was carrying a big secret around with me – a secret that Liv had gone to her grave not knowing, and that now I couldn't ever tell her.'

Mia put her head in her hands.

'Oh, God, Anna, I'm so sorry.'

'I tried to get you to confess,' she said, almost laughing. 'I even snogged Fraser 'cause I thought, for one mad second, that he'd snog me back and I could pretend that that kiss in Ibiza meant nothing and that – I don't know – he'd snog any of us if he was drunk enough!'

'Gee, thanks . . .' mumbled Fraser.

'But you probably all know about that anyway . . .'

434

Everyone looked at each other. 'Oh, my God,' said Anna. 'You didn't say anything, Fraser?'

Fraser smiled and shook his head.

'Doing the Buddhism thing kind of helped and hindered,' Anna carried on. 'At least Steve was someone to confide in and I told him everything. Steve's big on karma—'

'Steve's a fucking charlatan, Anna,' shouted Norm from outside, and Fraser wanted to hug him. Norm always cut to the chase. 'He's not a Buddhist, he's a bull-shittist,' and they all laughed, even Anna a little.

'Maybe, but he kept on about karma,' Anna continued, 'about how what goes around comes around, about how everyone gets their comeuppance in the end, about how nobody gets away with lying. And I listened to him – my head was a mess, I would have listened to *anyone* – and it seemed to make sense. But I didn't want anything bad to happen to you guys; I was *petrified* something else bad was gonna happen. So I tried to get the truth out. I felt like I owed it to Liv, to get to the truth. I know it sounds crazy.'

'It sounds crazy,' said Norm.

'I just felt . . .' Anna looked up at them all, her face dirty with smoke, make-up down her cheeks, and Fraser doubted he'd ever seen her look so small in his life. '. . . that I'd lost Liv, and now I was losing you all, and I couldn't bear it, because you lot are all I've got.

'Melody, you always had Norm and now that's broken up, you guys aren't *you guys* any more. Mia, we were close once but now you have Billy and *now* you seem to have Fraser and I miss you. I really miss you.'

435

'Oh, Anna,' said Mia. 'I miss you too. I'm sorry, darling, I had no idea you felt like this.'

'And me, who did I have?' Tears were running down her face now, dripping off her chin. 'I used to have Liv but now she was gone and I missed her so much, I *miss* her so much. I don't have a proper job, I don't have a baby, my friends were my life, my family, and I don't want it all to stop, I'm so shit-scared of it all just stopping.'

Perhaps the one person who acted like she needed them the least, needed them the most, thought Fraser. *He saw that now.*

Mia was stroking Anna's back, trying to calm her. Norm stuck one foot in the door; he wanted to get his facts straight.

'What, so you two snogged the night Liv died?'

Mia laid her head on Anna's knee, looked at Fraser and gave a defeated sort of smile. Fraser felt better, instantly. For some mad reason, just someone saying it out loud made him feel so much better. 'Yes,' said Fraser, 'and it's fucked with my head ever since. We've felt so guilty about it. Perhaps me more so than Mia—'

'Oh, yeah, because I don't care,' said Mia, sarcastically. 'I haven't got a conscience'

Fraser put his hand on her shoulder. 'You have, you're just much more sensible than me.'

'I knew what was done, was done, that's all,' said Mia. By now, Melody and Norm were both leaning on the doors of the ambulance, their faces aghast. 'And nothing would bring Liv back. I knew we'd never know if she saw, or what she felt. It fucked me up too – Christ, I was seeing a shrink for months! But I just could not go on beating myself up about it. We can't go on beating ourselves up. Liv wouldn't have wanted that. I know. She was my best friend.'

'Hey, we all know,' said Melody. 'And anyway, it doesn't matter now.'

It was the first thing that Melody had said, and everyone turned to look at her.

'It doesn't really matter who snogged who,' she said. 'Because Liv loved Norm.'

It took them a minute. '*What?*' Fraser said.

'Oh, yes, for quite some years, it turns out,' and she looked at Norm and smiled, but her eyes were watering. 'I know that's pretty hard to believe.'

Fraser looked across at Norm, who looked as if he might be sick, he looked so shocked, but there was also a flicker in his eyebrows that told Fraser it was true.

'I found this,' said Melody, and she took a piece of paper from her bag, 'when I was clearing all our stuff from the house.'

'Fucking hell,' said Norm, 'how did you manage that?'

'Oh, it wasn't hard, you didn't hide it very well. It was slipped in the sleeve of a Green Day CD.'

She unfolded it. There were just a couple of lines of writing and Fraser recognized them immediately, the elegant sloping, left-handed writing.

'Turns out there was a last thing on Liv's List,' said Melody. 'A number twenty-one.'

Norm had his mouth open now, gazing at Fraser. He very slowly put his teeth on his bottom lip.

'It's dated July the fifteenth.'

'That's Billy's birthday,' said Mia.

'And our wedding anniversary,' said Melody. 'She wrote this at our wedding. July the fifteenth, 2005.'

Fraser gave a shake of his head. That date had meant nothing to him when he'd seen it at the top of the List.

'Number twenty-one,' she read. 'Let go of Norm. He's gone now, it's over! You'll have to love him from afar. You've wasted far too many years wanting what you can't have. Enough now, Olivia. Must press on.'

She folded up the piece of paper and put it back in her pocket.

There was a long silence. Then, suddenly, Fraser started laughing as well as sort of crying.

'The sly bugger,' was all he could say. 'Olivia Jenkins, you sly bugger . . .'

Eventually, at around 1 a.m., the ambulances and the fire engines went, so it was just the five of them, standing on the pavement. They walked slowly back inside, the girls in front, Norm and Fraser behind.

'Well, that was a fucking turn-up for the books,' said Fraser. 'She kept that one quiet. *You* kept that one quiet.'

It all started to make sense now to Fraser, slot into place. Norm's obsession with the List, the rate he went on about Liv, like it was *his* girlfriend who'd died. The amount of time Liv used to spend with Norm, come to think of it, and he'd thought nothing of it; he'd thought it was perfectly innocent.

Norm stopped. 'I'm sorry,' he said. 'I don't know why I just didn't tell you. I thought you'd be gutted. I didn't know about any of this with you and Mia.'

Fraser turned to face him. The news had absolved him of some guilt, he couldn't lie, but there were still questions going unanswered. Things he needed to know: 'So what, did you sleep with her?' he said. 'Did you kiss her?'

'God, no,' said Norm. 'Never. I swear.'

The city was quiet now, just the odd drunken holler from somewhere, a wolf whistle, taxi on tarmac. The sirens long gone.

'Were you in love with her, then? Just tell me the truth. Not that it really matters now.'

Norm didn't say anything. Fraser felt his heart lurch.

'I don't know,' he said eventually, looking straight at him. 'I really do not know. There was maybe a time when I thought I was, but maybe I was just missing her. I missed her Fraser, so badly.

'We had a bond, basically. And maybe there were times when I thought that bond could have turned into something, but she was always with you and I was always with Melody, and I loved Melody, I really did. I thought she was It, but it didn't turn out to be, did it? When I saw that last thing on the List, I don't know, I was *flattered*. It was something that only Liv and I had.

'Things weren't going well with me and Melody. I never seemed to be good enough and I guess it was nice to know that I was special to someone. That someone thought I was *good*.'

Fraser was nodding slowly, taking it all in.

'I don't think she loved me either, not really. Not in the end. We were just *young*, mate. We were just working it all out.'

We were young, thought Fraser. *So young. So why was it sometimes he felt like he'd lived a lifetime?*

'She loved you, Frase,' Norm said eventually, stepping forward and taking his friend by the arms. 'At least, she only loved you at the time she died, that's what I think. I guess we'll never know.'

439

Nobody said anything for a minute. Fraser was trying to absorb it all.

Then, Norm said, 'I don't want this to come between us.'

Fraser nodded, slowly.

'Because those guys I went skiing with, those guys at the *Metro*? They're not my real friends. *You're* my real friends.'

Fraser looked at Norm, worry etched across his face, and for a second saw the awkward, chubby eight-year-old who'd shyly befriended him at Bury FC Under-11s twenty years ago and had never left his side since.

He took a step forward and hugged him. 'And you're my real friend,' he said. 'You're my real friend too.'

By 1 a.m., Mia, Melody and Fraser were all in the bar. Norm and Anna had gone to bed.

The drama and trauma of the evening had got to Fraser, and he felt exhausted and tearful, which was always when the old demons reared their heads. Anna swore Liv didn't see them kiss, that she wasn't on the balcony when it happened, but nobody could be a hundred per cent sure of it. Not that it seemed that relevant any more.

'I just should have been there for Liv,' he said out loud, biting his thumbnail. 'I should have been there for her, I wasn't there.'

'But, for God's sakes, Fraser,' said Mia. 'We were all drunk. None of us were there for her.'

Fraser looked at his hands. 'I saved Anna, though, didn't I? I didn't save Liv. Why couldn't I save Liv? And I still don't know if she was happy when she died. It kills me, that. Fucking kills me.'

440

They sat in silence. From across the room, Fraser could feel Mia's eyes on him. He lifted his head to see her close her eyes for a second, just a second, then give a little shake of her head, as if she'd been thinking something and now dismissed it.

He watched as she suddenly got up from her chair. 'I've got to go to bed,' she said quietly. 'Melody, you'll look after him, won't you?' Then she went over to Fraser and kissed him on the cheek, lingering there long enough for Fraser to feel her breath on his skin. 'You were amazing tonight,' she said. 'I'm so proud of you.' And then she kissed Melody on the cheek and left.

And so it was just Melody and Fraser now. The only sound, the whirr of the honesty fridge.

'Beer?' said Melody. 'I've got a fiver, I could leave them a fiver.'

She went to the fridge, came back holding two bottles of Bud and passed Fraser the opener.

Fraser cracked open his beer and sighed, a huge, long, weary sigh.

'And are you all right, Mels?' he asked, flopping back on the chair and looking at her. ''Cause, let's face it, nobody's asked you, have they?'

Melody kicked her shoes off and curled her feet underneath her.

'Yes, I'm fine,' she said. 'In fact, more than fine, I'm good.'

'And what about tonight's revelation? I mean, I know you and Norm are no longer together, but still, mate, that must have hurt like hell?'

She shrugged, 'Not really. And anyway, it's all in the past now, isn't it? Even if Liv had survived, Norm and

I still wouldn't have been right for one another. Maybe you and Mia would have ended up together, after all? It all comes out in the end.'

Fraser smiled, weakly. He hadn't really thought of that. How wise old Burgess was becoming these days. How strong she'd been about everything. He was really proud of her.

They drank their beer in silence. 'Can I say something?' said Melody after a while. 'Can I speak honestly to my friend?'

'I swear, if I hear any more honesty tonight . . . any more revelations . . . I swear I might keel over.'

Melody laughed, darkly.

'No, it's not a revelation,' she said. 'More a piece of advice. Fraser, you've got to stop thinking you had anything to do with Liv's death.'

Fraser bit his knuckle and looked at her, as if this would be a very hard thing to achieve.

'It was her death and her life. She's the one who lost her life, not you. To think that some kiss, that you or Mia had anything to do with it? It's just arrogant, frankly.'

Guilt is an arrogant and selfish emotion. It was Melody who'd said that to him, once, years ago. He remembered now.

He gave a short, ashamed laugh through his nose.

'We've got to let her go,' said Melody. 'We have to let Liv go.'

Fraser lay on top of his bed in his clothes, his mind racing, far from sleep. He wanted to talk to Mia. He had to talk to Mia. He picked up the phone on his bedside table, then sat there paralysed for a few seconds. Would

442

she mind if he woke her up? Would she even be asleep yet? He glanced at the clock: 1.45 a.m. He imagined her, alone in her bed, then imagined pulling back the sheets, slipping in quietly beside her, wrapping his arms around her soft warm skin and staying like that till dawn.

The thought, the desire, was so overwhelming that he sat bolt upright and decided that was absolutely what he must do. Then he realized that might scare her to death, so decided to call her instead. But there was no answer and, for a second, panic consumed him. Where was she? Where could she have gone at quarter to two in the morning? Maybe something was terribly wrong? Or maybe she was just ignoring him.

He went to the window on autopilot and pulled the curtains open. That's when he saw her. She was down below, sitting by the water's edge, her feet dangling over the side of the canal wall.

She was wearing one of the hotel's big fluffy robes over her coat for extra warmth, and Fraser smiled to himself. She looked as if she was on day release.

He gazed at her for a second – at her profile, the back of her neck, so elegant with her hair tied up – and felt a swell in his chest so big, he had to catch his breath. Then, without thinking about it too much, he grabbed his keys and left the room, taking the stairs two at a time.

He took the little alleyway at the side of the hotel, then crunched across the pebbles to join her, calling her name so he wouldn't scare her.

She turned around.

'Can I join you?' he said. 'I should have brought my fluffy robe, too. His and hers.'

She smiled at him.

'Wow, what a night, eh?' said Fraser, sitting down beside her, putting his hand on her leg. 'It's a quarter to two in the morning, what are you doing out here?'

'Just thinking' she said, 'about how we met, how so much has happened since then . . .'

Fraser sighed.

'Yep, and who'd have known what was in front of us, hey? When you jumped on me, hypnotised, on that fated day.'

Mia pressed her lips together and turned to him

'Fraser, I wasn't hypnotised . . .'

'You weren't?'

'Nope.'

'So why . . .?'

'You work it out.'

Fraser frowned at her and smiled, nervously.

They didn't say anything for a while, they just sat there, staring into the black water, their feet occasionally touching as they swung them.

'You're not tired yet then?' said Fraser eventually. 'I thought you'd be straight to bed.'

'Oh, you know,' said Mia. 'Didn't want to risk death by iron wheel. As a group of friends, we don't seem to have much luck.'

Fraser laughed.

'Yep, I think it's fair to say, we're not invincible. That you just don't know when it could all be over.'

Fraser turned to her.

'But it's not all over, is it?' he said.

She smiled at him. 'No, Fraser, it's not all over.'

'Do you ever feel like it is, though?'

444

They were looking straight at one another now, their faces centimetres apart.

'Yes, sometimes. But then I remind myself of the whole point of it.'

'To just enjoy it,' he said. It was a statement rather than a question, Mia noticed.

'Yeah, that's right, to just enjoy it.'

'And do the things that matter to us while we can.'

He could feel her breath on his face, her lips were almost touching his.

'And what matters?' said Mia, although Fraser suspected she knew the answer. 'What really matters to you?'

He leaned over and took her face in his hands.

'This,' he said, kissing her. '*You*.'

EPILOGUE

Summer 2009
Hest-Bank beach, Morecambe, Lancashire
No. 14: Swim naked in the sea at dawn

It is the beginning of August and just getting light. Too early even for dog-walkers, or horse-riders, but time for the sun to be slowly rising, gold and shiny as a brand-new penny.

The beach is ours, the only sound the car engine. I switch it off. Silence. If I listen hard, the faint roar of the sea.

We all get out, Billy between the two of us, and walk towards the water, which rolls gently towards us now, a silver carpet, dappled with light.

Over the shingle we crunch, then, taking our shoes off, barefoot over the mud flats. They're cracked and bone-dry after a long, hot summer, except for the tiny purple flowers, pushing up towards the sun.

We reach the sand; it's firm and wet and stretches

for miles, curving around us like a huge, sweeping cloak.

I stop and drink it in. I fill my lungs with salty air. This is no picture postcard, I think, but it is paradise to me: wild and barren and raw and real.

And now we are ready, our clothes are at our feet and we stand, the three of us, half blinded before the sun, like in Genesis, like the first-ever specimens of humankind.

I close my eyes and squeeze Billy's hand. I can hear the rush of the waves, the blood in my ears, and if I put my hand to my chest, the b-dum, dum of my heart. And now we are walking quickly towards the sea, the imprints of the waves in the sand, massaging our soles and propelling us forward.

Faster, faster, we go, walking, running. I squeeze my eyes shut, cry out and then . . .! The water is *freezing*, so cold it takes my breath away, and I pull Billy up by one arm, then the other, skimming him over the waves, Fraser swimming out in front of us, out towards the light.

And now I'm laughing and gasping, my feet flail on the shingle sea bed, my knees collapse and I have to push us up, towards the dappled surface. But it's beautiful, so beautiful, the sun rising higher by the second, turning the sky gold and pink.

I clutch Billy to my chest. I can feel the warmth of his feet on my belly, his head on my shoulder and the pull of the current beneath, running cool and fast between my legs.

It's getting deeper now, I can't touch the ground, and I have to kick my legs hard to keep us afloat. Fraser holds out his hand and I take it, then he pulls us towards him and into his arms. We wrap our bodies around one another for warmth, skin to skin, in the middle of the sea, and I can't feel where I end and the two of them start, where our skin meets the water, or the sea meets the sky.

I tilt my head back. When I lift it up again, Fraser is looking at me. Then suddenly, he pushes back, he is swimming backwards, out towards the horizon; a real-life infinity-pool, spilling over the edge of the earth. Kick, push, he goes. I watch a smile spread across his face and, behind him, the sun sailing higher. Another brand-new day.

A
Q&A
WITH
**KATY
REGAN**

1) What was the inspiration behind HOW WE MET?

When I was seventeen, a boy in my sixth form died suddenly. We weren't close friends but I went to his funeral, and the shock of his untimely death stayed with me for years. When I became a writer, it was something I always wanted to explore: how would the death of a friend, when young, affect you? Would you live your life differently? Friendship has always been a big theme in my life, too. I'm still close to friends from university and even school. (Also, I admit it, I've seen St Elmo's Fire and I wanted to write my own!)

2) Are any of the things from Liv's list on your list of ambitions?

Apart from the odd 'must-get-my-hair-dyed-professionally-before-I'm-forty' item, I don't have a list myself. I suppose what I was trying to say in HOW WE MET is that most of us are too busy with the messy business of life to really sustain this tick-box approach. The sad thing is that if Liv had survived, she probably wouldn't have bothered with any of these fanciful things, written in the flush of youth. In fact, she'd be looking down at her friends saying, 'What are you doing?' Sort out your actual lives rather than ticking off all these dreams!' Having said all that, I would love to be able to make a Roman blind.

3) HOW WE MET is also about the extraordinary moments in people's lives that help to define who we are and what's really important to us — were there any extraordinary moments from your own life that inspired you?

Yes, but I don't think they were found 'Climbing the Great Wall of China' (which I have done, and as I feared, it's so touristy, I've probably had more inspiring Chinese meals). Some of the extraordinary moments that have inspired or shaped me, I probably didn't realise were 'extraordinary' at the time, such as conversations with friends, words of encouragement or advice. Then there have been the obvious things, like becoming a single mother (albeit with much more help than Mia has), achieving my dream of becoming a writer and time spent with friends, knowing they are there through the rough and the smooth.

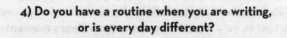

4) Do you have a routine when you are writing, or is every day different?

I really wish I was one of these writers who did a strict, 'thousand words before lunch, then lunch and swim, then a thousand words after', but my life – and my ability to write well – sadly, isn't that reliable! I tend to think I have a clear day to write, then remember my son has an assembly I said I'd go to, or I get up, all guns blazing, then hit a confidence crisis at 11 a.m. and manage three hundred words. The fact that I am so inefficient means I have to be writing or at least sitting at my desk thinking about it almost constantly to actually get it done in the end! That said, HOW WE MET came easier than any other book I've written so far.